Troubled Minds

Troubled Minds

GARY TAYLOR

CHARTRIDGE
BOOKS OXFORD

Chartridge Books Oxford
An imprint of:
Biohealthcare Publishing (Oxford) Limited
TBAC Business Centre
Avenue 4
Station Lane
Witney
Oxford OX28 4BN
UK
Tel: +44 (0) 1993 848726
Email: info@biohealthcarepublishing.com
www.biohealthcarepublishing.com

First published in 2010

ISBN:
978 1 907568 43 5

© G. Taylor, 2010

British Library Cataloguing-in-Publication Data.
A catalogue record for this book is available from the British Library.

All rights reserved. No part of this publication may be reproduced, stored in or introduced into a retrieval system, or transmitted, in any form, or by any means (electronic, mechanical, photocopying, recording or otherwise) without the prior written permission of the Publishers. This publication may not be lent, resold, hired out or otherwise disposed of by way of trade in any form of binding or cover other than that in which it is published without the prior consent of the Publishers. Any person who does any unauthorised act in relation to this publication may be liable to criminal prosecution and civil claims for damages.

The Publishers make no representation, express or implied, with regard to the accuracy of the information contained in this publication and cannot accept any legal responsibility or liability for any errors or omissions.

The material contained in this publication constitutes general guidelines only and does not represent to be advice on any particular matter. No reader or purchaser should act on the basis of material contained in this publication without first taking professional advice appropriate to their particular circumstances. Any screenshots in this publication are the copyright of the website owner(s), unless indicated otherwise.

Typeset by RefineCatch Limited, Bungay, Suffolk
Printed in the UK and USA.

This book is dedicated to the memory of a true gentleman:
my father in law and friend Harry Mills
1930 to 2010 R.I.P.

About the author

Gary Taylor is fifty years old and comes from a working-class background. Married with four daughters, he has lived in the West Midlands area in the UK all his life.

After leaving school, he trained as an engineer within a major bus operator, accomplishing, up to the date this book was written, thirty-four years of continuous service within the company. For the last twenty years, he has also been both a student and instructor within a prominent Midlands-based martial arts association, and still competes at European level.

This is Gary's second novel and is a very different genre from his first. The inspiration for the book came approximately five years ago, around 2005, after a very vivid and reoccurring dream that plagued his mind.

The author can be contacted via the publishers.

1

The birth

Jill Hennessey had been in labour for over sixteen hours; the contractions had started the previous evening. Her husband, George, as reliable as ever, had got everything that she required quickly into the car. They arrived at the maternity hospital within half an hour. As she lay on the bed waiting for the next contraction, her normally well-groomed, shoulder-length, fair hair was plastered against her forehead. She wished she hadn't been so hasty but had waited for a few hours until the contractions were stronger; it felt as if time was standing still.

George came back into the room, his swarthy complexion looking pallid on his stocky five foot nine inch frame, which was wilting slightly with fatigue. He had just been for a coffee in an attempt to wake himself up. Sitting down beside Jill, he took her hand and looked deep into her kind blue eyes, one of the things that originally attracted him to her.

'Won't be long now, love,' he said, gently squeezing her hand. She returned the gesture. At thirty-eight years of age, they had been married for almost twenty years. For most of that time, they had been trying to start a family, but after so long they had resigned themselves to believing it just wasn't meant to be. Then out of the blue they had a son, Charlie, and within two years Jill was pregnant again. Here she lay, about to deliver their second child at any moment.

It was unusual for the second child to take so long to arrive, but she had had a healthy pregnancy, so everyone thought it best to just let nature take its course. Both Jill and the baby were being monitored. They appeared to be doing fine; no sign of any stress. A scan had revealed they were having another boy, which pleased them both. They were not really bothered either way as long as the child was healthy, but another boy made sense financially. Wanting to give the baby every possible chance of a healthy start in life, Jill had insisted, just as she had done with Charlie, that the birth would be as natural as possible – no drugs for pain relief. A few years earlier she had witnessed the birth of a friend's baby for which pethidine had been used for pain relief. Jill had been shocked as the child appeared stillborn until another drug was administered to counter the effects of the pethidine.

Jill pressed on the buzzer above the bed; the contractions were now very close together. Jackie, a cheerful petite lady who had been Jill's midwife for the last six or seven hours, came into the room.

'Is everything OK, Jill?' she asked.

'I think it's nearly time, Jackie,' replied Jill.

After a short examination, the midwife said, 'Nine centimetres dilated, Jill; any time now.'

Jill squeezed her husband's hand. Having been through it once before, she knew what was ahead.

The previous day a maintenance engineer had been working on the Resuscitaire unit, which was in the corner of the room. Just before finishing, he was called away to another job and, thinking he would be back shortly, he didn't bother with a 'Do not use' or 'Out of order' sign. Theoretically, it shouldn't have even been in the room during maintenance, but these machines were in such shortage that staff were reluctant to let them out of their sight. Inside it, a small screwdriver lay across the disconnected cables, dangerously close to the supply terminal and machine body.

As the midwife prepared for the imminent birth, she pulled the Resuscitaire out of the corner; it was rarely used, but best to have everything in place, just in case. Unknown to her, as she pulled the Resuscitaire out, the screwdriver lodged against the machine body and the supply terminal, creating a circuit. If plugged in, a flick of the switch would make the whole machine live.

'OK, Jill,' said Jackie, 'you've done this before; I want you to push when you feel the contraction.'

Everything was going to plan, a little slow but nothing to worry about. Another hour passed and Jill was tiring; the baby's heart rate was becoming a little erratic. Without panicking the mother to be, Jackie called for assistance, and two more midwives arrived within seconds.

'What have we got here then?' asked Martha Simmons, a large West Indian woman with a beaming smile.

'I think the cord is a little tangled up,' Jackie replied.

'Right then, let's have a little look.' The West Indian midwife took charge; with hundreds of births to Martha's credit, Jill was in safe hands.

'Baby's nearly here, Mom; we just need to free up that cord a little.' Her presence made Jill feel safe. 'I just need to give a small tug.' The baby's head was now two-thirds out and the cord was visible around its neck. Jill felt an almighty tug inside her body as the midwife looped the cord over the baby's head.

'OK, my dear, one more big push and baby's born.' Jill felt the urge to push, and with teeth gritted she pushed with all her might. 'Mom and Dad, it's a boy!' declared the midwife with an even bigger smile.

'Is he OK?' asked Jill. There was no sound from the baby.

'He's a little tired and stressed, my dear, don't worry.'

Quickly, the midwife cut the cord and gave a couple of gentle taps on the baby's bottom; still no sound. The midwife placed the baby onto the Resuscitaire. Mother and father watched in silence, a glint of panic in their eyes.

'Plug us in please, Jackie;' said Martha, 'let's get some lights on.' Martha reached for a resuscitation pack as Jackie plugged in the machine. As she flicked the switch on the wall, sparks came from the back of the machine; the baby's body became rigid.

'Jesus Christ!' Martha jumped back, 'Turn it off, turn it off,' she shouted.

As Jackie wrenched the plug from the socket, Jill screamed and fainted, falling back onto the bed. The room was filled with the smell of burning. George couldn't believe what was happening. What should have been one of the happiest days of their lives had become a nightmare. Straight away, one of the midwives hit the emergency button on the wall, and Martha checked the baby's vital signs. The room fell silent. 'He's breathing,' she said.

A man in a white coat came running into the room. 'What's wrong?' he asked.

'The machine, Dr Moore; the baby got a shock from it,' Jackie told him, looking upset.

'Excuse me, ladies, let me have a look.' He put his stethoscope on the baby's chest. His heart sounded OK. He picked the baby up to turn him over. 'Whah, whah, whah!' Finally, the baby cried out.

'Nothing wrong with his lungs,' said the doctor with a grin, 'are you sure it wasn't a fit?'

'No,' said Jackie, 'as soon as I turned the Resusc on, sparks came out of the back, and his whole body went into spasm. Then there was a burning smell.'

Moore passed the baby to the midwife and turned his attention to Mr and Mrs Hennessey. Jill was just coming round. He checked her pulse; as her eyes opened, there was a look of fear in them. 'My baby!' she screamed out.

'It's OK, Mrs Hennessey, he's fine, everything's fine; try to relax.' Moore turned back to the midwives. 'Ladies, get Maintenance to move that machine from this room. Nobody is to touch it until there has been an investigation. Take care of Mrs Hennessey, and I want to get a full series of tests done immediately on the little one.'

Jill and the baby were kept in hospital for the next two weeks as a matter of precaution. But if anything, baby Karl became quite a star. The nurses and midwives commented that they had never seen a two-week-old baby so alert – it was as if he was constantly watching you. Meanwhile, the hospital authorities were taking no chances; they knew they would have to pay compensation. The investigation had found the cause of the incident, the guilty maintenance engineer had been dismissed, and the Hennesseys' solicitors were circling like a pack of hungry wolves. All the hospital could do was try to limit the damage.

2

Five years later

The first five years of Karl's life were happy but pretty ordinary. He had grown into a loving, well-mannered child, and his parents doted on him. His brother Charlie, now seven years old, had been at school for over two years. The coming September, it would be Karl's turn. He was so looking forward to it.

He hadn't had a great deal of contact with other children. His mother had taken him to a playgroup for a few months when he was three, but he hadn't interacted well with the other children, appearing so much brighter than the other kids his age. Some of the other parents resented him playing with their children. Although they were the same age, he always took over with jigsaw puzzles and games, completing them before the other children even got a look in. Jill had thought, 'OK, so he's clever.' She certainly wasn't going to hold him back just because he was bright.

It was just after lunch on a beautiful, sunny July afternoon. Jill was in the garden watching Karl, who was rolling on the grass holding two Action Man figures, imagining them in a fierce battle. Another week and the kids would break up for the summer holidays. Jill had explained to Karl that Charlie would be at home all day for several weeks. He couldn't wait – at last someone to play with. She spread a blanket on the lawn and lay on her back, the sun beating down on her face; if this was a taste of the approaching summer holiday, it was going to be a scorcher. Karl came over and curled up beside her. She placed an arm around his back and kissed the top of his head, feeling so content. Slowly they both dozed into a relaxed sleep, and it wasn't long before Jill began to dream.

She was standing by a river. The warmth of the sun was on her back, and the water looked so inviting. She kicked off her shoes and walked in. At its deepest point, it reached her knees. The cool water felt so refreshing; she couldn't remember being this relaxed. Then suddenly, from behind, a huge splash of water over her back took her breath away.

As she lay on the blanket, Jill's body twitched at the sensation of the cold water in her dream.

As she turned, little Karl was standing a metre or so behind her, a cheeky grin right across his face. Again, he splashed her, then ran away giggling. 'You wait, little man!' Jill gave chase. Every time she reached for him, he seemed to momentarily disappear, then appear again slightly out of reach. Although frustrating, it was a wonderful dream.

Slowly, Jill woke up, her back a little stiff from the uneven surface. Karl was already awake, his attention drawn once more to his Action Men.

'I've just had a dream about you, Karl,' said Jill.

Without turning from his Action Men, he said, 'But you couldn't catch me, could ya?'

Jill's brow furrowed in deep thought. Had she been talking in her sleep? 'How did you know that, Karl?'

'I was there, by the river; we had the same dream,' he said matter-of-factly.

Completely puzzled, she thought, 'Am I hearing this? We can't have the same dream, can we?' For the rest of the afternoon, it baffled her.

That evening, they all gathered to sit around the dining table. George always tried to get home in time for them to eat together. 'Something really strange happened today,' said Jill.

'What's that, love?' asked George, looking up from his meal.

'Karl and I had a nap in the garden today and somehow we had the same dream.'

George raised his eyebrows. 'That's unusual,' he said.

'Me and Karl do that all the time,' Charlie spouted up as if it was the most ordinary thing, his eyes not leaving his dinner for a second.

Jill put down her knife and fork and placed an elbow on the table, her hand rubbing her forehead. 'What do you mean, Charlie?' she asked.

He stopped eating and looked up. 'If I have a bad dream or a fun one, Karl gets into my bed and we dream together.' Jill and George looked at each other in disbelief. Karl was paying no attention at all to the conversation.

'Is this right, Karl?' asked Jill. Karl nodded his head, more interested in eating than talking. Jill turned her attention back to his brother. 'How long has this been going on, Charlie?'

'Always,' said Charlie, quite simply. Both parents took a long look at each other. 'What's wrong?' asked the little boy, 'It's not bad, is it?'

'No, son,' an endearing smile forming on Jill's face, 'it's just' – she thought for a moment trying to find the right words to use – 'it's a very unusual gift.' They were the best words she could come up with at that moment in time. Charlie went back to his dinner.

Five years later

Karl suddenly stopped eating and put down his fork, 'Am I the only one that can do it then, Mommy?' Jill saw something in Karl's eyes that worried her. At five years old, he actually looked troubled, as if he had all the problems in the world on his little shoulders. 'I'm sure there are lots of others who can do it, Karl,' Jill tried to pacify him. 'Don't worry, son, don't think about it now; eat up your tea.'

For the rest of evening Karl was very quiet, too thoughtful for Jill's liking. By 7.30 pm both boys were in bed and their parents settled in front of the TV, looking forward to the nice relaxed evening ahead of them. 'Do you think we should take him to the doctor's, George?'

George was staring at the television.

'George, are you listening to me?'

George jumped, breaking his concentration from the TV. 'Sorry, love, I was miles away.'

'What do you think about Karl?' Jill repeated.

George thought for a moment. 'I think the best thing we can do is have a quiet word with the doctor and see what he thinks.'

Jill sat back and stared at the ceiling. George could see she was really worried. He got up from his chair, went over to the sofa and sat down beside her. 'Come here, love.' He put his arm around her, pulling her close. 'Don't worry, we've always thought he was special. If anything it's some sort of gift, you wait and see.'

'I hope you're right, George. After I've dropped Charlie at school in the morning, I'll see if Kerry next door but one will have Karl for an hour while I pop down to the surgery.'

'Good, now sit back and try to relax.' George turned back towards the TV and was quickly engrossed in the programme. Unknown to him, however, for the rest of the evening Jill couldn't get the experience of the dream out of her mind.

The next morning as planned, Jill dropped Charlie at school and Karl at the neighbour's house. The surgery was busy, but the receptionist could see the concern on Jill's face and said she would try to fit her in between appointments. Jill sat nervously in the waiting room. 'How the hell am I going to handle this?' she thought.

Eventually, the receptionist called out her name. Jill got up and went to the reception hatch. 'The doctor will see you now,' said the receptionist, a gentle smile forming on her face. Jill thanked her and went along the hallway.

There were three doctors at the practice. The Hennesseys' GP was Dr Edwards, a man in his late forties. From past experience, he was a very understanding man. Years ago, when they had been trying for children, he had been very helpful and supportive. The last door in the corridor had a plaque with 'Dr Edwards' written on it. She knocked and Edwards called her in. He was sitting at his desk putting notes into the previous patient's file. He looked up and smiled. 'Hello, Jill, it's been a while since I've seen you; please take a seat.' Jill sat down, still wondering what she was going to say. 'How's . . .' he stopped for a second, searching his memory for her husband's name, 'George and the boys?'

'That's what I've come to see you about, Dr Edwards. You see, it's Karl.' Jill was obviously struggling for words.

'Go on,' he said, 'take your time.'

Over the next few minutes, Jill explained what had happened the day before, including what Charlie had said about it being normal to them. The doctor was intrigued. Karl had been closely observed for the first year of his life due to the accident at his birth, but all had seemed well. Edwards had never heard of anything like this before. 'I'll be honest with you, Jill, this type of case is completely out of my league. I'll contact the neurology department at the hospital and arrange an appointment. I know they are very busy, so the sooner I get a letter to them, the better. If they haven't contacted you in seven or eight weeks, give me a call and I'll chase them up.'

'Thank you, Doctor,' said Jill, getting to her feet.

'Try not to worry, Jill. I'm sure there's a simple explanation for what's happening to Karl.'

'I hope so, Dr Edwards, I hope so. Thanks for seeing me at such short notice.'

'You're welcome, Jill, any time. Bye for now.'

As Jill left the surgery her mind felt a little calmer; at least they had got the ball rolling.

The summer holidays came and went, and now that Karl had started school, Jill got herself a part-time job at the local supermarket and settled into a routine. The kids seemed happy enough, and nothing more was said about the dreams. Almost eight weeks to the day, a letter arrived with an appointment for Karl to be seen at the Queen Elizabeth Hospital, Neurological Studies Department. Suddenly, all the worries came flooding back into Jill's mind. Subconsciously, she had hoped the appointment would never arrive, but deep down inside she knew certain questions had to be answered, not for her sake but for Karl's.

Two weeks later Jill dropped Charlie at school and informed Karl's teacher that Karl had a hospital appointment. Karl was at home with his father; George had taken a day's holiday from work to enable him to accompany them to the hospital. As soon as Jill got back, it would be time to set off. George was in front of the mirror combing his hair, and Karl stood watching his father intently. George caught sight of Karl's reflection in the mirror and turned to him, smiling. 'Hello, little man, how long you been there?' Karl continued staring at him. 'What's wrong, cat got your tongue?' asked George.

'Daddy, why do I have to go to the hospital. Am I sick?'

George looked intently at him. It was the first time he had seen Karl looking stressed. 'Come here, son; sit down.' They sat together on the sofa. 'Son, I don't expect you to understand this, but you have a gift. I can't tell you why, but that's the way it is. You may not like it, but that's life. I'll help you cope with it any way I can, but I have a feeling it's for you to deal with, and when you realise it's a gift, make the most of it.'

Karl leaned his head against his father's shoulder, and George put his arm around him, pulling him close. 'Don't worry, son, don't worry.'

The sound of Jill's key in the front door brought the moment to an abrupt halt. 'You two ready?' she called, 'We'll have to get a move on now or we'll be late.'

'Come on, son,' said George. Karl smiled at him and winked, a private exchange they both used to say everything was fine. George returned the gesture.

The journey to the hospital didn't take long, but they were delayed parking the car – it seemed as if half the population had converged on the hospital all at the same time. George got a ticket from the pay and display machine and placed it on the dashboard.

'Right then, we all set?' asked George. Karl nodded.

Jill took hold of Karl's hand. 'Let's go son.' A brief smile and they set off across the car park towards the main hospital entrance.

The appointment had been made for 9:30 am and it was now just after 9:25, so they were pushing it a little. George looked at his watch. 'Hey, we'd better get a move on; you know how funny these people can be with appointment times.' They doubled their pace in an attempt to claw back a few seconds.

Just inside the main entrance two women manned computer stations behind a reception desk. 'Morning,' said George, opening Karl's appointment letter. 'My son has an appointment at 9:30.'

'Can I take a look, sir?' asked the receptionist, reaching for the letter. 'Ah yes, you want Neurology; it's in D wing. Go straight down the corridor' – she pointed across the way – 'keep going as far as you can, then turn right, all the way down that corridor, and right in front of you will be a lift. Go up to the second floor and you're there.'

'Thanks,' said George taking back the letter. He turned towards Jill.

'Did you get that?' she asked.

'Think so,' he said, raising his eyebrows slightly. They set off down the corridor at a hurried pace. The sheer size of the hospital overwhelmed them. By the time they arrived at the lift it was 9:40. George repeatedly pressed the button on the wall. 'It won't come any faster, love,' said Jill. Finally, the door opened and they stepped in, selecting the button for the second floor. When the door opened, they were faced with another reception desk, where a moon-faced woman looked up at them.

'Can I help you?' she asked.

'Morning,' said George. 'My son Karl has an appointment, I'm sorry we are a little late.'

She looked over the counter at Karl, a broad smile forming on her face. 'Hello,' she whispered to him, 'don't worry, everyone's late for the first appointment.' Then, turning to George, 'We are a little too well tucked away. Have you got his appointment letter?' George took the letter from the envelope and passed it over.

'Let me see.' She went down a list of names. 'Here we are – Karl Hennessey.' She read out his name, address and date of birth and Jill confirmed them. 'Right then, while you are waiting to be called in, fill out this questionnaire on behalf of Karl.' She passed over a clipboard with the questionnaire attached.

They had only half completed the form when a very smartly dressed young man came walking down the corridor. The receptionist immediately blushed. 'Morning, Dr Berrow,' she smiled.

'Morning Sandra, and how are you today?' he returned.

'I'm very well, thank you. Your first patient has arrived.'

Dr Berrow turned slightly to peer at the letter on the desk, and then immediately spun round.

'Good morning. Mr and Mrs Hennessey, I presume?' George stood up and shook his hand. The doctor then reached over to take Jill's hand. It was clear to see why the receptionist had blushed; he was a very handsome man, impeccably groomed with jet-black hair and piercing blue eyes. Jill self-consciously looked away, realising she was staring at him.

The doctor crouched down, 'And you must be Karl.' Karl clung on to his father's leg, not quite knowing how to take him. Berrow extended his hand towards the small boy.

'Shake hands, son,' said George. Slowly, Karl placed his little hand into Berrow's.

'Very pleased to meet you, young man; I've heard some good things about you. Shall we go down to my office? I've got some things down there you just might find interesting.' The doctor stood up, 'If you'd like to follow me to my office, Mr and Mrs Hennessey, we'll get started.'

'I haven't finished the questionnaire yet,' said George.

'That's fine,' replied Berrow, 'just leave it on the reception desk, we can finish that later. Shall we?' Berrow extended his arm to usher them in the right direction. 'Sorry it took so long to get the appointment out to you, only it's been very busy the last couple of months.'

'On the contrary, Doctor,' said Jill, 'we thought it was very quick.' They approached the end of the corridor and the doctor stopped, opening the last door on the left.

'Here we are.' Again he extended his arm. 'After you, Mr and Mrs Hennessey, and you, young man.'

They had expected a small office with a desk and a couple of filing cabinets but they couldn't have been more wrong. It was like entering Dr Who's Tardis. The room was almost thirty metres long, with the far wall covered in shelving stacked with folders, mostly patients' case notes. Berrow's desk was quaintly tucked away in a corner.

Dotted all around the room were expensive-looking high-tech machines; the Hennesseys couldn't even begin to imagine what they were for. Karl's eyes were quickly drawn to one particular area; it looked like a toy shop but with a difference: every toy was a puzzle of one kind or another, some more challenging than others.

'Do you like puzzles, Karl?' asked Berrow, observing the child intently.

'Speak up, son,' said George.

Jill jumped in. 'Give him a chance, George.'

The doctor knelt down in front of the little boy. 'I tell you what,' he said, 'how about you go and play with all those toys and I'll have a chat with your mom and dad?' A big smile beamed across Karl's face and he turned and ran in the direction of the toys. Berrow smiled reassuringly at Karl's parents. 'Shall we have a seat?'

They walked over to the desk and sat down. 'I've read the letter from Dr Edwards, and I have to say I've had some strange cases in the past, but if Karl can do what you say, it is truly unique gift. I've done some research and can't find anything documented that's even close.'

George and Jill looked stumped. They were hoping the doctor would say, 'Oh it's quite common; I see this from time to time.' But no such luck; he was as stumped as they were.

'With your permission, I'd like to start a series of tests.' Both of them sat up straight. 'Don't worry, Karl won't even realise the tests are taking place. Just a few sticky pads on his body while he attempts a few puzzles. Trust me, he'll think it's just a big game.' Relieved, Jill sighed audibly.

'How long before you start the tests?' asked George, glancing in Karl's direction.

'No time like the present,' replied Berrow. 'Let's go and see how he's getting on over there.'

They went down to the area where Karl was playing. 'Do you like these puzzles, Karl?' asked Berrow. Karl timidly looked up and nodded his head. 'I tell you what, let's play a game.' Berrow pulled over a machine mounted on a trolley and started unwinding some thin wires. 'See these, Karl?' Karl looked on intently. 'They're sticky – watch.' Berrow pressed a small pad to each of his own temples and attached a wire to each one. Reaching down, he plugged the machine in. As he turned the switch to the 'On' position, the needles on the gauges began to move.

'This is an electroencephalograph. That's a bit of a mouthful, so we just call it an EEG. Basically, Mr and Mrs Hennessey, it monitors brainwave activity. You see, there are five main brainwave patterns – I won't bore you with them individually – but what the EEG does is help us understand them a little better. It's completely harmless. Would you like a go, Karl?'

Karl nodded and smiled. Berrow turned off the machine and pulled the pads from his temples. 'Right then, let's put them on.' Karl stood up. Berrow carefully attached the pads to Karl's temples and switched on the machine. 'Whoa!' laughed Berrow. 'I think we need to recalibrate a little, not to worry.' Already the brainwave activity was nearly twice that of the doctor. He adjusted several dials and then turned to Karl.

'Right, let's try a puzzle. Mmm, which one?' Berrow scanned the shelves looking for a suitable puzzle. 'I wonder, this one is a little hard, but let's see how you get on.' Walking over to a nearby shelf, he picked up a Rubik cube. Karl's eyes were fixed on the puzzle as Berrow passed it to him. 'OK Karl, what you have to do is . . .' Karl instantly began rotating the cube, attempting to synchronise the colours. Berrow smiled and laughed. 'Feel free to start!'

The concentration on Karl's face was intense, and already the colours seemed to be falling into line. Berrow pulled up his sleeve and began timing Karl.

'Finished.' Karl held up the cube, smiling.

'That was the fastest I have ever seen a cube completed,' said Berrow. He turned to the EEG, which was rapidly printing out Karl's brainwave frequencies on a large sheet of computer paper. 'There must be something wrong with the calibration, it's way off the scale.'

Gently he disconnected the cables from Karl's temples, and the gauges instantly returned to zero. Berrow had a look of utter amazement on his face. 'Well, that's incredible. I've never seen frequencies that high before.'

Again he placed pads onto his own temples and connected the cables; the gauges were barely moving in comparison to Karl's recordings. Berrow seemed transfixed in his work, making adjustments to the machine's settings, trying to find an explanation for the phenomenon he had just witnessed. Jill and George looked at each other with increasing concern.

'Is everything all right, Doctor?' asked Jill.

Berrow's gaze remained fixed on the print out. 'From these figures I've just got from the machine, something amazing seems to be going on in young Karl's head. I think we need to make a few phone calls.'

George interrupted him. 'But is he OK, Doctor?'

'Mr and Mrs Hennessey, he's more than OK. Karl's brainwave frequencies are higher than those of any other patient I have ever seen, and from research I've done over the years, more brain activity than anyone else has ever seen. Could you bring Karl back at short notice?'

'Yes, of course,' replied Jill, 'but is he going to be all right?'

Berrow put his hand on her arm. 'I'm sure you have nothing to worry about. I'll make some calls then get straight back to you.' Berrow pulled the pads from the sides of his head and stood up. 'I have your number. There's a doctor based in London, a friend of mine; he specialises in this kind of thing. I'll give him a call. I feel sure he would like to take a closer look at Karl.'

Berrow smiled down at Karl and they all stood up. Berrow shook George's hand. 'Now remember, don't worry. I have a feeling Karl is a very special young man.'

'Thanks for your help, Dr Berrow,' said George as they all walked towards the door. As the door closed behind them, Berrow turned into his office, a broad smile beaming across his face. Squeezing his fists tight he raised his arms. 'Yes, yes!' he exclaimed aloud. He had spent his entire career waiting for a moment like this; Karl Hennessey could potentially put him well and truly on the map in his field of expertise.

3

The guinea pig

Berrow sat down at his desk, still grinning like a Cheshire cat. He flicked through his Rolodex to locate the business card of a Dr Wayne Clark. Clark had been one of Berrow's lecturers at university and was now a leading figure in their field of work. Selecting the card, he dialled the number; the phone rang out. After a short time, a woman answered.
'Hello, Dr Clark's surgery. Can I help you?'
'Yes, is Dr Clark available to take a call?'
'Who's calling please?' Berrow gave his name and was put on hold. He recalled something Clark had said to him at university: if you are really lucky, one very special patient will walk through the door and change your career for ever.
'Hello, Dr Berrow, I'm sorry Dr Clark is with a patient at the moment. Could I take a message?'
Berrow was still deep in thought. 'Oh sorry, yes, would you tell him that the one special patient has just walked into my surgery?'
'Sorry, Dr Berrow, did you say the one special patient?'
'Yes,' replied Berrow, smiling to himself, 'just say that, he'll know exactly what I mean. He has my number.'
'Thank you, Dr Berrow. Goodbye.' With that, he hung up.

Karl and his parents stepped out of the lift on the ground floor of the hospital. They walked back towards the main entrance with Karl between them, holding both their hands tightly and enjoying the extra attention.
'Well, son,' said George, 'he seemed like a nice man.'
'I liked his games,' said Karl, looking up at his father.
'Would you like to come back and do some more?' asked Jill. Karl turned to his mother, nodding his head up and down enthusiastically.
'Right then, let's get you off to school and we'll see what we can do.'
Within half an hour they arrived at Karl's school. After reporting into the office, they took Karl along to his class and he quickly blended into

the class activities. His parents informed his teacher of the pending tests, and then slowly made their way out into the corridor. They stood for a moment observing Karl through the classroom window, neither of them saying it but both thinking the same thing. What was in store for their special little boy? Only time would tell.

Later that day, Berrow was in his office, catching up on some outstanding paperwork in between patients. The phone rang. Scrambling through the case notes and papers, he picked up the receiver. 'Hello. Dr Berrow speaking.'

'Hi, Alan, it's Wayne Clark.'

'Dr Clark, it's great to hear from you.'

'Likewise. I've just got your message; sorry I didn't get back to you sooner – this new receptionist isn't up to speed yet. So, this patient; you think he's the one?'

'Absolutely,' replied Berrow eagerly, 'I've never seen frequencies like it. I asked him to attempt a Rubik puzzle. Well, attempt it is an understatement; during the process his beta frequency hit sixty Hertz!'

'I take it the EEG is in good order?' Clark was cautious.

'It was serviced last month, and I tested it on myself just minutes before him. The thing that excited me the most was the frequency of his theta waves – I've never seen a frequency higher than eight Hertz; his was over twenty, virtually off the scale.' Clark was impressed. 'But the best I haven't told you, Wayne,' said Berrow, lowering his voice, 'this is a five-year-old child.'

Clark sat back in his chair. If Berrow's test results were correct, this was an unprecedented case. He was keen to see this child. Berrow agreed to having Clark sit in on Karl's next appointment, secretly thrilled to have such a highly respected figure working alongside him.

An appointment was made for the following Thursday. George had been unable to get the time off work, so Jill agreed to take Karl to the hospital alone. Berrow and Clark had got together the previous evening; it started out as purely a business meeting, Karl being the subject in hand. But as the evening wore on, they both had a few drinks and started reminiscing about past colleagues, so very soon it became more social than business.

The following morning at 9 am prompt, Karl and his mother arrived at the hospital. Karl was so excited. Jill was pleased with how he was taking it all in his stride, but, if the truth be told, she was more than a little apprehensive. They made their way to the Neurological Studies Department and, as they stepped out the lift, Sandra, the receptionist, once again greeted them. She told them to go straight down to Dr Berrow's office, where he was waiting for them.

Karl happily skipped his way down the corridor, his mother warning him to stop running. Jill knocked on the door, and almost instantly it opened, as if Berrow had been standing behind it waiting for their arrival. Berrow greeted them, standing back from the door and gesturing with his hand for them to enter. Almost sheepishly, Jill walked through the door, Karl staying very close to her side, all his bravado now consumed by shyness. Clark got up from his seat by the desk and Berrow introduced him. 'Mrs Hennessey, Karl, I'd like you both to meet a friend and colleague of mine, Dr Clark.' Clark walked over to them, a friendly smile on his face.

'Alan, really, first names please. Wayne Clark, Mrs Hennessey, very pleased to meet you.'

'It's Jill,' she replied.

'Pleased to meet you, Jill, and you, young man, must be Karl. I've heard lots of good things about you.' Karl turned his face into his mother's skirt in an attempt to hide his shyness.

'Would you like a drink, Jill, before we get started?' asked Berrow.

'No, I'm fine, thank you,' she replied. Berrow was doing his utmost to try and relax both Karl and his mother. If he was to test Karl's ability to the extreme, he would have to gain the complete trust of his parents.

'OK then, if you're ready we'll get started. Right Karl, how would you like to show Wayne how you completed that puzzle I gave you last time I saw you?' Karl's face turned towards Berrow's and, with a smile breaking through, he nodded his head. 'Can we put those sticky pads on again?' asked Berrow. Again Karl nodded. Doing his best to make it as much fun as possible, Berrow attached the pads to Karl's head and switched on the EEG machine.

'Let's find that puzzle,' said Berrow. Scanning the shelves he quickly found the Rubik cube and turned it in a few directions to well and truly disarrange the various colours. 'Right then, young man, let's see what you can do with this.'

Instantly, Karl went to work turning the cube left then right, rotating it to and fro. Clark observed the machine; the frequencies were above average but no sign of overexaggerated wave activity.

'Finished!' exclaimed Karl.

'Did you find that easier than last time, Karl?' asked Clark.

'Yeah,' Karl replied, looking pleased with himself, 'I know how to do it now.' Placing the puzzle on the table, he sat back in his chair, squeezing his small hands together.

'Well, that was a little too easy for you, young man,' said Clark. 'Let's see if we can find something a little more challenging for him, Alan.' Berrow scanned the shelves looking for a puzzle Karl hadn't previously attempted in the hope they might just get a response.

'Let's try this one.' Berrow picked up a symmetrical ball puzzle. There was one key piece, but would Karl be able to work that out? He passed it to Karl, who instantly began rotating it in his hands, carefully scrutinising all the individual blocks. After thirty seconds, Berrow took back the ball, turned his back on Karl and slipped out the key piece. Instantly, the ball collapsed into a multitude of pieces in his hands. Turning back he placed all the pieces on the table. 'There you go Karl, try that one.' A frown appeared on Karl's small brow; Berrow wondered if he had overchallenged him.

Sitting back in his chair, Clark's eyes wandered to and from Karl and the EEG machine. Slowly, as Karl began to assemble the ball, the various frequency-monitoring needles flickered into action, then darted across the screen at an alarming rate. Clark's eyes widened. Within two minutes Karl had the ball assembled in two pieces with just the key piece to insert. He pushed them together and inserted the key piece, slowly rotating the two halves in opposite directions. Click. The piece locked it all together.

'Done it,' said Karl. He placed the puzzle on the table, again looking extremely happy. Clark was temporarily stuck for words; he sat back placing both hands on his head in amazement. 'Well done, Karl,' said Berrow, looking at Clark with a broad smile forming on his face.

Clark stood up. 'Remarkable, Alan. Have you seen those readings?'

'I told you he was special,' said Berrow quietly. They both looked at Karl, who drew his knees up to his chest, squeezing them tightly with his arms. With a cheeky grin on his face he asked, 'Shall we play some more?'

Over the next hour, Karl exhausted their supply of puzzles. The harder the task, the more he amazed them. They monitored him constantly, gathering valuable information. Eventually, Clark looked at his watch. 'I think that's enough for one day, Karl,' he said. 'What do you say Alan? We don't want to tire the young man out now, do we?'

Clark had been watching Karl's mother, who was becoming increasingly agitated; if they were to get the best out of Karl, the support of his parents was crucial. After reassuring Jill about the data they were collecting, Jill agreed to their proposal to let Karl rest for a few days and then try some sound therapy and see how it would affect his concentration.

Once Karl and his mother had left, the two doctors sat and discussed their findings. 'I've never seen anything like it, Alan.' Clark's excitement was obvious as he examined the EEG print-out. 'The frequency of his beta waves is unprecedented.' Berrow walked over to join Clark examining the print-out.

'Something else I'd like to try, Wayne.'

'What's that?' replied Clark, still deep in thought.

'The child's mother claims that when he sleeps he can not only enter other people's dreams, but he can take part in them.'

Clark's gaze moved from the print-out sheet. 'You mean actually be part of somebody else's subconscious?'

'That's what his mother claims,' Berrow replied. 'In fact, that's what he was referred to me for in the first place.'

Clark raised his eyebrows. 'I've never heard of anything like it before; this I have to see.' Clark again turned to the computer print-out. 'Look at his theta frequencies; even at rest they're three times that of anything I've ever seen; it's remarkable. If we are to monitor his sleep patterns, we need to go slow – did you see his mother today? She looked more than a little concerned at times, to say the least.'

'I agree;' said Berrow, 'we have to remember he is only five years old. It might be an idea to reduce the length of his appointments a little, maybe longer rest periods between appointments.'

'Good idea, Alan,' said Clark, scratching his head. 'I think we need to concentrate on winning over his parents a little. At the end of the day, without them we could lose Karl altogether.'

Over the next few weeks they put their plan into action, reducing the timescale and frequency of Karl's appointments. It proved to be a good move – Karl had seemed to be getting a little bored with their tests, but the less frequent and reduced length of his appointments seemed to be making him hungrier to take part. Trying various methods, they found that rhythmic sound had a profound effect on Karl's brainwave activity, disrupting his concentration so that at times he would become so frustrated that he would throw the puzzle to the ground, only to be scolded by his mother.

Both doctors agreed it was time to monitor Karl's sleep patterns. They had developed a good relationship with both Karl and his mother – it was now time to find out just how good. At the next appointment, they would put their plan to Jill.

Karl and his mother arrived as usual for his Thursday appointment at 9 am. Trying not to affect his school work, they kept to a rigid schedule, always getting him back to school for morning playtime. They arrived at Berrow's office to find both doctors sitting at the desk discussing some of Karl's previous test results. 'Morning, Jill; morning, young man. And how are we today?' asked Berrow, enthusiastically.

'Fine, thanks,' replied Jill. She always kept a smile on her face in their presence. The truth was that it was all becoming a bit too much for her. As far as she could see, the only people benefiting from any of this were the doctors carrying out their research. Clark was working virtually full time now, the case had intrigued him so much.

'What have you got for him today?' asked Jill, 'I haven't been able to keep him quiet since he had his breakfast.' Karl's face reddened; as his shyness surfaced he took refuge behind his mother.

'Well, Jill,' Clark got up from the desk, 'we were wondering, the tests we've been carrying out have given us lots to think about in relation to Karl's' – he hesitated for a second – 'shall we say, condition. But what we really need to do now is monitor him during sleep.'

Jill looked puzzled and automatically reached out to Karl, protectively. 'How do you plan to do that?'

'Well,' Clark replied carefully, 'if both you and your husband agreed, we thought we would set up a few pieces of equipment at your home. Once asleep, Karl would be none the wiser, just like the tests we have been carrying out here, except that we could get down to the root of the problem.'

Jill suddenly looked straight at him, fixing his gaze with a steely stare. Clark instantly knew he had offended her.

'*Problem*, Dr Clark? One thing Karl most definitely doesn't have is a *problem*.'

'I'm sorry, Jill,' Clarke replied quickly, 'it was a very poor choice of words and I apologise. Shall we say *gift*?'

Jill thought about it for a few moments – it would certainly be a relief to know what was happening to Karl. 'I'll have a word with Karl's dad,' she replied, 'and if he agrees, we'll do it.'

'Right, then,' said Clark cautiously, 'we'll leave it with you.' Not wanting to pressurise Jill, Clark's attention moved to Karl. 'Well then, young man, let's get down to work.'

That evening, George arrived home to his favourite dinner. As they sat down to eat, George smiled. 'Cottage pie; what have I done to deserve this?'

Jill looked up and smiled too. 'Karl's doctors want to monitor his sleep,' she replied.

'What's that going to prove?' asked George, putting his knife and fork down.

'Well, they hope it will enlighten us a little about Karl's gift.' Karl's eyes moved from one parent to the other as they spoke.

'I suppose it can't do any harm, can it?'

Jill shrugged her shoulders in response.

'Where and when do they plan to do it?'

'Here, if we don't mind. There will be a couple of machines under his bed and a few sticky pads on him; it's all automated.'

George picked up his knife and fork and continued eating his dinner. Looking over at Karl, he asked, 'What do you think, mate?' Karl shrugged his shoulders, impersonating his mother. 'Well, that's it then; if it's OK with Karl, it's OK with me. Now, can I get on with this cottage pie?'

The following day, Jill rang the hospital and informed Berrow that he could go ahead with the sleep monitoring. Enthusiastic to get started as quickly as possible, Berrow immediately arranged for the equipment to be taken to the Hennesseys' house and positioned as discreetly as possible by Karl's bed. Unfortunately, that meant imposing a little on Charlie's space but, unknowingly, Charlie was also to be included in the tests.

Berrow and Clark arranged to be at the house the following Monday evening at 7:30 pm, when the boys would be starting to settle down. Karl had gone through the process of being attached to the machines many times, so that wasn't a problem, but going to bed with the pads and wires on might just be a little more complicated.

When the doctors arrived, the boys were both upstairs getting ready for bed. The presence of the machines had made them both very excited, and they had been asked to promise not to touch anything. Clark rang the doorbell and looked at Berrow. 'Fingers crossed, Alan, this could be the breakthrough we've been waiting for.'

George opened the door. 'Good evening, Mr Hennessey,' said Clark.

'Please call me George.'

Berrow introduced Clark, and George firmly shook both doctors' hands before ushering them into the house, closing the door behind them. 'I must say, all that equipment looks a little complicated to me,' said George.

Berrow smiled, 'Honestly, George, there may be lots of wires and gauges, but it's not that complicated. It merely measures different types of electrical frequency.'

'As I said,' replied George, smiling, 'it looks complicated to me.'

As they entered the living room, Jill jumped to her feet. 'Good evening,' said the doctors in unison.

Jill acknowledged them. 'The boys are just getting their pyjamas on. Can I get you both a drink, tea or coffee?'

'I'm OK thanks, Jill,' said Clark.

'Likewise,' said Berrow. 'I'm trying to reduce my caffeine intake.'

'I do hope they haven't messed with any of your equipment,' said George with an anxious look. 'We made them promise to leave it alone.'

'Don't worry, George,' Berrow reassured him, 'they can't hurt themselves.'

'It's those machines I was worrying about,' replied George, and they all laughed.

'Do you mind if we go up?' asked Berrow. 'We need to set the calibration and make sure it's all working correctly.'

'No, Dr Berrow, you go right ahead. The boys will show you what room it's all in.'

Before they were halfway up the stairs, two small faces appeared at the top peering down at them. Clark smiled, 'Hello, boys. We know you're Karl, so you must be Charlie.' The boys chuckled and ran off to their bedroom.

Entering the room, the doctors were pleasantly surprised by the space they had to work in. Both boys were on one of the single beds, a quilt over the top of their heads, the chuckling sound of mischief coming from beneath. 'They must have gone, Alan,' said Clark, playing along with their little game. Then he grabbed a foot poking out from the quilt. 'Got ya!' With a squeal, the leg quickly retracted back under the quilt, followed by the sound of more laughter. It was pleasing to know that the boys were so relaxed about the tests.

Before long, all the wires were in place and the machines were calibrated ready to go. Jill came up with George close behind her; the boys were still giggling under the quilt.

'Right, you pair,' said Jill, 'get into bed.'

Both doctors stood up. 'She means the boys, Doctors,' quipped George.

'George!' said Jill, her cheeks reddening.

'Just a bit of fun, dear.' He raised his eyebrows at the two slightly embarrassed men.

Karl suddenly leapt from under the quilt and into the other bed.

'Right, young man,' said Clark, 'you know how these go; do you want to put them on yourself?' Karl took the pads one at a time and placed them on his head. 'Excellent, you'll be a doctor yourself one day, Karl.'

Clark turned to Jill and George, 'I was wondering if Karl and Charlie can interact with each other within their dreams? What do you think about letting Charlie join in? It would kill two birds with one stone, and you know it's completely harmless.' It was a gamble, putting them on the spot, but it might pay off.

The boys' parents looked at each other a little uncomfortably, and then shrugged their shoulders. 'If it can't hurt him, why not?' said George, so the doctor quickly attached extra cables to the secondary output sockets, and then one by one attached them to Charlie. To the relief of the doctors, as far as Charlie was concerned it was just a big game. If they were to keep the boys and their parents happy, they had to make the process fun.

They had ordered extra-long cables for the EEG machine to ensure they weren't overstretched and pulled off in the night. After a final check on the machines, the doctors said good night to the boys. Jill and George gave both boys a kiss, told them not to mess with the machines, and they all left the room, closing the door behind them.

'Well,' said Clark, 'we won't interrupt your evening any longer. What time do the boys normally get up?'

'Usually about half seven,' said Jill.

'Great, Jill; we'll get here for about quarter past seven. As soon as you wake them up, we'll get all the wires out of the way. Don't worry if they've pulled one or two off during the night. Right then, we'll bid you good night.'

Later that evening, as Jill and George went to bed, Jill stuck her head round the door of the boys' room. Karl had climbed out of his bed and into Charlie's, as he did from time to time. All the wires looked OK, and the boys looked so content she closed the door and went to bed.

The next morning at 7:15 am prompt, the doorbell rang. Jill had been up for half an hour or so, preparing breakfast and packing lunches for the boys. As she opened the front door she was greeted by two large, expectant grins. 'Morning, Jill,' said the doctors in unison.

'Morning, Doctors, come in. Can I get you a coffee?'

'That sounds great,' replied Clark. 'Coffee is my downfall, Jill; if there is one thing I need to cut down on, that's it.'

Berrow closed the door and they all went through to the living room. 'How did you get on then, Jill?'

'Fine; they haven't made a sound. Karl climbed into Charlie's bed, as he often does, but the wires looked OK so I left him there.'

'If you don't mind, Jill,' said Berrow, 'I'll go up and have a look at the results.'

'Of course not, Dr Berrow, they'll be awake by now.' Berrow went upstairs, closely followed by Clark. As they entered the boys' room, Karl was sitting up in Charlie's bed, removing the sticky pads, one by one, from his body. Berrow greeted him, and Karl replied with a yawn.

'Let me help you there.' Berrow removed the wires from their sockets on the EEG machine. Suddenly, Charlie suddenly sat up as if startled. 'Oh, you're awake young man; did you sleep well?'

'Yes, thank you,' said Charlie. 'Me and Karl went to the seaside.'

'I bet that was a nice holiday. Was it last summer?' said Clark.

'No,' said Charlie, 'last night.'

Both doctors stopped and looked at Charlie. 'What do you mean, Charlie?' asked Berrow.

'I had a dream about the seaside, and Karl came to play.'

Clark looked at Berrow in amazement. 'Is that right, Karl?'

'Yes,' he replied in a matter-of-fact way. 'We built sandcastles.'

Jill came in with two mugs of coffee. 'Here you go, Doctors; morning, boys.'

Clark turned and looked at Jill. 'Jill, the boys just said they had the same dream.'

'Yes, Dr Clark, this happens quite a lot; that's why I came to you in the first place.' She turned to the boys, 'Come on boys, breakfast.' The boys jumped out of bed and followed their mother out of the room.

Clark sat down on the bed, amazed at what he had heard. Berrow turned his attention to the printer, carefully stashed under Karl's bed. As he tore off the print-out, his eyes widened.

'Wayne, you're not going to believe this.' He handed the print-out to Clark. For a second, Clark thought there had been a malfunction with the machine, but the secondary read-out, which was Charlie's, was absolutely normal. Karl's frequencies had gone off the scale, and both doctors quickly realised they had witnessed something never seen before in their field of work.

4

Enough is enough

The two boys were sitting at the kitchen table tucking into bowls of cereal. Clark and Berrow appeared; Berrow was clutching the print-out sheets. 'Jill,' said Clark, 'do you mind if we ask the boys a couple of questions while they are eating breakfast?'

'No, Dr Clark,' Jill replied. 'Boys, listen to Dr Clark.'

'Hi, guys.' They both looked up from their bowls. 'Charlie, when you said you had the same dream as Karl . . .'

'No,' Charlie interrupted him, 'Karl came into my dream; I can't go into his dream.'

The doctor's attention was drawn to Karl. 'What do you do, Karl?' asked Clarke.

Karl raised his hand and placed it on Charlie's. 'You hold hands.'

Charlie suddenly burst into the conversation. 'He just has to touch me.'

Clark and Berrow were amazed.

Jill turned to them. 'It's happened to me as well, Dr Clark. I fell asleep in the garden with Karl lying next to me. Next thing I knew, I was dreaming and Karl was talking to me, just as I'm talking to you. Then, just like that, he was gone.'

'This is truly amazing, Jill,' said Clarke. 'I'd like to ask your permission to look deeper into this er . . .' – he hesitated for a second – 'phenomenon. It's the only word I can think of, Jill.'

'As long as it helps Karl to understand his gift, as we like to call it, it's OK with me and George.'

The doctors gathered up the rest of their paperwork, said their goodbyes and returned to the hospital. All their findings had to be recorded; it really was becoming very exciting.

George agreed with Jill to let the intensity of Karl's tests increase. Over the next two months, the doctors tried every test they knew, recording some incredible data but not really getting any answers. They decided to try using low-level sound from a machine in Karl's bedroom to see if it suppressed his ability to use his gift, just as it had with the puzzles. A few weeks into the tests, Karl began to complain to his mother that he was getting headaches, but, being unaware of the technical details of the tests, she was unable to make any link and anyway, why would she?

Jill was sitting at the kitchen table flicking through a magazine as she sipped her coffee; it was rare nowadays to get any relaxation time to herself. George was at work, and the boys were both at school. The phone rang; it was Karl's headmaster asking if it was possible for her to come in for a meeting with him. She was surprised and rather concerned, but he declined to discuss the matter on the telephone. As she had the afternoon off work, she could come in that same day. He agreed that sooner rather than later would be good. So much for a relaxing afternoon, Jill thought. She slugged back the remainder of her coffee, put the cup into the sink and went to get ready for the meeting.

When Jill arrived at the school reception, the secretary paged the headmaster over the tannoy. Mark Wilson had held the post of Principal at Karl's school for over 20 years. A highly motivated individual, he was respected by parents and children alike. As he came along the corridor towards the reception, he could see Jill sitting stiffly towards the edge of her chair. Hearing his footsteps, she turned and recognised him, instantly standing and smiling. As he approached, he extended his hand.

'Mrs Hennessey, so pleased you could make it at short notice.' Jill shook his outstretched hand, sensing the sincerity in his touch. 'Please come into my office; can I get you a drink?'

Jill declined, and Wilson ushered her into the office. As she sat facing the desk, Jill felt as if she was back at school, in trouble for some childish prank.

'I don't have to tell you, Mrs Hennessey, Karl is a very bright young man.' Jill nodded in agreement. 'But something concerns me. His form tutor, Mrs Beech, has seen a dramatic change in him over the last few weeks.'

The troubled expression on Jill's face said everything she wanted to say.

'Please don't be alarmed;' urged Wilson, 'this happens sometimes, especially with very bright children. Frustration sometimes overwhelms them if they are not receiving enough mental stimulation.'

'I can assure you, Mr Wilson; he gets plenty of mental stimulation. Over the last three months, he's probably had more than his fair share.'

'This is what concerns me, Mrs Hennessey,' Wilson replied carefully. 'I apologise if I'm talking out of line, but since Karl began undergoing these tests, he appears to be going backwards. His attention span has reduced and he's very bad-tempered, at times rude.'

Jill sat back in her chair; she appreciated the Principal's frankness, but at the same time felt a little offended.

'Please, Mrs Hennessy, anything I say is purely with Karl's interests in mind.'

'I'm sorry, Mr Wilson,' Jill replied, 'it was just a bit of a shock. I thought he was doing so well.'

Wilson stood up. 'Please,' he said, gesturing towards the door, 'take a walk down to Karl's class with me. Don't worry; he won't see us. I'd like to show you something.'

Jill followed Wilson out of the office and down the corridor. Every now and then, they would pass one or two children, each greeting the Principal very politely with a 'Good afternoon, Mr Wilson.' Each time, he returned the gesture with a smile. As they approached Karl's classroom, Wilson raised his hand. 'This is close enough Mrs Hennessey.' On the left side of the corridor, the windows were all covered with artwork produced by the children, barely an inch gap between pictures. Wilson peered through a small space. The children were in groups of four or five, busily working away at cardboard models. 'Take a look,' said Wilson.

Jill found a gap and looked through. At the rear of the class, Karl sat alone, frantically ripping pieces of card into small pieces, then throwing them, one by one, onto the floor.

'Karl,' shouted Mrs Beech, 'pick up that paper, I won't tell you again.' Jill couldn't believe what she was seeing.

'This is becoming a common occurrence,' said Wilson. 'In the last two weeks, Karl's been sent to my office three or four times. To say that I'm concerned is an understatement.'

Jill stepped back from the window and leaned back against the wall; the cold surface sent a shiver up her spine.

'I didn't have a clue,' she whispered. 'He's been a little quiet but I . . .' A tear rolled down her cheek.

'Please, I didn't mean to upset you, Mrs Hennessey.'

Wilson took a handkerchief from his pocket. Jill took it and wiped her eyes.

'Thank you, Mr Wilson. I thought the tests he was having were in his best interests; obviously, I was wrong.'

'Once again, Mrs Hennessey, excuse me if I talk out of line, but sometimes I think we should just accept people for what they are. There's no doubt Karl is a very special young man. One-to-one tuition may be the answer.'

Jill couldn't think of that just now. 'Mr Wilson,' she said, 'would you mind if I took Karl home early?'

'Of course not;' Wilson replied. 'I'll let Mrs Beech know.' He knocked on the classroom door and Mrs Beech looked up, instantly recognising Karl's mother.

'Karl,' she said, 'there's someone to see you.' As he looked towards the door, Karl's face transformed from frustration to euphoria, and he leapt over a small desk in an attempt to get to his mother as quickly as he could.

'Sorry to disturb you, Mrs Beech,' said Wilson.

'No problem at all, Mr Wilson; is everything all right?' asked the teacher.

'Nothing to worry about, Mrs Beech; Karl has an appointment this afternoon.'

The teacher's expression betrayed a look of relief that he was taking the rest of the day off. 'Get your coat, Karl;' she said, 'we don't want to keep your mother waiting.'

Karl didn't need telling twice; grabbing his coat and bag, he was ready to go in seconds. Mr Wilson walked them both to the main gate. Again, he reassured Jill that the situation would sort itself out. With a final goodbye, he headed back into the school.

Jill looked down at Karl, who smiled back at her, excited to be out of school early. 'What are we going to do with you little man?' she asked.

'What do you mean, Mommy?' he asked.

'Nothing, darling. Come on, let's go home.'

Later that evening, Jill was helping the boys into bed. It was taking increasingly longer to get them to settle at night. Karl was restless and seemed to have difficulty in falling asleep. Jill would read to him for twenty minutes or so, but he seemed stressed and even while sleeping looked anxious. George had requested a respite from the relentless testing, day in, day out. The disruption to the family routine was getting Charlie down and they could only imagine what it was doing to Karl, as the focus of the doctors' attention.

At last, Karl was finally asleep, and Jill quietly left the room and went downstairs.

'They both asleep, love?' asked George, glancing over his shoulder.

'Yeah, finally. You know George, there's something not quite right with these tests.'

George sat up straight. 'What do you mean?' he asked.

Jill sat down beside him on the sofa. 'I had a phone call today from Mr Wilson at the school. I had to go in for a meeting with him.' Jill fell silent. She could feel herself filling up with emotion and was unable to speak for a moment. George turned towards her. 'George,' she whispered, it's these tests; he's not the same little boy.' Tears began to roll down her cheeks. George was taken aback; he had been so engrossed with his work he hadn't seen what was going on right under his nose.

'Mr Wilson took me to watch him in his class.' Again Jill stopped to compose herself. 'George, he was sat at the back, all on his own, no friends, it was heart-breaking.'

George reached out and put his arm around her shoulder, pulling her close. 'How long has this been going on?' he asked.

'Weeks, George, it's been going on for weeks, and they've only just told us.'

He held Jill tightly. 'And it was going on right in front of me,' said George, 'poor little man.'

'He needs help, George,' replied Jill, 'and I don't mean from Berrow and Clark; I think they've done enough damage. He needs to be with people who can help him. He's special, and we aren't letting him grow.'

'We'll stop the tests,' said George, 'right now.'

'Too right we will,' replied Jill, 'but then what, let him fester in that school? George, they haven't got the resources to help him; he needs to be stimulated.' They sat in silence for what felt like an age. Jill raised her head and looked at George, 'What about his compensation money?' The money awarded for the incident at Karl's birth had been invested in a trust fund.

'I thought we agreed that was for when he grows up,' said George.

Jill's voice rose with impatience. 'Yes, but if he turns out like some kind of deranged juvenile delinquent . . .'; she suddenly stopped talking, hating herself for even thinking what she had just said. There was a long, uncomfortable silence, eventually broken by Jill. 'I'm sorry George,' she said wearily. George asked what she wanted to do with the money.

'We could use it to get him a good education,' she replied. 'There's eighty thousand pounds in that trust fund. I don't know how far that will go in terms of private schooling, but it will give him one hell of a head start.'

'You mean like boarding school?' asked George. Jill nodded. 'I can't imagine him not being here at night,' said George, uneasily.

'Me neither,' replied Jill, 'but we have to think of Karl's well-being long term. I know one thing for certain: I'm going to see Dr Berrow first thing in the morning; it's the end of those bloody tests.'

The following morning, Jill got the boys off to school and went straight to the hospital. They had agreed that George should go into work so as not to jeopardise his job; the last thing they needed was financial instability. Jill knew exactly what she was going to say and told George not to worry.

Walking into the hospital, all Jill could think about was the previous day's meeting at Karl's school. Looking through the classroom window, seeing Karl sitting alone like a small, lost soul; it had enraged her to see her younger child looking so sad and lonely, and anger was burning inside her even now. She knew it wouldn't do anyone any good to have a slanging match and told herself to remain as calm and civil as possible, but she was determined that whatever the doctors said to try and persuade her, it was definitely the last they would see of Karl.

The lift opened, and Jill walked straight up to the reception desk. Sandra, the receptionist, saw Jill approaching and quickly looked down at her appointment sheet. She always familiarised herself with the day's appointments and was sure the Hennesseys weren't on the list.

'Morning,' said Jill, 'I haven't got an appointment, but if possible I'd like to talk to Dr Berrow; it's about Karl's tests.'

'I thought it was strange to see you here today, Mrs Hennessey,' replied Sandra, making polite conversation. 'If you take a seat, I'll see if he's available.'

Jill sat down wondering how Berrow would react; they had spent an awful lot of money on Karl's tests, but at the end of the day it was Karl's welfare she was concerned about, and no amount of money was that important.

Sandra put the phone down and looked up. 'Mrs Hennessey' – Jill stood up – 'he's with a patient at the moment but will see you as soon as he's finished.'

Jill thanked her and went back to her seat. On a corner table, she saw a pile of magazines; rummaging through them, she chose one and sat back down, flicking through the pages to kill the time. Around fifteen minutes later, Jill heard the click of Berrow's office door opening. She heard him arranging his patient's next appointment, and finally, bidding the patient goodbye, he came into the reception area.

'Jill, how are you?' asked Berrow.

'I'm fine, thank you,' replied Jill, automatically.

'How is Karl?' he asked.

'That's what I've come to see you about.'

A worried expression crossed Berrow's face. 'Right then,' he said, 'shall we go into my office?'

Jill got up, placed her magazine back on the pile and followed Berrow down the short corridor to his office. Berrow closed the door behind them, and before he could say a word, Jill spoke. 'We have decided to stop Karl's tests.'

Berrow's eyes widened; he was dumbfounded. 'But Jill, we are just starting to get somewhere.'

'Exactly where is "somewhere"?' Jill began, adding, before Berrow could speak, 'As far as I can see, the only thing that is happening is that Karl is becoming a bad-tempered and depressed little boy.'

Berrow moved over to his desk and sat down. 'Please, Jill, take a seat.'

'Thank you, but I'd rather stand,' replied Jill, not wanting to be drawn into a debate on the subject.

'How long has Karl been showing these symptoms, Jill?' Berrow asked.

'Since your tests started,' she replied sharply, then lowering her eyes realising how loudly her voice had risen.

'It must be a side effect of the sound treatment,' said Berrow, almost under his breath.

Jill quickly looked up, making eye contact with Berrow. 'What sound treatment?' she asked.

'Don't worry,' replied Berrow, 'it's completely harmless; we just tried some high- and low-frequency sound with the monitoring.'

Jill was trying to control her temper. 'You told us you wouldn't do anything without consulting us first. Basically, you have been using my boy like a lab rat.' Jill was fuming.

'It's not like that, Jill, it's harmless . . .' Berrow stood up, trying to calm the situation down.

'It's Mrs Hennessey, to you.' Jill hadn't intended to go down this road, but after finding out about the sound tests, she frankly didn't care any more. 'I want those machines out of my house by this evening or I will put them out.' She turned and walked out of the door, through reception and straight into the lift. She heard Sandra call goodbye to her but was too angry to reply. Berrow chased after her, but the lift door closed before he caught up.

'Is everything all right, Dr Berrow?' asked Sandra.

'Don't ask, Sandra, don't ask,' Berrow replied shaking his head. He walked thoughtfully back to his office and closed the door behind him.

As the lift descended, Jill took a deep breath. Her hands were shaking and she clasped them together to control the rage she felt. Reaching the ground floor, she took one more deep breath, stepped out of the lift and headed towards the hospital's main exit.

Later that afternoon, two technicians arrived at the Hennesseys' house and took away all the equipment. Jill stood over them, making sure that every last cable and clip was removed; she didn't want them to have any reason to return. A few weeks passed and Karl seemed to be back to his old self. Every few days, the boys would tell their mother about dreams they had had together, but she tried not to make a big issue of it. The school Principal had kept in touch, with reports on Karl's attitude, and although it had improved immensely, he still felt that Karl needed a little more than the school could offer him.

One Saturday afternoon, George watched at the kitchen window as the boys played happily together in the garden. Being two years older than Karl, Charlie always had the edge when it came to their boyish games. Charlie had Karl pinned down on his back. Karl fought like mad to escape, but it was futile. Occasionally, Charlie would let Karl win. As soon as Karl thought he was in control, he would sit, proud as punch, mounted on Charlie's chest. Charlie would roll him off and again take control and playfully taunt him.

Jill was still convinced that private education would be the best thing for Karl. Unknown to George, Jill had that morning printed off at the local library a prospectus for a boarding school she had seen advertised in a magazine. 'Marshdown School for Gifted Boys, set in a hundred acres of beautiful Shropshire countryside, approximately five miles from the village of Highley,' she read. The main school had originally been a Victorian manor house, purchased by a private consortium in the late 1940s, to become Marshdown School for Boys. Over the years, the school had developed a very good academic reputation. At ten thousand pounds a year, it wasn't the most expensive boarding school, but it was very selective, maintaining that only gifted children would be considered. The pupils' ages ranged from five to eighteen years, and all were full-time boarders.

Jill had read the prospectus and that morning had rang the school's enrolment officer to ask all the questions that were, understandably, on her mind. She hated going behind George's back, but knew that it was best to investigate thoroughly first; if nothing came of it, why give him any undue stress?

George heard the front door close as Jill arrived home. 'I'm in the kitchen, love,' he called out. Dropping her coat on the back of the living room sofa, she went through to the kitchen.

'You've been a long time,' said George.

Jill had the prospectus in her hand. 'Have the boys been OK?' she asked, glancing out of the kitchen window towards where they were playing.

'Yeah, look at them; they've been rolling all over the place out there for the last hour. I know one thing, they will definitely need a bath tonight,' said George with a contented smile across his face. He looked down at the brochure in Jill's hand. 'What's that you've got there?' he asked. Jill passed it to him. He read the front cover out loud: 'Marshdown School for Boys.' He looked up from the cover directly to Jill. 'You've spoken to them about Karl.'

Jill pursed her lips and raised her eyebrows. 'Have a read, George; I think it could do him the world of good.'

Without replying, George looked back down at the folder, went into the living room, sat down and started reading.

Jill had been in the garden with the boys for well over an hour when George appeared at the back door. 'What do you think?' she asked.

'I don't know;' replied George, 'it's a big decision.'

'Once the boys are in bed tonight, we can have a long talk about it,' said Jill. 'Now, let's get something to eat.' She turned back to the boys, 'Who's ready for their dinner?'

'Me, me, me, me, me!' the boys shouted excitedly. Jumping to their feet, they ran to the back door, almost knocking their father flat on his back. Regaining his balance, George laughed and followed them into the house.

5

Marshdown

That evening, when the boys were finally tucked up in bed, Jill and George once more scanned through the school prospectus. Whether it was a good school or not wasn't really the issue; it was more a case of being able to cope with not having Karl at home and, more importantly, whether he could cope without his family around him. It was a tall order to ask of a child who was not yet six years old. And even if they agreed to send him, he still had to pass the entrance exam. What kind of entrance exam a five-year-old would sit they couldn't imagine. But the school insisted that they took on only gifted boys, and if that was the only criterion, Karl would pass with flying colours.

They seemed to be going round in circles: one minute it all felt positive, the next they were having doubts. George sat back in his chair. 'I think I'm going to call it a day, love,' he said, half yawning and raising his arms to stretch.

Jill looked at George's face; the frown lines on his forehead accentuated the fact that he was finding the whole thing very stressful. 'You go on up, love,' she said. 'I'll lock up.' Jill began putting all the prospectus paperwork into a folder.

'See you up there,' replied George, lethargically trudging towards the stairs.

Jill placed the closed folder on the coffee table; her eyes stared a little longer than necessary at the package. With a deep nervous breath, she stood up, went into the kitchen and secured the bolt on the back door. After putting away a few kitchen utensils from the drying rack, she clicked off the living room light and went upstairs, that evening's discussion still playing heavily on her mind. George was at the top of the stairs, leaning against the door frame of the boys' room.

'Are you all right, George?' asked Jill.

'Yeah, fine; I was just watching them sleep,' George replied quietly. Karl had got out of his bed and was cuddling up to his brother. 'I was just wondering,' he said, 'do you think they are having the same dream?' The couple stood in silence, staring at the boys, deep in their own thoughts. Finally George said, 'I think we owe Karl this chance.' Jill looked at him with a loving smile. 'Come on, let's go to bed.'

The following day, they agreed to give the school a call and arrange an appointment. By pure luck, the school had an open day that coming Saturday. Jill thought it would be a good idea for the whole family to go over there and see if the school was as good as its prospectus. She tried to explain to Karl that it meant staying away from home, and he seemed fine about the whole idea. But she thought it might be a completely different story if the time came for him to board. She made a call to the enrolment officer she had met the previous Saturday and it was all arranged; they were to be at the school on Saturday for 10:30 am.

The week dragged. Karl was completely oblivious to what could potentially change his whole life as he knew it. Jill and George had so many questions going round in their heads, things like how does a child of not even six years old learn to cope without his family, what if he wakes in the night, who does he turn to? It really was a worry, but they knew the school would reassure them, and at the end of the day he wouldn't be the first child to go to a boarding school.

On Saturday morning at 8 am prompt, the family set off in the car; it was a good two-hour drive, and they wanted to be there with time to spare. It was a tedious drive down many narrow roads and lanes, but the beauty of the Shropshire countryside took them both aback. George spotted a sign indicating Marshdown School next left. The school perimeter was surrounded by a higher than normal dry stone wall that looked impeccably maintained. Turning in at the entrance, they were confronted by a huge wrought iron gate. Mounted on the wall was an intercom system with two CCTV cameras above the gate. George wound down his window and pressed the button. A few seconds later, a voice asked, 'Hello, can I help you?'

Leaning a little closer than was necessary, George replied, 'Hi, it's Mr Hennessey. I've brought my son along to the open day.' There was an uncomfortable silence. Looking at Jill, George said, 'they must be checking our name on a list.'

'At least we know they have good security,' replied Jill.

The intercom gave a loud bleep. 'Welcome, Mr Hennessey; follow the road up to the main school building.'

With no more than the hum of a small motor, the huge gates began to open. George selected first gear and slowly drove through the entrance.

The winding road took them up to the school through a thick, mature woodland, so dense that it gave the impression that it was much later in the day. The boys had fallen asleep on the journey and were just starting to stir as the car cleared the woodland. Jill had also been very quiet for the last half an hour or so of the journey, feeling a little apprehensive of what they were getting themselves into.

Before them, about four hundred metres across a large expanse of beautifully manicured lawn, stood Marshdown. With its Victorian facade and towering chimneys, it was a most imposing building. There were already a number of other cars parked on the gravel in front of the school. Some other potential pupils and their parents were walking towards the main entrance.

George parked the car, and as he pulled on the hand brake, he looked over his shoulder at the boys, smiled, then winked. 'Right then, let's go and see what they have to offer us.'

The boys looked a little worried after waking up in a strange place. George locked the car, and they all trudged through the excessively deep gravel towards the main entrance, both the boys holding very tightly to their parents' hands.

Just inside the doorway stood a man in traditional black master's robes; he was balding slightly with a small pair of spectacles placed precariously on the end of his broad nose, looking as if they could fall off at any moment. In his hand, he held a clipboard with a list of that day's potential pupils. As the Hennesseys approached, his eyes raised over his spectacles.

Offering his hand, George smiled and said, 'Good morning – Mr and Mrs Hennessey, we are here for the open day.'

'And a very good morning to you, sir,' replied the Master, shaking George's hand. He then turned and looked at Jill; 'Madam.' He nodded slightly. They had the impression he was trying a little too hard. 'I'm Mr Fletcher, Head of Science, very pleased to meet you. Now, let me see.' He scanned down the list on his clipboard, 'Ah yes, Karl Hennessey.'

'That's right,' said George.

'Straight through the main corridor, into the assembly hall,' said Fletcher. 'Headmaster will be giving an introduction at 10:30 prompt.' George thanked him, and they made their way along the corridor, looking up at the many grand portraits on the walls, presumably past masters and school benefactors. It was all very regal; the ceilings were covered in ornate plasterwork, coving and archways that wouldn't have looked out of place in a palace.

'It's very posh,' whispered Jill.

'You can say that again,' George whispered back, his eyes still trying to take in all the grandeur.

Both the boys stayed very close to their parents as they entered the main assembly hall. Just as in the corridor, the assembly hall was filled with fine pieces of art and group photographs of pupils assembled in rows outside the school. At the front of the hall, there were five rows of chairs with a gap in the centre, facing a raised stage. Approximately twenty other family groups were gathered in the hall; some of the children were as young as Karl, while others looked as old as eleven or twelve. Mingling among them were five or six men in master's robes, chatting and welcoming the families. One of them excused himself from the parents he was talking to and came over to the Hennesseys. He was very tall and painfully slim, so slim that he actually looked ill.

'Good morning,' he said enthusiastically, 'John Fitzpatrick, Head of Languages.'

'Mr and Mrs Hennessey; pleased to meet you,' said George, shaking the master's extended hand. After they had introduced the boys and partaken in a few minutes of light conversation, Fitzpatrick glanced at the large clock at the end of the hall. 'It's just about time to take our seats; will you please excuse me?'

George and Jill nodded their heads, and Fitzpatrick walked over to the stage, 'Ladies and Gentleman and potential pupils of Marshdown School for Gifted Boys,' the experienced teacher's voice rang out, commanding the attention of all present, 'please take a seat; Headmaster will be with you shortly.'

Parents and children alike shuffled their way into the rows of chairs and sat down. A number of masters appeared on the stage and sat in a semi-circle behind the main podium. With perfect timing, the door of the main hall opened as the last master sat down. The Headmaster, Mr Giles Pendlebury, entered the hall, clutching a leather-bound folder. With bolt upright posture, at well over six feet tall, he was a very intimidating figure; some parents appeared to be shrinking in their seats as he strode determinedly up the centre of the hall between them and took the steps onto the stage.

Pendlebury was fifty-three years of age, always impeccably dressed, a small moustache lining his top lip but otherwise perfectly clean-shaven and his jet-black hair showed no sign of age. He had held the position of Headmaster at the school for nearly five years, and the school exam results were proof enough of his ability to lead. As he reached the podium, there was absolute silence. He opened his folder and placed it on the oak rest before him. Towering above the parents, he raised his eyes from the folder, a broad grin appearing on his face.

'Good morning ladies and gentlemen,' he paused for a second and, looking at the faces turned upwards towards him, he added, 'children.' His air of unforced authority filled the room.

Pendlebury talked for almost an hour. Each time Jill and George thought of a question they would like to ask, he seemed to cover the subject. He was obviously very experienced and anticipated questions that would surely be on the minds of every parent in the room, even answering questions that they hadn't thought of, but which were extremely relevant. Finally, he asked for any questions. The parents appeared to be racking their brains; he had been so thorough that they could not think of anything further to ask. He closed by dividing the group up equally amongst all the masters on the stage, and sent them on a guided tour of the school, arranging for everyone to meet for lunch in the dining room at 1 pm.

The various groups set off. Each master had a specific route to take in an attempt to reduce congestion in the corridors. Most of the boarders had gone home for the weekend but, as usual, a few boys had been left behind. Some lived a long distance away from the school and it just wasn't practical to go home every weekend, while others had parents living or working abroad, so they would stay on and continue working towards forthcoming examinations, relaxing or taking part in weekend activities arranged for them. In the Hennesseys' group, there were two other boys of Karl's age. The Headmaster had attempted to match up the families whose children would be spending time together should they become pupils of the school.

The under-tens' dormitories were located on the top floor of the main building. Fitzpatrick, the master who was showing them around, thought it best to start at the top and work their way down. Each room had eight children, but looking at the size of the room, six would have been a better number. Beside each bed was a small cabinet for personal belongings, together with a chest and a wardrobe. The room adjacent to the youngest pupils' dormitory housed a master. On a weekly rotational basis, the masters would take their turn sleeping there, to reassure the younger boys should they wake in the night. The classrooms were on the first and second floors, while the ground floor had the dining room, kitchens, assembly hall and various other recreational rooms and offices. At the rear of the building were extensive outbuildings. After a slow walk around, Fitzpatrick answered any questions they had, finally leading them to the dining room for a drink and a much-needed bite to eat.

The parents were beginning to relax now that their questions had been answered, and the hum of conversation as they introduced themselves and chatted filled the dining room. After the buffet lunch, parents wishing to pursue the application process were asked to return to the main assembly hall. Those who were unsure could either leave or make an appointment to discuss any further questions they had. The Hennesseys took a slow walk back to the assembly hall where about seventy per cent of the parents remained. Through the windows of the Great Hall, they could see families getting into their cars and unhurriedly driving back down the gravel path towards the tree line, their reasons for leaving very much their own.

Fletcher, the master they had first met on entering the school, was handing out enrolment forms. George was sure the precariously balanced spectacles would fall off at any moment. During the next two hours, the Headmaster and Deputy Headmaster interviewed each family in an attempt to determine each child's needs. No decisions would be made that day by parents or the school. The older boys would sit a written examination some time within the next two weeks to determine their academic ability. The younger boys would have a further interview with their parents to determine whether they where suitable.

On arriving home that evening, there was a lot to talk about. They were very encouraged by what they had seen, and Karl appeared to like the school; he had quickly made friends with the two other small boys who had accompanied them on the tour of the school.

Dropping onto the sofa, George untied his shoelaces and kicked off his shoes. 'Ooh, that's better,' he said, stretching out his legs.

'They were very posh. I felt a little out of place,' said Jill.

'Nonsense,' replied George lying back, looking up at the ceiling. 'When we pay Karl's fees, it makes us just as good as they are.'

Jill instantly turned to George. 'Does that mean we're going to send him?'

'Jill, in my opinion, that school will give Karl a better start in life than anything we can offer him. He'll make friends who will open doors for him in the future, you see.'

'God, I hope you're right, George, I hope you're right.'

One week later, a letter arrived addressed to the parents of Master Karl Hennessey. It was the appointment they had been waiting for to meet the Headmaster at Marshdown. The interview would be in two weeks' time, once again on a Saturday morning. The weekend was a good time to hold the interviews, as it did not interfere with the day-to-day running of the school and usually enabled both parents to attend.

As the Hennesseys sat eating breakfast, Jill was still a little apprehensive of whether Karl really understood the significance of what joining Marshdown School would really mean to his life. 'Karl,' said Jill – his eyes looked up from his cereal bowl – 'we've had a letter from Marshdown School.'

'What did it say, Mommy?' he asked.

'They want you to go for an interview with me and Daddy to talk about you going to school there.'

'Are we going?' he asked.

'Do you want to?' asked George. Karl vigorously nodded his head. 'You know it means sleeping there all week if they accept you?' Again he nodded. 'And you'll only see us at weekends?' Karl glanced at Charlie, who was just finishing his bowl of cereal.

'You'll miss him, won't you, son?' said George looking across at Karl's brother.

Charlie put his spoon in his bowl. 'Why does Karl have to go away to school and I don't?' asked Charlie.

George drew in a breath; he knew these questions were inevitable. 'Well, son, you know Karl has a gift?' Charlie looked directly at his father and nodded. 'Well, we think this school may be able to help Karl understand it, and he can learn things there that he can't at school just now.' The answer seemed to pacify the boys and it was the best their father could come up with for now. Jill looked over at George and smiled, obviously pleased with his attempt to explain the unexplainable.

Jill hit the table with the palms of her hands, startling George and the boys. 'Right, then,' she said, 'let's make a move or we will all be late.'

The boys jumped up, hurriedly placing their bowls in the kitchen sink and dashing off upstairs to wash and clean their teeth. 'It's times like this I will miss if he does go to that school,' said Jill.

'Me too, love, but it's for the best. I'm sure.' George reached over the table, smiled and squeezed Jill's hand. The gesture of reassurance seemed to work, for now anyway.

The day of the meeting couldn't have come sooner. The previous week had mentally tormented Jill; should they or shouldn't they send him? – he's so young. Every waking moment since the letter had arrived, the question had consumed her mind. They had to get to the school at the same time as the open day, but at least this time they knew exactly where they were going. On reaching the gate, George once again used the intercom, and the large uninviting wrought iron gates slowly opened.

There were fewer cars parked outside the school this visit. Jill's eyes focused this time on the grounds and the meticulously tended flowerbeds; somebody obviously took great personal care in attending to them. They trudged through the gravel into the main entrance, where a sandwich board stood inside in the doorway with a notice attached: 'PARENTS AND CHILDREN PLEASE GO TO MAIN ASSEMBLY HALL.'

They went along the corridor to the assembly hall. In front of the stage, Mr Fletcher was sitting at a large desk, his eyes scanning over some paperwork. Chairs had been placed around the edge of the hall, and two other family groups sat filling out what appeared to be some kind of questionnaire. Jill noticed both the boys that Karl had made friends with last time sitting quietly with their parents. Karl waved at them, and the boys both smiled and waved back excitedly. As the Hennesseys crossed the hall towards Fletcher's desk, they were aware of the other families discreetly glancing at them, each probably wondering who their own child would be spending the rest of his school days with.

'Good morning,' said Fletcher as they approached the desk.

'Morning,' replied George. 'Mr and Mrs Hennessey; we've brought our son Karl for his interview.'

'Excellent,' replied Fletcher, stabilising his glasses on the end of his nose. 'Could I ask you to fill out this questionnaire? Headmaster will be with you as soon as he can. There are two other interviews before you.'

George thanked him, and they moved to the seats at the edge of the hall, giving a nod and a brief good morning to the other families they had met at the open day tour. One by one, the Headmaster called the families into an office at the far end of the hall. Just over an hour later, the Headmaster came out of his office and called the Hennesseys' family name. George, Jill and the boys all stood up and made their way down the hall to the door where the Headmaster was waiting. He greeted them and gestured with his arm to enter his office. Closing the door behind him, the headmaster walked over to a huge desk positioned by the window. All around the walls were leather-bound sets of books, which looked as if they were purely for display purposes only.

'Please take a seat, Mr and Mrs Hennessey,' said Mr Pendlebury.

George and Jill positioned themselves on two of the three chairs in front of the desk; the boys perched together on the remaining chair.

'First,' he continued, 'may I say how extremely pleased I am that you have chosen Marshdown for your child's education.' George and Jill both returned a pleasing smile. 'Now,' he said, 'which one of you young men is Karl?' Pendlebury's eyes flicked across the paperwork on his desk over to the boys. He quickly held Karl's gaze. 'Five years old, it must be you, young man.' Karl nodded. 'Very pleased to meet you,' said the Headmaster.

Instantly his eyes diverted back to George and Jill, still holding his friendly, smiling expression. 'With younger boys, I like to think we are very lucky; I see it as a blank canvas is to an artist.' George wondered how many times he had said that today. 'I see from your application that Karl has an aptitude for puzzles.'

'Yes,' replied George, 'he can do puzzles faster than the doctors had ever seen.'

'Doctors, Mr Hennessey?' – the Headmaster appeared confused.

'Yes,' George explained. 'Karl was having tests at the Queen Elizabeth Neurological Centre. We didn't really finish with them on good terms, but I feel sure they would vouch that Karl has something quite special.'

'I see,' said Pendlebury thoughtfully.

'He was being observed by Dr Alan Berrow,' George continued. 'I'm sure he wouldn't mind if you gave him a call.'

'I don't think that will be necessary,' said the Headmaster. 'Anything we need to know will be included in Karl's GP's medical report. Now then, what exactly gave you the idea to bring Karl to Marshdown?'

'We thought he was being held back at his present school,' said Jill. 'They just can't stimulate him.'

The Headmaster sat back in his chair and looked at Karl. 'Hmm, it seems to me Karl that you are a clever young man. How do you feel about staying with us here at Marshdown?'

There was a few seconds' silence. 'Speak up son,' said George.

'Give him a chance, George,' replied Jill quickly, agitated by his impatience.

Karl shyly raised his eyes to look at the Headmaster. 'Yes, I'd like to come.'

'Well, I never. Young man, you are the first five-year-old I have had an answer from today; good for you.' Turning to George and Jill he said, 'You know, sometimes the young ones find me a little intimidating.' 'I wonder why?' George thought to himself.

Pendlebury continued, 'As you have probably read in the school prospectus, with the younger pupils we vigorously enforce the three Rs. The younger boys are assigned a mentor who will read with them on a daily basis. We find using this method gives great results, and the older boys acquire house points. So they really do push them as more house points means more social time.' George and Jill were both impressed with their methods.

'Right then,' said Pendlebury, 'we now come to the subject of fees. You are familiar with our fee structure?' George nodded. 'This year we are introducing the opportunity to pay an annual fee, which of course will incorporate a reduction.'

George interrupted him. 'As soon as we find out whether Karl has a place at the school, we'll make a decision as to what method of payment we will choose.'

'Excellent,' said Pendlebury. 'Now, is there anything at all you would like to ask me?'

'We will probably think of something when we get home,' replied Jill, and they all laughed.

'Well, you have the school number; anything at all, please don't hesitate to contact us. I know it's a big decision, especially with one so young.' Again he looked at Karl and smiled. 'But you can trust me on this, if Karl is accepted, he will get the best possible education here at Marshdown. We will contact you within the next fourteen days, Mr and Mrs Hennessey, but I'll be frank with you now, Karl is a perfect candidate for Marshdown.'

They thanked the Headmaster, shook hands and began their journey home, feeling that their minds had been put at rest and wondering what the post would bring over the next two weeks.

6

A new beginning

Every morning after the interview, George and Jill had anxiously watched the post. It had been over a week now, so the letter could arrive at any time. Unlike his parents, Karl was still taking it all in his stride. The family routine had continued as normal; each morning they would have any early breakfast, George would go off to work, and Jill would take the boys to school. Her job in the local supermarket, three days each week during school hours, was not very well paid, but it helped provide a few family creature comforts.

That morning, as the family were finishing their breakfast, the familiar rattle of the letterbox alerted Charlie. He was halfway across the living room before the post hit the floor. Gathering up the letters, he hastily made his way back to the kitchen.

'Let's have a look then, son,' said George, anxious to see what had arrived. He flicked through the letters with Jill looking on nervously. 'Bill, bill, junk mail . . .' Suddenly he stopped, his eyes fixed on the next envelope. 'This is it!' he exclaimed.

The boys didn't look too bothered, but panic was written all over Jill's face. 'Open it, then,' she said.

George picked a knife up from the kitchen table and slid it along the edge of the envelope. Quickly, he removed the contents and unfolded the letter. 'Dear Mr and Mrs Hennessey,' he read aloud, 'I am writing with regard to your son, Karl . . .' He stopped reading aloud and started mumbling to himself as he read the letter.

'For God's sake, George, will you read it out loud, please?' shouted Jill.

George stopped and looked straight at his wife. 'He's in; they've accepted him.'

Jill didn't know whether to jump for joy or cry. Something inside her was hoping they would turn him down; at least then, when he was older, they could tell him they had tried to get him into Marshdown School. But now that wasn't the case; the decision was made the minute George opened the letter.

The school informed them that the new intake of junior and infant pupils would start after the Christmas holiday. If they wanted Karl to take up his place at the school, his fees for the first two terms would have to be paid in advance before Christmas. The fees were paid, Christmas came and went, and all the items on Karl's uniform list were purchased. All that was left to do now was wait for the big day.

On the first day of term, two very nervous parents double-checked Karl's list, making sure every item was in his case. Jill had helped Karl into his new uniform. Marshdown had a strict dress code; Karl was standing in the living room wearing a black blazer with blue piped edges, black flannel trousers, white shirt with blue school tie and the school coat of arms boldly displayed, just below the knot. Most of the younger boys were still trying to master their shoelaces, so Windsor tie knots were definitely asking a little too much and they were allowed preformed elasticised ties. Jill stood in front of him and looked him up and down a couple of times. He looked so grown up; she felt a lump in her throat but managed to control herself before Karl realised there was anything wrong, and she just gave him a broad smile.

George had taken a day's holiday to drive Karl into school. They dropped Charlie off at school and then set off for Marshdown, arriving just after 10:30 am. With all the pupils on site, the school had a totally different feel. Parents were arriving with new pupils, returning parents and pupils were greeting each other after the Christmas break, and it was truly bustling. The school policy on days such as these was to reassure the parents of new pupils then get them to leave as quickly as possible.

George carried Karl's case into the assembly hall; Karl was walking closely behind, holding his mother's hand. Year ten boys had been rallied to help transport all the cases to the correct dormitories. A plan of the sleeping arrangements for the younger boys' dormitories lay on a large desk at the end of the hall. Daniel Wilkes, a very young looking master, had been given the task of supervising the influx of new pupils. Senior boys approached the desk with a case and name, Wilkes would give them a location, and then the case was whisked off to the correct dormitory. It all seemed to be working very efficiently.

George found himself intently observing the young master. He was very tall, well over six feet, with no sign of facial hair and a spare physique; he looked as if he had not yet filled out. If it were not for his height, he could easily have passed as a senior boy. George thought it was probably because he was getting older himself; policemen, teachers, they all seemed to be getting younger.

Wilkes stood up from the desk. 'Ladies and gentlemen, boys, could I have your attention?' The murmuring stopped and everyone turned to look at the young master. 'In five minutes, I will ask all the new boys to assemble at the front of the hall. Senior boys have all been allocated specific dormitories to assist the boys to settle in. So, Mums and Dads, don't worry; they're in good hands. It's our policy to get the boys settled in as quickly as we can, thank you.'

The parents began their goodbyes, and there were a few tears around the room, but no more than usual. George crouched down to face Karl. 'Well, son, this is it, a whole new beginning for you. I'll be here on Friday to collect you.' George felt a surge of emotion rising in his body, 'You be a good boy and do as you're told.'

'Yes, Daddy.' replied Karl, looking very calm and not at all upset.

Jill was finding it hard to hold back the tears; she simply said, 'Be a good boy Karl.' Anything more and she would have cracked up. She knelt down to hug him and then kissed his cheek. Taking a deep breath she said, 'Love you, son.'

'Love you too, Mommy,' replied Karl.

Once again Wilkes stood up. 'OK, will all the new boys come to the front of the hall, please?'

Frantically, parents and children gave final hugs and kisses, finding it hard to let each other go. Karl smiled at his mother; Jill wiped her nose with a paper tissue and said, 'See you Friday, son.'

Karl then turned to his father, smiled and winked; George struggled to compose himself in awe of the confidence his young son was showing. George winked back. 'See ya Friday, little man.' Karl walked over to the rest of the boys gathering at the front of the main hall.

'Listen out for your names, please,' said Wilkes, and began calling out the names of the new pupils. There were twenty-four new boys with ages ranging from five to eight years. They had been arranged into three dormitories, eight boys in each. They were led off in a straight line with one year ten boy at the front and one at the rear, making sure they didn't lose anyone. It was the job of the year ten boys to get the newcomers settled into their dormitories. Finally, the last eight, including Karl, marched off. Some parents made a last attempt to get a final wave or smile from their child as they disappeared into the corridor at the back of the hall.

'Right then, Mums and Dads,' said Wilkes. 'Firstly, don't worry; your boys are in very good hands. If there are any problems whatsoever, you will be contacted. Please have a safe journey home, and we will see most of you on Friday; thank you.' He smiled and began collecting up the paperwork on his desk, indicating that it was time for the parents to leave.

'That was a little abrupt, wasn't it?' said Jill.

'Well,' replied George, 'I think he is being cruel to be kind looking at some of the mothers in here. Come on, let's get off.'

Slowly the hall began to clear, although some parents seemed a little reluctant to leave their children.

Karl and the other boys followed the seniors upstairs to the third-floor dormitories, where their spaces had already been allocated, with their belongings placed on top of their beds.

'Right, lads,' said the senior boy who had led Karl's column from the assembly hall. His name was Kyle Higgins, a short stocky lad, with a severe case of acne. Now fifteen years old, he had been at the school since the age of six and knew just how the boys were feeling at this moment in time. That was probably why he had been chosen for the task of making the boys feel welcome. 'Take off your blazers and start emptying your cases into your wardrobes. If you need any help, just shout.'

As the boys set about the task, Higgins and the other senior boy tried to encourage them to talk. Once they had unpacked, they all sat on the beds. Higgins stood in the middle of the room, 'Lads, I think we need to introduce ourselves. You guys are going to be spending a lot of time together so you might as well be friends. Right then, let's start here.' He randomly pointed at a fair-haired boy with a freckly complexion, sitting on his bed with his legs crossed. 'What's your name?'

'William Campbell, but my mom calls me Billy.'

'Nice to meet you, Billy.' said Higgins. 'And the next.' He pointed at Karl.

'Karl Hennessey, but my mom just calls me Karl.' Both senior boys laughed. 'Well, I'm pleased to hear that, Karl; nice to meet you also.'

Higgins went round the room asking each of the boys to introduce themselves. It really was a good idea, and by the time he had reached the last one he couldn't shut them up.

'OK, boys, listen now. In a minute we are all going down to the assembly hall, and the Headmaster will give us his usual first day speech. Don't talk when he's talking or you'll see a side of him you'd rather not. Then you'll be introduced to the masters, we'll all have some lunch, then no doubt start work, OK?' They all nodded in reply. 'Right then, boys, blazers on and we'll head down. Keep close in a straight line on the way down; we've got this far and I don't want to lose anyone now.'

The rest of the day went without a hitch. Karl and the other boys in his dormitory got to know each other a little better. Although Karl was not to know it at the time, Billy Campbell, the freckly little boy in the next bed to him, would become a very close friend for many years to come. The first night for the new boys had a few homesick tears, but the duty master soon calmed everything down. As the days passed, the boys quickly settled and got into a routine. George and Jill collected Karl each Friday evening and returned him on Sunday, enabling him to be ready for school first thing Monday morning.

The weeks and months rolled by, and Karl became more and more independent. At weekends he would take care of himself, making his own bed, washing and cleaning his own teeth without any prompting. The school was teaching him well, not just in that department, but also academically. His reading and writing had moved on in leaps and bounds, and he always brought a selection of books home with him at the weekend. The school's senior pupil mentor programme appeared to have been a master stroke. He was already moving away from Charlie at an astonishing rate, even though he was two years his junior. Karl Hennessey was becoming a very bright and intelligent young man.

If all the attention Karl received at the weekend bothered Charlie, he didn't show it. The boys would always end up sleeping in the same bed, still greatly enjoying each other's company. Karl was reluctant to use his gift at Marshdown, not really knowing how the other boys would react to such a phenomenon, so he took every opportunity to share Charlie's dreams. Always trying out new things, he quickly realised that if he concentrated hard enough there were no limits to what he could achieve within the dreams. He now realised that if he woke in the night and Charlie was still asleep, he could look into Charlie's dreams merely by touching his hand. But unless he slept, he couldn't interact with them. Who knows what he would be able to achieve in the future; only time would tell.

7

Years later

Karl had been at Marshdown for over seven years. At slightly above average height, he was extremely thin, looking as if he desperately needed a good meal. He kept his dark hair very closely cropped; low maintenance, as he referred to it. His clear complexion showed no signs of adolescence. Although he really didn't know any different, he had been very happy at boarding school. He threw himself whole-heartedly into his education and spent every weekend and holiday with his family. But increasingly he found himself divided from them, some weekends feeling that he would rather stay at school to source the vast amount of knowledge available to him in the well-stocked library. Thankfully, common sense always prevailed and told him to stay close to his family, especially his brother Charlie, who, if the truth were known, had missed Karl immensely in his first few years at Marshdown.

A new master had taken a position at the school and was having a huge influence on Karl's education. Martin Blakeway was in his mid-forties, a slightly built but athletic man with shoulder-length fair hair. He was not the type of teacher usually found in a boarding school, but when he had applied for the position, the Headmaster had been so impressed with his CV and references that he felt he could not miss the opportunity to secure such an intelligent and experienced individual. With a Master's degree in psychology and a string of other subjects to his name, he would be a very useful person to have on his staff.

At the rear of the main school building was a large green with benches strategically placed to provide views of the beautifully manicured flowerbeds.

These were painstakingly tended by a very old gardener who went by the name of Mr Diggle, endearingly known to the boys as Digger, due to the fact they rarely saw him without a spade in his hands. It was Friday lunchtime, and Karl was sitting on one of the benches, taking in the view at the back of the school. In the summer months, he liked to sit on the lawn and read, but with the autumn once more upon them, it was a little too cold to stay out for long. Two more classes after lunch and his father would come and collect him for the weekend.

'Hello, Karl.' Blakeway's voice startled Karl, who turned quickly to look at him.

'Hello, sir, I didn't see you there.'

'You looked miles away,' said Blakeway.

'I was just wondering what time my father would arrive this afternoon.'

'Do you mind if I sit with you, Karl?' asked Blakeway. He always called the boys by their Christian names, even though the school policy was to address pupils by their surnames.

'No, sir, please.' Karl moved up the bench. Blakeway sat down and leaned back, stretching his arms across the back of the bench as he gazed across the fine lawn and flower beds that stretched before him.

'These grounds are such a credit to old Digger,' said Blakeway. Karl tried to control the broad grin forming on his face; it was strange to hear a schoolmaster talking so openly. 'Tell me, Karl, I get the feeling you are not all that enthusiastic about going home these days.' Karl looked down at the floor, alarmed that his feelings were so obvious. 'Is everything OK at home?' asked Blakeway.

Slowly, Karl raised his head and looked at the master. 'I know I have my parents to thank for bringing me to Marshdown in the first place' – he paused, his eyes focusing on the ground somewhere in front of him – 'but I have nothing in common with them any more. If it wasn't for my brother Charlie, I don't know what I would do.'

'You're not the first to feel like this, Karl,' said Blakeway gently. 'I've had the same conversation with half a dozen boys over the years. I think the public school system alienates us from normal family life. But it will change, I promise you.' Karl found the words reassuring.

Blakeway stood up and straightened his jacket. 'Walk with me, Karl,' he said. Taking the pathway away from the main school building, Karl and Blakeway talked about everything and nothing, the master not yet realising the extent of the influence he would have on the young man's outlook on life.

As time passed, Karl had moved out of the junior dormitories. Of the eight boys in his original dormitory, there were only two left: Billy Campbell and himself. Billy was not the brightest boy at school – Karl frequently had to finish his homework for him to bail him out – but he was easily the funniest. The other boys had sometimes referred to them as joined at the hip as they were very rarely apart in the first few years at the school. Billy was the only boy Karl had told about his gift. Billy thought he was pulling his leg, until one morning when Karl told him all about the dream he had had the previous night. At first Billy was shocked and, if the truth were known, a little frightened, but just like Karl's brother Charlie, Billy found that it really was good fun when he allowed Karl to interact with him.

Recently, Karl had begun to walk around the dormitory in the dead of night, touching the hands of other boys in the dormitory. He had developed his gift to such a degree that he could enter their dreams while he was still awake. It wasn't quite the same as when he was asleep; more like being a fly on the wall, not yet able to interact while awake.

One of the boys, Jerald Sanderson, had been very homesick. He was a chubby little boy with greasy brown hair, and other boys constantly took the mickey out of him. Sometimes Karl would hear him crying at night, but he would never show any sign of weakness in the presence of other boys. Jerald's father was a merchant banker, and his work took him to many countries. During one of his father's trips abroad, his mother had run away with a wealthy client, leaving Jerald to fend for himself, hence why he had ended up at Marshdown. Jerald was not particularly gifted academically, but his father's wealth ensured him a place at the school.

It was almost 2 am and Karl was lying awake in bed. He was intrigued by Blakeway's background in psychology and would take every opportunity to observe the other boys, trying to weigh up what was going on in their minds. Karl climbed out of bed and tip-toed over to Jerald's bed. He looked as if he had a fever; the sweat was running down his face, staining the pillowcase. As Jerald slept, Karl could see the rapid eye movement under his closed eyelids; he was obviously dreaming and Karl couldn't resist.

Being very careful not to wake him, Karl placed his hand on the back of Jerald's. As soon as Karl closed his eyes, it was like being transported out of his own body. Suddenly, there was Jerald; he was in some kind of storeroom. Karl looked around and realised it was the school gym stores. There were tears running down Jerald's face and he looked frightened. Why on earth was he in here?, thought Karl. Suddenly, the door opened and Mr Mortiboys, the school physical education master, came in holding a long, thin cane. How Karl hated him; he was a real bully of a man. Not that tall, about five feet nine inches, but very powerfully built, he always picked on the boys who showed no inclination towards sport, Jerald being one of them, ridiculing them at every opportunity.

Mortiboys turned and locked the door, and then walked over to Jerald, tapping the cane on the palm of his hand. 'Right, Sanderson, you snivelling little shit, you know what you have to do.' said Mortiboys. Jerald turned away, his hands covering his face as Mortiboys swished the cane through the air. Tensing with fear, Jerald slowly turned round. Karl half expected Jerald to raise the palm of his hand to be punished, but what happened next horrified him. Mortiboys opened the cord in his tracksuit trousers and pulled them down, exposing his partially aroused penis. Although Karl wasn't actually in the dream, he was gripped with fear as he watched Jerald fall onto his knees and take hold of Mortiboys' now erect penis. Karl released Jerald's arm and fell backwards, bumping into the bed directly behind. 'Who's that?' shouted the boy in the next bed.

Suddenly, everyone was waking up. Karl tried to quickly get back to his bed when, CLICK, the light was switched on. Karl squinted his eyes, trying to adjust to the light. In the door way stood Mr Preston, a no-nonsense master who normally only dealt with year ten boys.

'You, boy,' said Preston in a stern voice, 'what are you doing out of bed?'

Karl was still in shock; Jerald was sitting up looking straight over at him. 'I must have been sleepwalking sir,' replied Karl.

'Get into bed now,' said Preston. Jerald, soaked in sweat, stared straight over at Karl, as if he knew Karl was aware of his dream.

'Now all of you, go to sleep,' said Preston, 'or there will be what for tomorrow morning.'

Karl pulled the sheets up to his neck and turned onto his side. The light turned off and the door closed. Karl lay in the darkness wondering what was going on in Jerald's head; was it just a dream or was he reliving something beyond any child's worst nightmare? It was a good hour before Karl finally fell asleep, and considerably longer for Jerald.

Over the next few weeks, Karl watched Jerald very closely; he seemed on edge. Unable to contain himself any longer, Karl decided to ask Jerald if everything was all right. Karl spotted Jerald sitting alone eating his lunch. Seeing his opportunity, he quickly made his way over to Jerald's table.

'Hi, Jerald.' Karl put his tray down on the table next to Jerald and sat down. 'God, I hate this cottage pie.'

Karl moved his food around on his plate, hoping to get a reply, but Jerald just carried on eating. Karl thought, stuff it, in for a penny in for a pound. 'Is everything all right, Jerald?'

There was still no reply from Jerald, but he seemed to absorb Karl's question. Suddenly Jerald put his knife and fork down. 'What were you doing by my bed that night?' Karl knew exactly which night he meant.

'I told you all, I was sleepwalking,' replied Karl.

'You were touching my hand.' Jerald stared at his food.

'I don't remember that,' replied Karl, trying to hide his embarrassment.

Suddenly, Jerald jumped to his feet, pushing his seat back away from the dining table.

'Calm down, mate,' said Karl, shocked by Jerald's response.

'Firstly, I'm not your mate,' said Jerald, 'and secondly, stay away from me, you got that?'

Karl was completely taken aback by the outburst. Raising both his hands in a submissive gesture, he said, 'OK, I'm sorry I spoke.'

By now all eyes in the dining room were watching the commotion unfold. The normal dinnertime din had turned to an uneasy silence. Jerald slowly glanced around the room, his face bright red with both anger and embarrassment. Then, without another word, he walked out of the room. Billy Campbell had been at the food counter watching from a distance. He picked up his tray, went over to Karl's table and sat down.

'Karl, mate, from where I was standing it looked like you were having a problem with the art of conversation.' Billy, always clowning, had a grin right across his face.

Karl gave out a huge breath and shook his head. 'Not now, Billy,' he said, 'not now.'

Karl picked up his knife and fork to resume eating, and quickly the lunchtime chaos returned.

It seemed that no sooner than Karl arrived back at school on a Sunday evening, it was Friday again. Most people long for Friday evening, the end of the school or working week, but Karl was exactly the opposite and he couldn't wait to get back to school. It was a quiet journey home. With the incident with Jerald still at the forefront of Karl's mind, he had little to say. He didn't like falling out with people, and he remembered Blakeway telling him that life was too short to hold grudges; say what you think and ninety-nine per cent of people will respect you for it.

George pulled up outside the house, pleased that the journey was over and already dreading the return trip Sunday evening. He had made the journey so many times he felt that he knew every square inch of road between their house and the school.

'Come on, son,' said George, 'your Mom will probably have a meal ready for us.' Jill liked them all to sit down for a meal on Friday evening; it kind of reaffirmed the family group feeling, and each of them would tell the others what kind of week they had had. Opening the front door, George shouted, 'We're home,' and with both hands on Karl's shoulders, 'go on, son, in you go.' Karl was only half way across the living room when Charlie came out of the kitchen.

'How you doing, bro?' Charlie would be fifteen soon, and it would not be long before he would leave school or go on to further education. As the boys had grown, their features had remained very similar, and facially they were almost clones of their father. But physically they were very different. Charlie had been into weight training for some years and had stacked on a fair amount of muscle. Karl was quite the opposite; his insatiable appetite for knowledge and spending most of his time reading did nothing for his stature. Charlie grabbed Karl and with one arm around his neck pulled him down into a headlock.

'Charlie, pack it in,' said George. Charlie made a fist with his other hand, and rubbed his knuckles on top of Karl's head. Karl struggled but was no match for his brother.

'Charlie, for the last time now, pack it in,' George raised his voice a little.

'OK, OK,' laughed Charlie, releasing the lock around his brother's neck.

Karl smiled, knowing he meant no harm. 'What do they feed you on, gorilla?' said Karl.

'Raw meat,' replied Charlie, raising an arm to display a well-defined biceps, 'it's all meat, bro, all meat.'

Jill came through from the kitchen, 'Come here, son.' She gave Karl a typical motherly hug, the type that would embarrass any young man.

'OK, Mom,' said Karl, 'I've only been gone for five days.'

'Well, I miss you,' she replied, pleased to have him home.

'When's tea ready, Mom?' asked Charlie.

Jill looked over at Charlie shaking her head. 'Don't you think of anything other than your stomach?' Charlie just grinned. 'You get yourself changed, Karl; tea will be on the table in ten minutes,' said Jill, smiling.

'Come on, bro,' said Charlie, 'I'll carry your bag; you don't look as if you could manage it up the stairs!'

Karl pulled a face, 'Yeh, yeh, meat head.'

The boys went upstairs, engrossed in friendly banter.

The evening passed as any other Friday evening, and the boys eventually went up to bed. The bedroom had hardly changed. Charlie had not been allowed to take over the whole room, making sure that every time Karl came home, he actually felt that he was home and not just a visitor. As Karl lay in bed, he couldn't get the situation with Jerald out of his mind. He needed to tell someone about the dream, and Charlie was the perfect shoulder to lean on.

'Charlie,' he said, 'I've been working on my gift just lately.'

That got Charlie's attention. 'Nice one, bro, what can you do now, then?'

'Well,' replied Karl, 'I've learned to go into people's dreams when I'm still awake.'

Charlie turned on to his side to face Karl, 'That sounds wicked,' he said.

'I can't interact in the dream,' Karl continued, 'but I can watch what they're doing.'

'I tell you what, bro,' Charlie was impressed, 'you could make a fortune with that gift of yours.'

'Something's happened at school; it was really scary.' Karl told Charlie all about Jerald's dream. Charlie was now sitting up, enthralled by Karl's account of what happened.

'Well, I see it like this,' Charlie put his back against his headboard and pulled his knees up, 'he's either queer or he's being abused.'

'Exactly what I thought,' replied Karl. 'So what do I do, Charlie?'

Charlie sat for a few moments, deep in thought. 'Got it;' said Charlie, 'ask him straight out, no messing just ask him.' Charlie looked pleased with his contribution to the problem. 'But if he says he's a queer . . .' Charlie went quiet.

'What?' asked Karl.

'Be careful if you bend down to pick the soap up in the shower!' Charlie laughed.

'What are you like, Charlie?' They both laughed and said goodnight. Karl lay in bed thinking about what Charlie had said. He would do it; as soon as he got Jerald on his own he would confront him, and hopefully that would be the end of it.

8

The confrontation

Karl arrived back at school late Sunday afternoon; after saying his goodbyes to his parents, he went up to his dormitory. Most of the other boys arrived back at school on Monday morning, so Karl spent Sunday evenings relaxing in the dormitory or else would go down to the television room for a couple of hours. It was school policy not to allow TVs in dormitories. Karl didn't mind; he would sooner read a book anyway.

Karl knew that Jerald had stayed at school that weekend and, fingers crossed, he might just catch him alone and confront him. As the evening passed, Karl stood by the dormitory window looking down at the school forecourt. More boys were arriving, but still there was no sign of Jerald or any of the other boys from their dormitory.

Feeling bored, Karl decided to empty out the trunk at the bottom of his bed – to say it was overcrowded was an understatement. All his schoolbooks and a few personal belongings were strewn out over the dormitory floor when the door opened; it was Jerald. Karl turned and acknowledged him with a nod of his head; Jerald returned the gesture in the same manner. As Karl was putting his books away, he tried to think of a way to break the ice and make conversation without getting into another argument.

Jerald sat on his bed flicking through an old sports car magazine. Karl decided to try and turn the onus on himself by telling Jerald about his gift, initially not telling him what he had seen in the dream. Karl put the last few books away and took a deep breath. Here goes he thought to himself.

'Jerald,' said Karl.

Jerald looked up from his magazine. 'What?' he replied abruptly.

'Can I tell you something?' Karl waited for his answer.

'Depends what it is,' replied Jerald. Karl went over and sat on the bed opposite Jerald's.

'You know that night I was over by your bed?' Jerald gave a nod. 'I have a confession.' Karl looked down at the floor in an attempt to stop Jerald feeling uncomfortable. 'I have a gift.'

Jerald looked intrigued. 'What sort of gift?' he asked.

'It's one of the reasons I got sent to this school in the first place. If I touch people when they are asleep, I can dream with them.'

'You're winding me up,' said Jerald, irritated.

'No, I'm not,' said Karl. 'I've been able to do it since I was very young. I don't know how I do it, I just can.'

'So that's why you were touching my hand that night?' Jerald lowered his head. What Karl had said finally sunk in; if he could do what he claimed, then he knew all about Mortiboys and the abuse he had sustained. 'So you're telling me you know what I was dreaming about that night?' Tears began to sting Jerald's eyes. Karl nodded and the tears ran down Jerald's cheeks; he put both hands over his face and lowered his head.

'How long's it been going on?' asked Karl. Jerald continued to stare at the floor, tears dripping off the end of his nose, pooling on the floor in front of him. He sniffed, clearing his nose then rubbed his eyes.

'Start of term. He started making me clean out the storeroom, but then . . .,' Jerald stopped talking, finding it hard to continue. 'Then he started touching me. I was so frightened I couldn't . . .' Again Jerald went quiet, pausing to compose himself, 'Now he's making me touch him. I refused at first, but he hurt me.' Jerald stood up and pulled up his shirt; 'Yesterday he did this.' He turned to show Karl his lower back. Karl was shocked to see a very painful looking weal about half an inch wide and virtually the full width of Jerald's back.

'Jesus, Jerald, how the hell did he do that?'

'He hit me with a cane.' replied Jerald, pulling down his shirt and sitting back down on the bed.

'I'll come with you; let's go and see the Headmaster,' said Karl.

'No!' There was panic in Jerald's voice. 'He won't do it again; he looked really worried when he realised he'd marked me.'

'Jerald, you have to speak up. He has to be stopped.'

'I will, I will, just let me do it in my own time, please,' Jerald was almost begging.

'OK,' said Karl, 'just make sure you do, 'cause if you don't, I will.'

'Just one thing, Karl,' Jerald looked straight at him, 'stop calling me Jerald; my mom and dad call me that and I hate it – Jerry will do.'

Finally, Jerald had opened up. Karl felt as if he had helped share a huge burden with his new-found friend. Karl's father had told him that one day he would find out why he had been given the gift; he was now beginning to understand.

The confrontation

The next week flew by. Jerald's father was still working away, so it meant another weekend at school. Karl was beginning to get on really well with him and could tell he wasn't looking forward to spending another weekend potentially at the mercy of Mortiboys. On Thursday evening, Karl, Billy and Jerald shared a table in the dining room. True to his word, Karl had said nothing about what Jerald had told him.

'I'm going to ask if I can stay at school this weekend,' said Karl.

'Why would you want to do that?' asked Billy as he forced more food into his mouth.

'Apart from seeing my brother, its boring as hell,' Karl replied.

'Won't your mom and dad mind?' chirped Jerald.

'Probably,' said Karl, 'but I'll just say I've a lot of work to catch up on.'

Inwardly, Jerald was chuffed he hadn't got to face another solitary weekend in school, and it was very unlikely Mortiboys would try anything when he wasn't alone. Karl made a phone call home. Jill wasn't pleased but accepted that he needed time to complete his studies. She was pleased that after all this time he still showed such a lot of enthusiasm for his schoolwork.

On Friday afternoon after the last lesson, parents began arriving and Karl and Jerald went back to the dormitory to keep out the way. By 7 pm everyone who was going home had gone. Both boys were lying on their beds reading when the click of the door catch caught their attention. Simultaneously, they looked over the top of their books and saw Mortiboys standing in the doorway.

'Hennessey, I thought you'd gone home.'

'No, sir,' said Karl, 'I'm staying at school this weekend.'

Mortiboys looked over at Jerald. 'Sanderson, I need you to help me sort out some kit in the gym.'

'I don't feel very well, sir,' replied Jerald.

'Nonsense, boy,' said Mortiboys, 'you look fine. The exercise will do you good.' Again, Jerald pleaded illness but it was no good. 'Fifteen minutes, in the gym,' snapped Mortiboys. The look on his face said 'Or else.' He closed the door behind him as he left the room.

Karl looked over at Jerald. 'You're not going, are you?'

'I've got no choice,' said Jerald.

Karl couldn't believe his ears. 'Let's go straight to the Headmaster and sort this out once and for all.'

'I told you I'll deal with it,' said Jerald. It was obvious he was in some form of denial, just hoping the problem would just disappear, but Karl knew better.

Fifteen minutes later Jerald was standing outside the gym door trying to pluck up the courage to go in. Unknown to Jerald, Karl had followed him, just staying out of sight. Jerald pushed the door open and went in. Mortiboys was throwing a basketball at a hoop. Bouncing the ball on the spot, Mortiboys called out, 'Go into the storeroom, Sanderson, and wait.' With fear in his eyes, Jerald did exactly as he was told. Mortiboys threw the ball through the hoop once more then walked over to his office at the end of the gym.

Karl peered round the edge of the gym door; he could feel his heart pounding in his chest. They must be in the storeroom, he thought. He was just about to push the gym door open when he saw Mortiboys come out of his office. Karl jumped back pressing himself against the wall. 'Shit,' he said under his breath.

Peeping through the crack at the edge of the door, his eyes fixed on the perverted master. Mortiboys walked across the gym, in his hand the cane that had inflicted the injuries to Jerald's back. The master opened the storeroom door, glanced behind and then went inside, closing the door firmly behind him.

Karl began to panic; what could he do? He couldn't confront Mortiboys alone. He had to tell, but who? Karl turned and ran; the Headmaster was usually in his office till at least 7 pm. If this animal was to be caught in the act, he had to move fast. Karl entered the rear of the main school building, still running as fast as he possibly could, his face soaked with sweat. Turning into the staff room corridor, which was normally out of bounds to pupils, he ran straight into Mr Blakeway, who was just about to leave for the weekend. Folders, paperwork, books all went up in the air, and both of them ended up flat on their backs.

'My God, Karl, what the hell is going on?' said Blakeway. Considering what had just happened, he was actually very composed.

'Jee Jerry Sese Sanderson, sir.' In his panic, Karl was stammering trying to get his breath back.

'Slow down, slow down,' said Blakeway, in an attempt to get Karl to calm down.

'In the gym storeroom, sir, Mortiboys has got Jerry.'

By the alarm and panic in Karl's voice, Blakeway thought he should investigate. Leaving all his paperwork where it had fallen, he pulled Karl to his feet. 'Show me,' he said.

Again Karl set off at full speed, Blakeway in hot pursuit. They burst into the gym and Karl stopped and pointed. 'They're in the storeroom.'

Blakeway dashed over, pressed down on the handle and shouldered the door open, expecting to find an injured pupil. What he found disgusted him; Mortiboys was semi-naked, wielding a cane above his head. Jerald was cowering in the corner, his face gripped in fear. In a futile attempt to

The confrontation

take control of the situation, the young boy had refused to perform the sexual acts Mortiboys tried to force upon him and had paid for it agonisingly. The cane had already struck four or five times across Jerald's back.

Before Mortiboys could turn, Blakeway saw his chance and, grabbing his shoulders, he dragged him backwards out of the storeroom. They both stumbled, trying to stay on their feet. Mortiboys spun round, swinging the cane at Blakeway's head, but the faster and leaner master saw it coming and ducked. As the cane went over his head, Blakeway bobbed up and threw a skilled right hook, hitting Mortiboys square on the chin. Dazed but not beaten, Mortiboys got to his feet and ran at the lighter master. Blakeway lashed out with a well-aimed boot, catching Mortiboys in his exposed groin. His face said it all; mouth wide open he fell to his knees, the colour instantly draining form his face.

'Karl,' shouted Blakeway. Karl was standing by the main door, shocked but at the same time impressed by his mentor's actions. 'Get the Headmaster. I'll look after Jerald.' Karl didn't need telling twice. Without saying a word, he turned and sprinted off in the direction of the Headmaster's office.

Pendlebury was in his office, relaxing in his high-backed leather desk chair. Reaching into the bottom draw of his desk, he pulled out a bottle of Jack Daniels. He wasn't what you would call a drinking man, but on Friday afternoons when all the boys who were going home had left and the school fell quiet, he liked to sit alone in his office and pour a glass of the amber liquid. It was an hour when he could relax and take his mind off the general running of the school.

He held up his half-filled tumbler towards the late afternoon sunlight, turning it slightly and gazing at the prism of colour that flashed across the pattern cut into the crystal. 'Bottoms up,' he said, smiling. The glass touched his lips and he felt the warming sensation flow over his tongue and touch his throat. Suddenly, the door loudly burst open and Pendlebury sat upright, spluttering his drink. Karl stood in the doorway.

'What on earth do you think you are doing, boy?' shouted Pendlebury, pulling a handkerchief from the top pocket of his jacket to wipe himself down.

'It's urgent, sir; Mr Blakeway needs you in the gym straight away.' The look of panic on Karl's face drew an instant reaction from the Headmaster, who immediately rounded the desk and ran towards the gym.

Pendlebury pushed the door of the gym open, and he and Karl rushed inside. Blakeway and Jerry were on the far side, perched on a long exercise bench. Blakeway had his arm around Jerald's shoulder attempting to comfort the traumatised young man. There was no sign of Mortiboys; as soon as Blakeway had gone to attend to Jerald, Mortiboys had struggled to his feet and made his escape.

In the main car park at the front of the school, Mortiboys' Range Rover engine burst into life. Where he was going he didn't know; all he knew was that he had been caught red-handed and had no choice but to escape. As he left the gym, he had made his way to his locker and had quickly thrown on some clothes, grabbed a few personal belongings and run straight out of the building to his car. The Range Rover's wheels spun across the deep gravel on to the path, heading for the tree line.

There was only one way out. Mortiboys knew the gates would be locked and the security staff certainly would not open them for him. As he approached the gates, instead of reducing his speed he accelerated – forty, fifty miles an hour. The gates had been there along time and were a testament to Victorian craftsmanship. The Range Rover slammed into them. An average-sized saloon probably wouldn't have had any effect, but the sheer power and weight of the Rover meant it punched its way through, sustaining huge damage to both the gates and the vehicle. The vehicle momentarily came to a halt as Mortiboys recovered himself from the impact. With smoke billowing from the crumpled bonnet, the car disappeared off into the distance.

Back in the school, the Headmaster had taken Blakeway and the boys to his office, where they were quickly joined by the security officer who managed the main gate CCTV, reporting the incident with Mortiboys' Range Rover. The police were immediately informed, as were the boys' parents. Although the welfare of the boys was the Headmaster's prime concern, he couldn't help thinking of the damage the appalling business would do to the credibility of the school. He just hoped they could recover from it.

9

Heart to heart

The police arrived and statements were taken from all involved. Normally, they would have waited for both boys' parents to arrive, but in the circumstances, with Jerald's father being half way round the world, the Headmaster was theoretically his guardian. The school had finally managed to contact his father, but even catching the next available flight meant it would be the following day before he arrived.

Karl's parents arrived within two hours, leaving immediately after they had received the phone call. After an in-depth conversation, Karl had told his parents he was fine; it was Jerald who needed taking care of. If they didn't mind, he wanted to stay at school with Jerald, at least till his father arrived. George and Jill were so proud of him – he showed such great strength and maturity for a boy so young.

A warrant had been issued for the arrest of Mortiboys. The officer in charge said it wouldn't take long to pick him up as the damage to his car as he had rammed the gate meant it wasn't going very far. He had also probably sustained personal injury upon impact and would turn up at the nearest A&E unit.

They intended to leave a police officer in a squad car at the school's main gate overnight. The gates had been severely damaged and would need attention the following day to once again fortify the school's security. It was very unlikely that Mortiboys would return, but, just in case, there would be an officer at hand. Finally, the police had collected all the required information and went about their search for Mortiboys.

Pendlebury sat in his office; what had meant to be a relaxing glass of whisky had turned out to be a real nerve-calmer. Now he had the unpleasant task of compiling a letter for the parents and guardians of the entire school.

The boys went back to the their dormitory. Blakeway made three mugs of hot chocolate and took them up to the dorm; normally this would never happen, but given the situation, it seemed appropriate.

Considerately, he knocked on the door before entering and found the boys lying on their beds. Jerald had already fallen asleep, but Karl sat up, swinging his feet down to the floor.

'Here you go, Karl,' said Blakeway smiling, as he passed him a mug of chocolate. Karl took it with both hands and thanked the master. 'He's flat out,' said Blakeway, glancing over at Jerald. 'It's probably the best thing for him.'

Blakeway took a sip of his chocolate and looked at Karl. 'Are you all right Karl?'

'I'm fine, sir,' replied Karl. 'I told Jerry to speak up about Mortiboys when I first found out what was happening.' Karl took a drink of chocolate, 'He begged me not to tell; I should have told sooner.'

'It was a terrible position for you to be in; you must have been scared stiff.' Blakeway again took a large gulp on his drink. 'How did you find out it was going on?' he asked. Karl didn't want to lie; Blakeway was a good man and a very clever man. If Karl lied, he knew he would see straight through him.

'I have a gift,' said Karl.

'What sort of gift?' replied Blakeway, intrigued.

'I can see people's dreams.'

Blakeway straightened up and placed his mug on the chest at the bottom of Karl's bed. 'What do you mean?'

'When people sleep, if I touch them I can see what they are dreaming.'

Blakeway raised his hand to an already furrowed brow. 'Wait a minute, Karl; you're telling me' – Blakeway paused and smiled – 'you can see what other people are dreaming?' He didn't know whether Karl was trying to wind him up; he certainly looked serious.

'Yes, sir, that's how I found out; I saw Jerry being abused, he was having a nightmare.'

'You are being serious aren't you, Karl?' said Blakeway, mystified by Karl's answer.

'Yes, sir, I touched his hand while he was sleeping. At first he wouldn't talk about it, but when I told him about my gift, he told me all about it.'

Blakeway shook his head; he still couldn't believe what he was hearing. He had always known that Karl was a special young man, incredibly academic, but this was just amazing. Karl spent the rest of the evening telling Blakeway about the tests he had undergone when he was younger and how, over the years, he had developed his gift. They talked late into the night, developing a mutual admiration. Fascinated, Blakeway asked if he could help Karl to research his gift and hopefully develop it even more. Karl was over the moon, quickly accepting the master's offer; it felt good to have finally talked about what had been such a closely guarded secret.

On Monday morning, boys began arriving back at the school, to be welcomed by the press. The main gates had been temporarily repaired but had to be operated manually until a major overhaul could be carried out. This kept the press out of the grounds, but the reporters and freelance photographers plagued anyone arriving at the main gate. In an attempt to reassure parents and boys, the Headmaster had letters ready for every parent returning their child to his custody, but the onerous task was made even more difficult by the presence of the journalists. A few parents opted to take their children home, but the majority had faith in the Headmaster, who assured them that this was an isolated incident and had been taken care of. Every child would have the opportunity talk to an independent counsellor and discuss any thoughts or concerns they had.

Andrew Mortiboys had been hiding out in an old barn just outside the village of Chelmarsh, no more than a mile from a small cottage he rented. Cold, hungry and experiencing acute depression, he was on the verge of suicide. He couldn't believe what he had done to the young boy; being placed in a position of authority, it was unforgivable. When he was caught, as he knew he eventually would be, what would happen to him? He would definitely go to prison, and what then? He had heard all sorts of stories about child sex offenders being beaten, abused and even raped by other inmates. He couldn't face a life like that.

After ramming the school gates he had driven to a reservoir not half a mile from where he now sat. He had hauled himself out of the car, blood oozing from a gaping wound on his left shin, and in excruciating pain from his right forearm which, by the look of the deformity, was certainly fractured. With his last ounce of strength, he had pushed the battered and smoking car into the reservoir's murky depths, hopefully throwing the police off his scent, at least for a short while. It was Monday now, and, under cover of darkness that night, he planned to get into his cottage. What he would do after that he didn't know, but at least he would be warm.

Jill and George sat down to their evening meal; normally, Charlie ate with them, but on this particular evening had gone out with friends. Jill had been doing some financial homework on Karl's school fees and was pleased they were alone on this occasion. Squeezing tomato sauce onto her pie and chips, she said, 'I had a letter from Marshdown today.'

'What was that about, then?' asked George, rolling round a particularly hot piece of meat in his mouth.

'George, in the last five years the fees have gone up nearly three thousand pounds, and that's without uniform.' Jill put her knife and fork down. 'There isn't enough money left in Karl's compensation account to complete his education. I reckon we have enough for another eighteen months.'

George stopped chewing and swallowed hard, relieving his mouth of a tough piece of meat. 'Overtime,' said George, hoping to continue his meal in peace.

Jill shook her head. 'Overtime? Do you know how much money we are talking about, George?', her voice rising.

'OK, OK, no need to shout!' said George, wiping his mouth with the back of his hand. 'We've done the best we can for that boy; at least he's had a head start, and I'm sure he'll be able to finish his studies in a state school.'

'It's not quite the same though is it, George?' said Jill vindictively.

'Have you got any other ideas, then?' George replied. They finished the meal in silence.

Mortiboys waited until late evening, making sure that any passing vehicles would not detect him. Awkwardly, he got to his feet and, engulfed by darkness, made his way around the edge of the field towards the open road. He stopped every now and then to ease the pain from his leg; infection was rapidly taking hold of his body. The wound needed to be cleaned and dressed, and an immediate course of antibiotics was essential. In another twenty-four hours it would be too late; his body would succumb to septicaemia.

He hobbled along the road. There was no footpath, and if a car had passed him, he would not have been able to duck into a hedge to hide as he was too immobile, but had no choice but to take the risk. Only another four hundred metres and he would be home. In the distance, the glare of a car's headlights came round the bend. With every last ounce of strength, he stood up straight, trying to hide the fact he was injured and in great pain. As the car approached, he placed his back against the hedge, as if avoiding the path of the vehicle. The driver glanced at him and waved a hand, thanking him for standing back in the darkness. Mortiboys waved his good arm, grimacing with pain, and the car disappeared down the road and round the bend.

Leaning against his front door, Mortiboys struggled to get his key out of his pocket, every movement producing great pain. Before closing the door behind him, he checked left and right. The cottages either side of him were very rarely used in the winter months; both were second homes for city dwellers. As he closed the door, he leaned back against it, a wave of relief washing over him. By the look of the place, the police had already searched the cottage – either that or he had been burgled.

With the light on, he could see the severity of the cut on his leg. It had stopped bleeding, but looking into the gaping wound he could see the glistening white bone of his shin. His head began to spin and, as quickly as his injuries allowed him, he sat down in an armchair, the sight of his own bones instantly sending him into shock. As soon as he was able, using the furniture for support, he made his way into the bathroom. Staring into his own eyes in the bathroom cabinet mirror, he became ravaged with guilt. Facing the world after what he had done was no longer an option.

He hobbled over to the bath, put the plug in and turned on both taps. His face contorted as he slowly removed his clothes. By now the bath was three-quarters full, and the steaming warm water looked so inviting. Taking a small pair of nail scissors from the cabinet, Mortiboys turned off the taps and slowly lowered himself into the water, for an instant so comforting. He lay back with tears stinging his eyes; then, taking the closed scissors in the fist of his good hand, he raised his injured arm. Gritting his teeth, he plunged the pointed blades of the scissors into his wrist and, with his eyes closed and teeth still gritted, he plunged again and again. Seven, eight times, maybe more, he didn't know. His wrist became a bludgeoned mess; crimson fluid squirting from his wrist each time the scissors were raised. His head flopped back in the bath. Dropping the scissors onto the floor, he lowered his shoulders below the surface of the water. The warmth was now feeling even more comforting, and slowly he lost consciousness and slipped beneath the crimson-coloured water.

It was Wednesday lunchtime and Karl and Billy were in the school dining room, Billy as usual being his annoying self. Each time Karl looked away from his food, Billy would endeavour to steal some from right under his nose. It was funny at first, but as usual Billy didn't know when to stop.

'Next time you touch my food, Billy, see this fork?' Karl raised his fork gripped tightly in his clenched fist and menacingly pointed it at Billy.

'Karl Hennessey!' came a loud shout from the entrance door of the dining room. It was the head boy, Benjamin Knight, an impeccably dressed eighteen-year-old. Now in his final year, it wouldn't be long before he left Marshdown. He was elected as head boy more for *who* he knew, rather than *what* he knew. Coming from a very wealthy family, his father had always made sure his contributions to the school fund were recognised in one way or another.

Karl quickly put his fork back down on the table and stood up.

'Headmaster's office, straight away,' shouted Knight; then he turned and walked out of the door.

'That will teach you to raise your fork at me,' said Billy with some delight.

'Don't be stupid,' replied Karl. 'I wonder what he wants me for; I'd better get down there. Looks like you got my dinner after all.'

Karl pushed his plate towards Billy, who wasted no time devouring what was left. Karl hastily made his way to the Headmaster's office, wondering what was in store for him. Two good knocks on the door, and Karl waited to be beckoned in. 'Enter,' came the familiar voice from within. Karl pushed the huge door open and peered around the edge; the Headmaster was sitting behind his desk, and in front of him sat Mr Blakeway.

'Ah, Hennessey,' said the Headmaster, 'come in, shut the door behind you and take a seat.' Karl did as he was ordered. Blakeway gave him a welcoming smile.

The Headmaster sat up straight, both hands placed flat on his desk. 'I thought it only right that both of you heard the latest developments before all sorts of stories start flying around.' Looking straight at Karl, the Headmaster continued, 'Hennessey, when I have finished, I would like to ask a small favour of you.'

'Anything, sir,' replied Karl.

'Good man.'

Karl was sure he saw a glint of a smile on the Headmaster's face. 'I had a visit earlier today from Detective Inspector Moran, the officer in charge of tracking down Mr Mortiboys.' The Headmaster briefly paused and took a deep breath. 'He was found this morning at his cottage, he'd committed suicide.'

Karl's and Blakeway's mouths fell open; they had expected him to say that Mortiboys had been taken into custody.

'I don't know what to say, Headmaster,' said Blakeway.

'Unfortunately, there is no more to say; what's done is done.' The Headmaster's face showed no compassion for his deceased member of staff. Turning to Karl, the Headmaster again attempted a half smile. 'Jerald Sanderson will be returning to school next week, Hennessey. As he is in your dormitory and you know what he has been through, I would appreciate it if you would keep an eye on him for me; any problems come and see me straight away.'

'Certainly, sir,' replied Karl, feeling quite proud that the Headmaster had entrusted him with the task.

'You conducted yourself excellently at the weekend, Hennessey; we were all very proud of you.' Karl thanked the Headmaster but could feel himself blushing. 'Right then, you can get back to your lunch break.'

As Karl got up to leave the room, Blakeway turned to him. 'I have a few books that will interest you, Karl. Come and see me at the end of school today.'

'Yes, sir, thank you,' replied Karl, and he left the room pulling the door closed behind him.

10

Nightmares

As soon as school had finished, Karl usually went back to the dormitory to get changed ready for the evening meal. On this occasion, he went straight over to Blakeway's classroom; he loved reading and couldn't wait to see what the master had for him. There were a few boys still in the classroom, so Karl waited outside. Blakeway saw him through the window and waved a hand, beckoning Karl to come in.

As Karl approached the desk, Blakeway picked up a pile of books. 'Here you go, Karl,' said the master. 'Have a read of these. I've briefly gone through them, and I think you will find them very interesting.'

Karl took the books with both hands and then quickly placed them on the nearest desk as they were quite heavy. 'Thank you very much, sir,' he said enthusiastically.

Blakeway smiled; it was strange to see such excitement in the eyes of a student so young, when being presented with enough reading material to last most people three months. One by one Karl read the titles aloud, '*The Power of Dreams* by Gustav Heinz, *Understanding the Mind* by David Studley, *Telepathy: Fact or Fiction?*' He looked at Blakeway. 'Another by David Studley,' almost as if he had heard of the author. Finally, he picked up the last book, '*How to Control your Dreams* by Chloe Masterson.' Again he turned to Blakeway; 'I like the sound of that one.'

'I thought you might,' said Blakeway. 'You can keep them as long as you like Karl.'

'Are you sure, sir?'

'Absolutely,' Blakeway continued, putting paperwork in his briefcase. 'Let me know what you think. If they are of any help, I will see what else I can dig out for you.' Karl thanked him once again.

Blakeway looked at his watch. 'Right, take those books up to your dorm and get over for your evening meal. You need to eat well if you're going to keep that brain of yours in tip-top condition.' He gave Karl a jovial smile.

Without hesitation Karl gathered up the books, unconcerned now about their weight, and headed back to his dormitory.

After his evening meal, Karl went back to the dormitory and began reading; just like being engrossed in a good thriller, he couldn't put them down. Reading as much as he did, he had acquired an ability to speed-read at a phenomenal rate, only putting his books down when other boys in the dormitory complained that the light was keeping them awake. Friday afternoon quickly came around, and Karl took the last book home with him to read over the weekend. Some things in the books gave him ideas – the problem he had was finding willing subjects to try them out on; he didn't want to attract too much attention, not yet anyway.

Arriving back at school on Sunday evening, Karl realised that he had spent so much time reading the books Blakeway had lent to him that his schoolwork had been neglected. Quickly, he set about getting up to date. He had been working for about an hour when he heard voices outside on the landing. The door opened; it was Jerald accompanied by the Headmaster and another man. Karl didn't recognise him but assumed that it was Jerald's father; although quite chubby in stature, the hair gave it away, being neatly cut and the same colour as Jerald's, but greasy as hell, obviously a family trait. Karl stood up and the two boys greeted each other, obviously pleased to see each other.

'Ah, Hennessey, I'm so pleased you're here,' said the Headmaster, 'this is Jerald's father.'

'Pleased to meet you, Mr Sanderson,' said Karl.

'I'm pleased to meet you, Karl. Jerald's told me so much about you. I wanted to thank you personally for helping in this terrible ordeal.'

'It's nothing,' replied Karl, feeling awkward.

'Oh it is, young man; we greatly appreciate what you did, and won't forget it.'

Karl blushed a little, embarrassed by the attention.

'As you can see, Mr Sanderson,' said the Headmaster, 'they're a close-knit little group in the dormitories; they always have their friends at hand, should they need them.' Karl thought the Headmaster was going a little over the top, but he was obviously trying to smooth things over with Jerald's father.

'I must be frank with you, Pendlebury,' said Jerald's father, 'Jerald asked to come back. It's his welfare and happiness I'm concerned about; if it had been my choice he wouldn't have set foot in this school again.'

'I completely understand, Mr Sanderson,' said the Headmaster, trying to hide his embarrassment. 'The safety of the children is and always will be paramount.' The Headmaster rubbed his hands together, a habit that surfaced when he was a little nervous. Few, if any, of Jerald's friends realised that his father was a very powerful man in the world of finance, but the Headmaster was acutely aware of this and the fact that he had many influential friends and colleagues; a word from him could ruin the reputation of the school and end Pendlebury's career.

They continued in polite conversation for about fifteen minutes, and then Jerald's father announced that he had to leave as he had a flight to catch in the early hours of he morning. After a rather unaffectionate goodbye to his son, both he and the Headmaster left Karl and Jerald in their room.

Later that evening, Karl was scanning through the borrowed books, and Jerald had fallen asleep. As it was Sunday, they were alone; Billy and the other boys in the dormitory wouldn't arrive until the following morning. Karl heard Jerald talking in his sleep; he was constantly moving around in his bed, being very fractious. Climbing out of bed, Karl went over and stood next to his friend, it was so tempting to reach out and hold his hand, but after what had happened last time he thought it best not to. His friend looked increasingly troubled.

'Jerry,' said Karl. Jerald mumbled, obviously still dreaming, his face lathered in sweat just as before. Karl leaned down and shook Jerald's arm. 'Jerry, wake up.' He called a little louder this time and it did the trick. Jerry woke with a start.

'What's wrong?' Jerald asked, looking alarmed.

'You were dreaming;' said Karl, 'talking to yourself.'

Jerald sat up and wiped the sweat from his forehead. 'I keep dreaming about Mortiboys. It was bad before, but now he's dead, it's like he's haunting me.' Jerald raised his hand and rubbed his eyes. 'I haven't slept a night through since I was told he'd killed himself.'

'I've got an idea Jerry; if you'll let me, I'd like to try and help.' This was the opportunity Karl had been waiting for. Armed with all the exercises and ideas from the books he had read, it was a great chance to test it out.

'What do you want to do?' asked Jerald, a little suspiciously.

'All you have to do is go to sleep. When I'm sure you're asleep, I'll hold your hand and go to sleep myself.'

Jerald was at once doubtful, but excited. 'You really think this will work, Karl?'

'I know it will; I've done it with my brother since I was small. I've been reading books about dreams; it's all about your frame of mind when you go to sleep. If you think hard enough about a place in your subconscious, you can go there.'

Jerald looked amazed. 'You really believe you can do this, don't you?'

Karl nodded.

'OK,' said Jerald, 'what have I got to lose? Let's give it a go.'

Jerald moved the bedside cabinet and Karl pushed two beds together; then they both climbed back into bed.

'Right, Jerry, just go to sleep; when I'm sure you're asleep, I'll hold your hand.'

Apprehensively, Jerald lay back and closed his eyes. About ten minutes later, Jerald sat up. 'I can't sleep now, Karl.' There was no answer. 'Karl.' Still no answer. 'Typical.' said Jerald; Karl had fallen asleep. Nervously, Jerald took hold of Karl's hand and lay back, eventually drifting off to sleep.

Almost like stepping out of an extremely dense fog, Karl appeared in what he knew was Jerald's dream. He was standing alone in the school gym; there was no sign of Jerald. The door to the storeroom was closed; if Jerald was reliving the same nightmare, Karl knew that's where he would find him, probably at this very moment being compromised by Mortiboys. Slowly, Karl walked over to the door, when suddenly, without any warning, the door flew open. Jerald came running out with that look of terror in his eyes. Looking straight at Karl he shouted, 'Run, he's coming.' Jerald ran straight past, gaining pace, his face gripped with fear. Startled by the sudden commotion, Karl shouted after him, 'Wait, Jerry wait!' But there was no stopping Jerald. He disappeared out of the door and down the corridor.

Karl turned back to the storeroom to see Mortiboys coming through the door, fastening the cord on his tracksuit bottoms, the same thin cane he had used on Jerald under his arm. He looked directly at Karl. 'What's your problem, Hennessey?'

This was a first for Karl. Although he knew Mortiboys was merely a figment of Jerald's imagination, it was still very frightening. Mortiboys raised the cane, aiming a blow at Karl. As the cane swished through the air, Karl closed his eyes. Almost instantly, Karl disappeared and then reappeared outside Mortiboys' range. Again Mortiboys came forward, this time attempting to grab Karl by the scruff of the neck. Again Karl closed his eyes, but this time he thought about Jerald. Instantly, he reappeared standing behind Jerald in the school grounds. Jerald had run out of the rear entrance of the school and was hiding at the side of an outbuilding.

'Jerry,' said Karl.

Jerald spun round, almost toppling over with panic, 'Jesus Christ, Karl, what are you doing? You nearly gave me a bloody heart attack.'

'You have to face him Jerry; it's the only way to stop the nightmare.'

'I can't.' Breathlessly, Jerald shook his head. 'I can't.'

'You have to, Jerry; that's why I'm here. Remember, it's all a dream.'

Jerald looked confused, it was as if he was struggling to understand what was real and what wasn't.

Mortiboys came running out of the school's rear entrance. 'Where are you Sanderson?' he shouted. 'I'll find you, and when I do . . .' Jerald was petrified; he splayed himself against the wall of the building.

'Come on, Jerry, let's face him.' The look on Karl's face said 'We can beat him.' But Jerald was terrified.

'I can't,' he said. Edging towards the rear of the building, he stumbled over a pile of bricks. Mortiboys heard him fall, turned, and ran in their direction. Again, Jerald panicked and ran for it, but Mortiboys saw him and gave chase. Mortiboys was closing on Jerald, and Karl could see it wasn't going the way he had planned. He had to wake up and quickly.

Closing his eyes, he concentrated; this was a trick he had done many times with his brother. His eyes opened and he concentrated on Jerald. 'Jerry,' he said aloud. Quickly, he turned to see Jerald, sweating profusely, his head moving from side to side, his body rigid with fear. God only knows what was happening within his subconscious at that moment in time. Karl began shaking him. 'Wake up Jerry, wake up!'

Suddenly, Jerald's eyes opened wide and he gulped in a huge breath.

'Karl,' said Jerald, 'he was chasing me.' The terrified boy paused for a second and looked away, then slowly turned back and looked straight at Karl. 'You *can* do it;' he said in amazement, 'you were there.'

Karl stared back. 'Jerry, something told me you just had to face him. If you're going to rid your mind of this nightmare, it's got to happen. Don't ask me how I know, I just do.'

Suddenly, a wave of tiredness washed over Karl; he felt so tired that he thought he was going to pass out. 'Jerry,' he said weakly, 'I need to rest.' The dream had taken a lot out of Karl. Usually, when he interacted in dreams it was fun and relaxing, but Jerald's dream had been far from that. Karl could barely get back to his own bed; his legs felt like lead as he staggered round to it.

'Karl, are you OK?' asked Jerald.

'I'll be fine,' Karl replied. He rolled onto his bed and was asleep in seconds. This had been a whole new experience; he had just found out that gifts like his did not come cheap.

Lessons began promptly at 9 am. Normally, the boys got up at 7:30 am, had breakfast at 8:15, then collected the necessary books and went straight to lessons. On this particular Monday, Karl and Jerald were still sleeping soundly at 8:30 am. Fortunately, Billy Campbell was early for the first time in his life. In his usual loud manner, he barged through the dormitory door and then spotted Karl.

'What have we got here then, Sleeping Beauty?' He turned towards Jerald. 'And Rip van Winkle! Come on sleepy heads, it's nearly nine o'clock.'

Both boys woke simultaneously and sat up. Karl picked up his watch from the bedside cabinet. 'Shit, it's nearly quarter to nine, Jerry.' He leapt out of bed and began dragging his clothes on. Jerald followed suit, albeit a little more slowly.

'Don't worry Karl,' he said, 'we'll make it, but we aren't going to get breakfast.'

Billy was looking inquisitively at the two beds, which were still pushed together. 'What was going on here last night then? Two beds together, two boys alone, nudge nudge, wink wink, something you lads aren't telling me?' Billy struck an effeminate pose.

'Don't be a twat, Billy,' said Karl as he tied his shoelaces. 'I interacted in Jerry's dream.' Jerald looked over, catching Karl's eye. 'It's OK, Jerry, I've interacted with Billy before; he won't tell anyone.'

Jerald finished dressing.

'Let's get that bed back where it should be or they'll all be asking questions,' said Billy, realising it wasn't something he should be making fun of. Quickly they got everything back into place, gathered up their books and went to their first lesson.

Karl hadn't been himself all morning and he was relieved when lunchtime finally arrived. He had tried to concentrate during lessons, but his mind kept wandering back to the dream. When Jerald had left the gym, Karl had found himself facing Mortiboys alone. Every time he had interacted in somebody else's dream, the host had always been present, because in theory if they weren't there, there wasn't a dream. He was baffled. It was as if he was powering the dream with his own thoughts. He tried to explain what was troubling him to Jerald and Billy, but it was more than they could comprehend.

'Karl,' came a voice from behind him; it was Blakeway. Karl stood up. 'Sit down, sit down,' said Blakeway, 'I don't wish to interrupt your lunch, I just wondered if you have had time to look at any of the books.'

'Yes, sir,' replied Karl, 'I'll return them after school.'

'No, I don't need them just yet; wait until you have had time to read them all.'

'I have, sir; I've finished them.'

Blakeway was astonished. 'You never cease to amaze me, young man. Drop them back after school. I have two more for you to look at, and we can discuss your findings.' Blakeway made his way out of the dining room, acknowledging other masters and pupils on his way to the door.

'We have to try again, Jerry,' said Karl.

Jerald put down his fork. 'When? We can't do it with all the others in the room; it would be all over the school by morning.'

'You're right.' Karl rubbed his forehead. 'Think,' he said out loud. 'I know, what if we stay at school for the weekend?'

'Don't forget me, you pair,' said Billy; he didn't like the idea of being left out on something exciting. 'If you oversleep again, you'll need someone to wake you up.'

'Ok, that's it, then,' said Karl, 'we'll all phone home and say we are having a revision weekend. All three of us agreed?'

'Agreed,' replied the other two boys.

After school Karl took the books back to Blakeway, and, in confidence, he explained what had happened in Jerald's dream. Blakeway found it absolutely incredible, but at the same time he was a little worried as none of them really knew what they were getting involved with. He knew he couldn't stop Karl; the only thing he could do was give him as much information as he could on the subject, and just hope he was equal to the task.

After a long, tedious week, Friday finally arrived. Karl had one or two ideas he wanted to try in the dream and told Jerald that on Friday night, provided Jerald did exactly as he asked, it would be the end of Mortiboys once and for all. Jerald was still a little apprehensive and twice that week had woken soaked in sweat after experiencing a dream similar to the one Karl had interacted in. On both occasions, he couldn't find it within himself to do as Karl had advised and face Mortiboys; he just hoped Karl would be the influencing factor that evening.

After their evening meal, the boys went back to the dormitory. Karl had noticed that the more tired Jerald was, the less he seemed to have the nightmares. That evening he told Jerald that he shouldn't stay up too late and that once he became sleepy, he should concentrate on Mortiboys. They pushed the beds together and stretched out, talking about what they planned to do when they left school. All three of the boys were bright, even Billy with his overexaggerated sense of humour and clumsiness, but Karl had excelled academically. If everything went to plan and he continued at his present rate, he would achieve a degree in psychology before his eighteenth birthday. It would be a new school record, and, although Karl would never admit it to anyone, it was a record he wanted.

By 10 pm they were all becoming tired. Billy lay on his side looking across the room at Karl and Jerald, who were lying next to each other, their hands already loosely holding on to each other. Slowly, they drifted off to sleep.

Karl suddenly found himself with his brother Charlie. He was no more than about six years old and they were in the garden of his parents' house. As usual, Charlie had him pinned on his back and was squirting water onto Karl's face from an old washing up liquid bottle. Karl remembered the incident well; he had struggled for so long and had been unable to move his brother. In the dream, Karl thought, if only I was a little stronger. Concentrating on the thought, he pushed against Charlie's chest and to his amazement he picked him up like a baby, dropped him on his back and sat on his chest.

Suddenly, he woke. It was like a light bulb turning on in his head. Glancing round at the other boys, he could see that they were both fast asleep. Jerald had released Karl's hand and had turned over, curled up in a ball. At least he was sleeping soundly. Now Karl knew how he could help Jerald to defeat Mortiboys.

The next morning the boys woke early. Although disappointed with the previous night's experiment, they decided to give it another go when Karl told them about his dream. Karl spent the day reading the new books Blakeway had given him, while Billy and Jerald lounged about in the games room playing pool and watching television.

After their evening meal and a visit from the duty master making sure all was well, the boys settled down for the evening. Again they pushed the beds together and then lay chatting until, one by one, they drifted off to sleep. As Karl felt his eyes becoming heavy, he took hold of Jerald's hand. He found himself sitting on a bench in the school grounds. The sun was on his back and felt very relaxing. He often sat there in the summer months reading or just relaxing, taking in the sunshine. But was this dream his or Jerald's? Karl closed his eyes and thought of Jerald. When he opened them he was still in the same place. Suddenly, from the hedges some twenty metres behind him, he heard someone call his name. He turned but saw no one. Again, somebody called him. He got up and walked over to where the voice was coming from. Through a small gap in the hedge he saw a face.

'Jerry, is that you?'

'Yes, quickly, he might see you,' replied Jerald.

'I want him to see me, Jerry. Remember what we said? You have to face him. Come on out.'

Jerald scrambled from under the thick hedge.

'Let's finish it, Jerry.'

As if he had materialized out of thin air, Mortiboys appeared on the other side of the green, armed with the cane that Jerald had felt so often. 'You piece of shit, Sanderson, get over here now,' he shouted. Jerald was physically shaking, and Karl could see him wilting before him.

'Jerry, be strong;' said Karl, 'don't listen to him.'

Mortiboys began walking towards them, raising his cane ready to strike. Tears ran down Jerald's face and his bottom lip quivered like that of a small child being disciplined by his parents. Karl sensed that Jerald was about to run, and he had to think fast. Turning towards him he told Jerald to hold both his hands, close his eyes and think of nothing. Anxiously, Jerald took his hands, but he was too afraid to close his eyes.

Karl closed his eyes and thought of the dormitory; instantly, they both appeared in the room. 'Now listen, Jerry, as soon as you think of him, he'll be here.'

Karl looked into Jerald's eyes; he was terrified. Somehow Karl had to do this for him, if that was possible. From the hallway came the sound of heavy footsteps. Jerald looked left and right trying to find an escape route. His eyes fixed on the window.

'No, Jerry!' said Karl, gripping Jerald's hands tightly, 'When he comes through that door, stand still; I'll deal with him.'

Jerald was physically shaking. A wet patch appeared on the front of his trousers, slowly spreading down the right side of his leg and finally dripping onto his shoe. Not wanting to embarrass his friend, Karl turned to face the door. Instead of fear, Karl felt a rage stirring inside him. The door flew open and Mortiboys stood in the doorway, holding the cane in his right hand.

'I've got something for you, Sanderson.' An evil smirk appeared on his face. Through his tracksuit bottoms the boys could see the outline of his engorged manhood; he grabbed it with his left hand and moved it up and down.

'You know what to do with this, Sanderson; you can teach that little shit.' He nodded towards Karl.

Mortiboys raised the cane and moved towards them. Jerry cowered backwards but Karl stood his ground.

'You first then, Hennessey.'

As the cane swished through the air towards Karl, he focused on Mortiboys' arm. A look of shock seized the pervert's face. As hard as he tried to force his arm down it wouldn't move; his whole body was rigid. With amazing composure, Karl slowly stepped behind Mortiboys and leaned close to his ear.

'Not this time, Mortiboys' – Karl's voice was calm and even – 'you're finished.'

Jerald was still cowering down with his hands on his face. 'Jerry,' said Karl, 'Jerry, look.'

Through his fingers, Jerald glimpsed at the spectacle in front of him. As Jerald's hands fell from his face and he got to his feet, Karl could see his confidence growing. Taking the cane from Mortiboys, Karl snapped it over his knee and threw the thin strips of wood to the floor. 'Told you he was nothing,' said Karl.

A tear ran down Jerald's cheek and he turned to look at Mortiboys. His fear had gone and all that remained now was anger. With lightning speed, Jerald ran at his tormentor, his right foot smashing Mortiboys square in the groin. Released from his frozen state, Mortiboys collapsed in a heap, retching and vomiting as he hit the floor. Karl smiled; they'd done it.

'Come on, Jerry, we haven't got to worry about him any more.'

They moved towards the door, but then Jerald stopped, turned and ran at Mortiboys. Not content with the injury he had already inflicted, he slammed his foot into Mortiboys' lower back once, then twice.

'Bastard!' he shouted at the top of his voice. Mortiboys moaned, pulling his legs up into the foetal position. Jerald finally looked content. Silently, the boys left the room, closing the door behind them.

Almost instantly, Karl woke up. He looked over at Billy, who was sitting with his knees pulled up to his chest; he looked as if he had been watching a late-night horror movie. 'What the hell was going on with you two?' he asked, 'I thought at one time Jerry was going to fall out of the bed.'

'We did it,' said Karl, 'Jerry faced him; it's over.' Karl leaned over and shook Jerald. Slowly he stirred and sat up, leaning on one elbow. Looking over at Karl, he smiled. 'Thanks, mate.'

'You're welcome,' Karl replied, 'but I should sort that out.' Karl gestured towards Jerald's bed sheets, which were soaked, and a small puddle that had gathered under the bed. Jerald still managed a smile; it was a small price to pay to rid himself of his nightmares.

It was the last time Jerald would ever dream of Mortiboys. The night had taken a lot out of Karl, and while he was excited by his achievement, he was also exhausted. For three days, he remained weakened by the experience but was at the same time pleased for his friend.

Karl recounted the weekend's events to Blakeway. It was impossible to understand what was happening; was it the power of suggestion, or could Karl really participate in and direct the dreams of others? Whatever the explanation, Blakeway was enthralled and determined that he would support Karl in every way he could.

11

Affairs of the heart

Two years had passed since the night Jerald had faced his demons, and the experience had brought the boys closer together. They would often stay at school together over the weekends. Karl continued to develop his gift, now finding that he could interact in others' dreams just by touching them and closing his eyes, but he was always more in control when he slept.

Billy and Jerald planned to leave Marshdown after their examinations, taking their 'A' levels a year early. Karl, on the other hand, had taken 'A' levels two years earlier and was now taking additional subjects, together with an Open University degree in psychology, closely watched by his mentor, Mr Blakeway. Eighteen was the maximum age for the boys at Marshdown; pupils usually went direct to university from the school. Karl planned to complete his degree and then go to university for his Master's.

Unknown to Karl, however, finances at home were getting desperate; his father worked every hour God sent, but it still wasn't enough. The compensation money had run out, and unless they found money from another source, Karl would have to complete his education in the state system. It was putting massive pressure on his parents' relationship; they hardly saw each other from one day to the next, and when they did, they always seemed to be arguing. That coming Friday, Karl was going home for the weekend. It was becoming a less and less frequent occurrence; he sensed the tension between his parents and chose to stay at school either with friends or just to study.

George phoned the Headmaster and arranged a meeting with him before school finished that Friday. As usual, the Mr Pendlebury was only too happy to accommodate them. George and Jill set off for Marshdown after lunch, giving them plenty of time to get there for the meeting. On arrival, they went to the Headmaster's office, stopping twice along the way, greeted by masters who had tutored Karl over the years. George knocked the Headmaster's door. Looking nervously at Jill, he straightened his jacket. They had always found the Headmaster a little intimidating, but at the same time they were pleased that someone in his position should have such an attribute.

Pendlebury had anticipated their arrival, and, rather than calling them in, got up and opened the door. 'Good afternoon, Mr and Mrs Hennessey,' Pendlebury welcomed them with a broad smile, 'please, come in.'

George thanked him as they entered the office and Pendlebury closed the door behind them. They sat down, exchanging pleasantries about their journey. 'I must say, young Karl is making tremendous progress with his degree; Mr Blakeway is expecting nothing less than an Honours.' Pendlebury beamed. Jill looked so proud, but at the same time a feeling of sadness besieged her.

'Well, Mr Pendlebury, that's what we've come to see you about,' said George. Pendlebury sat up looking concerned.

'You see, Mr Pendlebury,' Jill explained, 'we financed Karl's education through compensation he received from an accident when he was born, and unfortunately it has run out.'

Pendlebury sat back in his chair looking genuinely upset. 'Oh dear, that is awful.' He took a deep breath. 'I really would like to say that he could finish his time with us on a scholarship, but although I have tried in the past with other exceptional students, we have never been able to secure funds.' The meeting suddenly became very sombre.

'I'll keep trying to raise the money,' said George, 'but . . .' His body language said it all.

The Headmaster could see the disappointment on both their faces. 'Of course,' he said, 'I will endeavour to try and influence the board of governors, but I have to be frank with you, Mr and Mrs Hennessey, I am not confident of success.'

Jill smiled, appreciative of his honesty. 'Thank you, Mr Pendlebury,' she said. 'If he has to finish his education in a state school, then that's the way it has to be.' An uncomfortable silence followed.

'Right, then,' said George. 'Well, thank you for your time, Mr Pendlebury; we will keep you informed of the situation.'

The Headmaster stood up. 'Mr Hennessey, my door is always open.' He offered George his hand, and both men returned a firm handshake. After a brief goodbye, they left the Headmaster with his thoughts. As they crossed the main hall, other parents were waiting for school to finish. Soon small groups of pupils began arriving; then, one by one, they drifted off home for the weekend, leaving the Great Hall in an eerie silence.

Pendlebury sat back in his chair, his usual Friday afternoon glass of Jack Daniels in his hand. 'Great pity;' he said to himself, 'showed enormous potential that boy.' He slugged his drink then raised the glass to eye level, enjoying the warmth of the liquor as it passed down his throat. A knock on the door startled him, and quickly he stood the glass in the opened bottom draw of his desk. 'Come in,' he called.

Blakeway's head appeared round the edge of the door. 'Sorry to disturb you, Headmaster. I just wanted to discuss Karl Hennessey's progress plan for his degree.'

'Ah yes, Hennessey,' said the Headmaster scratching his chin. 'Please, Mr Blakeway, come in; I have something you need to know.' Blakeway closed the door and sat opposite the Headmaster. 'I've just been informed that it's very unlikely Hennessey will be with us next year.'

'But he will have completed his degree in two years, possibly eighteen months.' Blakeway was stunned by the news.

'Unfortunately, Mr Blakeway, his parents' finances no longer make it possible for him to continue at Marshdown. As you know, a scholarship is out of the question, so, unless his parents can come up with the money, I'm afraid that's the end of it.'

Blakeway was devastated and sat shaking his head. 'The system stinks,' he said, raising his voice a little too loudly as he stood up. Pendlebury knew the master had a special bond with the boy and was just venting his frustration. Blakeway turned and walked towards the door.

'Mr Blakeway.'

Blakeway stopped and again faced the Headmaster. 'That information was confidential. I don't think the boy knows himself yet, and you never know, they might just raise the money.'

Blakeway knew by Pendlebury's tone it wasn't going to happen; it was almost as if he was trying to pacify him. Closing the door behind him, he went back to his classroom. Deep in thought, he gathered up the paperwork from his desk and went home for the weekend.

Karl's journey home was very quiet; once again he sensed the tension between his parents. It was dark when they pulled up at the house, and, hearing the car, Charlie went out to meet them. Charlie had finished school that year and landed himself a job with a local electrical contractor. The money wasn't good, but it had great prospects, and he had been attending college on a day release basis to attain the necessary qualifications. Although it was not an indentured apprenticeship, he could still become a qualified electrician, and, most importantly, he really enjoyed what he was doing.

Karl was the first out of the car. 'You're late,' called Charlie; Karl rolled his eyes and flicked his head to one side, indicating that his parents were not talking. They went into the house, Jill going straight to the kitchen to prepare the evening meal.

'Mom,' Karl called out, 'I'll put my washing in the basket.' He was just about to dash upstairs when George called him back.

'Son,' he said, 'we have to talk.'

'What now?' asked Karl. Uninterested in whatever might be going on between his parents, he just wanted to catch up with his brother.

George thought about it for a second and then changed his mind. 'Over dinner, son; you sort your stuff out.'

Karl took the stairs two at a time and found Charlie lying on his bed.

'How you doing, bro?' Charlie greeted him.

'What's up with Mom and Dad?' asked Karl.

'You tell me,' replied Charlie, shaking his head. 'They're like this all the time now; at least you're at school all week; I've got them 24/7.'

As Karl began putting his dirty washing into the laundry basket, Charlie quietly rolled off his bed and tip-toed over. Before Karl could do anything about it, Charlie grabbed him around the neck. 'Aha, you thought you'd got away without a bit of a rough up!' laughed Charlie as he pulled Karl to the ground and sat on his chest.

'Pack it in, you gorilla,' replied Karl. Suddenly, a dream flashed across Karl's mind in which he effortlessly picked his brother up, throwing him off his chest like a baby. Then, instantly, it was gone and he flashed back to reality.

'Come on you, soft lad;' goaded Charlie, 'at least try to escape.' Unknown to Charlie, that was Karl's best effort.

A voice in the doorway distracted them. 'Get off him, you ape.'

Karl saw his opportunity and, catching his brother off guard, pushed against his chest with all his might. Charlie toppled backwards, landing flat on his back, and George roared with laughter. 'That will teach you; well done, Karl.'

Charlie sat up and put his hand out to Karl. 'Well done, bro, that was a first.' A slightly reddening face confirmed Charlie's embarrassment as Karl grabbed his hand and pulled him to his feet.

'Dinner's ready in five minutes, lads,' said George as he went back downstairs with a smile on his face, so pleased that two brothers with such different upbringings could be so close.

Over the evening meal, Karl's parents explained the situation with the school fees. Karl was mature enough to understand that if there was no money in the kitty, that was the end of it. He could not imagine life without Marshdown; he had had some good times there. Still, it was not the end of the world; he could continue his education in the state system, and, with luck, the Headmaster might be successful in securing further funds.

That evening, Karl's dilemma was at the forefront of Blakeway's mind. After he had eaten, he sat down with a copy of the school prospectus package; looking at the fees section, it was clear that the school aimed to attract more affluent people. It annoyed him that someone with Karl's potential could miss out on the last few years of education just because of his bank balance. He couldn't and wouldn't stand by and watch all that talent go to waste.

On Saturday morning, Karl woke late. Pulling on a T-shirt and tracksuit bottoms, he went downstairs, where he found Charlie in the living room, lying on the settee watching some kid's television show. Charlie greeted him without looking away from the screen. 'Morning, bro.'
'Where's Mom and Dad?' asked Karl, rubbing sleep from his eyes.
'Shopping and working. Mom will be back dinnertime, but we won't see Dad much before six o'clock.' George had gone into work early, never missing the opportunity for overtime.
'Tea?' asked Karl.
'I've been lying here for over an hour waiting for you to ask me that question,' Charlie stretched and yawned. 'A piece of toast wouldn't go amiss either.'
'Lazy git,' laughed Karl. Charlie never did very much on Saturdays, reckoning that he worked hard all week and deserved his 'recuperation time', as he referred to it, at the weekend. The boys sat watching TV until lunchtime, when Jill returned from the shops. Heavily laden with plastic shopping bags, she struggled into the house, putting all the bags down in a heap on the kitchen floor. Karl got up and went into the kitchen. 'I'll put it all away, Mom; you have a sit down.'
'You're a good lad, Karl,' said Jill. 'More than I can say for some lazy sods,' raising her voice so that Charlie heard, but it was like water off a duck's back; Charlie carried on watching the television.
Later that afternoon, Charlie went out to see friends, and Karl was stretched out on his bed with another of Blakeway's books. Jill saw her opportunity, and, piling the cushions at one end of the settee, she slipped off her shoes and put her feet up. It was a rare occurrence. Pointing her toes, she gave out a long yawn and lay back. It didn't take long for her to fall asleep; it had been a very busy week and tiredness had finally caught up with her.

Feeling a little peckish, Karl came downstairs; he had spied some nice biscuits while putting the shopping away. He saw his mother fast asleep on the settee and remembered back to when he was a little boy interacting in his mother's dreams, not really knowing how he did it but enjoying every moment; they were always fun times. He saw her face twitch, a sure sign that she was dreaming. Karl had read many books on the subject of sleep and, along with his gift, he had become something of amateur expert on the subject.

The urge to hold his mother's hand and become involved in her dream was overwhelming. Trying to resist, he went into the kitchen and took a biscuit from the tin. As he stood looking out of the kitchen window, a voice in his head was saying, Go on, do it. 'What the hell,' he thought. The urge finally overtook him.

Quietly, he went into the living room where his mother was still fast asleep. Kneeling down, he gently held her forearm and closed his eyes. Next thing he knew he was standing at the bottom of the stairs. He could hear something from one of the bedrooms, and, turning his head to one side, he held his breath in an attempt to hone his hearing. It sounded like panting or heavy breathing. Slowly, he climbed the stairs, being as quiet as he could. As he reached the top, the noise became louder and he hoped it wasn't what he thought it was; it would be very embarrassing walking in on his mother and father.

But the urge to identify the sound was too great to resist, and, creeping along the landing, he reached his parents' room. The door was half open. On the bed, he could see his mother moving up and down in the throes of passion. He wanted to back off, but for some reason he had a compelling urge to watch. Faster and faster she moved up and down, her moans getting louder and louder until finally she climaxed, rolling over onto her back lathered in sweat and exhaled loudly. Suddenly, Karl felt his heart miss a beat; the man she had been so passionately entwined with was not his father, but his so-called best friend from work, Brian Jackson. This was the man who was making it possible for Karl's father to acquire so much overtime.

The shock must have made Karl increase his grip on his mother's arm as, within the dream, she looked straight at him. Karl instantly opened his eyes and released her arm, quickly running towards the stairs. Jill opened her eyes and touched her forearm, which felt painful. Looking down, the reddened imprint of Karl's grip was quite clear. 'Oh no,' she said to herself.

By now, Karl was in his room with the door firmly closed. Jill went up to see him; she had to face him now while they were alone. Standing outside Karl's bedroom door, she swallowed hard, her throat feeling dry and constricted. 'Karl,' she called. There was no answer. 'Karl, we need to talk.' She waited in anticipation. Slowly, Karl got off his bed and opened the door.

'All I want to know is,' said Karl, 'was it a dream or are you and him . . .' Karl lowered his head, unable to continue or look at his mother; it was the most embarrassing moment of his life.

'Karl, your father and I haven't been getting on for some time now,' Jill started, awkwardly.

'Stop there; what you're telling me is that you and Jackson are . . .' he stammered, unable to find the right words.

Jill nodded her head. Karl felt tears welling in his eyes.

'I was going to tell him,' said Jill, 'but when all the problems with your school started . . .'

Karl felt enraged. 'Don't use me as an excuse!' He felt his temper rise. 'That's why he gives Dad all the overtime, so you and him can . . .' Karl stopped short. Tears ran down his face.

'It wasn't like that, son.'

'Well, it looks like that to me.' Karl grabbed his jacket off the bed and pushed past his mother.

Anxiously, Jill called after him. 'Where are you going?'

Karl stopped and looked straight into his mother's eyes. 'Tell him, because if you don't, I will.' At that moment in time he felt no love for his mother, just resentment. All his life he had put her on a pedestal, and in a matter of a few minutes it had all gone. Karl took the stairs two at a time, almost stumbling near the bottom. Jill ran after him but couldn't keep up.

'Karl, wait, please listen to me.'

Heading for the front door, he gave no reply. Fumbling with the latch, he pulled the door open as Charlie came in.

'Hi, bro,' said Charlie, in his usual jovial manner.

Karl pushed past him without saying a word.

'Whoa, what's the hurry?' Charlie stood back against the wall to let Karl pass. Jill quickly followed him.

'Karl, please!'

'What's wrong, Mom? What's going on?' asked Charlie.

Karl rushed through the front gate and disappeared round the corner. Charlie looked down the road after Karl then back at his mother. 'Mom?' Jill just shook her head and went back into the house.

By six o'clock that evening, Jill was beginning to get worried. George would be home soon, and it was such a mess; she knew it was all coming to a head. Perhaps it would be better for everyone once it was out in the open. Charlie was in his room; he could sense that whatever was wrong, it was serious. Jill sheepishly went up and knocked his door. 'Charlie, can I come in?'

'Yeah,' came the reply. He lay on his bed with one of Karl's books, not really reading it, more in thought.

'Will you go and look for Karl for me? Your Dad will be home soon, and we have things to talk about.'

'It can't be that bad can it, Mom?' The sadness in his mother's eyes frightened him. 'I think I know where he's gone;' said Charlie, 'won't be long.' He rolled off the bed to his feet and hurried down the stairs.

When the boys were young, Jill and George would take them most weekends to an adventure playground on the Edgemere Estate, not ten minutes' walk from home. It was one of those play areas made purely of tubular steel climbing frames and slides, designed to be vandal-proof. Karl used to love going there; it was a real novelty for him after being cooped up at school all week. Charlie had a good idea that's where he would find him.

It had been a long time since Charlie had been in that area. As he approached the playground, he noticed one or two hostile-looking groups of kids sitting around just beyond the perimeter railings. On the slide at the far end of the playground, he could see Karl lying down with his hands behind his head. As he got closer, Karl looked up.

'What's up, bro?' asked Charlie, attempting his usual cheerful tone. Karl made no reply. 'You know it's not a good idea to hang around here on your own; if the police don't pick you up, they will' – Charlie turned and nodded towards the group of boys, concealing their identities with hoodies pulled well over their heads, secured with baseball caps, and scarves wrapped around their faces.

'Mom's having an affair,' said Karl. Charlie sat down on the other end of the slide and stared at the floor beneath his feet. 'Did you know?' asked Karl.

Charlie looked up at him. 'I had an idea; just by the way they've been with each other. I hoped it would just blow over.'

'I told her to tell him or I would,' said Karl.

'I don't think that's a good idea, bro.'

'Well, I'm not just going to sit there and watch her humiliate him.'

Charlie shook his head and took a deep breath. 'Come on, let's get out of here before those wasters start taking an interest in us.'

Karl climbed down off the slide, and as they walked towards the playground exit, Charlie put a reassuring arm on Karl's shoulder. 'Don't worry, bro; whatever happens, things will work out for the best in the end, you'll see. Come on, I'll stand you for some fish and chips.' And they walked off in the direction of the local chippy.

It was after 7:30 when they arrived home – Charlie thought it was a good idea to let Karl calm down a little more before he saw his father. They found the house in darkness.

'Mom, Dad,' shouted Charlie. He clicked on the living room light, but there was no sign of them. Karl turned on the light above the stairs, and, just as in the dream, he went up, crossed the landing, then peered through the half open door of his parents' bedroom. The light from the hall illuminated the figure of his mother lying on the bed.

'Is that you, Karl?' she asked, quietly.

'Yeah,' he replied, 'where's Dad?'

'I told him. He's gone out.' She gave a loud sniff, and it was obvious she had been crying.

'Where did he go?'

'I don't know, but he was very upset.'

Having nothing else to say to her, Karl turned and went downstairs.

By eleven o'clock, there was still no sign of George, so the boys decided to go and look for him. He rarely drank, but not knowing where to begin, the two local pubs, The Acorn and The Chestnut Tree, seemed a good place to start looking. As they crossed the island at the end of the street, The Acorn was right in front of them. A few stragglers were still coming out, but it was almost empty and the landlord was about to lock the door.

'Excuse me, mate,' said Charlie. 'I'm looking for a bloke with black hair, thick-set fella about my height; I think he might have been in a bit of a mood.'

'He certainly was that,' said the landlord.

'You've seen him, then?'

'About nine o'clock, he started playing up with a couple of the local lads. Picked on the wrong boys, didn't he?'

'Where did he go?' asked Karl.

'Last time I saw him, he was staggering down towards The Chestnut, but he wouldn't have got in there, not in that state.' The landlord slammed the door shut and firmly secured the bolts.

'Let's walk down to The Chestnut; if we can't find him there, we'll call the police.' Charlie could see Karl was becoming upset. 'Don't worry, bro; we'll find him.'

About four hundred metres down the road, something caught Karl's eye. Someone was sitting in the line of trees that fronted the houses on the opposite side. They crossed the road. 'Stay behind me,' said Charlie. As they got closer, they could see in the darkness the silhouette of a man leaning against a tree drinking from a bottle. Charlie approached, prepared to defend himself should the man become aggressive. Realising that they were approaching, the figure staggered to his feet and raised a half empty bottle of whisky.

'Come on, then, I'll fuckin' brain ya,' he slurred, as he staggered backwards, tripping over a tree root and dropping the bottle before falling onto his backside.

'Dad!' cried Charlie. It was a real shock for the boys to see their father like this, and for Karl it was the first time he had ever heard him swear.

'Charlie,' said the dazed George, 'what the fuck are you doing out at this time of night?' They held his arms and pulled him up. In the blueish light of the street lamps, they could see that both his eyes were swollen and a small trail of blood ran from his nose.

George looked at Karl. 'He's clever, he is, you know, Charlie, really clever. Goes to a posh school and all that.'

'I know, Dad;' said Charlie, 'now, let's get you home.'

It was too much for Karl; he tried not to show it, but tears stung and glistened in his eyes. By the time they reached home, George was literally out on his feet. They lay him on the settee, pulled off his shoes and, after covering him with a blanket, went to bed.

After a restless night, Karl washed and dressed before going downstairs; Charlie was still fast asleep. Not knowing what to expect, Karl cautiously looked in on his father. George was still asleep with the blanket pulled over his face in an attempt to cut out the light. In the kitchen, Jill was sitting with a cup of tea. As he came in, she looked up.

'Want some tea and toast?'

'I can get my own, thanks,' replied Karl. He made two cups of tea and went into the living room. Putting the cups down on the coffee table, he shook his father. 'Dad, wake up.'

Slowly, George pulled the blanket from over his head, exposing two black eyes. 'Jesus Christ, my head,' said George, squinting.

'I'm not surprised,' said Karl.

George put his hand to his forehead. 'Sorry, son, you shouldn't have seen me like that.'

'Here,' Karl passed him a cup of tea, 'drink this.'

'I bet you can't wait to get back to school.'

Karl smiled; his father had always been a tower of strength to him. This was the first time he had ever seen him weak and vulnerable; he had a feeling it wasn't going to be the last.

12

Work commitments

A sombre atmosphere lay over the Hennessey household for the remainder of the day. Charlie spent most of his time lying on his bed, preparing for what he referred to as another exhausting week ahead. George had not spoken to Jill since she had confessed to her affair with his so-called friend. Karl collected his schoolbooks together and, without advertising it, packed all of his socks, pants and a few extra T-shirts. He had no plans to return for the next couple of weekends. The thought of watching his parents' relationship fall apart before his very eyes didn't appeal to him, and anyway, if they had time and space, they might just be able to work things out.

George was sitting in the living room; he had wrapped a bag of frozen peas in a tea towel and was nursing his swollen, panda-like eyes. Gathering the last few items he needed for school, Karl walked through.

'What time do you want to get off to school today, son?' asked George, peering at him with one eye open the other masked by the pack of frozen veg.

'I'm easy, Dad;' replied Karl, 'any time you like.'

'Can we get off a little earlier, then, only I want to get back before dark if I can. My eyesight isn't a hundred per cent at the moment.'

'Sure, I'm ready when you are, Dad.'

Unknown to Karl, his father had an ulterior motive for wanting to leave early; inside he was crushed by what Jill had told him the previous day. Brian Jackson of all people. George needed a drink to free his mind of the images that kept appearing in his mind's eye. Jill had gone out earlier that day without so much as a goodbye, and George was convinced she had gone to him. At the moment, he was keeping his rage in check, but for how long he didn't know.

Karl loaded his bags into the back of his father's car. After being called several times, Charlie managed to drag himself off his bed to say goodbye, twice putting his younger brother in a headlock before they reached the front door. Karl got into the car and fastened his seat belt.

'OK, son, you ready?'

'As I'll ever be,' replied Karl.

Charlie was leaning against the frame of the front door. Karl stared at his brother, looking for some kind of emotional farewell. As the car engine burst into life, Charlie suddenly raised a hand, beckoning them to wait. Reaching into the pocket of his jeans, he searched around.

'Hang on, Dad,' said Karl.

George put the handbrake back on. Charlie's hand came out of his pocket with two fingers raised in a V gesture, a large smug grin spreading across his face.

George shook his head. 'He's a first class prat, your brother.'

As they drove off, Karl couldn't help chuckling to himself; Charlie was a clown, but he wouldn't have him any other way.

They arrived at Marshdown. It was always quiet there on Sunday afternoons. George didn't hang around, once again telling Karl that he wanted to get back before dark. Karl watched his father's car disappear down the road and into the small wood that led to the school's main gate. Once the tail lights were out of sight, Karl went up to the dormitory. Carefully folding his clothes, he neatly stowed them in the chest at the end of his bed. He was pleased that he had taken the time to clean it out the previous week; with the amount of clothes he had brought with him, he would have struggled to fit them all in. It would be a good couple of hours before Jerald would arrive at school, so Karl got out his course work, sat on his bed and immersed himself in his work.

It was nearly nine o'clock when Jerald finally arrived; his father had another business trip planned for the following weekend so he had spent a little more time with Jerald, trying to pacify his guilty conscience. Karl told Jerald all about what had happened with his parents that weekend, including the dream. Jerald sympathised with him as his own parents had split up a few years ago. As the boys settled down for the evening, Karl thought that a good night's sleep in what he referred to as his own bed would do him the world of good. He had had enough of dream interacting for the present.

Karl quickly fell into a deep sleep and soon began dreaming. He was in his parents' house; the similarities between this and his mother's dream were uncanny. Just as in her dream, he could hear a low moaning sound coming from upstairs. Just as before, the urge to investigate was overwhelming. Slowly, he climbed the stairs, the sound becoming louder with each step. Was it possible he had absorbed the dream into his own subconscious? This was a totally new experience.

Work commitments

Cautiously, he crept along the landing in the direction of his parents' room. The door was half open, just as in his mother's dream. He peered into the room and saw his mother writhing on top of a man, only this time her upper body was covered in blood. Karl felt the hairs on the back of his neck stand up as she stared at him, a grotesque grin across her face.

Suddenly, the man raised himself up onto his elbows and looked towards Karl. Karl's bottom jaw dropped open as the shock hit him; the man was Mortiboys, the dead schoolmaster. As Mortiboys pushed himself up to a sitting position, blood poured from open wounds on his wrists. Still looking at Karl, Mortiboys laughed loudly, his hands all over Jill's upper body as she writhed in ecstasy, their bodies entwined. Now they were both looking at him, grinning, laughing, mocking him; it was the worst nightmare he could imagine.

'No!' he shouted. Instantly he woke, finding himself sitting upright, his heart pounding.

'Karl,' called Jerald from across the room, 'what's wrong?'

Karl lay back against his pillow, which was damp with sweat. 'It's OK, Jerry; I just had a bad dream.'

'You shouted out loud,' said Jerald.

'Sorry, mate, go back to sleep.'

Karl lay in his bed trembling; the dream had really frightened him. He felt as if he had no control, just like when Jerald first faced Mortiboys. Karl racked his brains, what had caused the two dreams to combine, and why was Mortiboys bleeding? Karl had never been told how Mortiboys had died, just that he had committed suicide. Had the Headmaster or Mr Blakeway said something that he had unknowingly absorbed, or was he just so worried about his parents that his mind was playing tricks on him? He lay there for what seemed like hours as vivid pictures of the dream appeared in his mind. Finally, he slowly slipped into a restless, uneasy sleep.

George had been drinking until almost two in the morning. After being asked to leave the pub just before 10 pm, he had gone to the local off-licence and purchased a bottle of scotch. Drowning his sorrows was having an adverse effect on his problems, and all he could think about was Jackson with his hands all over his wife. When he arrived home, another blazing row with Jill confirmed her decision as to whether or not their relationship was worth another go.

George was due in at work at 7 am, but at 7:30 he was still fast asleep on the settee. Jill would usually have been up and about by now, but after the previous evening's row, she had decided to stay in bed until George had gone to work. Charlie got up and ate his breakfast. Before leaving for work, he looked in on his father. Gently, he shook George's arm. 'Dad, what time are you in work?'

George slowly turned on to his back, his mouth was bone dry, and the now familiar pulsing headache stopped him from opening his eyes. 'What time is it?'

'Nearly quarter to eight,' replied Charlie.

'Shit,' said George, 'I'm late.'

'The kettle's on; I'll see you later.' Charlie pulled on his jacket and walked down the hall and out of the front door, closing it firmly behind him. George turned over and went back to sleep.

Some time later, the noise of the front door slamming shut finally roused George. Jill had seen him asleep on the settee, but after their exchange of words the previous evening, she decided to leave him where he was. For the past six months, Jill had been doing two jobs trying to raise the money for Karl's school fees. Between 11 am and 3 pm she worked in the local supermarket, and from 4 to 8pm she had been working at the local secondary school as a cleaner. As far as George was concerned, both jobs were on a Monday to Friday basis, but in reality, the evening job had only been two days a week for the last three months; the other three evenings had been spent in the arms of her lover. Jackson had always made sure that there was overtime available for George on those evenings, in an attempt to keep him occupied.

George got to his feet, a sudden loss of balance making him reach for the arm of the chair. He grimaced at the familiar throbbing in his head and reached down to pick up a whisky bottle. It was empty, but he held it to his mouth and tipped it up, craving the last drip. He made his way unsteadily to the kitchen, where he turned on the cold tap and swilled his face. The shock of the cold water made him gasp.

Drawing in a deep breath, George knew he had to go to work. More importantly, if he was to keep his job, he had to stay in control, as he knew that with one word from Jackson, he would be out. Reluctantly, he changed his clothes and set off to work. Passing through the main gate, the security guard waved in acknowledgement from his booth.

Each day, one hour after the start of the shift, the clock cards were gathered up and taken into the office. The reason for this was that if anyone was more than an hour late, they were obliged to ask permission to start work. There were three foremen spread across two shifts, one of them being Brian Jackson. George crossed the shop floor; it was like being back at school and being told to go to the headmaster's office. Cat calls rang out from every direction – 'Who's been a naughty boy then?',

'You'll get your legs slapped.' Normally, George would have accepted it as a bit of friendly banter, but today the circumstances were very different.

A few metres ahead through the office windows, George could see two men in white cow gowns: John O'Connor, a middle-aged man he had known for the best part of twenty years, and Brian Jackson. Already he could feel his blood boiling. 'Take control,' George said to himself, 'take control.' He tapped the door and went into the office.

'Afternoon, George,' said O'Connor, 'pleased you could make it.' It sounded sarcastic, but it was just his dry humour.

'I've had a bit of trouble,' said George. Jackson kept his head down, focusing on his paperwork to avoid joining in the conversation.

'Sorry to hear that, mate; anything we can do to help?' asked O'Connor, oblivious to the situation between the two men. The statement hit a raw nerve, and George couldn't resist firing back a sarcastic statement.

'I think certain people have done quite enough.'

Jackson looked up. 'We didn't mean it to happen, George.'

O'Connor looked at Jackson and then across to George, scratching his head with bewilderment. 'Have I missed something here?' he asked.

George strode over to Jackson's desk, his temper rising with every step. 'Didn't mean it to happen?' George was barely able to control himself. 'You have the audacity to give me overtime when you know I'm trying to keep my boy in school, then you go round and shag my wife!'

O'Connor couldn't believe what he was hearing. 'Gentlemen,' he said, trying to calm things. 'I think you should take this out of the workplace.'

'He's no gentleman,' hissed George.

Jackson stood up. 'If you'd paid her more attention, it wouldn't have happened in the first place.'

This was too much for George, and with gritted teeth, he unleashed a well-timed right cross. It was so swift and accurate that Jackson did not see it coming. George's fist hit him square on the jaw, and as his legs buckled, he was already out cold, slumping into a heap behind his desk. O'Connor, with his mouth agape, couldn't believe what he had just witnessed.

'For fuck's sake, George, you've done it now, mate; they'll sack you for this.'

'Fuck it,' said George. 'I resign.' Straightening his jacket, he turned and left the office, adrenaline still rushing through his body.

Through the office windows, George's work colleagues had seen everything. This time, as he walked across the shop floor, the silence hung so heavily that the sound of the proverbial pin dropping would have been ear-splitting. Every eye in the factory was fixed on him as he left the building.

As George arrived home, the adrenaline levels in his body were returning to normal, but he realised that something was wrong with his right hand. The middle knuckle was swelling at an alarming rate, and, as he attempted to make a fist, it became pretty obvious that at best he had cracked it. He took a bag of peas from the freezer, wrapped it in a tea towel and pressed it to the back of his hand. He had not been in the house fifteen minutes when two police officers knocked at the front door. 'Mr Hennessey?' asked one of the officers,

'Yes,' replied George.

'Mr George Hennessey?' George confirmed his name.

'We have had a report of an assault' – the officer pulled out his note pad and turned to the first page – 'on a Mr Brian Jackson.' The ice pack wrapped around George's hand didn't help his case.

'He had it coming,' said George.

'Mr George Hennessey, I am arresting you on suspicion of assaulting Brian Jackson. You do not have to say anything, but it may harm your defence if you do not mention when questioned something you may later rely on in court. Anything you do say may be given in evidence.'

George couldn't believe it; he had heard the words on television, but now they applied to him and he was in deep trouble. One of the officers took out a pair of handcuffs. 'Is that really necessary?' asked George.

'You tell me, Mr Hennessey.'

George gently smiled and shook his head. 'All right if I get my jacket and keys?'

The policemen nodded; they knew George had no previous record, and the violent incident appeared to have been well out of character. Five minutes later, George was in the back of a police car on his way to the station.

Back at the factory, an ambulance had been called for Brian Jackson, but fortunately for George, the only injuries he had sustained were a blow to his pride and a nasty contusion to his lower jaw. The paramedic attending wanted him to be checked out at the hospital, but Jackson refused. He also said he didn't want the police involved, but as the assault had taken place on company premises, he was given no choice in the matter. Even so, he refused to press charges, which infuriated the company area manager.

It was almost 8 pm, a good seven hours after the incident, and George was sitting in a cell wondering what the hell had gone wrong with his life. In a matter of a few weeks, it had all fallen apart. The sound of the key turning in the lock released him from his self-pity, and an officer came in swinging a huge bunch of keys on a chain.

'Right then, George' – the friendly approach from the officer made him feel at ease – 'you're free to go. The gentleman you thumped doesn't want to press charges.'

As George stood up, the officer towered above him. He placed a hand on George's shoulder. 'Listen, George,' he said, 'I can see you're a law-abiding sort of bloke, and I don't know what's been going on between you and this other chap, although I have a pretty good idea. But the answer isn't knocking him out, because next time you won't be so lucky.'

'Huh, so this is lucky is it?'

'Come on,' said the officer, 'let's get you booked out.'

After another talking to by the desk sergeant, George went home, dreading what kind of welcome he would receive when he arrived there.

The house was in darkness. He shouted to Charlie, but there was no reply; he had probably gone out with his friends straight from work, thought George. Switching on the hall light, he moved through the house; the familiar feeling of comfort had gone, it felt cold and empty. A feeling of loneliness overwhelmed him, and almost overcome by emotion he went into the kitchen. On the table, propped up against a coffee mug, was an envelope with his name on it. He picked it up, but before opening it he looked at it carefully and sadly. Was this the only way he could now civilly communicate with his wife? He ripped through the fold of the envelope flap with his finger, taking care not to damage the contents.

Dear George, I received a phone call today from John O'Connor. He told me what happened at work. If there was any chance of saving our relationship, your actions today have made me realise it has come to an end. I am truly sorry it has come to this. I also realise that my actions mean Karl will have to leave Marshdown, but I think that was inevitable. Both the boys are survivors. I know it will take some time, but they are both growing up quickly and will soon be making their own way in life. I deeply regret ending it like this, but I think long term it will be the best for both of us. I hope at some time in the future we can once again talk without any animosity towards each other.

Jill

George felt a lump in his throat. So that was it, he thought, she's gone. Tears welled in his eyes, then trickled down his cheeks. Throwing the letter onto the table, he rubbed his eyes. Minutes later, he pulled out his wallet and examining its contents, found a ten pound note. 'That's enough,' he said to himself. Half an hour later, George returned from the off-licence and, without bothering to use a glass, sat down at the kitchen table and began drowning his sorrow; the bottle was slowly becoming his only friend.

It was after eleven when Charlie came home. A work friend had arranged a double date with a couple of girls they had met the previous weekend. They had been to the cinema and finished up in the local pizza bar. Charlie had had such a good night he had arranged to take one of the girls out the following weekend. Feeling really pleased with himself, he bounded into the house.

'Mom, Dad,' he called out. No reply. That's strange, he thought; the TV was turned off. Walking into the kitchen, he found his father slumped face down on the kitchen table, beside him an empty bottle of whisky. What had been a great evening was rapidly deteriorating.

Charlie shook his shoulder. 'Dad.'

George did not move. The letter on the table caught Charlie's eye, and he reached over to pick it up and read it. It was something he had known was coming. Although he had tried to prepare himself for the inevitable, it still hit him hard, and putting his thumb and index finger to his eyes, he resisted the urge to shed a tear. His mother had made her bed, and if anyone was going to salvage the remainder of this family it was him.

'Come on, Dad!' he shouted, as he shook George's arm vigorously. George finally began to stir, oblivious to his surroundings. 'Come on, let's get you to bed.'

Charlie pulled him to his feet. After a struggle, he managed to get George upstairs and onto his bed. Pulling off George's shoes, Charlie covered him with a quilt and went to his own room.

The following morning, Charlie was up by 7:30 am. He could tell from the letter that something had happened the previous day at his father's work, but had no idea just how serious it was. The last thing Charlie wanted was his father out of work; it would just compound the problem. Once again, he stood over his father, a mug of tea in one hand, shaking him with the other.

'Dad, wake up, wake up; you'll be late.'

George's eyes opened; he looked awful.

'Here, drink this,' said Charlie, frustrated by his father's lack of response.

'Thanks, son, what time is it?' At last.

'Eight o'clock. If you don't get up now, you'll be late again.'

George sat up and gratefully took the mug.

'Something I have to tell you . . .' George was interrupted by someone banging on the front door. Charlie ran downstairs and opened the door; it was a courier with a letter.

'Can you sign, please?'

Charlie took his pen, signed the sheet and dashed back upstairs, two at a time, with the letter, addressed to George.

'It must be important; I had to sign for it.'

George ripped the letter open. As soon as he saw the letterhead, he knew what it was. Due to the assault on a member of staff, his employment was terminated on the grounds of gross misconduct. He read no further, just passed it over to Charlie. Charlie mouthed the words as he read the letter, then sat down on the bed. 'Jesus Christ, Dad, what have you done?'

'I'm sorry, son, I was trying to tell you.'

Charlie got to his feet. 'I'd better get to work or we'll have nothing coming in.'

George lowered his head as Charlie walked over to the bedroom door. Before leaving, he stopped and turned. 'Stay off the drink, Dad, please, for me.'

Without waiting for a reply, Charlie went to work.

13

The benefactor

Although George had signed on to claim benefits, the next few weeks were hard. Charlie and George's joint incomes were not enough to pay all the bills, and little by little they were getting deeper into debt. George insisted that he had stopped drinking, but, fortunately, Charlie knew better than to believe him. More and more frequently, he found empty whisky bottles hidden at the bottom of rubbish bags.

Charlie had written to Karl explaining that their parents had finally gone their own ways. Not wanting to worry him, Charlie only included in the letter what he wanted Karl to know. Karl couldn't do anything about the drinking and the financial problems, so what was the point in burdening him with them?

After reading the letter, Karl decided to stay at school for the next few weeks; realising this could be his last year at Marshdown, he wanted to complete as many modules of his degree as possible. The summer was fast approaching, and Karl's fees were paid up until Christmas. The school insisted on payments being made a term in advance, which meant that if Karl's fees weren't paid by the end of September, he would not be returning in the New Year. Losing a pupil was not a big issue for the school as it was increasingly oversubscribed, meaning that there were always new pupils waiting to fill spaces, especially sixth-form pupils.

It was lunchtime at Marshdown. The Headmaster encouraged the other masters to each lunch in the dining room with the boys whenever possible. He thought it was one of the few areas of school life at which discipline could have sometimes been a little better, but whenever he was present, it wasn't a problem. On this occasion, he sat alone enjoying an extremely large portion of shepherd's pie.

After selecting his lunch, Blakeway picked up his tray and scanned the dining room. Seeing the Headmaster sitting alone, he made his way towards him; it was an ideal opportunity to ask him a few questions that were on his mind. 'Ah, Headmaster, mind if I join you?'

The Headmaster looked up from his lunch. 'Not at all Blakeway, please.' The Headmaster courteously rose slightly from his seat, gesturing Blakeway to join him.

Placing a napkin across his lap, Blakeway glanced over at the shepherd's pie the Headmaster was eating, then looked back at his own plate. 'Do you have shares in the catering department, Headmaster?' he asked jovially.

The Headmaster looked at Blakeway's meagre portion and then back to his own. 'It is a little embarrassing, I know; I think one of those young ladies has a soft spot for me or my position.' They exchanged a friendly smile.

'Tell me, Headmaster, have you had any feedback from young Hennessey's parents concerning his future at the school?'

'Not a word,' replied the Headmaster. 'I'm pleased you mentioned it; I will have to get a letter out to them before the summer break.'

A few tables to the right, two boys were laughing a little louder than the Headmaster found acceptable. 'Excuse me, Blakeway.' The Headmaster stood up, his chair screeching on the floor as he pushed it away from his legs. 'You boys' – the dining room fell silent as Pendlebury stared directly at the two boys who had been causing the commotion – 'if I hear another noise from either of you two, you will be spending this evening standing in silence outside my office, do you understand?'

'Yes, sir,' they whispered in unison.

'Yes, Headmaster,' corrected Pendlebury, insisting on the proper use of his title. The boys lowered their heads, visibly shrinking in front of their peers. Blakeway didn't realise it, but he was staring at the Headmaster. He could be a pompous arse at times, thought Blakeway, but he got results, and that was why, year after year, the governors renewed his contract. The Headmaster sat down and continued eating his lunch.

'So, there's no joy with the scholarship, then?' continued Blakeway.

Pendlebury swallowed a mouthful of food and dabbed his mouth with his napkin. 'Can I tell you something in confidence Blakeway?'

'Of course, Headmaster.' Blakeway leaned towards the Headmaster, intrigued.

Pendlebury glanced briefly around checking whether anyone was within earshot. 'There is no scholarship;' he said quietly, 'there never has been and probably never will be.'

Blakeway put his knife and fork down. 'But you told Karl's parents you would investigate the . . .'

Pendlebury interrupted Blakeway, the use of a student's Christian name visibly annoying him. 'I did, Blakeway, but I knew it was a futile exercise.'

Blakeway sat back in his chair. 'What if someone else put the money up for his fees?'

The Headmaster looked directly at Blakeway. 'I hope you're not thinking what I think you are, because it would be quite out of the question.'

'I'm sorry, Headmaster, I don't know what you mean.'

Their eyes met, and Blakeway held the stare, trying hard to conceal his intentions. After a few moments he stood up. 'Would you excuse me, Headmaster? I need a little fresh air.'

'Good day, Blakeway.' said the Headmaster, the tone of his voice dismissing the younger man. Blakeway picked up his tray and nodded his head in respectful acknowledgement and then left the dining room.

Charlie had a dilemma. It had been two weeks now since his father had lost his job, and it was becoming increasingly obvious that George was drinking excessively. Some days he didn't bother to wash or dress and ventured out only to feed his habit. Charlie hadn't a clue where he was getting the money from. Karl was coming home this weekend for the first time in a month and was in for a real shock, but Charlie couldn't keep it from him forever.

Bills were beginning to pile up that Charlie couldn't pay; as a trainee electrician, Charlie earned very little. They needed money and fast. After making some enquiries, a friend at the gym had told Charlie that the local foundry was taking on workers; it was heavy work and long hours, but the money was good, and there was the opportunity for overtime should he want it. Charlie really enjoyed his present job, but if he didn't do something, and fast, they would lose everything.

As the weekend approached, it was clear that George would be in no condition to collect Karl from school. Charlie phoned Marshdown pretending to be his father and arranged for Karl to be taken to a local railway station, saying that his car was off the road for repairs. Blakeway saw his opportunity to speak to Karl's parents and, unaware of what was going on in Karl's home life, told Karl that he was visiting a friend in the Midlands; with only a small diversion could easily drop him home on the way. That evening Karl called home and told Charlie about the master's offer, which Charlie gratefully accepted.

On Friday afternoon, Karl gathered up most of his clothes. Billy had been taking some of Karl's washing home for the last few weeks, his mother sympathising when he explained that Karl's parents had separated and he had preferred to stay at school. Karl was packing up his last few things when Blakeway knocked on the dormitory door. 'Hi, Karl, you nearly ready?'

'Yes, sir, just putting the last few things in my bag.' Karl was struggling to pull the zip closed on his holdall.

'Here, let me help.' Blakeway took hold of the sides of the bag, pulling it together, allowing Karl to easily pull the zip across.

'Ready when you are, sir.' Karl picked up his bag and followed Blakeway out of the dormitory and down the stairs. Once outside, they crossed the gravel to the staff car park, and Blakeway bleeped the alarm on his new Ford Focus.

'Nice car, sir,' said Karl.

'Unfortunately, Karl, it's a necessity. I've never been much of a car enthusiast, but yes, it's one of the better ones I've had.' They walked over to the car. 'Boot's open, Karl; put your bag in.'

Karl lifted the tailgate and put his holdall in. 'Where's your bag, sir?' said Karl inquisitively. Blakeway hadn't thought of that; as he was going home after seeing Karl's parents, it hadn't crossed his mind.

'I have to come back tonight,' said Blakeway thinking on his feet, 'it's just a fleeting visit. Right then, shall we go?'

Reaching into his glove box, Blakeway pulled out a portable satellite navigation system.

'TomTom,' observed Karl.

'Yes, great, aren't they,' replied Blakeway. 'I don't know how I'd get on without it. I got your parents' postcode from the office.' Using the suction device, he attached the device to the windscreen and turned it on. 'Right then, postcode.' Blakeway entered the postcode and selected 'route'. A firm voice gave an instruction, 'Turn around when possible.'

'Well, that's a good start,' said Blakeway, 'we haven't even left the car park yet.'

Karl laughed as Blakeway started the engine and pulled off the gravel, heading in the direction of the main gate. With a wave to the security guard, they were on their way. The satellite navigation system finally identified the road and selected the fastest route. Blakeway eased back into the driving seat, trying to get as comfortable as possible for the journey ahead. Keeping his eyes on the road he said, 'Tell me Karl, what do you plan to do when you finish your education? No,' he added, momentarily glancing at Karl, 'I'll rephrase that. What are your ambitions?'

Karl turned towards the master. 'Ambitions? Oh that's easy, sir, I want to be a psychologist.'

'You know, I had a feeling you were going to say that,' said Blakeway.

'I suppose long term, sir, I'd like to have my own practice, but the way things are going at the moment, I'll be lucky to finish my degree, let alone take a Master's.'

Blakeway almost told him not to worry about that, but bit his lip just before he opened his mouth. 'Yes,' he said, carefully selecting his words, 'the Headmaster told me that the financial situation at home isn't good; fingers crossed it will all sort itself out.' Blakeway concentrated on the road.

'I hope so, sir.' said Karl. 'I really hope so.'

They each retreated to their own thoughts. Blakeway was considering how he was going to offer Karl's parents enough money for their son to complete his education at Marshdown. Karl, on the other hand, could only think about what was in store for him now that his mother had left them. Just over an hour later, they pulled up outside Karl's parents' house. Raising his hands and placing one to his mouth, Blakeway yawned and stretched.

'Here we are, then,' said Blakeway.

Karl knew he had to ask him in, but he was a little apprehensive of the welcome they might get. The front door opened and Charlie stepped out; he had been watching at the window for them to arrive. Raising his hand in a welcoming gesture, he walked down the path to the car.

'That's my brother, Charlie,' said Karl.

Blakeway turned off the engine, unclipped his seat belt and got out of the car. Looking over the roof he called out, 'Charlie, Karl's told me all about you.'

'That's done it, then,' joked Charlie in reply.

Blakeway laughed and walked round the car to him. 'No, no, young man, on the contrary, it was all good. Sorry,' he said, offering his hand, 'I'm Martin Blakeway.'

'Nice to finally meet you, Mr Blakeway.'

'Please call me Martin.'

'Now I can say Karl has told me a lot about you; it's Mr Blakeway this and Mr Blakeway that.'

Karl was now out of the car. 'Shut up, Charlie,' snapped Karl, his complexion giving away his embarrassment.

'Well, that's charming,' mocked Charlie, making a grab for Karl, who, anticipating the manoeuvre, smartly jumped back out of range.

'Next time,' said Charlie with a smile. 'Come in, Martin,' he added, 'you must be parched after that drive.' Blakeway agreed and accepted Charlie's offer of a coffee.

Karl lifted his bag out the boot, and they all went into the house. As soon as they were inside, Karl knew there was a problem. He didn't know how he knew; maybe it was another side to his gift he had yet to explore. The house felt sad, or maybe the occupants' personas were making it feel like that.

'Are your parents about, Charlie?' asked Blakeway.

'I'm afraid not,' replied Charlie, 'they've gone out for the night.'

That's strange, thought Blakeway. Karl hasn't been home for four weeks and they go out on the very day he comes home.

'Oh that's a shame, I wanted to have a chat with them both.'

'It will be late when they get back. Do you take sugar?'

'Two please,' replied Blakeway.

Leaving Blakeway in the living room, Karl and Charlie went to the kitchen. As Charlie flicked the switch of the electric kettle, Karl dropped his bag down in front of the washing machine.

'Why are you lying to him?'

'We don't need to tell other people our business,' replied Charlie, in almost a whisper.

'He's not other people, he's my teacher, and he's not stupid.' Karl began loading the washing from his bag straight into the machine.

Charlie crouched down facing him and, still in a half whisper and said, 'Now listen to me, Karl, if he knows what's been going on in this house, you'll probably be out of that school Monday morning.'

Behind them there was a loud cough; Blakeway had been standing in the doorway listening to their muted conversation. 'I think we need to have a chat, lads.'

Charlie finished making the drinks, and they all went into the living room and sat down.

Blakeway broke the silence. 'I take it your parents have not gone out after all.'

'Oh no,' said Charlie, 'they've definitely gone out. Dad can be found about half a mile up the road in the Acorn pub, drunk as a skunk.'

'What about your mother?' asked Blakeway.

'She went out about three weeks ago and hasn't been seen since.'

Blakeway shook his head. 'How have you been coping, Charlie?'

'As best I can, really. Dad got into a fight at work and lost his job. That was the final straw for Mom; she just packed her bags and left, bless her.' Charlie's voice was full of sarcasm. 'Dad's been on the bottle ever since.'

Blakeway could see that Karl was upset by what Charlie had said. In attempting to shield Karl, Charlie had made the impact of the whole situation a little too much for him to take.

Karl stood up. 'Excuse me, sir,' he said and rushed upstairs, not wanting to break down in front of his mentor.

Blakeway waited, listening for Karl to be well out of earshot. 'Charlie, while Karl's upstairs, I need to have a chat with you. I guess theoretically you are not only his brother now, but also his guardian, well the only responsible one anyway.'

'Never thought of it like that,' said Charlie, 'but yes, I suppose I am.'

'Well, do you know his school fees will run out this Christmas?'

Charlie didn't look surprised. 'Yeah, I remember Mom and Dad saying that if they couldn't raise the money, he was going to finish his education at a state school.'

'That's exactly what I want to talk to you about,' said Blakeway. 'You see I have a proposition I would like to make, but Karl mustn't know about it.' Charlie thought it was strange, but it didn't hurt to listen. 'I would like to be Karl's benefactor.'

Charlie looked confused. 'What do you mean?'

Blakeway sat forwards, placing his forearms on his knees. 'I'd like to pay for him to finish his education at Marshdown.'

Charlie sat back and took a deep breath. 'Jesus Christ, Martin, that would cost you a fortune.' Charlie was bewildered. 'I'm not being funny, but why would you do that?'

Blakeway smiled. 'I'm sure I don't have to tell you that Karl is a very special young man, and I refuse to stand by and watch a brilliant student fall by the wayside because his education can't be financed.'

Charlie took a good look at Karl's potential saviour; was he genuine?

'Why can't Karl know?' asked Charlie, still apprehensive.

'If the Headmaster found out, I would be out of a job.'

Charlie nodded his head understandingly. 'As far as Karl is concerned, he will have a scholarship. As long as we keep it to ourselves, he will be none the wiser. All that is important is that he finishes that degree, and I will spend as much extra time as I can to make sure he achieves that goal.'

Charlie clasped his hands together and looked down at the floor, deep in thought. Blakeway wondered what was going through his mind.

After a few moments, Charlie raised his head. 'But how would you pay the money?' he asked.

'I will give you a cheque to pay into your account. All you have to do is write a cheque of your own and send it to the school.' Charlie was touched; this man turns up with his brother, offering to pay thousands of pounds towards his education and wanting nothing in return; it really restored his faith in human nature.

'I don't know what to say,' said Charlie.

'How about, it's a deal?' Blakeway smiled and offered him his hand.

Charlie looked into his eyes; there was no sign of deceit, just friendship. 'If you're sure,' said Charlie.

'I've never been so sure of anything in my life, Charlie.'

'In that case, it's a deal.'

They shook hands.

'I wish my parents could be here to thank you for your kindness.'

'Never mind that, Charlie, you just look out for him. He is a very clever young man, but he's still very vulnerable, and this problem with your parents, it's going to hit him hard.'

'I know,' replied Charlie, 'I could see it in his face when I told you about Dad.'

Blakeway got to his feet. 'Listen' he said, 'I'm not going to stick around; I have to be somewhere else. Give me a phone number I can contact you on and I will make all the arrangements for Karl's fees.' Charlie wrote down their home phone number, and gave it to Blakeway. 'Excellent,' said Blakeway. 'Right, I'll get off,'

They walked to the front door. 'I won't say goodbye to Karl. If he is a little upset, I wouldn't want to embarrass him.'

Blakeway stepped out of the front door and then suddenly stopped and turned round. 'The Headmaster is going to send your parents a letter concerning Karl's fees. I would make sure you deal with it before your father.'

'Don't worry, will do,' Charlie assured him, 'and thanks again, Martin.' Once more they shook hands, holding on a little longer than normal.

'I'll be in touch,' said Blakeway as he got into his car and fired up the engine. With a quick wave of his hand, he pulled away. Charlie thoughtfully watched the car disappear out of sight and then closed the front door.

Karl was lying on his bed, his pillow damp with tears. On hearing Charlie coming up the stairs, he wiped his hands across his eyes in an attempt to hide the fact he had been crying. Charlie stood in the doorway, leaning against the frame; Karl had his back to him but Charlie sensed he was awake. 'You all right, bro?'

'Not really,' replied Karl. 'Why didn't you tell me about Dad?'

'What good would it have done? It wouldn't have changed anything.' Charlie stepped into the room and sat down on Karl's bed. 'I'm relying on you to get us out of this mess.'

'What do you mean?' asked Karl, intrigued by Charlie's reply.

'Well, your teacher was just telling me you've got a scholarship.'

Karl suddenly jumped up putting his feet to the floor. 'You're joking.'

'I'm not; he wanted to tell Mom and Dad, but due to the circumstances he told me instead, so bro, that means only one thing.'

'What?'

'I'm in charge!'

Before Karl could even think, Charlie leapt forward, grabbing his younger brother around the neck. 'I've missed this,' said Charlie.

In a muffled voice due to Charlie's muscle-bound arm being wrapped around his neck and partially covering his mouth, Karl replied, 'Once a gorilla, always a gorilla.'

Unexpectedly, Charlie let go. 'Ha, and guess what else?'

'What?' asked Karl.

'I might just have another job.'

Karl was taken aback, 'But you love your job, and you haven't finished your training yet?'

'That doesn't matter, this one pays a lot better, and we need the money now Dad's not working.'

'I could get a job,' said Karl.

'You just dare. Now you have this scholarship, you have to get the best results you can. Hopefully, in a few years' time, you'll be able to keep me,' laughed Charlie, squeezing the back of Karl's neck with two fingers.

'Come on,' said Charlie, 'let's get something to eat. Dad will be home later; then we'll have our hands full.'

14

A dead-end job

It was just after 11 pm. Karl was asleep on the settee, and Charlie was watching a movie, albeit through heavy eyelids. The sound of slurred singing alerted Charlie; their father was home and, by the sound of things, had had another alcohol-fuelled evening. His ability to open the front door in a drunken state was improving. Some nights he would come home laughing and joking; other nights he would be overwhelmed with grief – there was no set pattern.

As he came into the living room, he saw Karl fast asleep on the settee. 'Here's my boy!' he shouted.

The commotion startled Karl, who quickly sat up looking at his father. The man he had doted on for so long was a shadow of his former self. Karl found it hard to find the words to talk to him.

'Come on then, lad,' said George, 'give your dad a hug.'

Karl got up and George grabbed him, pulling him close. Losing his balance, George fell backwards against the wall, taking Karl with him.

'Take it easy, Dad,' said Charlie. 'You're pissed. Sit down before you fall down.'

The smell of alcohol revolted Karl; he had always thought of his father as a proud man, not the drunken fool standing before him. George staggered round the settee and slumped down.

'Do you want a coffee, Dad?' asked Karl. Charlie looked up at Karl and shook his head, as if to say, You're wasting your time.

George replied in a slurred, almost whispering voice. 'I have a little drink here.' Reaching inside his jacket pocket, he pulled out a small bottle of scotch and waved it at Karl. With a smile on his face, George took the top off and held it up. 'Purely medicinal,' he said, then took a large slug on the bottle.

His eyes flickered, and he looked as if he could pass out at any moment. His head wobbled from side to side as he attempted to secure the top back on the bottle. Finally succeeding, he pushed the bottle back into his inside pocket. Leaning his head back on the settee, his eyes appeared to roll around in his head; then gradually he fell asleep or lost consciousness, the boys weren't really sure which.

It was just before midnight, and all three of them had fallen asleep. Charlie was lying across the armchair, his head on one arm and his legs hitched up over the other. Karl was on the settee next to his father, when something woke him; probably the sound of George's snoring. Rubbing his eyes, he looked over at his brother sleeping soundly. Then he turned his attention to his father.

George's mouth was slightly ajar, and under his closed eyelids Karl could see occasional rapid eye movement, which from Karl's experience usually meant he was dreaming. He couldn't resist it. Slowly, he took hold of his father's hand and closed his eyes. What happened next was a completely new experience.

He was in a pub, and George was sitting at the bar with a bottle of scotch and a single glass in front of him. Karl struggled to focus, the faces of the other people in the bar were distorted; it was like trying to look at the world through the bottom of a jam jar. He tried to walk over to his father, but his legs gave way, not completely, just enough to make him reach for the support of the nearest chair. The room began to spin. What was happening to him? He had to get out of there. His stomach churned, it felt as if he could be sick at any moment. Quickly, he closed his eyes to escape his father's dream, and almost instantly was back in the living room. He opened his eyes to see Charlie looking at him.

'What happened?' asked Charlie.

Karl placed his hand on his stomach and took a deep breath. 'I thought you were asleep,' replied Karl.

'I was, but you started making funny noises; it woke me up.'

'God, that was awful,' said Karl, 'I was nearly sick; I won't do that again in a hurry.'

Charlie sat forward in his chair. 'What happened then? I saw you holding his hand.'

'Everything was spinning, just like I was drunk, I suppose. I couldn't even walk straight. If I hadn't came out when I did, I would have been sick.'

'He's like that 24/7 now,' said Charlie.

Karl rubbed his eyes, still a little subdued from the experience.

'Come on,' said Charlie 'let's get him off to bed. You look like you could do with it yourself.'

Without trying to wake him, the boys pulled George to his feet and, in a semi-conscious state, with a son under each arm, he staggered to the stairs. Eventually, after a considerable amount of gentle coercion, they made it to his bedroom. Laying George on his bed, Charlie slipped off his shoes. The boys covered him – still fully clothed – with a quilt and turned off the light, closing the door behind them.

On Saturday morning, Karl woke just before eight o'clock. Having been at Marshdown for so many years, his body clock had set precisely, and he rarely slept after eight in the morning. The house was silent. Considering the condition his father had been in the night before, it was very unlikely he would be up before lunchtime. As for Charlie, he just liked his sleep. After some tea and toast, Karl put the television on and put his feet up on the settee.

It was a good hour before Charlie stirred. He came down yawning and rubbing his head. 'Morning, bro; you been up long?'

'Couple of hours,' replied Karl.

Charlie glanced up the hall towards the front door. 'Letters,' he said aloud as he walked down the hall and gathered them up. 'Junk, Dad, junk, junk, ah, one for me,' he said as he flicked through them. Putting the others on the table, he tore open his letter; it was from Mitchell and Slater, the aluminium foundry. 'Things are looking up, bro; they want me to go for an interview Monday morning,'

'It's a bit short notice, isn't it?' asked Karl.

'Yeah,' replied Charlie, 'but the sooner I get the job, the sooner we get some good money coming in.'

Karl wasn't happy about Charlie throwing away his opportunity to qualify as an electrician, but something deep inside told him that if he could complete his degree, one day he would be able to pay him back.

The rest of the weekend was very quiet. George was still in no condition to drive, so Karl caught the train back to school. It was only about an hour's journey, and, if the truth were known, he actually enjoyed travelling on the train for a change.

Charlie's interview was scheduled for 10 am on the Monday. He didn't own a suit – it wasn't really the way he dressed – but a jacket and trousers were smart enough, and, he thought, at the end of the day he wasn't applying for a position in a bank.

It was about a thirty-minute bus journey to the foundry. Earlier that morning, Charlie had phoned in to work with a cock-and-bull story about cricking his neck and not being able to come in. He wasn't one for taking time off, so they had no reason to doubt his story. He arrived at the foundry with a good twenty minutes to spare, and the security guard directed him up a flight of stairs that led to a suspended Portacabin. Charlie knocked the door and waited.

A very pleasant-sounding voice called him in, and he opened the door to see a young girl, not much older than himself, sitting at a desk. She was very attractive, with long brown hair and the most beautiful green eyes he had ever seen. Without realising it, he was staring into her eyes, almost mesmerised.

'Can I help you?' she asked with a smile.

Charlie snapped out of his trance-like state. 'Sorry, yes, my name's Charlie, Charlie Hennessey.'

'Hello, Mr Hennessey,' she replied.

'Please call me, Charlie.'

She continued to smile at him. 'Mr Slater will be back in just a minute, please take a seat.'

Charlie thanked her and sat down while the girl went back to her work. He found himself being drawn to look at her from the corner of his eye. She turned and smiled, sensing that he was looking at her. Uncomfortably, he returned the smile and moved awkwardly on the chair. Just then, the door opened.

'I don't know why I bother. Bloody contractors. My kids could have painted out those offices by now; anyone would think it was the bloody Forth Bridge.'

Ken Slater was in his late thirties, the eldest of three sons. Balding and overweight, his body was beginning to show the strain of taking over the business from his elderly father. His father had retired three years earlier, due to ill health. His two brothers showed no interest in the family business, but were both successful businessmen in their own rights.

'Mr Hennessey has arrived, Mr Slater.'

'Thank you, Susie.' Slater turned to Charlie. 'Mr Hennessey.' Charlie stood up and offered his hand, which Slater shook firmly. 'Pleased to meet you, Mr Hennessey. I like that in a young man, a firm handshake.'

Slater opened the door. 'Shall we?'

As Charlie stood up, he made eye contact with the office girl and, for a few moments, they held each other's gaze; he was sure she blushed. As they walked down the stairs, Slater said, 'Two weeks we've been in this glorified shed. Two days they told me they would take to revamp and paint, bloody contractors.'

Slater fell silent, and Charlie could tell he was under a great deal of stress.

'Sorry, Mr Hennessey, you must find my ranting very boring.'

'It's Charlie, sir, and no, I can imagine it's very annoying.'

'Anyway,' said Slater, 'I'll take you down to the foundry.'

As they walked Slater continued talking. 'I won't beat about the bush, Charlie, I need a man ASAP. I've just had to let a young man go, completely unreliable.'

'Well, reliable is the one thing I am, Mr Slater.'

Slater looked into Charlie's eyes. 'I believe you are, Charlie.'

As they entered the main building, Charlie felt the rise in temperature, 'It's warm in here,' he said.

'This is nothing,' replied Slater. 'The aluminium is poured into its castings at over a thousand degrees centigrade. Foundries are very dangerous places; on the health and safety side, there is no room for error. Every member of my staff has to go on an in-house training course. Then and only then are they let anywhere near the molten metal.'

As they walked around the foundry, there were catcalls and whistles, typical factory banter. Every now and then, employees would walk past Slater and acknowledge him; he would either nod or raise his hand, returning a friendly gesture. The environment was shocking, dust everywhere and a horrible smell; Charlie asked what it was.

'Ah yes, you see we put sodium tablets into the metal to purify it. Don't worry, you'll get used to it.'

They passed two men, one driving a forklift truck carrying a pallet, the other walking beside it making sure the castings on the pallet didn't tip off.

'Your job would be what we call a shot blaster,' said Slater. 'These castings' – he nodded towards the metal objects on the forklift – 'are taken over to that machine.' He pointed at a large box-like contraption. 'The casting is placed in there, then sandblasted to get rid of any rough bits. Then it's polished, and the process starts all over again.'

'That sounds straightforward,' said Charlie.

Slater's eyes scanned the shop floor, as if he was searching for someone specifically. Charlie now knew what Slater meant about the heat; as they approached the furnace it was almost unbearable.

'Mr Cartwright,' shouted Slater. A man about thirty metres away raised his hand in acknowledgement. Pulling his gauntlets off his hands, he walked over to them,

'Morning, boss.' Alex Cartwright was one of Slater's team leaders. He earned an extra pound an hour for taking charge of the shop floor. Charlie looked at the man's arms; he had never seen such powerful forearms. Working in the foundry for the last ten years had developed them massively out of proportion to the rest of his body. Slater introduced Charlie, and Cartwright nodded. 'All right, son.'

'Give him the once round, then send him back up to the office will you please, Alex?'

'Will do, boss.'

Charlie turned to Slater. 'Does this mean I have the job?'

'Well, do you want it?' asked Slater.

'Yes please.'

'Then it's yours. Listen to Alex; he'll explain your job in more depth. Then I'll see you back at the office. Thanks, Alex.'

Again, Cartwright nodded. Slater took out his mobile phone and walked off in the direction they had come from.

'Right then, Charlie, let's show you round, introduce you to a few of the lads.'

Over the next half an hour, Cartwright walked him around the foundry, showing him where he could go and, more importantly, where he couldn't go. When they arrived back at the office it was nearly lunchtime. Charlie's clothes felt damp; if he was like that after less than an hour, what would he be like after an eight-hour shift? Again he knocked at the door and was called in by that soft pleasant voice.

'I was told to come back to the . . .'

Before he could finish talking, the girl pointed down to the other end of the office. Slater was sat at his desk, browsing through some paperwork. He looked up. 'Ah Charlie, everything OK?'

'Yes, thank you, Mr Slater.'

'Right then.' Leaning over his shoulder, Slater looked up at the year planner. 'Next Monday, eight o'clock. Susie will sort out all the paperwork, and we'll get you started.' Charlie thanked him. 'Work hard and we'll get on really well.'

'I will, Mr Slater, thanks again.'

Charlie turned and walked towards the door. 'Bye, Susie.' He felt a little cheeky using her first name, but what the hell.

She looked up at him. 'Bye.'

She blushed and looked down again at the paperwork on her desk. As Charlie closed the door, he looked back at her; they made the slightest of eye contact, but it said so much.

At Marshdown, the day had started pretty much as it always did. One or two boys were usually late on Mondays, and the Headmaster found it extremely annoying. His theory was that it was just as easy to be five minutes early as five minutes late. But unfortunately, due to the distance some of the parents were coming, he just had to accept it.

Karl, on the other hand, found himself full of zest, enthused by the opportunity to finish his degree at Marshdown. He didn't advertise the fact that he was getting a scholarship, just in case the other boys felt it was like free-loading or, worse still, favouritism. Blakeway took most of Karl's lectures as he was overseeing Karl's degree. The other boys were still studying 'A' levels, which was the norm at their age. While Karl and the other boys in the group were ardently studying the pieces of work prepared for them, Blakeway sat at his desk looking through the school prospectus, in particular the leaflet explaining the schools fee structure. He had worked out that, with no hitches, Karl would complete his degree at his eighteenth birthday.

Blakeway looked down at his watch; it was just twelve o'clock. Placing the prospectus into his desk drawer, he stood up. 'Lunchtime boys.'

The familiar sound of books being closed and chairs squeaking filled the room, and within a few moments the boys had left, apart from Karl. Karl was still at his desk, his pen fervently filling another page of work. Blakeway called his name. Karl's head popped up from his desk. 'Yes, sir?' he asked, with a startled look on his face.

'Look around you, Karl.' said Blakeway. Karl was clearly unaware that the others had left. 'They've gone to lunch Karl, as you should.'

'Right, sir; sorry, sir.'

Karl closed his books and pushed them into his bag a little more quickly than normal. As he reached the door, Blakeway called his name. Karl stopped and turned.

'I admire your enthusiasm, young man, but don't overdo it.'

'No, sir, I won't.' Karl opened the door.

'One more thing, Karl,' said Blakeway, stopping him in his tracks. 'Please, come a little closer.' Karl walked over to the desk. 'As far as your scholarship is concerned, please keep it to yourself. It's a first at this school and may not happen again. We don't want people stirring things up, you know, the jealous types.'

'I thought exactly the same thing, sir.'

'Good man,' said Blakeway. 'Now, go and get something to eat.'

Once Karl had left the room, Blakeway pulled out the prospectus. He had worked out that, for Karl to remain at the school until his eighteenth birthday, it would cost fifteen thousand pounds. Blakeway was not a wealthy man, but after the death of his father a few years earlier, he had been given a small inheritance. His father's property had been sold and the proceeds shared out between him and two other siblings. It had sat in his bank account gaining interest, waiting for the day it might be needed. Today was that day.

Taking out his cheque book, he filled out the necessary amount and sat back with a feeling of pleasure. The thought of potentially changing a young person's life in such a positive way felt great.

15

Dreams fulfilled

It had been three weeks now since Charlie had begun working at the foundry, and for the first two days, true to his word, Mr Slater had sent him on a health and safety at work course. Once Charlie started his own job, he realised the importance of the course; there was danger around every corner. After four days working alongside Alex Cartwright, the team leader, he was left to his own devices.

It was heavy work. As a shot blaster, it was up to him to collect the castings and make sure they were all sandblasted and polished. Every morning for the last fortnight, Charlie had woken up stiff and tired; it would take time for his body to become accustomed and conditioned to the continuous bending and heavy lifting day in, day out. Still, the money was good, and already he was working overtime, quickly finding out it was part and parcel of the job, with some men working as much as sixteen hours a day. It was the first time in months they had managed to pay the household bills on time, no thanks to George, who was still hitting the bottle hard, apparently oblivious to the situation they were in.

Some weeks earlier, Charlie had received a letter from Mr Blakeway containing the cheque to cover Karl's fees for his time left at Marshdown and his Open University course. As soon as the cheque cleared, Charlie filled out all the necessary forms and sent them off to the school, accompanied by a cheque of his own. The fact that Charlie sent the cheque rather than his father did not concern the school; as long as they got their money, that was all that mattered. As the deadline for school fees approached, the Headmaster received a weekly financial print-out from the secretary. He liked to keep an eye on the school's budget; at the end of the day, if the school was not financially viable, both he and his staff would all be out of a job.

On this occasion, he scanned the print-out, reading the names alphabetically, 'Grant, Hatfield, Hennessey,' he stopped. 'Well, I never,' he said aloud. Straight away, his mind was doing overtime: how does a working-class family who only a short time ago didn't know how they were going to pay their child's fees suddenly come up with a full year's payment? 'I wonder,' he said to himself.

Later that day, Pendlebury went to lunch in the school dining room. After receiving his usual oversized portion from a more than pleased to see him dinner lady, he scanned the room. On the other side of the room, he spotted Blakeway sitting with two other masters: Mr Cunningham, a short man with a pointed face who taught mathematics, and Mr Bridges, a powerfully built ex-military man, who had taken the position of physical education master after the Mortiboys fiasco.

As Pendlebury edged his way around the dining room, all the boys in his proximity seemed instantly to fall quiet as he passed their tables. Out the corner of his eye, Blakeway saw him approaching. 'Good day, gentlemen;' said the Headmaster, 'do you mind if I join you?'

'Not at all, Headmaster,' said Cunningham, moving his tray and chair over to give him a little more space at the table. All three of the masters stared at Pendlebury's oversized lunch. He saw them looking and, finding it quite embarrassing, quickly made conversation to distract their attention.

'We have a large number of students taking 'A' level maths this coming year, Cunningham.'

Hearing his name, Cunningham dragged his eyes from the Headmaster's lunch. 'Er, yes Headmaster; one or two exceptionally gifted individuals.'

Cunningham turned to Blakeway. 'I must say, Martin, I wish your prodigy, young Hennessey, had time to further his mathematics. Remarkable young man. I get the feeling he could achieve a very high standard whether I was in the classroom or not.'

'Oh, that reminds me, Blakeway;' interrupted the Headmaster, 'it seems that Hennessey will be staying with us a little longer after all.'

Blakeway tried to look surprised. 'That's wonderful, Headmaster.' Blakeway continued with his lunch as if it was no big deal.

'Yes,' Pendlebury continued, 'a full twelve months' fees paid just last week.' Pendlebury took a large mouthful of his lunch and then put his knife and fork down. 'I must admit, I didn't think he would still be with us after Christmas, not after the conversation I had with his parents.'

Blakeway could feel the Headmaster's eyes boring into him. He looked up from his plate. 'I am pleased for him; he truly is a remarkable young man. It would have been terrible if just a year's fees had stood in the way of what could potentially be, well, let's face it, the best thing that's happened to this school in years.'

'Oh, come off it,' jumped in Bridges, 'it takes more than one boy to build a reputation such as this school has.'

'Hear, hear, Bridges,' said the Headmaster.

'Yes, well,' Blakeway dabbed his mouth with his napkin, 'at least now he will get the chance to fulfil his potential.'

Blakeway stood up. 'If you will excuse me, gentlemen, I have a little paperwork to complete before this afternoon's lectures.'

Bridges and Cunningham both courteously nodded as Blakeway picked up his tray, but Pendlebury held his gaze, almost testing him. He wanted to ask him straight out, but at the same time didn't want to know. A rare and sardonic smile passed across the Headmaster's lips, saying a silent 'Touché.'

Blakeway returned the gesture. He crossed the dining room, placed his tray on the far end of the food counter, and disappeared through the door.

Walking towards his classroom, Blakeway's mind was still on the conversation he had just had with Pendlebury. By the Headmaster's mannerisms, he obviously knew Blakeway was Karl's benefactor; he either couldn't prove it or didn't want to. Hoping it was the latter gave him a little more faith in human nature. Arriving at the classroom, Blakeway looked through the glass pane in the door and saw Karl sitting at his desk, already ardently back at his work. As Blakeway opened the door, Karl glanced over his shoulder.

'Don't you ever take a break, young man?' asked Blakeway as he walked over to his desk.

'I just wanted to finish this piece of work, sir, while it was fresh in my mind.'

Blakeway shook his head and sat down as Karl continued with his work. Blakeway sat looking over his desk at Karl. He was amazed at his hunger for knowledge; it was almost bordering on an obsession.

'Tell me, Karl,' said Blakeway, 'I'm intrigued to know, what is it like when you enter other people's dreams?'

Karl stopped working and put his pen down. He sat back in his chair and looked out through the classroom window, deep in thought. After a few moments, he said, 'It's hard to put into words, but until recently it was just like being awake.'

Blakeway tapped his mouth with his index finger. 'What do you mean, *recently*?'

'Well,' said Karl, leaning forward eagerly, 'I've been trying some new things just lately. Billy and Jerry let me enter their dreams; they think it's great fun. I've learned to do all sorts of things. I can appear and disappear as I wish. I can even control the dream.' Karl was now sitting on the edge of his seat.

'Last week, I watched a documentary about the Great Barrier Reef. It was amazing; I'd never seen anything like it. So, the other night I was interacting with Jerry, and the dream was a bit boring. I thought about the Barrier Reef, and suddenly we were there, just like I had seen on television, the same place! We were on a boat, sailing along with dolphins swimming all around us. The sea was beautifully clear and blue; it was paradise.'

Blakeway was absolutely speechless. Listening to Karl speaking so passionately about his gift made him realise even more how right he was to finance this amazing young man's education.

'If you want to,' Karl spoke cautiously, 'I'll interact with you, sir.' Ever since he had first heard about Karl's gift, he had wanted to experience it. But after what had happened with Mortiboys, sleeping in the same room as a pupil was not a good idea. 'We could do it on a Sunday evening, sir; there will be only me and Jerry here till Monday morning.'

It was a gamble, thought Blakeway, but the temptation was just too much. 'OK, Karl, if you like, next time I'm covering the weekend, we can do some extra course work; maybe on the Sunday, we'll give it a go.'

'Great, sir.'

The door opened and a crowd of boys filed into the classroom, ready to start the afternoon's work.

Charlie was in the works canteen; he had just finished a BLT sandwich and was sitting back, drinking a carton of milk. Lunch breaks were staggered and nearly always spent alone at the foundry, due to the fact that the furnace had to be continuously monitored. On this rare occasion, he was joined by Alex Cartwright.

Alex was asking him how he was settling in when the office girl, Susie, walked in. Charlie's gaze was instantly drawn towards her. Alex could see that something or someone had caught his eye, and as he turned to see what or who it was, he saw the young girl smile in their direction. Glancing back to Charlie, he realised there was some chemistry going on between them.

'Hi, Charlie,' called Susie, and Charlie raised a hand to acknowledge her.

Looking at Charlie, Alex slowly shook his head. 'Ooh, you want to be careful there, son.'

'Why's that, then?' asked Charlie, anxiously.

'Don't you know?'

'Know what?' Charlie was now leaning forwards, giving Alex his complete attention.

Alex almost whispered, not wanting her to hear what he was saying. 'It's the gaffer's niece; the name gives it away a little – Susie Slater.'

'You're joking,' said Charlie, looking shocked.

'Close your mouth, son.' Alex took a drink from his coffee mug and leaned towards Charlie. 'Last bloke who asked her out has been on the sick for the last four months.'

Alex sat back in his chair, alarm bells ringing in his head. 'You mean the gaffer had the bloke sorted out?'

'No, you clown,' replied Alex, 'he got a splash back from a crucible; the metal went all down the back of his leg and into his boot. Down to the bone they reckon; had to have grafts and all sorts. Be a good two to three months before he gets back to work, if he ever does.'

Again, Alex took a slug on his coffee. 'Anyway, she turned him down flat. Word is she won't go out with work colleagues; nice looking bit of stuff as well.'

Susie paid for her lunch, and Charlie sheepishly glanced over. After what he had just been told, he really doubted his chances.

She picked up her sandwich and a bag of crisps. Turning to leave, she glanced over with the hint of a smile in Charlie's direction.

Alex instantly picked up on it. 'You're in there, son.'

As the door closed behind her, Alex added, 'It takes a good two minutes to reach the office from here. If you go now, you'll catch her.'

Charlie took a deep breath and, picking up his carton of milk, quickly headed out of the canteen.

The canteen was at the top of two flights of stairs leading off a long passageway. Taking the stairs two at a time, he quickly reached the bottom. As he turned into the passageway, he could see Susie a little way down, reading the notice board. He wondered if she had waited on purpose, anticipating that he would come after her. What was he going to say? Normally his banter with the opposite sex was pretty good, but this girl was something else; she was so stunningly beautiful he felt tongue-tied. As he approached, she turned and looked at him.

'Hello, Charlie,' she smiled.

He couldn't speak. Come on man, he thought to himself, talk.

'Hi Susie.' Thank God; he'd managed to force out a couple of words.

'Are you enjoying your new job?'

As she spoke, she looked straight into his eyes, and he was dumbstruck. Her eyes seemed to consume him; it felt as if he had stood there for an age.

'It's hot,' he heard himself say, and cringed as the words came out. You blithering idiot, he thought to himself, why did you say that?

Susie laughed. 'Well, it is a foundry.'

'I'm sorry,' said Charlie, 'that was a stupid thing to say.'

For a good ten minutes they talked, not about anything in particular, just a kind of get to know you conversation.

Susie looked at her watch. 'God, look at the time, I'll have to get back or I'll be in trouble.'

Charlie didn't want to miss his chance. 'Its probably a bit forward of me, but if you aren't doing anything this weekend, would you like to go out for a drink or maybe something to eat?' His stomach was doing somersaults, expecting her to say, 'With you? You're joking of course.'

'I'd love to,' she replied, 'only this weekend I'm going away with my parents.'

'Oh, never mind,' said Charlie, thinking it was just a gentle way of turning him down.

'I can make it the following weekend though,' she said. 'I'll give you my phone number; give me a call at home, and we can arrange to meet up.'

'That would be great.' Charlie couldn't believe his luck. Inside, he wanted to jump for joy, but kept his excitement in check.

'Listen, I have to go; talk to you later.'

'Yeah OK, see ya,' said Charlie.

As she walked down the corridor towards the forecourt, she turned and smiled. Like a besotted schoolboy, he returned the smile. As she disappeared through the door, Alex came down the stairs.

'Charlie, old mate, you still here? Did you catch her?'

'Week Saturday,' announced Charlie with a broad grin.

'What about a week Saturday?' Alex looked flummoxed.

'I'm taking her out.'

'You old fox,' said Alex putting his huge arm around Charlie's shoulder and squeezing him. 'You're a real dark horse you are. Come on, let's get back in the oven before we're missed.' They both walked swiftly down the passage and across the forecourt.

'If I was you,' said Alex, 'I'd keep this to yourself; when it gets back to Mr Slater, and it will, he'll be watching you like a hawk.'

That weekend, Karl and Jerald both stayed at the school. When Karl told Jerald that he was going to interact with Blakeway, Jerald replied that even if he had planned to go home he would have cancelled it, as he wouldn't miss it for the world. Blakeway told Karl that he was on duty at school all weekend and could go over some course work.

Karl knew little about his mentor's life outside school. He was a very private man, not revealing much about his background to anyone; even the other masters were a little baffled by his secretive nature. Karl wondered if his dreams might reveal a little more about him.

They worked until just after five o'clock and, without any outside interference, managed almost to complete another module of Karl's degree. Feeling very pleased with the day's work, they went off to their evening meal. Although there were no staff in the kitchens, they always made sure there was access to the kitchens when senior pupils and masters stayed at school over the weekend. The cook usually plated up and froze the remnants from Friday's lunch; if nobody ate them, they were always discarded first thing Monday morning.

Blakeway, Karl and Jerald sat in the dining room, in front of them generous portions of vegetable lasagne.

'So tell me, Jerald,' said Blakeway inquisitively, 'when Karl interacts in your dreams, do you have to be in a certain frame of mind?'

Jerald thought for a moment. 'I don't think so, sir.' He looked at Karl. 'I don't think you've ever failed to interact, have you Karl?'

Karl shook his head as he tried to cool down a particularly hot mouthful of food. Finally managing to swallow, he replied. 'It's usually straightforward. The worst I ever experienced was when my father was drunk. If that's what it's like when you drink too much, I don't think I'll bother.'

Blakeway laughed. 'Good decision, Karl. There's nothing clever about excessive alcohol; trust me, I've been there.'

'Sorry, sir,' said Karl wondering what he meant, but not daring to ask.

'It was another life, but what you said is interesting,' said Blakeway, trying to move the conversation away from something he would rather not to talk about. 'You actually took on his mental state?'

'When Karl first started with me,' said Jerald, 'it felt as if he was just another person in my dream. But now I feel as if I'm a character in *his* dream; does that make sense?'

Blakeway ate another mouthful of lasagne and put his knife and fork down. 'I'm not sure,' he replied, 'but I think Karl's ability is maturing with age and knowledge. It's just like working a muscle – the harder you work it the stronger it gets.'

Jerald looked up from his plate. 'It's another world, sir.'

In one short statement, Jerald had summed it all up.

By 9 pm, they had all settled down for the night. Blakeway had no intention of staying in the dormitory all night; it was bad enough *being* there. If another pupil came in the following morning and he was still there, it would be the end of his time at Marshdown, and probably the end of his career. But the urge to experience such a phenomenon was just too overwhelming; like a kid in a sweet shop, he had to try some. Pulling two beds together, Blakeway and Karl lay down.

'Just relax, sir,' said Karl, suddenly assuming the confidence and authority that his gift had bestowed upon him. 'Jerry is going to stay awake and make sure nobody comes in.' Jerald had already wedged a chair against the doorknob, so that it couldn't be opened from the outside.

'Great,' said Blakeway, as the situation was doing nothing for his nerves. 'I can just see somebody finding us in here with a chair keeping the door shut. I'll be spending the next ten years behind bars.'

Lying there thinking the worst was not helping, so Blakeway decided to just lie back and try to blank his mind. Nearly half an hour later, sleep finally began to take over him. Karl saw his eyes begin to close and very gently placed his hand on the back of Blakeway's.

Some time later, Karl found himself in a park, close to a child's play area. From experience, Karl knew it was not his own dream, but he was not able to locate Blakeway. Suddenly he saw him. He was at the far side of the playground pushing a small boy on a swing. At the side of the swing, a woman was leaning against the frame enjoying the whole experience. The sun was shining, giving the dream a real sense of relaxation. Blakeway lifted the boy off the swing and, like any small child, he darted off to investigate his surroundings. The woman said something to Blakeway and then went and sat down on a nearby bench. The little boy moved from one climbing frame to the next, a little too small for the apparatus really, but enjoying himself nevertheless.

Blakeway started walking towards a building that looked like a public toilet, and Karl waved in an attempt to catch his attention. Finally, Blakeway looked over and turned towards him. Standing in front of Karl, Blakeway looked a little confused.

'Hello, sir,' Karl said, 'shall we go?'

'What do you mean?' asked Blakeway. 'I'm dreaming. I know that because I've had this dream before, but you weren't in it.'

Karl smiled. 'Hold my hands, sir, and close your eyes.'

Blakeway did as Karl instructed and, taking hold of his hands, closed his eyes. When Blakeway opened his eyes, which was no more than two or three seconds later, he had been transported from the park and was on the deck of a boat, gently sailing along. He could feel the sun bearing down on his back, the sea was crystal clear, and at the bow dolphins skimmed in and out of the wake produced as the boat cut its way through the ocean. Karl came up the stairs from the small inside cabin carrying two tall drinks. He passed one to Blakeway, whose mouth was slightly gaping, finding it hard to absorb what was happening.

'Where are we, Karl?'

'Australia, the Great Barrier Reef; it's beautiful, isn't it, sir?'

'But we were just in the park!' Blakeway was struggling to comprehend the magnitude of what was happening to him.

'That was your dream,' said Karl, 'this is mine.' Karl took a sip of his drink. 'Do you remember, sir; I said if I have a good enough realisation of a place, my imagination can produce it. Just like seeing something in your mind's eye. Only because you're in my dream, you're seeing it too; it's simple really.'

Karl again sipped his drink, while Blakeway looked at the contents of his glass and shook it. 'I don't know about simple, it's incredible,' he replied.

'Come on, sir, drink up; we have to go somewhere else.'

Blakeway took a slug of his drink. 'Cranberry juice, my favourite drink.'

'I know, sir,' said Karl grinning. 'Don't forget, it's my dream. Now, we have to go, sir. Close your eyes, and don't open them till I tell you.'

Blakeway did as he was told. Within a couple of seconds, Karl asked him to open his eyes. It was pitch black. They were both lying flat on their backs looking up at a galaxy of the most dazzlingly shining stars.

'Ayres Rock, sir; I saw a documentary that said it's one of the best places in the world for stargazing.'

Blakeway was lost for words. Karl pointed up to the sky. 'Over there, a little to the left, that's the constellation of Sagittarius. The cluster to the right is Scorpio, and, do you know, sir, they are over thirty thousand light years away. Amazing, isn't it?'

Blakeway just lay there in silence as Karl continued to impress him with his detailed knowledge of the stars. How long they were there Blakeway didn't know, but it seemed like hours. He was feeling so completely relaxed, and then Karl said it was time to go. Blakeway took a deep breath and closed his eyes. Instantly, he was transported back to the park, standing at the exact location he had first seen Karl.

'It's time to wake up now, sir,' said Karl, and then, in the blink of an eye, he was gone. Slowly, Blakeway opened his eyes. Karl and Jerald were sitting on the bed next to him.

'What time is it?' asked Blakeway, rubbing sleep from his eyes.

'Eleven o'clock, sir,' said Jerald.

'How long were we away?'

'Away, sir?' asked Jerald.

'Um, you know what I mean.'

'You slept for about an hour. It's good, isn't it, sir?'

Stuck for words Blakeway simply replied, 'Amazing.' He could not believe what had just happened to him. He had experienced some things in his life, but this was the most profound thing ever.

16

Family confrontations

Blakeway didn't hang around long in the dormitory that night; he had already pushed his luck a little further than he should have, being there in the first place. Still, he was pleased he had, as it was a night he would never forget.

Blakeway's dream had intrigued Karl too: who were the woman and the little boy? Blakeway had never mentioned being married, or that he had any children. Perhaps it was something he yearned for. Karl had found out long ago that people's dreams could tell you a lot about them, but Blakeway's had baffled him. When Karl entered people's dreams, if the host was in a happy state of mind, he would sense it. For some reason, even though Blakeway's dream appeared to be happy and tranquil, Karl sensed anxiety. It was a little akin to the first time he interacted with Jerald – his sixth sense was telling him that all was not right with his friend and mentor.

Back home, Charlie's life had taken a turn for the better. His job was going well, although the hours were very long and tiring. Also, his relationship with Susie was beginning to flourish; from their first date, they just seemed to click. While becoming very close outside the workplace, they decided to keep it quiet from their work colleagues, for now anyway. Charlie wrote a letter, which was out of character for him, telling Karl all about Susie and his new job. That coming weekend, Karl planned to go home and meet her; if anyone could make Charlie put pen to paper, she must be worth meeting.

On Friday evening, Karl arranged a lift to the railway station. Once he got off the train, it was only a ten-minute taxi ride home, and Charlie said he would deal with the fare when he got home. Unknown to Karl, Charlie had arranged to meet him at the station. Susie had volunteered the use of her new car, a bright red Mini Cooper, bought for her six months earlier by her father as a gift for passing her driving test.

As the train pulled into the station, Charlie and Susie were waiting at the platform entrance. Karl struggled off the train, a rucksack on his back and a very heavy holdall in his right hand. As he walked towards the ticket collector, Susie spotted him, instantly seeing the family resemblance. 'My God,' she said, 'he's like a thin version of you.'

'I'm not that ugly, am I?' joked Charlie. Susie smiled and nudged him with her elbow.

Karl, not expecting his brother to be there, didn't see him. As the ticket collector clipped Karl's ticket, Charlie shouted out, 'Bro, over here!' Instantly, Karl looked up to see where the voice had come from. Surprised to see his brother at the back of the crowd, he raised a hand in acknowledgment and started pushing his way through the crowd, eagerly trying to exit the platform. Finally, Karl emerged from the platform, pleased to see his brother.

'I didn't expect to see you here; I was going to get a taxi.'

'Susie offered to collect you.'

Karl turned to the young girl standing next to his brother; he was stuck for words. In Charlie's letter, he had said she was gorgeous looking, and he wasn't kidding; she was absolutely stunning.

'Hello, Karl. Charlie's told me a lot about you.'

As she smiled at Karl, he was dumbstruck; her green eyes were almost hypnotic. Finally, he broke his stare. 'Likewise, Susie; pleased to meet you.'

'Come on, then,' Charlie chipped in, 'let's get off home.' He picked up Karl's bag, and they headed towards the car park. They chatted all the way home. Karl was very impressed with Susie's new car, telling them a few too many facts about the vehicle's background. Charlie stopped him in his tracks, telling Susie that Karl spent too much time reading and was consequently full of useless information. Karl picked up on the fact that he was boring them and quickly changed the subject.

That evening, they decided to go out together, a kind of family bonding evening. Susie suggested ten-pin bowling, and Charlie, with a keen competitive nature, couldn't resist. He was especially eager since Karl had only been bowling once before, so a trouncing was on the cards. Karl didn't mind as it was great just to relax and spend time with them.

The evening went really well, with not quite such a trouncing as expected. Karl held his own in the first two games, only losing by a large margin in the third through boredom, which he did his utmost to conceal. They finished the evening off in a buffet-style Chinese restaurant. Over the last six months, Charlie's voracious appetite had got him on first-name terms with the proprietor. The weekend special offer was eat as much as you liked for £7.95. Charlie referred to it as 'eat as much as you can', which he did. Feeling bloated, they finally arrived home just after eleven o'clock.

Susie came in to finish the evening off with a coffee before making her way home. They sat in the living room drinking tea and coffee, with the boys firing friendly banter at each other over the bowling. Susie laughed; she found it hilarious that a simple thing like a game of bowling could make Charlie so fiercely competitive.

The sound of a key fumbling in the front door lock and the door crashing open instantly stopped their conversation. Karl shot a look over at Charlie, both of them realising their father was home. Susie, startled, had still not had the pleasure of meeting George; Charlie had always made sure he was out when she came round. Having told her about his father's drink problem, she was a little anxious about meeting him, to say the least.

Well and truly intoxicated, George staggered down the hall and into the living room. Oblivious to the fact that three people were in the room, and without saying a word, he carried on into the kitchen, bouncing off the settee and sideboard as he went. Without speaking, they scanned each other's faces, Susie's expression being one of panic. Charlie gave her a reassuring smile to calm her nerves a little, but the sound of glasses clinking and the glug of liquid being poured from a bottle alerted them to the fact he wasn't finished drinking just yet.

'I'm going to get off home,' whispered Susie, picking up her bag.

'OK, darlin',' said Charlie, and the couple stood up.

'It was nice to meet you, Karl,' said Susie.

Karl jumped to his feet. 'Yeah, same here, and thanks for picking me up at the station and letting me come out with you both tonight; I had a great time.'

Susie walked over, put her arms round him and gave him a long hug. A little taken aback by her show of affection, he looked over her shoulder at his brother. His face was saying hug her back, which Karl did, and it felt great. He couldn't remember the last time he had felt human contact, especially from the opposite sex.

George stood in the kitchen doorway clutching a glass of whisky. 'Who the fuck are you?' he slurred.

'Dad, watch your language,' snapped Charlie, 'and be a bit more civil, this is Susie, my girlfriend.'

'Hello, Mr Hennessey,' said Susie timidly.

George stared at Susie and looked her up and down. Charlie could see she felt intimidated and decided to get her out as quickly as possible. 'Come on, Susie, I'll see you out to your car.'

'Bye, Mr Hennessey; bye, Karl.'

Karl smiled and nodded his head, still feeling warm from her contact.

As she walked past George, he grabbed her shoulder. 'Where's my hug, then?'

The smell of alcohol in her face made her feel nauseous. Charlie reacted instantly, pulling his father's hand from her shoulder and pushing him back towards the kitchen door. 'Take your hands off her.' George stumbled back, spilling his drink, just managing to catch hold of the door frame with his spare hand. It was the first time in his life that Charlie had shown anger towards his father.

'Temper, temper,' said George, draining what was left in his glass.

Charlie put his arm round Susie's shoulder and led her to the front door. 'I'm sorry, Susie,' he said.

'It's not your fault, Charlie, but you know he needs help, don't you?'

'Yeah, the problem is convincing him of it.'

She gave him a hug. 'I'll give you a call tomorrow.'

After a gentle but very reassuring kiss, Susie got in her car and drove off.

Charlie was fuming. He went back into the house, where George was still using the kitchen door frame for balance, and squared up to him. George looked back at him as if to say, what have I done?

Finding it difficult to control his rage, Charlie said, 'If you ever touch her again, I'll knock you out.'

Karl looked over at his big brother; he had never seen him looking so angry in his life, and could tell he meant every word. Without saying another word, Charlie went upstairs to bed.

Karl went over to his father, feeling very emotional, and said, 'Dad, if you don't sort yourself out, you're going to lose the only people who still care for you.'

For a brief second or two, they made silent eye contact, and then Karl followed his brother to bed. George sat in the kitchen staring at an empty glass and a half full bottle of whisky. It seemed like hours, although it was really no more than fifteen minutes. Like a cat sitting next to a bowl of cream, he licked his lips in temptation. As his hands shook, he squeezed his fists tight, then, suddenly undeterred by his son's words, he grabbed the bottle, filled the glass two-thirds full and slammed the bottle back down on the table. He lifted the glass and began drinking; within half an hour, the bottle was empty and George was slouched over the table fast asleep.

The next day, little was said about the previous evening. George probably couldn't remember what was said anyway. Susie offered to take Karl back to school on Sunday to save him a boring train journey, and she was dying to see what these public schools were like.

Just after lunchtime on Sunday, Susie and the two boys set off for Marshdown. It took a little longer than normal, as none of them was particularly good with a map, but two or three wrong turns later, they finally arrived at the school gates. After a quick once over by security, the gates were opened, and Susie drove through. They cleared the tree line, revealing the main school building in all its glory.

'Wow,' said Susie, 'it's like a stately home or something.'

'Well, it is really,' said Karl. 'Before it became a school, it was owned by gentry.'

The car rolled up to the main entrance.

'Can I come in,' asked Susie, 'or are they a bit funny about girls?'

'Well, they are,' replied Karl, 'but there's only one or two members of staff here till Monday morning.'

Susie smiled at Karl, then Charlie, and said, 'Well, let's go in then.'

Karl and Charlie grabbed a bag each. Susie bleeped the central locking on the car and followed them into the main entrance. They walked down the long corridor, walled with portraits of people associated with the school, various past governors and headmasters, and into the Great Hall.

'This is cool,' said Susie, spinning round taking in all the pictures and architecture.

'Keep your voice down,' said Charlie. Susie smiled and raised a hand to her mouth.

'Come on,' said Karl, 'I'll take you up to my dorm.'

They both followed Karl through a doorway at the rear of the hall, which led to a spiral staircase. 'This isn't the normal way up,' he told them; 'it's part of the fire escape route, but it's quicker.'

Round and round they went. At every fourth spiral, there was a caged exit onto each floor. It had been years since Charlie had visited the school, always opting to stay at home when his father dropped Karl off.

'Come on,' called Karl, who was a few spirals higher than Susie, 'I'm on the top floor.'

Susie was already out of breath and Charlie pushed her on from behind. 'Nearly there now, darlin'.'

Finally reaching the top, Susie leaned against the wall, out of breath. 'I wish you'd told me about that, Karl;' she gasped, 'I'd have waited in the car.'

Pulling open a heavy, spring-loaded fire door, Karl led them into a passageway with three doors.

'Mine's the last room;' said Karl, 'come on.' He pushed the door open to reveal Jerald lying on his bed, reading a magazine. He looked up.

'Karl, you're early.' He turned the magazine towards Karl. 'Look at the tits on that!'

Susie stepped through the door, and Jerald quickly closed the magazine, his face rapidly reddening, and stuffed it behind his pillow. Susie smiled. 'Boys,' she murmured, looking around the dormitory. Karl dropped his bag on his bed.

'Jerry, this is my brother Charlie and his girlfriend Susie.'

Embarrassed, Jerald mumbled a quiet hello to them.

'Don't worry, mate,' Charlie smiled, 'it could have been a lot worse.' They all laughed, seeing the funny side of it.

Karl and Jerald took them on an unofficial guided tour of Marshdown, ending up in the canteen. Family members were welcome to eat with their children at weekends, especially after a long journey, and a box at the end of the serving counter gently encouraged them to leave a small contribution towards the cost of the food. After a not very exciting dinner of microwaved steak and kidney pie and chips, Susie and Charlie said their goodbyes. Karl and Jerald walked them to the car.

'Nice car,' said Jerald, walking around the vehicle to inspect it.

'OK, Jerry,' said Charlie, 'Karl's told us everything we ever need to know about Minis.'

They all laughed except for Jerald. 'Have I missed something?' he asked.

'I'll tell you later, mate,' said Karl, still laughing.

'Right then, bro, we're off. Keep swotting lads.'

Susie again gave Karl a long hug. 'See you soon, Karl,' she said.

Karl smiled back at her and she turned to Jerald. 'You're not getting away without a hug.' She pulled him close. and Jerald couldn't believe his luck.

'Bye, boys,' said Susie as she climbed into the car. Charlie pulled down the window and shouted, 'Go on you two, back to work.'

'Charlie!' Karl shouted. Charlie looked over his shoulder, to see Karl reach into his pocket and pull out two fingers in a victory sign. As the car drove off, Charlie laughed out loud.

'What's so funny?' asked Susie.

'Nothing; it's just something between me and Karl.'

As the car disappeared into the trees, Jerald stared after it. 'Jesus Christ, Karl, I'm in love.'

'She's a cracker, isn't she?' said Karl. Jerald was still looking towards the trees.

'Hellooo,' Karl had his hands to his mouth, like a loud hailer. 'Jerry, are you still in there?' Jerald snapped out of his trance.

'Come on,' said Karl, 'I've got some new ideas I want to run by you that we can try out with my gift tonight.'

The two boys ran up the stairs back into the school.

17

An unhappy reunion

As the weeks and months rolled by, Karl only occasionally went home, preferring to stay at school with Billy and Jerald. Charlie sent him letters on a regular basis, letting him know about any developments at home. Charlie had been promoted to team leader in the shot blasting department; it meant more responsibility but, more importantly, more money. From the way he wrote about Susie, it seemed that their relationship was getting pretty serious. Karl was pleased for him; he deserved a break. Having to stay at home night after night watching their father fall apart was more than Karl could have coped with.

In just over a month Karl would be seventeen, leaving him just twelve months to complete his degree. Blakeway told him that, if he continued at his present rate, he would graduate at the end of the following summer term. The weekends spent at school were giving him plenty of time to work on his gift. Jerald and Billy took turns to stay over most weekends.

Occasionally, when Karl stayed at school alone, he would have nightmares. They always involved people from previous interactions, often his mother and father. But Mortiboys was the nightmare that frightened him the most, always laughing at him, with blood pouring from open wounds to his wrists. Jerald had been told by his father how Mortiboys had committed suicide. Not wanting to talk about it, he had pushed it to the back of his mind, but somehow Karl had unknowingly extracted it from Jerald's subconscious. How he had done it was just another on a long list of questions Karl had yet to find an answer to.

For Karl, it was like having two lives, using his dreams to subconsciously travel. Jerald and Billy were happy to be part of the experiment. Karl would read a book or watch a documentary, then somehow replicate it in his dreams.

The only downside was the tiredness. Karl would study all day for his degree and then experiment with his gift in the evening, and for a young man not yet eighteen, he was beginning to look considerably older. Karl's birthday came and went. He received cards from both his parents with a twenty pound note in each. They were obviously sent by Charlie as the serial numbers on the notes were in sequence. Karl didn't really care, but it made him appreciate his brother even more.

It would soon be Christmas and that meant that, like it or not, he would be at home for almost three weeks while the school closed down for the festive season.

As Christmas approached, the atmosphere at school changed. Karl had experienced it many times before, but this time for him it felt a little sombre. The excitement, especially in the younger boys, was obvious to see. That coming Friday, Charlie and Susie would be coming to collect him from school. He couldn't wait to see them, but at the same time he dreaded going home to see his father.

By Friday lunchtime, all the boys had been sent back to their dormitories to bag up all their dirty washing and personal belongings. In less than an hour, parents would begin arriving to take their children home for Christmas. The traditional end of year assembly was already over so, theoretically, they were already dismissed. The Headmaster always waited by the main entrance to greet the parents, particularly those who were more influential, as they arrived. Charlie and Susie had both booked a day's holiday at work and Charlie hoped they would arrive early.

The excited boys gathered in the Great Hall, together with their assorted bags and cases. The presence of half a dozen masters kept the boys reasonably quiet, but it was a happy time and they relaxed the rules. Parents began arriving, some staying a little longer than others, chatting to masters and socialising with other parents. There were still twenty or so boys left in the Great Hall when Charlie and Susie arrived, and the older boys' eyes were instantly drawn towards the skin-tight T-shirt and jeans that showed off every curve of Susie's slender body. Karl noticed several of the masters taking a sneaky peek when they thought nobody else was watching.

'Bro, what's happening?' shouted Charlie at the top of his voice.

The Headmaster shot a glance of displeasure as he chatted to a pupil's father, who happened to be running for a seat in Parliament. Karl cringed as he picked up his bags and went over to them. Karl didn't want to stay a minute longer, especially after the look he had just received from the Headmaster.

'Do you think I should have a word with your Headmaster before we go, just check everything's OK? Only he keeps looking at me.'

An unhappy reunion

'Please, Charlie,' replied Karl, 'don't say a word. Let's just get out of here.' Susie gave Charlie a look as if to say, stop winding him up. A few minutes later, they were in the car and on their way home.

The traffic was heavy all the way, and the journey took over two hours in all. They arrived home to find the house in darkness. George had taken to hanging around in the local park with some so-called friends. 'Winos' was the best description Charlie could give them, but they would drink anything they could get their hands on. Sometimes their binges would go on into the early hours, and occasionally George would not come home at all.

They decided to have a quiet night in, and Charlie phoned through an order for a couple of pizzas. He was told to expect the delivery in about an hour, maybe a little longer, as it was a very busy night. It didn't matter; they weren't going anywhere. About half an hour later, there was a knock at the front door. 'That was quick,' said Susie jumping to her feet, 'I'll go.'

'Money's on there, darlin',' said Charlie, pointing towards the sideboard.

She picked up the money and counted it out as she went to the door. 'There you go, £13.40 . . . oh!'

Expecting to see the delivery man, Susie was surprised to be confronted by a woman who clearly had nothing to do with pizzas. 'Can I help you?' asked Susie.

'Is George in?'

'No, I'm sorry he's out. I don't know what time he'll be back. Would you like to leave a message?'

'Yes, please tell him Jill called.'

As the woman turned to walk away, Susie realised who she was.

'Wait,' Jill turned round, 'are you Charlie and Karl's mom?' The woman nodded. Susie took a deep breath and wondered what to do. Charlie had told her about their mother, but Susie had never seen her. All existing photographs had long been removed and put away.

'I'm Susie, Charlie's girlfriend; please come in.' Jill smiled and followed Susie into the house.

'Did you have to go to the shop for them?' quipped Charlie. But Susie's face told him something wasn't right. Susie moved to one side and Jill appeared. Karl looked gobsmacked, and Charlie jumped out the chair.

'What the hell are you doing here?'

'Hello, boys,' said Jill sheepishly.

'What do you want?' demanded Charlie, showing not the slightest respect.

'Charlie!' said Susie. She had never seen him like this; he had always shown respect and courtesy to everyone in front of her. Karl remained quiet, and Jill gently smiled at him.

Charlie couldn't contain himself any longer. 'Has he thrown you out? You're wasting your time coming back here.' Susie went into the kitchen, not wanting to get involved.

'No, Charlie, it's quite the opposite,' Jill replied. 'I want your father to give me a divorce.' She took a breath. 'Brian has asked me to marry him.'

It was too much for Charlie. 'Well, that's great,' he sneered, 'I hope you're both fuckin' miserable together. Now get out.' Charlie strode over to his mother and pushed her towards the door.

Susie saw what was happening and rushed in. 'Charlie, don't!' She grabbed his arm, tears running down her face. 'Please Charlie, don't!'

Seeing Susie's tearful face stopped him in his tracks; she was the last person in the world he wanted to upset. 'OK, OK, I'm sorry.' He stepped back.

Jill was just about to walk out but turned back to them. 'I am truly sorry this happened. I hope one day in the future, we'll be able to talk and put this behind us.'

'Never,' snapped Charlie.

Jill turned to Karl, looking for some kind of clemency. Karl stood up and walked over to his brother, standing firmly by his side; he had made his stand. Eyes full of sadness, Jill turned and opened the front door.

A man was standing right on the doorstep. 'Two pizzas for Hennessey.'

Tears were now running down Jill's face.

'I'm not that late, am I?' he joked.

Without saying a word, Jill edged her way past him and disappeared down the road. Jill's appearance at the house had opened up some partially healed wounds, and to say that the rest of the evening was a little solemn was an understatement.

That Saturday morning, Charlie went into work early on overtime. He only worked until lunchtime at weekends, but it really made a difference to his money now that he was on a higher rate of pay. Karl was lounging about, flicking from one TV channel to another, unable to find anything worth watching. George came down the stairs and was probably the most sober Karl had seen him since their mother left.

'All right, son?' he asked, as he walked past into the kitchen. After putting the kettle on, he sat down at the kitchen table. Karl got up and joined him in the kitchen.

'Do you want some toast, Dad, I'm having some?'

An unhappy reunion

'No, not for me, son,' George replied, 'a coffee's all I have in the morning; have trouble keeping my breakfasts down just lately.' The truth was, his alcohol addiction had almost reached the point of no return, and if he didn't stop soon it would be too late.

'You really should eat, you know, Dad.'

'Later maybe, son, later.'

Karl made the coffee and some toast for himself, and then sat at the table next to his father.

'Mom came round last night.'

George suddenly stopped drinking his coffee and looked at Karl. 'You mean she was here, at the house?'

'Yeah, it's all right though; Charlie told her exactly how we feel.'

'What do you mean?' George was beginning to look agitated.

'He threw her out,' said Karl.

George raised his hand to the side of his head, grimacing as if suddenly overwhelmed by pain. 'You mean she finally started to see sense and your half-wit gorilla of a brother told her to sling her hook?'

Karl was shocked by his father's reaction. 'It wasn't like that, Dad.'

'What do you mean, it wasn't like that; what do you know?' George got to his feet and started pacing around the kitchen, squeezing his fist in the palm of his other hand. 'She might want to come home; she's probably dumped that twat Jackson.'

Karl was getting worried; his father was acting very strangely. 'Dad, she said they are going to get married.'

George flipped. At the top of his voice he shouted, 'MARRYING THAT BASTARD? SHE'S MY WIFE!' He picked up his coffee cup and slammed it against the wall at the other end of the kitchen. Karl reacted by putting his hands on the back of his head, as shards of the cup splintered all around the room. George stormed out of the kitchen shouting 'I'LL GIVE THEM FUCKING MARRIED!' Grabbing his coat, he stomped down the hall and through the front door, slamming it behind him.

With his hands still on his head, Karl began to cry. He had not felt this sad since the day his mother walked out. The sooner he got out of this place and made his own way in life the better.

When Charlie arrived home, Karl was still sitting in the kitchen, coffee and pieces of mug littering the floor.

'Shit, what's happened here?'

'It was Dad,' said Karl. 'He went mad when I told him about Mom last night.'

'You've been crying,' said Charlie, noticing Karl's reddened eyes.

'I got upset when he started shouting,' said Karl, embarrassed.

'He's a stupid bastard; why doesn't he just let her go?'

'Charlie, I'm worried. I think he's going to do something stupid.'

Charlie put his hand on Karl's shoulder. 'Bro, don't worry; he'll go out have a few drinks and come back with his tail between his legs, you'll see.'

Karl couldn't get it out of his mind all afternoon. Charlie had not seen the temper George was in when he left the house. By nine o'clock in the evening, Karl was beside himself with worry. Over time, Karl had learned to listen to his senses and had found that he had an uncanny knack of knowing when things weren't right. Charlie was nodding off on the settee.

'Charlie, I'm worried.'

There was no reply. 'Charlie,' Karl called out.

Flinching, Charlie turned his head. 'What? I was asleep then.'

'I've got a bad feeling about Dad,' said Karl.

Charlie sighed. 'Look,' he replied irritably, 'if he's not back by eleven o'clock, I'll go and have a look for him, right?'

Karl sat back and folded his arms, a little annoyed at his brother's lack of interest.

Charlie soon fell asleep, and Karl sat there, watching the hands inch their way slowly around the clock; it felt as if time was standing still. All sorts of things were going through his mind, and he had visions of his father murdering his mother and her lover. 'Stop it you fool,' he said to himself.

The minutes ticked by and finally, at five to eleven, he couldn't wait any longer. 'Charlie, Charlie, it's eleven o'clock and Dad's still not home.'

Slowly, Charlie opened his eyes and yawned. Glancing up at the clock, he rubbed his eyes, threw his legs off the settee and sat upright. 'Come on then, I have a good idea where we'll find him.'

It was bitterly cold outside. In less than a week, it would be Christmas Day, and the weather forecast had announced a fifty/fifty chance of snow; not a good time of the year to be drunk, lying in a ditch. Half a mile down the road, the local park had become a favourite haunt for the local winos and junkies. Charlie thought that if George was short of money, he would probably go down there to try to scrounge a drink. Approaching the park, the gates were locked.

'How do we get in?' asked Karl naively.

'Same way they do,' replied Charlie, 'come on.'

An unhappy reunion

Karl followed his brother along the line of the fence. One by one, Charlie pushed the panels until one of them, as if on a hinge, pushed back, creating a large hole. 'There we go.'

Karl looked at his brother and shook his head. 'I'd never have thought of that.'

Charlie smiled, 'You know what your problem is, bro?' Karl looked at him, his mouth slightly ajar. 'You're too clever.'

They both climbed through the hole, making sure they replaced the panel.

'Right, now listen; these geezers can be a bit rowdy, especially when they're pissed, so if I say run, do it, right?'

'OK,' said Karl, nodding his head a little more quickly than necessary.

It was pitch black. As they moved into the park, Karl felt the change in terrain as they went down a steep hill. In the distance, silhouetted against the night sky, there was what looked like a small copse. From deep inside, they could see the glow of a fire.

'Don't worry about making a noise;' said Charlie, 'it's better they know we're coming. When Dad first got involved with these wasters, I had to come and get him one night.'

As they got closer, Charlie broke a few sticks, advertising the fact that they were coming.

'Who is it?' came a deep, gruff voice from within the copse.

'Charlie Hennessey and his brother; we're looking for our dad, George.'

A torch clicked on and shone straight into Charlie face; he raised a hand to his eyes to shield the glare. The boys walked over towards the fire, where six or seven men sat close by, surrounded by bottles, cans and a few hypodermic needles.

'Hi, guys,' said Charlie, 'how's it going?'

'Fuckin' cold,' replied a haggard-looking man with tattoos on his face and neck.

'Have you seen me dad tonight?'

'Tonight?' said the man with the gruff voice. 'He's been scrounging drink off us all day.'

Wanting to stay on their good side, Charlie reached into his pocket and took out a screwed up ten pound note. 'Here, get some drink on me.' Two of the men quickly jumped to their feet; the opportunity for easy money didn't come often. 'That's all I've got, but you're welcome to it if you can tell me where me dad's gone.'

The tattooed man stood up, holding a bottle upside down by its neck and pointing it towards the others.

'Sit down, or you'll have me to deal with.' The two men cautiously sat back down, their eyes scanning the boy's like hyenas in search of an easy meal. Charlie gave the man the ten pound note, which he quickly stuffed into his trouser pocket.

'Over there.' He pointed towards a pile of boxes.

'What, you mean he's in the boxes?' Karl was shocked.

'Well, he was before dark; he was out of it.'

Karl ran over to the boxes, followed by Charlie, and one by one they pushed and kicked them out the way. Lying there in a heap was George.

'Is he still breathing?' asked Karl.

'Yeah, but he's very cold. Come on, help me get him up.'

As the boys dragged him to his feet, the men around the fire paid no attention. They were more concerned with keeping themselves warm than with whether George lived or died. The next hour and half was the hardest struggle either of the boys could ever remember. It had been a struggle the last time they had to carry George home, but trying to get him up the hill and through the park fence was a nightmare. Once or twice on the way home, he regained consciousness, but only briefly. Passing motorists glanced at them unsympathetically, and there was no way they could expect any help in the way of a lift.

Finally, they arrived home, dragged George upstairs and lay him on his bed. Not bothering to remove his clothes, they dropped his shoes onto the floor and covered him with a duvet.

'Come on, bro,' said Charlie, 'we can check on him later, give him chance to warm up a little.'

'OK, Charlie, put the kettle on; I'll be down in a minute.'

Charlie went down to the kitchen, and Karl sat on his father's bed. He had to know what was going on inside his father's head; drunk or not, he had to interact with him. He could hear the familiar sounds telling him that Charlie was filling the kettle and taking cups from the shelves.

Reaching under the edge of the quilt, he took hold of his father's hand and closed his eyes. Almost instantly, he found himself standing in a dark field. It was very cold and a little hazy. A feeling of anxiety swept over him and felt as if it could overwhelm him at any moment. He could hear the sound of running water in the distance and was drawn towards it; something was telling him to go to the water. As the sound became louder, he knew he was close, but still couldn't see it. Turning to his right, he saw the silhouette of a bridge. Standing on the top, looking over the edge, was a man. It was George. Karl ran to the edge of the bridge. 'Dad, Dad!' he shouted at the top of his voice. George turned to him, gave a brief smile and then began climbing up onto the edge. Karl ran up alongside him.

'Dad, what are you doing?'

'I've had enough, son;' replied George, weakly, 'it's for the best.'

'Listen to me, Dad, don't do it, I can help you. Just take my hand.' Tears rolled down George's face. 'You have to trust me, Dad. Just take my hand and it will all feel better, believe me.'

Looking into his son's eyes, George smiled again. 'You're a good lad, Karl.' Then he looked down at the torrent of water some fifty feet below. Karl knew he had to do something and fast. Lunging forwards, he grabbed his father's hand. He closed his eyes, concentrating and focusing all his mental power.

A sudden feeling of warmth engulfed his body. Opening his eyes, he found that they were sitting on a beach. To his left, a huge stone arch jutted out into the sea; Lulworth, he thought to himself. Years ago, a friend of the family who had a caravan at Lulworth Cove in Dorset would rent it to them for a week during the summer. The holidays were some of Karl's fondest memories.

Partially in shock, George stared at Karl. 'How did I get here?'

'Don't you remember the bridge, Dad? You looked like you needed a little help.'

George lay back, his elbows disappearing into the sand, still finding it hard to comprehend what was happening. He gazed across the beach, recognising the place where they had spent many happy days. 'We had some good times here, son, I remember them well; it feels like it was a lifetime ago.'

Karl picked up a pebble and threw it into the sea, watching it bounce across the surface three or four times before disappearing. 'You can't go on like this, Dad.'

'I know, son, I know. You and your brother have stood by me through thick and thin, and I know I don't deserve it. For that I'll always be thankful to both of you.' George lay on his back and looked up at the sky. 'I can't understand it; when we left the bridge I was drunk.'

Karl smiled. 'That was your dream; this is mine.' George looked confused. 'That's the best explanation I can give you, Dad.'

They sat silently for a while.

'Karl, when you see your brother, thank him for being as strong as he is and remind him that you two are the world to me.'

'Tell him yourself in the morning; he'd appreciate it.'

George smiled. There was a look of contentment on his face, as if he had just left a confessional box and been exonerated of the worst possible sin. Slowly, his eyes closed and he drifted off, back into his own subconscious. Karl stayed within his dream and watched his father for a few minutes. George began to look relaxed and was soon sleeping comfortably. Karl closed his eyes and opened them again; he was back in his father's bedroom, sitting on the bed at his father's side.

Gently, he released his father's hand. 'Good night, Dad,' he whispered, and quietly left the room, glancing back as he pulled the door closed behind him.

18

A time to mourn

Sunday morning was Charlie's one morning lie-in of the week; unless he was seeing Susie, it was very rare for him to be up and about before 10:30 am. Karl woke just after eight and looked over at Charlie, who was sleeping soundly. As quietly as he could, he tip-toed out of the bedroom and went downstairs to the kitchen. He yawned and scratched his head, squinting slightly at the intensity of the daylight beaming through the window.

Although bitterly cold, it was a fine day and he couldn't believe Christmas was only a few days away. There was no sign of festive spirit in the house – not a card or a Christmas tree in sight – and after the previous evening, festive decorations were the last things on his mind. He made some tea and toast and went into the living room, slumping down on the settee in front of the television. The time dragged as he flicked from channel to channel, trying to find something worth watching.

It was just after ten o'clock when Charlie finally stirred. 'Morning, bro,' he said in a throaty voice, as he shuffled into the living room and fell into an armchair.

Karl acknowledged him, picked up his cup and plate and went into the kitchen. Placing the crockery in the sink, he called out, 'Want some tea and toast Charlie?'

'Nice one, bro; marmalade on the toast please, two sugars in the tea.'

'Would you like me to feed you as well?' Karl's sarcasm was like water off a duck's back to Charlie, who made no reply. A few minutes later, Karl took him in his breakfast. Charlie had his feet up across the arm of the chair watching the television.

'Anything else, master?' asked Karl.

'Not just yet,' said Charlie, 'but stick around and I'll think of something.'

'I bet you will; I'll go and see how Dad is.'

Charlie looked up from the TV. 'You telling me he's not up yet?'

Karl shook his head.

'Well, that's a first; he never stays in bed, no matter how much he's had to drink the night before.'

Alarm bells immediately rang in Karl's mind, and he started up the stairs taking two at a time. He stumbled at the top, falling onto his knees. He thought back to the conversation he had within his father's dream. Composing himself, he got to his feet and gently knocked on the door, leaning his head towards it to listen for a reply; there was no answer. Slowly he opened the door, just enough to put his head round.

As he looked in on his father, panic overwhelmed him. Lying flat on his back, George had congealed vomit over his face, neck and mouth. Frozen to the spot, Karl screamed for Charlie at the top of his voice. He heard the sound of Charlie's feet bounding up the stairs. Reaching the bedroom he pushed past Karl.

'Oh no, for fuck's sake no!'

Karl stood frozen in the doorway, but Charlie rushed over to the bed, frantically trying to wipe the vomit from around their father's face and mouth, in a futile attempt to resuscitate him. Turning to Karl with panic in his eyes he shouted, 'Phone an ambulance; go quickly!'

Karl knew it was too late, but just in case there was the slightest glimmer of hope, he dashed down the stairs and dialled 999. Paramedics were on the scene within fifteen minutes, and almost immediately they confirmed what the boys already knew. They did not attempt to resuscitate George as he had been dead for a considerable amount of time. The drink had finally taken him. Almost definitely, he had choked on his own vomit, but official confirmation was for the coroner to decide.

The police arrived and spent some minutes talking to the paramedics and taking notes. Both boys were clearly overcome with grief, and the officers compassionately offered their condolences and said that they would return for a statement from them at a later date. George's body was taken to the hospital mortuary to await an autopsy.

Charlie phoned Susie; he couldn't think of anybody else to call, and he realised in his moment of grief just how much she meant to him. She came straight over, and when Charlie opened the door, she put her arms around him and held him tight. All his emotions came to a head and he wanted to burst into tears, but that wasn't his way. Bottling it all up, Charlie bit his bottom lip, hoping to portray that he had it all under control.

In the living room, Karl sat in silence, his eyes sore from the tears he had shed. Punishing himself, he thought that if only he could have interpreted the grief his father was feeling, just maybe he could have saved him.

Later that evening, Karl and Charlie sat together in the living room. Susie had offered to stay, but Charlie told her to get off home as she had to work in the morning. There was an eerie silence about the house, as if it had died with George. If they had somewhere else to go, they would have done so, as the house had nothing but bad memories for them.

Karl looked over at his brother. 'Charlie, can I tell you something?'

Charlie turned to Karl without speaking, but his eyes told Karl to continue.

'Last night when we put Dad into bed and you went downstairs, I interacted in his dream.'

Charlie suddenly looked interested. 'What happened?'

'I think he knew he was going to die; in fact, I think he committed suicide.'

'Don't be stupid. How can you commit suicide in your mind?' Charlie looked agitated.

'When I first went into his dream, he was going to jump off a bridge; I stopped him and took him away from it.' Karl paused trying to find the right words. 'It was just the things he said, Charlie. He told me to tell you he loved us and that he was sorry for everything he had done; it was like he was saying goodbye.'

Both boys sat in silence with their own thoughts. At least Karl had had that last moment with their father; for Charlie, the last memory he had of him was that of a pathetic semi-conscious drunk.

Christmas did not arrive at the Hennessey household that year; no presents or cards were exchanged, there was no tree in the house, and cards arriving by post were put in the bin. Due to a backlog at the coroner's office over the festive period, the autopsy could not take place until after the holiday, adding to the boys' grief. Finally, the cause of death by asphyxiation was confirmed, and their father's body was released.

Charlie arranged for the funeral at the local crematorium; it was a very low-key affair. A few of George's old work colleagues turned up, who remembered him in better days, and Susie and her parents were there to support the boys. Their mother made a brief appearance, but from the looks Charlie gave her, it was obvious that she was not welcome. Not wanting to cause a scene, she didn't hang around. Leaving a small wreath at the rear of the church, she slipped quietly through the door, choosing to deal with her own grief alone.

Two weeks passed, and the new term at Marshdown started, but Karl was nowhere to be seen. Still overwhelmed with grief, he had spent the last fortnight wallowing in self-pity. If he had only interpreted his father's dream differently, he could have prevented his death. Of course it was not true, but if you tell yourself it is for long enough, you eventually start to believe it. Charlie had taken a week's bereavement leave. He was on full pay as his leave was due to the death of an immediate family member; the last thing they needed now was financial problems.

The school phoned two or three times, leaving messages that Karl deleted and chose to ignore. But Charlie picked up one of the messages before Karl had time to delete it. As soon as Charlie realised what Karl had been doing, he contacted the school. The Headmaster gave his most sincere condolences and asked if he could be kept up to date with Karl's progress, as it was his last year at the school.

Pendlebury immediately called a meeting with Blakeway to explain the situation; Blakeway was extremely concerned. He knew that things would be difficult for Karl as he had been aware of the problems surrounding George's drinking. Not wanting Karl to throw away his future, he decided to give it another week; if he had heard nothing by then, he would pay him a visit.

Anxiously, Blakeway waited. Each morning, when he went into the classroom, he hoped to see his young prodigy sat at his desk, eager as ever for knowledge. Just to receive a simple letter in the post or a message from the Headmaster would have sufficed. By Thursday, he knew it was not going to happen. With only seven months left to the summer break, which was theoretically the end of Karl's time at Marshdown, Blakeway knew he had to intervene. That Saturday he would go and visit Karl; at least then he would know that he had tried his best.

On Saturday morning, just before lunch, Blakeway set off. Having been to Karl's house once before, he was confident he could retrace his steps. His trusty sat nav system was in the glove box, just in case. He had no idea what to expect, but kept his fingers crossed that the journey would not be a futile one.

He knocked on the door, hoping for a warm welcome, but after a few minutes there was no reply. He knocked a little louder. Still nothing. Walking round the front of the house, he peered through the bay window, straining his eyes to see through the net curtains. It looked as if they had not been cleaned for some time, making it virtually impossible to identify if there was anyone in the house. Deciding that there was nobody at home, he wished that he had called before setting off on such a long journey.

Raising the letterbox, he peered down the hall and just caught sight of Karl disappearing into the kitchen. 'Karl!' he shouted. Karl was obviously trying to avoid any contact. Once again he shouted but louder this time. 'Karl, it's Martin Blakeway. I know you're in there, let me in.' Still no reply. 'I've come a long way today and I'm not going anywhere till I've spoken to you. Five minutes, that's all I want.'

Blakeway dropped the letterbox flap and stood up straight, stretching his now aching back and contemplating what to do next. Suddenly, a click from the front door lock caught his attention. As the door opened, Karl's face appeared; he looked desperately tired, as if he had not slept in days.

'Karl, how are you? Can I come in?'

There was a slight hesitation; then Karl stood back from the doorway, allowing Blakeway access. Karl offered him a cup of tea, which Blakeway gratefully accepted. Leaving Blakeway in the living room, Karl went into the kitchen and turned on the kettle. As he prepared two cups, Blakeway came and stood in the doorway. Leaning against the door frame and feeling a little uneasy, he said, 'I was very sorry to hear about your father.'

Karl said nothing, but poured water into the cups and stirred the tea bags round. Blakeway sat down at the kitchen table and looked up into Karl's face, attempting to get some eye contact. 'It gets easier you know.'

Still not speaking, Karl squeezed out the tea bags and slid a cup in front of his tutor.

'Thank you,' said Blakeway, picking up the cup and sipping the hot tea. 'Oh, I needed that.'

Karl sat down next to him. Blakeway placed his cup back on the table. 'You probably think, what does he know?'

Karl suddenly turned to him. 'I would never think that, sir.'

At last, Blakeway had got a reaction. 'Can I tell you something, Karl?'

'Of course, sir.'

'Do you remember when you interacted in my dream, Karl, and you asked me who the boy and the woman were?' Karl nodded, now giving Blakeway his full attention. 'That was my son Bradley and my ex-wife Angela.'

Karl was flabbergasted. 'I didn't even know you were married, sir, let alone have a son.'

Blakeway smiled. 'Not many do; you see, he was killed, knocked down by a car. That very dream is a nightmare I have harboured in my mind for nearly ten years, since the accident.'

Karl was shocked. He remembered feeling uneasy within his tutor's dream; it was something else he had learned to understand within other people's dreams, even before anything bad happened.

'He was just four years old when it happened. My wife thought he was with me, and I thought he was with her; I only went to the toilet. He wandered off in the park, stepped out in front of the park attendant's van . . .' Blakeway had tears in his eyes. 'He was so small, the man driving the van didn't realise he had hit him until a woman screamed, seeing his little broken body on the floor behind the van.'

Karl's face was aghast his mouth partially open. 'I'm so sorry, sir.'

Blakeway rubbed a tear from his eye. 'That's why I said to you that it gets easier; time is a great healer, Karl.'

'What happened to your wife?'

'Ah, dear Angela. We tried to work it out, but unfortunately it was the stress of it all. You see, we blamed each other; the one time in our relationship we should have been strong together, and we fell apart. Eventually, we went our own ways.'

Karl's head was down in deep thought.

'Can you see what I'm trying to tell you, Karl? Like it or not, life goes on. Sometimes it's terribly hard, but it still goes on. What you do in the next few months will determine your whole life.'

Karl knew what he meant, but was finding it hard to find the enthusiasm. Just then, the front door opened and Charlie walked in, having finished his Saturday overtime. Recognising Blakeway's car outside the house, he came straight through to the kitchen.

'Martin, nice to see you, how's things?' He thrust an outstretched hand towards Blakeway, who stood and shook it firmly.

'I was very sorry to hear about your father; thought I'd come and see how you were both bearing up.'

The three of them sat down at the kitchen table and chatted for a good hour. Charlie agreed with everything Blakeway said about Karl getting on with his life, but Karl was finding it difficult to snap out of his frame of mind. Blakeway finally prepared to leave, but he asked Karl to have a good think about what he had said, and Karl promised he would.

That evening, Charlie had arranged to go out with Susie. Karl was sitting in the living room, his head firmly pressed into his hands, feeling sorry for himself. Charlie pulled on his jacket. As he checked his pockets, he looked at his brother and shook his head. 'Bro, can I have word?'

Karl said nothing, just looked up.

'Remember when Mom and Dad first split up?'

Karl nodded.

'I've never told you this, but I was really pissed off when I had to leave my other job. Especially the first few weeks in the foundry; it was really hard. The long hours and heavy work nearly killed me, but it kept us going. In the back of my mind, I thought, when Karl finishes his education, he'll help us out of this shit.'

Karl's head sank a little lower as he realised he wasn't only letting himself down but Charlie also.

'So the thing is, bro, if you don't go back and finish that degree of yours, everything I threw away in my old job was for nothing.'

Karl looked up at Charlie; his normal rock of a brother had watery eyes. All the time he had been wallowing in self-pity, he hadn't realised exactly what effect it was having on his brother and best friend. An urge to protect his sibling soared through his body, and he felt sure it was just how Charlie had felt the day he handed in his notice, taking a job he didn't want, purely to care for his family.

'I'm sorry, Charlie.' A single tear ran down Karl's cheek, but he quickly stopped it with the back of his hand as there was no time for tears now. 'I'll go back to school on Sunday. When I get that degree, I'll earn enough money to get you out of that place, you see.'

Charlie smiled. 'Just get the degree, bro; we'll worry about the rest of it later.'

The boys shook hands firmly. 'Right then,' said Charlie, 'I've got to get off; I'm meeting Susie in town. See you later.' Grabbing his jacket, Charlie checked his pocket for his wallet and hastily left. Karl spent the rest of the evening getting his clothes and books together. It would probably be a few weeks before he came home again; having missed three weeks, he had a lot to catch up on.

That Sunday afternoon, Charlie was asked to work overtime. It was unusual for him to work on Sundays, but there had been talk of redundancies if certain contracts weren't won, and if the workforce put in the time and effort, they might just be able to avert any job loses. Susie offered to drive Karl to school. Karl loved spending time with her. They passed the journey having a real heart-to-heart about Charlie, and Karl had the feeling it wouldn't be long before the sound of wedding bells would be heard; she was obviously besotted with him. Before she left at Marshdown, Karl got his usual hug, which was the highlight of his day.

The next morning, all the boys in Karl's dormitory were pleased to see him, and gathered together to fill him in on everything that had been going on since the start of term. Just before a quarter to nine, Blakeway parked his car, gathered up his books for the morning's lessons and grabbed his briefcase. As he walked through the school, he said good morning to one or two groups of boys gathering in the halls. After a brief conversation with Mr Bridges the PE master, he arrived at the classroom. Through the glass panes in the classroom door, he could see Karl sitting at his desk. A feeling of jubilation embraced him; he wanted to run in and jump for joy, but in the circumstances a more temperate approach was required.

Walking past Karl, he placed his briefcase and books on the desk. Karl looked up and Blakeway smiled. 'It's good to see you, young man.'

'Likewise, sir.'

'Are you ready to start?'

Karl nodded his head. 'You bet, sir.'

19

A friend in need

As the weeks rolled by, Karl was relentless in his studies and the long hours with little food were starting to take their toll on him. Once or twice, to the annoyance of his tutors, he had fallen asleep in class. Each time a student stayed in school for the weekend, it was logged. Every now and then, the Headmaster would go through the journal and initial each page. On this occasion, as he scanned through, he noticed that Karl had not been home for eight weeks; with all the trauma in the young man's life, it concerned him.

He decided to call a meeting with Blakeway to discuss the situation. Lunch had just finished and Blakeway had a free period, so they arranged to meet. Armed with Karl's progress reports to date, Blakeway arrived at Pendlebury's office. Karl had already caught up with the weeks he had missed at the start of term, and was progressing at an even faster rate than expected.

Blakeway knocked the door and, choosing not to wait for the familiar call of 'Enter', opened the door and peered round the edge. Pendlebury looked up from his desk, a little annoyed that Blakeway had entered without permission, but at the same time, too concerned with the reason for the meeting to comment. 'Please come in Mr Blakeway, take a seat.'

Blakeway closed the door behind him and, fumbling with a large bundle of folders, he made his way to the desk and placed them on the edge.

'As you can see, Headmaster, with regard to young Hennessey's work, I couldn't ask any more of him, it's all of an exceptional standard.'

'Please, Mr Blakeway, sit down.'

He did as he was asked.

'I know Hennessey is an exemplary student; that's not what I'm really concerned about. You see, it's one thing having a student with the highest possible exam results, but it's another thing when he might have a nervous breakdown achieving them.'

Blakeway sat back in his chair; he certainly hadn't expected this kind of reaction from the Headmaster.

'Did you know, he hasn't been home for eight weeks? Considering that his father died in dramatic circumstances only a few months ago, wouldn't you say that was a little strange? He's also been falling asleep in classes and looks very drawn.'

Before responding, Blakeway took a deep breath and thought for a moment. 'I fully agree with you, Headmaster, but Hennessey's circumstances are considerably different from those of most young men of his age.'

The Headmaster sat back, tapping his hand on the desk, contemplating Blakeway's statement. Before the Headmaster could reply, Blakeway said, 'I paid him and his brother a visit after their father died, just to give my condolences and check they were coping. You see, when their mother walked out on them, his nineteen-year-old brother, Charlie, became his guardian; it's a lot to ask of one so young.'

'I see;' said Pendlebury, 'but I'm still amazed.'

'What's that, Headmaster?' asked Blakeway looking quizzical.

'Well, we should have been informed about his change of guardianship, but also, with all this going on in the family, how on earth did they manage to raise the boy's school fees?'

Blakeway maintained steady eye contact; he could tell by the expression on the Headmaster's face that he knew where the money had come from, but even if he had wanted to prove it he couldn't.

'Anyway,' said Pendlebury, 'that's not important at the moment, but we have to keep a close eye on him. I am going to insist that he goes home for the next couple of weekends.'

'I couldn't agree more, Headmaster,' replied Blakeway. 'He needs to relax. He's well ahead with his studies, and a break will do him good.'

'Excellent, Blakeway; that's just what I wanted to hear. He thinks highly of you, he'll listen.'

'I have a lecture with him later this afternoon, and I'll have a word after class.'

Pendlebury sat up tall, slapping both palms of his hands on his desk. 'Right, I think we are both in agreement, we'll leave it at that.'

Blakeway stood up, gathered his folders from the desk and pushed them, none too securely, under his arm. 'Good afternoon, Headmaster.'

Pendlebury nodded in acknowledgement as Blakeway left for his classes.

Later that afternoon, Blakeway asked Karl to stay behind after class. As the boys filed out of the classroom, Karl remained at his desk. As one classmate passed him, he jovially shook his head and whispered, 'You're in for it now.'

'Yeah, yeah,' Karl replied nonchalantly.

As the last boy pulled the door closed behind him, Blakeway looked up from his desk. 'Karl, it's nothing to worry about, I just wanted to bring to your attention something the Headmaster and I have discussed.'

Karl sat up straight in his chair, a look of concern on his face.

Blakeway picked up on it straight away. 'Don't panic, we are very happy with your work; in fact, we are so happy that we would like you to relax a little.'

Karl was a little confused. 'But, sir, I haven't finished my course work yet.'

'I know that, but you're well on schedule; in fact you're about two months ahead. Look Karl, the Headmaster has insisted you go home for the next two or three weekends, just to relax and recharge your batteries.'

'But, sir, I can do that here.'

'Karl, you're not listening to me; the key word was *insists*.'

Karl fell silent and lowered his head; his parents' house held nothing but bad memories, and if he never went back there it would be too soon.

'I'm free this weekend,' Blakeway continued. 'If you like, I'll drop you home, save putting Charlie out.'

Karl resisted grinning; he enjoyed his mentor's company outside class. 'That would be great, sir, thank you.'

'That's settled, then. Friday afternoon, as soon as school finishes, we'll get off.'

Blakeway stood up and closed the books on his desk. 'I believe you have PE with Mr Bridges next, don't you, Karl?' Karl nodded. 'Then I would hurry; with his military background he has no time for poor punctuality.'

Karl glanced at his watch, and his eyes widened. Gathering his books as quickly as he could, he dashed out of the classroom and rushed towards the gym.

Blakeway sat back down in his chair, and his mind wandered back to his own son; since talking to Karl about him, he seemed to have been at the forefront of his mind. He would have only been a few years younger than Karl, and for some time Blakeway sat there, reminiscing over memories of happier days.

Friday quickly came around. After eight weeks without going home and being more focused on his studies rather than taking his clothes to the school's laundry, Karl had amassed quite a lot of washing. Placing his bags into Blakeway's car, he slammed down the boot and got in the passenger side door.

'All set?' asked Blakeway.

'As ready as I'll ever be, sir.'

'Let's go then.'

Flicking up gravel, the car moved a little too quickly towards the tarmac road. Once or twice on the approach to the main gates, they had to pull over close to the trees to avoid the influx of parents' vehicles arriving to take their sons home for the weekend. Once clear of the school, they sped off on their journey.

They had not been travelling for long when Karl turned to Blakeway. 'Sir, do you remember telling me about your son and wife?'

Blakeway nodded.

'I was wondering about that recurring dream you have. I know you can't change the past, but what if the outcome of your dream was different, do you think you would sleep better?'

Blakeway took a deep breath and shuffled in his seat. He thought about it for a few moments, then said, 'It's a good question, Karl; it was a poignant time in my life.'

Karl could see that it was painful for Blakeway to talk about it, but continued. 'I have an idea, sir' – Blakeway glanced at him – 'what if I interacted in your dream and changed its outcome, so it wasn't a nightmare any more but a pleasant experience?'

'How could you do that?'

'Stop Bradley's accident happening.'

Blakeway turned sharply to Karl; it was difficult to tell if he was shocked or offended. He maintained his gaze on Karl a little too long.

'Sir, the road.'

Quickly, Blakeway focused on the road ahead, narrowly missing the kerb.

'I'm sorry if I offended you, sir.'

'No, Karl, I just didn't expect it. Do you think you could do that?'

Karl nodded. 'I think so; it might take a couple of sessions, but yes, if you like; you could stay over at my house. Charlie wouldn't mind; and it would be safer there.'

The idea intrigued Blakeway – not just the thought of Karl changing the outcome of the dream, but to get the chance to interact with him again; the last time had been an incredible experience. He longed to do it again, to the point where it felt addictive. 'Let me have a think about it, Karl.'

The rest of the journey was relatively quiet; both of them appeared lost in their own thoughts. Finally, after a long struggle through the Friday afternoon traffic, they arrived at Karl's home. Charlie was still at work, but Karl had his own key. Gathering up his bags from the boot of the car, they went into the house. Emptying a bag of dirty washing onto the kitchen floor, Karl offered Blakeway a cup of tea.

'I'll get it, Karl; you get that washing machine started.' Blakeway put the kettle on and then mooched around for the tea bags.

'In the end cupboard, sir,' said Karl, seeing Blakeway struggling to find the tea and sugar. The washing machine burst into life, and, armed with two cups of tea and a packet of digestive biscuits, they went into the living room for a much-needed sit down.

They had not been sitting down more than ten minutes when the front door opened and Charlie and Susie appeared. 'Martin, how are ya?' beamed Charlie. 'Who's this you've bought with ya? It looks like our Karl, but its been that long since he's been home that I'm not sure any more.'

Susie slapped his arm as if to tell him to stop playing him up.

Blakeway, forever the gentleman, jumped to his feet. 'Hello Charlie and . . .' He looked at Susie.

'Susie,' she replied.

'Pleased to meet you, Susie.' Blakeway moved a little closer and offered his hand.

'Sorry, Martin,' jumped in Charlie, 'this is my girlfriend Susie.'

'Too slow, you big chump,' said Karl with a big smirk on his face. As Charlie edged his way round the settee, Karl pulled his legs up in a feeble attempt to avoid some form of brotherly inflicted pain.

'They're like this all the time, Martin,' said Susie.

Blakeway laughed. It was good to see this more natural side of Karl, and the break from studying would do him the world of good. Once the brothers had calmed down, they all sat down and talked about what they had been up to for the last couple of months. Once they had caught up, Susie suggested that they all went out to eat that night, hers and Charlie's treat, and it was agreed.

'We could go bowling first,' added Charlie. 'I haven't beaten Karl in months; he must be due another good hiding.'

Blakeway laughed; he did find Charlie amusing.

Karl came back at him. 'I think you might just have a shock; I've been practising.'

'Practising?' said Charlie sarcastically. 'They haven't knocked down your library and built a bowling alley, have they?'

Karl tapped two fingers on the side of his head, and Charlie knew exactly what he meant. 'It's not the same, bro.'

'We'll see,' said Karl, 'we'll see.'

Charlie turned to Blakeway. 'You up for it, Martin?'

'I don't know; I've never been bowling. and I can't really go in my work suit.'

'No problem,' replied Charlie. 'You can borrow some of my gear. My shirts might be a little big, but everything else should fit.'

Blakeway thought about it for a moment. 'What the hell, why not? I'm only going back to an empty flat. I'd love to come. Thanks for the invitation.'

Charlie looked at Karl and rubbed his hands together. 'OK, that's it then; another chance for nipper over there to see the master at work.'

Karl shook his head.

'Don't listen to a word of it, Martin;' said Susie, 'he's like a big kid.'

The evening went really well, especially for Karl. For the first time in any physical activity, he had beaten his brother, not once but twice. Charlie wouldn't accept it; if they had let him, he would have played all night until he had won a game. But time was not on his side, and everyone was hungry. They spent the rest of the evening in a local pizzeria. Karl enjoyed the moment, constantly reminding Charlie of his victory. Susie drove them all home but did not come in as she was going out shopping early the following morning with her mother and decided to call it a night.

As it was getting late, Charlie insisted that Blakeway should stay over for the night and went upstairs to put clean linen onto what had been George's bed, which had been left bare since the room had been cleared out.

As Karl and Blakeway sat in the kitchen drinking coffee, Karl decided to bring up Blakeway's dream. 'It would be a great opportunity sir, to interact in your dream.' All evening, Karl had been respectfully calling Blakeway 'sir'.

'Karl,' said Blakeway, 'outside school, call me Martin; it's much less formal.'

'Are you sure, sir?'

Blakeway smiled. 'Martin.'

'Sorry,' replied Karl, 'Martin.'

'Just don't forget at school, if the Headmaster found out I would be for the high jump. As far as the dream's concerned, if I'm staying the night I'm willing to give it a go.'

'Brilliant,' said Karl, 'all you have to do is think about the dream as you go to sleep. It doesn't always work, but I've found it to be the best way.'

'Right then;' said Blakeway, 'on that note, if it's OK with you two, I'll turn in.'

Charlie showed Blakeway up to his room, leaving Karl in the kitchen, thinking about the dream interaction that was to take place later that night. When Charlie came back down, Karl told him about Blakeway's dream and what he was going to try and do. If he were successful, he would be taking his gift into a whole new dimension.

Half an hour or so later, Karl and Charlie quietly made their way up the stairs. Even in a strange environment, it should have been long enough for Blakeway to get off to sleep, especially after the long drive and the evening's bowling. Karl slowly opened the bedroom door, holding his breath and squinting as the door squeaked. With the door half open, he peered round the inside. Blakeway appeared to be sleeping soundly. Karl tip-toed in, closely followed by Charlie. Cautiously sitting on the edge of the bed, Karl looked up at Charlie. 'Here goes, then.'

'Good luck, bro,' whispered Charlie.

Karl reached out and very gently took hold of Blakeway's hand. As he closed his eyes, he was instantly transported into Blakeway's subconscious.

Karl was standing on a beautifully manicured lawn. In front of him, two elderly gentlemen dressed in white flannel trousers and crisp white shirts happily rolled bowling balls in Karl's general direction, apparently oblivious to his presence. Karl walked in their direction, but, as they passed, neither acknowledged the other; they either couldn't see him or chose not to.

Hearing the sound of children playing, Karl broke into a gentle trot down an adjacent path. Following the noise, he turned left past a large hedge. He was in the same playground he had previously seen in Blakeway's dream, but had approached it from the other side.

Quickly scanning the play area, he spotted a woman on the bench, presumably Blakeway's wife. She was sitting back with her eyes closed and seemed very relaxed. There was no sign of Blakeway or his son; was he too late? Again he scanned the area. On the far side, he could see the public toilet building. He had to assume that Blakeway was already in there, as that's where he had been going the last time he interacted with him. Time was not on his side; he had to find the boy quickly.

Starting to panic, he ran across the playground trying to remember what Bradley had been wearing. His preparation was poor; he should have asked these questions before he interacted. Running along, he tried to think; Bradley was run over, so I have to get onto the road.

The playground was surrounding by tall hedgerows, and behind them, unknown to Karl, was the fateful tarmac road. Bradley was on all fours crawling through a hole in the bottom of the hedge. To a child so young, it was a great adventure. On the other side, driving at no more than four or five miles an hour, the park warden scanned the opposite field for two teenage boys, reportedly throwing bricks into the pond. Bradley came out of the hedge just as the van passed, his little frame, still on all fours, invisible to the passing van. As the infant disappeared under the side of the van, the rear right-hand wheel rolled straight over his back, not even giving him a chance to cry out, finally crushing his neck as it rolled off his little broken body. 'Bloody rocks,' said the warden to himself. Oblivious to the little boy at the side of his van, he continued scanning the fields.

He had not gone more than five metres when a woman walking her dog saw the horrific sight. Hearing her screams, Karl dashed down the pathway towards the van, but he knew he was too late. Arriving at the scene, he saw the child's crumpled body spread-eagled on the tarmac, the side of his head partially crushed by the sheer weight of the vehicle rolling over his body. Karl turned away in shock, trying to control the urge to vomit. The park warden stood at the back of his van, his hands trembling as he tried to use his radio to call for help. People were beginning to appear from everywhere, coming to see what all the commotion was. There was nothing Karl could do. Soon, Blakeway and his wife would be here, and the fullness of his mentor's nightmare would be realised.

Not wanting to see him reliving his grief, Karl closed his eyes tightly, and in a flash he was back in the bedroom. Blakeway was still fast asleep. As gently as he could, Karl released his grip on Blakeway's hand.

Charlie was sitting on the dressing table stool. As quietly as he could, he whispered, 'What happened? It's only been a few minutes.'

Without speaking Karl pointed to the door, and they both tip-toed out of the room, quietly closing the door behind them.

Once in their bedroom, Karl sat on the bed and lowered his head. 'I was too late.'

'What happened, then?' asked Charlie, anxiously wanting to know the details.

'By the time I found him, the accident had already happened; it was terrible.' Karl pinched the top of his nose with his thumb and index finger.

Charlie could see it had really stressed him out. 'It was a dream, bro.'

'I know, but it really happened to Martin and his wife; it must have been terrible.'

'Look at it this way, bro, you'll know what to do next time.'

Karl thought about what Charlie had just said. He was right; the first time was more like reconnaissance. Now he knew what was going to happen, he could change the outcome. They both got ready for bed, and within minutes Charlie was asleep. It took considerably longer for Karl, who could not get the image of the little boy's crumpled body out of his mind.

The following morning, Karl was up early, having not slept well at all. As he sat in the kitchen drinking a cup of tea, his mind wandered back to Blakeway's dream. Now he had seen the outcome, he wanted to go straight back in and put things right, but he knew it wasn't that simple. Blakeway came down the stairs and into the kitchen, flattening down his hair with the palms of his hands. He looked as if he too had had a restless night's sleep; it was the first time Karl had seen him anything but impeccably turned out.

'Morning, Martin; tea and toast?'

'That would be nice, thank you, Karl.'

Karl pushed down the button on the kettle and dropped two slices of bread into the toaster.

'I had the dream again last night,' said Blakeway.

'I know;' replied Karl, 'I was there.'

Blakeway looked surprised.

'I saw the accident, but it was too late to do anything. If you'll let me try again, I know what to do now.'

The toast popped up, making them both jump. Karl buttered it and placed it in front of Blakeway with a cup of tea. Blakeway was quiet. He picked up a slice of toast and was just about to take a bite when he said, 'Every time I have that dream, it's like living through the whole experience again. When I wake in the morning, for the first fifteen or twenty minutes I feel just as I did on the day after the accident.' Blakeway bit his toast and looked into his mug of tea. Karl had a feeling what his friend had just said was a cry for help; next time, he would put it right.

Blakeway left just before lunch. He offered to come back on Sunday evening to take Karl back to school, but it had already been arranged that Susie would take him. They agreed that Blakeway would again bring Karl home the following Friday, and once more Karl would attempt to interact in his dream. For the rest of the day, Karl did exactly as he had been told, completely switching off from his schoolwork and just relaxing in front of the television. That evening Charlie took Susie out for a meal, inviting Karl along too, but he declined, feeling that he was intruding on their relationship.

When Charlie returned home, Karl was half asleep on the sofa.

'You still up, bro?' said Charlie, throwing his jacket over the back of a chair. Karl stirred slightly and rubbed his eyes.

'Yeah, I was thinking about Martin and his wife. Can you imagine how hard it must have been to lose a child like that? No wonder they split up.'

'Bro, you're taking it to heart. I think the only way Martin has coped with it is by putting it to the back of his mind, so should you.'

'I know, I know, but he's my friend, and I feel like I need to help him.'

'Look,' said Charlie, 'go to bed and for now forget about it. Get a good night's sleep, and it will all look a little clearer.'

Karl knew Charlie was right. He said goodnight and went up to bed. As he brushed his teeth, he looked at his reflection in the bathroom mirror. How he had aged. Swilling out his mouth, he spat into the sink and looked a little closer into the mirror. He raised a hand to his left temple; although his hair was very short, it looked grey. He rubbed it with the tip of his fingers. Sure enough, he was getting grey hair and not yet eighteen. Shaking his head at his own image, he went to bed.

As much as he tried, Karl couldn't get Blakeway's dream out of his mind. Finally, he fell into a restless sleep. How long he had been asleep he didn't know, but suddenly startled, he opened his eyes. He felt a presence in the room. The room appeared darker than usual, so dark that he couldn't even see Charlie's bed. Straining his eyes, at the bottom of his bed he could just about make out the silhouette of a small figure. As his eyes adjusted to the dark, the figure became clearer. Karl's heart began to race. Rigid with fear, Karl stared into the eyes of Blakeway's son.

Barely big enough to see over the bottom of the bed, the small boy came round the side towards Karl, his head grotesquely deformed from the accident. Gripped with fear, Karl backed up to the wall and pulled his legs up, hugging his knees. The little boy stood no more than three feet away. After what seemed an age, he said in a voice that didn't appear to be his own, 'Why didn't you help me?' Karl felt the hairs stand up on the back of his neck; he tried to speak, but no words came out. The boy looked angry. At the top of his voice, he shouted, 'WHY?'

Karl closed his eyes and suddenly sat up and shouted, 'I TRIED!'

Within seconds, the bedroom door burst open and Charlie flicked the light on. Karl was soaked in sweat.

'He was here, Charlie; Bradley, he was here!'

Charlie looked around the room. 'Karl, there's no one here; you were dreaming.'

'I'm telling you, Charlie, he was here.' Karl lay back down on his pillow, cold and damp with sweat.

'Go to sleep, bro. I'll be up in a minute.' Charlie turned the light off and went downstairs. Lying in the darkness, Karl was too afraid to close his eyes. If it had been a dream, he couldn't tell the difference between it and reality, and that was really frightening.

As the days at school rolled by, the dream played on Karl's mind more and more. He knew that the only way to rid himself of this mental turmoil was to do as the small boy had asked and help him.

After school on Friday afternoon, Blakeway drove Karl home. They said very little on the journey, both consumed by their own thoughts. The house would be empty that evening as Charlie and Susie were going to the cinema. Susie knew nothing of Karl's gift. He was also concerned she would find it a little weird that his lecturer came home to stay for the weekend, so they had concocted a story about Karl having some extra tuition in a more relaxed environment while coming to terms with his father's death. When the time was right, he would tell her the whole story.

Sometime after 10 pm, Blakeway conceded to his tiredness and said goodnight. All he had to do was go to bed and once more concentrate on the dream. Karl's dilemma was knowing how to interact in the dream so that he would be in the right place at the right time to take control. If he mentally forced Blakeway to relive the dream from the way Karl saw it, it truly wouldn't be Blakeway's dream. Karl had to make sure he stayed in Blakeway's subconscious.

He waited about the same length of time as he had the previous week, to ensure that Blakeway was in a deep sleep. Like some kind of déjà vu experience, he tiptoed into Blakeway's bedroom and sat on the bed. Gently, he took hold of Blakeway's hand and closed his eyes, thinking about the place where the accident had taken place.

In a flash, he was standing on the path where he had seen the van. He looked around, but there was no sign of Bradley or the van. With haste, he walked down the path to the bend and, some three hundred metres away, he could see the warden, leaning out of his van talking to a man out walking his dog. Scanning the hedge, Karl tried to find the point where Bradley must have crawled through. It must have been near the bend or the warden would have seen him as he drove up the pathway. The warden's van very slowly started up the path. Where was he? Karl dodged up and down trying to find the hole, but it all looked the same. The van was almost there, and Karl could feel his heart pounding in his chest as he started to panic.

Suddenly, a rustling of leaves caught Karl's attention, some twenty metres down the path. The van was only a few metres away. Waving his arms, Karl ran down the middle of the path. 'STOP, STOP!' he shouted at the top of his voice. From the smallest of holes, a little boy's head popped out. Karl's heart was in his mouth; the van was almost on him. There was no way the warden could see him. Almost sprinting. Karl slammed his hands onto the bonnet of the van, 'STOP, GODDAMMIT!'

The warden slammed on his brakes and looking shocked, leaned out the window. 'What do you think you're doing, you fool? I could have run you over!'

Karl came round the side of the car; right below the warden's arm, little Bradley was on all fours. 'That's why I stopped you,' said Karl, pointing at the small boy literally under the sill of the van. Reaching down, he scooped him up.

The warden looked as white as a ghost. He got out of the van and, taking a deep breath, put both hands on his head and leaned against the side of the vehicle. 'I couldn't see him.' The realisation of what had just happened was hitting home.

Karl smiled at Bradley. 'Your mommy and daddy are looking for you; shall we go and find them?'

Bradley nodded, unaware of the danger he had just been in. Karl put the little boy down, and, holding his hand, they walked back towards the entrance to the playground, leaving the bewildered warden with his thoughts.

Turning into the playground, Karl could see Blakeway and his wife; she was crying, and another woman was trying to console her. Blakeway was turning around, panic in his eyes, scrutinising every child. Karl released Bradley's hand; 'Go on, Brad, there's Mommy and Daddy.' The little boy dashed as quickly as his little legs would carry him towards his parents. They both saw him at virtually at the same time; his mother hugged him so tightly that the little boy could hardly breathe. He'd done it.

Karl now knew why, all those years ago, his father had said to him, 'One day, son, you will find out why you have this gift.' And he was right; it was the best feeling in the world.

Blakeway stood looking at Karl with tears in his eyes. He said nothing, but he didn't have to; Karl could feel his thoughts. Karl raised his hand in acknowledgement, turned and walked away, leaving his friend to enjoy his family, albeit only in his dreams.

Karl opened his eyes. He was sitting on the side of Blakeway's bed, still holding his hand. Gently, he released his grip on his friend's hand. A feeling of contentment overwhelmed him; even when he had helped Jerald to face his demons, he had not felt this way. Quietly, he left the room. Although still charged with emotion, he was totally exhausted. Leaving his clothes in a small mound, he climbed into bed and was asleep in seconds.

20

Graduation

Blakeway woke. A piercing ray of sun shone through the bedroom window; it was remarkably warm for early March. As he rubbed the sleep from his eyes, he glanced at his watch; it was just before 9 am. Throwing back the quilt, he couldn't remember having such a good night's sleep.

Charlie had long since risen and gone to work for his Saturday morning overtime. Blakeway dressed, made the bed and walked along the landing towards the stairs. As he reached Karl's room, he noticed that the door was slightly ajar. Very quietly, he pushed the door half open; Karl was sleeping soundly. Not wanting to wake him, he pulled the door closed and quietly went downstairs to the kitchen. The outcome of his dream was still at the forefront of his mind. He searched around for something to write on. Unable to find anything he ripped a piece of card off a cereal box. On it he simply wrote, 'Thank you, Martin,' and then gathered up his belongings and left, closing the front door securely behind him.

It was another good hour before Karl stirred; it wasn't like him to stay in bed. As he lay there, his hearing became acutely attuned to any sounds within the house, but all was deathly quiet. He climbed out of bed and put on his dressing gown. Charlie's bedside clock revealed just how late it was, a quarter to eleven; it was unheard of for Karl still to be in bed at this time. Poking his head around the door to Blakeway's room, he saw that the bed was neatly made, as if it hadn't been used.

Before going downstairs, he swilled his face. Even though he had been in bed for the best part of twelve hours, he still felt sleepy. He took a long look at his face in the bathroom mirror. His eyes looked deep set, like some kind of half-starved concentration camp victim. He had never carried much weight, but even so he was beginning to look haggard. Is that what Blakeway and the headmaster had seen? Was he ageing at an alarming rate or just overdoing it? Whichever it was, it didn't feel good.

Karl went downstairs to the kitchen. The first thing he spotted was Blakeway's note on the table. As he read it, he smiled. It was little things like that, that made him forget about the image in the bathroom mirror.

Easter was only four weeks away, and at least half of the boys in Karl's year would not be returning after the break. That included his friends Jerald and Billy. Both had achieved the required 'A' level grades to go to their chosen universities, and until September they would be taking a well-earned break from their education. Even if Karl finished his degree ahead of schedule, he wouldn't be leaving until the summer break. He didn't mind. As he told Jerald, it would give him the opportunity to finish off the few books in the library he hadn't already read.

On Sunday evening, Charlie and Susie drove Karl back to school; it was teatime when they arrived. They didn't hang around as it would soon be dark and Susie wanted to get back. As he waved them off, another car came up the drive. A very expensive-looking black Mercedes rolled into the car park, and Karl was intrigued to know who was in it. The front doors opened and two familiar faces appeared; it was Jerald and his father. Karl raised his hand in acknowledgement.

'Hello, Mr Sanderson.'

Jerald's father came round the car, his hand already extended. 'Good to see you, young man.' He shook Karl's hand a little overenthusiastically. 'I was sorry to hear about your father; please accept my condolences.' Karl thanked him. 'I hear you're staying on till the summer?'

'Yes, sir, I will have completed my degree by then.'

'That's excellent; psychology isn't it?'

'Yes, sir.'

'Well, I can't give you a job in that area, but if you need a character reference for any job applications, let me know.' He turned to his son; 'Jerald.'

'It's Jerry, Dad.'

'Sorry, son. I'm pleased that Karl's here. I have to be in London by this evening, so I'll get off and leave you and Karl to it, if that's OK with you.'

'Sure, Dad; I'll just get the rest of my stuff out of the boot.'

Karl offered to help, and the two boys pulled the bags from the cavernous boot space. Slamming the boot lid down, Jerald's father went round to the driver's door. 'See you a week on Saturday, Jerald. Bye, Karl; nice to see you again.' Karl raised his hand in reply.

As his father climbed into the car, Jerry sighed and under his breath he said, 'It's Jerry, Dad.' The Mercedes engine fired up and the boys watched as it slowly rolled off the gravel and onto the tarmac, picking up speed as it found the firmer surface.

'Nice car,' said Karl.

Jerald wrinkled his nose. 'He's had better.'

Karl's knowledge of cars was such that he knew the basic price for an S-Class Mercedes saloon was in excess of fifty-five thousand pounds, but to Jerald it was just another car. What very different worlds he and Jerald came from. 'One day,' Karl thought to himself, 'one day, I'll have a car like that.'

The boys lugged the bags up to the dormitory.

'Last time,' said Jerald. Karl looked at him quizzically.

'Go on,' said Karl, 'give me a clue what you're talking about.'

'Last time before I leave this place.' Jerald sat on his bed and looked around the room. 'It will be strange not being here.'

'Tell me about it,' replied Karl, 'after the Easter break when you guys leave, I'm on my own in this dorm.'

Jerald checked out the other beds, and pointed at each one. 'Billy uni, Ryan uni, Mark working for his dad, Ian uni, me and you. God, mate, I didn't realise; you're going to be bored out of your head. Come on,' said Jerald, 'leave the bags; let's go down to the kitchen and raid the dessert fridge.'

'Sounds good to me,' said Karl and they set off down the stairs, all thoughts of leaving school pushed to the back of their minds.

The next few weeks dragged by. Karl had only one module of his degree left to complete; he could easily have finished it in a couple of weeks if he had put his mind to it, but there was no rush. The boys who were leaving at Easter were already pulling pranks on each other, to the displeasure of the Headmaster. It was no different from any other year, with water bombs and superglue being very much a favourite.

Blakeway was sitting at his desk catching up on some outstanding paperwork. Karl sat at a desk in front of him, finishing off a piece of work. The other boys had gone to lunch a little early; having completed all their exams and coursework, it was just a matter of killing time before the end of term. Karl glanced up at Blakeway.

'Sir, I was thinking.'

Blakeway raised his eyes from his notes. 'What were you thinking, Karl?'

Karl sat back in his chair, the end of his pen resting on his chin. 'When I graduate, I was thinking of establishing a psychology practice.'

Blakeway was taken aback. 'Don't you think that's a little bit like trying to run before you can walk?'

Karl thought about it for a few moments, 'Well, sir, with my gift, I've kind of got a bit of a head start.'

'That is one way you could look at it, but if you want my personal opinion, I'd advise you to continue with your education. A Master's in psychology, or, if you feel that way inclined, we can investigate the psychiatry route. Both, I feel, will help you to understand your gift on a, shall we say, more educated level.'

Karl had great respect for his mentor, and carefully he absorbed everything Blakeway had said.

'Anyway, I think that's enough for one morning; let's go and get some lunch.'

Still in deep thought, Karl closed his book. Slowly, they walked together towards the dining room, Karl's future still very much the topic of conversation.

It was the Friday of the Easter leavers' assembly. Each boy that was leaving went up onto the stage and received a dictionary from the Headmaster; it was a tradition the school had maintained since first being established. After the assembly, all the proud parents gathered with their sons in front of the entire school for a final get-together. Then the Headmaster walked amongst them, telling them what wonderful, well-mannered, educated sons they had, hoping to secure their younger siblings to a life in boarding school.

Karl had witnessed the event year in year out. Usually, it was like watching paint dry, but this time it was slightly different – most of the boys leaving were his friends. As he was not leaving with them, he felt somehow alienated from the celebrations. His friends said that they would come back for the summer leavers' assembly, as a kind of mini-reunion. How true to their words they were, Karl would find out that coming summer.

As Karl waved off the last few of his friends, it felt as if another chapter in his life was coming to an end. Trying to avoid being roped in to tidying up the Great Hall, Karl went the back way up to the dormitory. He planned to stay at school for the weekend as Charlie had partially moved Susie into the house on Friday and Saturday nights. Not wanting to feel like a gooseberry, he thought he would stay at school and read a little.

As the door closed behind him, the quietness of the room engulfed him; he couldn't remember ever feeling so lonely. Lying on his bed, he reached over to the bedside cabinet and picked up a book. Looking at the cover he read out, '*The Definition of a Tortured Mind*'; very appropriate, thought Karl, as he opened the book at the first page.

The sound of deep, uneven breathing caught Karl's attention. The room appeared darker than usual; it was only 5 pm, yet it felt more like midnight. Karl shivered; the temperature seemed to have dropped significantly. Looking over at Jerald's bed, he could just make out through the gloom the shape of someone lying with the sheet pulled up high, the chest rising and falling. Karl was rigid with fear and could feel the hairs rising on the back of his neck. Who could it be? All the other boys had gone home.

Slowly, Karl forced himself to stand up and, step by step, he cautiously approached the bed. Something inside him was screaming out, telling him to run, but in the same breath, something else told him that he must look, pull the sheet back. Standing just out of reach, Karl slowly extended his arm and took hold of the edge of the sheet. Now absolutely gripped with fear, he pulled at the sheet, which slid straight off the figure. Lying on the bed, partially dressed, was his father, dried vomit smeared over his face and neck. Karl closed his eyes tightly, then opened them again. George was still there. Was it real or a dream? He didn't know.

Suddenly, his father's eyes opened, and the grotesque form turned to look at him. Karl stumbled backwards, and in an attempt to get away, he fell onto his backside. His father sat up, still staring at Karl and began to speak. 'You could have saved me.' Lifting his feet off the bed, he stood up.

Karl got to his feet and backed away. Again he closed his eyes tightly and thought about waking up. Opening his eyes, again he saw his father reaching out for him, just a few feet away, his face contorted with anger. Summoning all his energy, Karl turned and ran for the dormitory door. He pulled it open and ran through but there was nothing there, just darkness. He was falling and could feel his heart pounding in his chest.

'Got to wake up, got to wake up!' he told himself. With a start, he sat up in bed, his book falling off his chest onto the dormitory floor. It was still light. Rapidly, his eyes searched every corner of the room, expecting to see the spectre of his father waiting to attack him, but it had just been a dream. Getting to his feet, Karl picked up his book and placed it on the bedside cabinet. Slowly, he felt his heart rate returning to normal. Opening the dormitory door, he almost expected to find blackness, but no, it was the same old hall. At times like this, his so-called gift felt more like a curse.

Although Karl's evenings were mostly spent alone, the weeks passed surprisingly quickly. As the weather improved, he spent lunchtimes sat out in the grounds, occasionally joined by his mentor, Blakeway, to discuss a wide variety of subjects, but somehow always returning to Karl's gift. It seemed that Blakeway was even more intrigued by it than Karl had initially thought.

Karl completed his degree, and now all he had to do was kill time and wait for the summer leavers' presentation. He had been tipped off that the school planned to make a big event of it as Karl had done so well, and a couple of local papers planned to send photographers over for the presentation. The Headmaster was over the moon; as far as he was concerned, all publicity was good publicity. It was a great honour for the school as no other pupil had ever achieved such a high qualification at such a young age, and the Headmaster had his fingers crossed that it would encourage another successful September intake of students.

The day finally arrived, and a far greater number of parents turned up than usual, mostly parents of Karl's friends. Charlie had even bought a new suit for the occasion. The Great Hall was full of students past and present, not a spare seat in the house. The front row consisted of all the masters, with the pupils who were to receive awards sitting behind them. The stage was lined with governors and dignitaries who were only seen on such prestigious occasions, the Dean and Headmaster taking the central positions. As usual, the Headmaster set the proceedings underway by welcoming everyone to the school, then introducing the Dean.

The Dean was an Old Etonian by the name of Donald Shaftsbury, an overweight man with thinning grey hair in his late fifties. His ruddy bulbous nose gave away his penchant for fine wines and malt whisky. Standing at the podium, he went through all the usual end of term acknowledgements, finally arriving at the academic achievements. One by one he called the boys up to be presented with their certificates; parents, pupils and masters alike clapped and applauded each and every one of them.

Finally, there was only one pupil left. The Dean delivered a speech to rapturous applause and asked Karl to come up and collect his scroll. As Karl made his way to the front, the sound was deafening; everyone in the hall was on their feet clapping and cheering. Once he had received the scroll, the chant from the hall was, 'Speech, speech!' It was the first time that Karl had ever found himself in such a position.

Silence fell in as Karl approached the podium. 'What can I say?' He collected his thoughts. 'Thank you, Mr Blakeway, for your constant support. And thank you to all the other masters who have helped me achieve this.' Karl waved his scroll. 'I'd like to say a big thank you to my brother, Charlie. A lot has happened in my home life over the last few years, and without his support, I don't think I'd be here today; thanks bruv. Finally, I'd like to thank the school for keeping me on for these last twelve months. Without the scholarship, I would have had to seek my goals elsewhere.'

A murmur swept across the hall, and Karl wondered what he had said to stir them up so. The Dean leaned over to Karl and whispered, 'We don't do scholarships.'

Karl's eyes instantly fixed on Blakeway, who was sitting in the front row with his arms crossed. The penny dropped. 'I'm sorry,' said Karl, 'if I could rephrase that, thank you to my benefactor. I am truly grateful, thank you.' Karl nodded his head in Blakeway's direction, and Blakeway calmly returned the gesture, unconcerned by the Headmaster's glare.

Karl left the stage to the sound of his friends clapping and cheering, much to the annoyance of the Headmaster, who was trying to call the assembly to an end. As everyone filed out Karl received many handshakes, slaps on the back and congratulations. Through the crowd, Karl saw his benefactor leaving in the direction of his office and called out to him. Blakeway stopped and turned. Pushing his way through the crowd, Karl made his way towards him. 'You knew I wouldn't have accepted charity, sir.'

'Correct again, Karl, but I couldn't stand by and watch talent go to waste.'

Karl smiled, 'I'll make it up to you one day, sir, not just financially.'

'Karl, just make sure that whatever you choose to do, be successful. That's all the reward I need.' They shook hands, their grip tighter than usual, reinforcing what was already a formidable bond.

Charlie and Susie followed Karl up to his dormitory. 'Last time,' said Karl as he climbed the last few stairs. He had already packed up his belongings, and it was just a matter of picking up his bags.

'Right, then,' said Charlie, 'let's get off then.'

Karl stood looking around the room, which held so many memories. After a moment, Charlie placed a hand on his shoulder. 'Come on, bro, time to move on.'

Walking down to the car Karl was very quiet, lost in his own thoughts. Once everything was stowed away in the car, Susie drove towards the line of trees. Looking up at the rear view mirror, Susie saw Karl glance over his shoulder, back towards the school building, and slowed down.

'All right, Karl?' she asked affectionately, realising that for him it was like leaving home. Karl nodded; a whole new chapter of his life was about to begin.

21

Redundancy

The journey home was a quiet one. Karl was contemplating what his next move would be as he had to start earning money. Sensing the impact that leaving school was having on him, Charlie and Susie quietly left him with his thoughts. As they pulled up outside the house, Charlie made a deep, sighing noise, tinged with a touch of sarcasm 'Home sweet home.'

'Don't be like that;' said Susie, 'anyway you've got to show Karl your handiwork.'

'Oh yeah, come on, bro; we've made a few changes.'

They got out of the car and, laden with Karl's bags, made their way up the path.

'I'll put the kettle on,' said Susie, going straight through to the kitchen. 'Help Karl upstairs with his bags.'

As they climbed the stairs, Karl sniffed. 'Fresh paint! I never thought I'd see the day you did any decorating.'

Feeling very pleased with himself, Charlie replied, 'You haven't seen anything yet.'

Karl went first and opened the bedroom door; the whole room had been transformed. The floor had been laminated, a new pine bed replaced the old one, the back wall now housed a fitted wardrobe, and pride of place was given to a matching desk with a leather swivel chair. Karl could tell from the curtains and bed linen that Susie had obviously had quite an input. He couldn't help smiling. 'Its great, Charlie.'

'You can blame Susie for all the girly stuff,' Charlie replied.

'I guessed that. Where are you sleeping?'

Charlie grinned, 'I was hoping you'd ask that.' He flicked his head, indicating that Karl should follow him. Charlie went ahead, down the hall to what had been their parents' room. Charlie pushed the door open and extended his arm. 'Please, enter my boudoir, young man,' using an exaggerated, plum-in-the-mouth accent.

Karl shook his head. 'Clown.'

Walking into the room was like going into a show home. As in Karl's room, the floor had been laminated, making the room appear more spacious than Karl remembered it. Everything had been replaced. Karl gazed around the room at a huge and expensive-looking pine bed with a range of matching furniture. Once again, Susie's influence was all over the soft furnishings.

'I take it Susie's moved in, then?' said Karl, his eyes still scanning the room.

'I thought you'd be pleased for me.'

Karl suddenly turned to look at his brother. 'I am, I am; I didn't mean to sound selfish, I'm really pleased for you. It's just a bit of a shock seeing Mom and Dad's room changed so.'

With that, Susie came upstairs. 'What do you think, Karl?'

'It looks great, Susie. I'm really pleased for you both.'

Susie felt suddenly emotional. 'Oh, come here.' Putting her arms around Karl, she hugged him in the way only she could.

'I'll have to watch you two,' laughed Charlie.

Susie smiled and slapped the top of his arm. 'What are you like? Come on, I've made some tea downstairs.'

Karl and Charlie sat down in the living room. Susie brought in a tray of tea and biscuits and placed it on the coffee table before sitting down.

'What's the plan then, bro?' asked Charlie, sitting back with a cup of tea in one hand and a biscuit in the other.

'Well,' Karl picked up his cup, 'I'll have a look in the papers and see what jobs are out there. The sooner I start earning, the better. I'm not really sure what's going to be available to me, but I'm sure the Job Centre will advise me.'

Susie leaned forwards. 'Before you go to the job centre, you should sign on the dole. It takes a couple of weeks before they give you any money, so the sooner you get your name down the better; it all helps.'

'Let's hope it doesn't come to that,' said Karl.

'Take your time, bro,' said Charlie, 'find the right job. Another few weeks isn't going to make any difference.'

Karl spent the rest of the weekend settling back into the house. It was the first time in his life he had had his own room. It felt strange having privacy and his own territory, but it was nice.

Karl was up and out early on Monday morning and made his first stop at the Social Security office to sign on. He hated the idea of taking money from the State, but until he got himself sorted out, it was the only way he could contribute to the household bills. Now that he was no longer at school, he had to help Charlie in anyway he could.

His next stop was the Job Centre. If he wanted to drive a forklift truck or be a store security officer, he could have had a job the same day. It seemed his downfall was his lack of experience. Even the lower levels of social work required experience and references that he just didn't have. He was beginning to realise that even with a degree, the type of work that interested him required specific, often lengthy training, starting at the bottom and working up. It had really been quite naïve of him to think he was going to walk straight into a well-paid job, but it wasn't going to stop him trying.

As the weeks went by, Karl applied for position after position. Each time, he had the same reply: we will keep you on file, should any other positions become available. When he did get an interview, he had the feeling it was more out of politeness and the position already had somebody else's name on it.

Charlie said nothing, but he knew that Karl was kidding himself if he thought he was going to walk into his ideal job. Then suddenly, out of the blue, Charlie received a letter informing him that the foundry would be laying off a small percentage of the workforce. There had been talk of it on the shop floor for some time, but even Susie was shocked by the letter; she had not heard a thing at home or in the office. Charlie had only worked at the foundry for two years. The usual process was a call for voluntary redundancy first, then last in first out, so it wasn't looking good for him. A meeting had been called for the following day and the union had a full-time official coming in to chair the meeting.

At lunchtime that day, all the workers except for a couple in essential positions, gathered in the canteen. The full-time official, a man by the name of Arthur Dowling, sat at the far end of the room flicking through documents he had prepared for the meeting. Dowling had been a working man all his life. With only ten years to go before his own retirement, he had been offered the position as a full-time official within the union. He couldn't believe his luck and quickly snapped up the opportunity. After twelve months, he still looked uncomfortable in his high-street suit, his large, leathery hands and thick forearms a tribute to his working-class background.

Alex Cartwright, the team leader, came into the room and made his way over to Dowling, stopping now and then to talk briefly to other members of staff. Finally, he shook hands with the official and stood beside him, ready to address the workforce.

'Gentlemen, can I have your attention?' The din in the room quickly dissipated as all eyes focused on Cartwright. 'For those of you that don't know him, this is Arthur Dowling, our full-time official. Arthur's been negotiating on our behalf with Management. With that, I'll hand you over to Arthur.'

Dowling stood up. 'Thank you, Alex. Afternoon, gentlemen. I wish I was here on other business, but you know the situation. We hope to resolve this problem on a voluntary basis. I've been having talks with Management, and there is a package on the table.' Around the room, a few despondent heads raised. 'The basic package is twelve weeks' severance pay. Also, on top of that, anyone volunteering within a given period of time will get an extra three thousand pound incentive.'

Around the room, talking broke out in every corner. Charlie scanned his work colleagues; virtually all of them were family men. It wasn't hard to work out that, if it came down to compulsory redundancy, he was very high on the list, if not at the top. For over an hour, the official was bombarded with questions. Charlie listened, but every which way, it seemed his time at the foundry was coming to an end.

When Charlie arrived home, Karl was preparing a meal. 'Two mins, it'll be on the table,' Karl shouted from the kitchen. There was no reply. Karl put his head round the kitchen door to see Charlie, sitting on the settee looking a little dejected.

'You all right?'

'Yeah,' sighed Charlie, 'I'll tell you over tea.'

Sitting down to their evening meal, Karl was wondering what had made his brother so low. He set about pouring excessive amounts of tomato sauce onto his pie and chips. 'Go on then, what's up?'

Without any hesitation, Charlie told him he was going to be made redundant. Karl put the bottle down, taken aback by Charlie's unexpected announcement. Charlie explained what had been said at the meeting, adding that if nobody else volunteered for redundancy by the end of the week, he would have to. It was the only way to secure the extra three thousand pounds. If the company had to lose five people from the shop floor on a last in, first out basis, Charlie would definitely be one of them. By that time, the extra three thousand pounds would probably be off the table. They both agreed that it wasn't the preferred choice, but if nobody came forward and volunteered, then Charlie would.

Karl was desperate to put his knowledge and gift into action. Over the past weeks, he had been developing an idea that would enable him to do so; if Charlie was made redundant, it would be the perfect opportunity to put it into action. The question was, would Charlie be willing to put his hard earned cash forward to finance it?

Over the next few days, Charlie waited anxiously to see if anyone would volunteer. Susie, trying to glean as much information as possible, reported that there had been no inquiries at all, let alone volunteers. There was only one thing for it; Charlie asked for voluntary redundancy. It was accepted, and he was told to finish at the end of the week. To say that Charlie's mood was a little sombre was an understatement. The regular income had given him a feeling of security, and although it was hard work, he had enjoyed his time working at the foundry. Karl decided that the time was right to put his idea to his brother; that evening after tea he would talk to him.

If Charlie was worried about money, he wasn't showing it. As Karl washed up the plates from the evening meal, Charlie watched some cheesy American sitcom on television. From time to time, the sound of his laughter rang through to the kitchen. Karl quickly finished his task, thinking that as Charlie was in a good mood, it would be the perfect time to talk about his idea.

Drying his hands on a tea towel, he went through to the living room. 'Can I talk to you Charlie?'

'What about?' Charlie's eyes remained fixed on the television.

'I've had an idea.'

'Idea? As long as it involves making lots of money and doing little work, I'm all ears.' Karl remained quiet. 'I'm only joking; go on, spit it out.'

'What about if we open a practice?' replied Karl, a little sheepishly.

Charlie looked confused. 'What kind of practice?'

'A psychology practice. With my academic knowledge of psychology and my gift, it could work. All we need to do is rent a couple of offices.' Karl sat down opposite Charlie and continued eagerly, 'We could do home visits, put some ads in the paper, a bit of office furniture. I reckon that with your three thousand pounds redundancy payment, we could be up and running.'

Charlie said nothing, and for a moment, Karl thought he had offended him.

'You know something, bro?' – Karl had no idea how his brother would respond – 'I knew that one day you'd come up trumps, but you've got to remember that you're the brains of the outfit, I'm just putting up the money. Deal?' Charlie put out his hand and Karl grasped it firmly.

'Deal! I won't let you down, Charlie; you won't have to do a thing. I'll get started first thing in the morning.'

'Whoa, slow down, bro; I won't get the money till I finish at the weekend.'

'OK then, first thing Monday morning. Meanwhile, I'll begin looking online to see what we can get for our money.'

'Good idea. Now I'm just going to give Susie a call before I go to bed.'

One of Susie's friends had just got engaged, and they had gone out to celebrate and show off the ring. Their conversation turned to the subject of the new business he and Karl planned to set up. Charlie had not told Susie of Karl's gift; it was hard enough for him to understand himself, let alone explain to someone else. But Susie was aware that Karl had a special understanding of psychology and thought it all sounded very exciting, instantly offering her help in setting it up.

After saying goodnight to Susie, Charlie began to make his way up to bed, but he was cornered by Karl, his mind racing with ideas. 'I think it's important that the waiting and consulting areas look professional but relaxing.' He already had a good idea of what he wanted. 'Susie has good taste when it comes to décor, and her touch will make all the difference.'

Charlie put his hands up, as if to try to stop Karl from talking. 'Sleep on it, bro;' said Charlie, 'there's plenty of time to talk about it, and I'm up early again tomorrow.'

As Charlie went upstairs to bed, Karl sat back on the settee. How could he possibly sleep now? He just couldn't wait to get the ball rolling.

22

The practice

On Monday morning, Karl was up bright and early. Leaving Charlie lying in bed, he headed into town. He planned to register himself with as many estate agents as possible; if the right office was out there, as he was sure it was, the more people that were searching. the better. Starting at one end of the High Street, he went methodically, one by one, into each estate agency, leaving his details. He felt that some appeared more interested than others, and after being shown the details on one or two possible properties, he quickly realised that his budget of three thousand pounds was not going to last long. Feeling a little dejected, he slowly walked back down the High Street, his mind wandering back to his school friends Billy and Jerry. He wondered what they were up to; it wouldn't be long now before they both went off to university. He decided to call them as soon as he got home and wish them well.

It was lunchtime when Karl finally arrived home; Charlie was sitting in the garden reading a newspaper, taking a well-earned rest after finishing work at the foundry on the previous Friday. Seeing Karl in the kitchen, Charlie closed his newspaper and called out to him. Karl leaned against the back door frame.

'I've given my details to all the estate agents on the High Street, and they say they'll give me a call as soon as they have something.'

What Karl didn't say was that the chances of getting anything half decent with the money they had was very slim, to say the least.

'I'm going to give Jerry and Billy a ring, see what they're up to.'

'Before you do, a cup of tea wouldn't go amiss.'

'Lazy git,' Karl replied with a smile, and went back into the house. He switched the kettle on and went through to the hall. Picking up the phone, he selected Jerald's number. It rang for quite some time, and he was about to hang up when a woman answered in broken English.

'Señor Sanderson's residence; can I help you?'

'Hello, is Jerry there?' asked Karl a little apprehensively.

'Err, you want Señor Jerald?' Who the hell is this?, thought Karl.

'Yes please.'

'I get him.' Karl heard the sound of the receiver being put down, followed by a high-pitched voice.

'Señor Jerald, Señor Jerald, telephone!'

A few seconds later the phone was picked up. 'Hello?'

'Is that you, Jerry? It's Karl.'

'Karl! How you doing? Hang on, mate . . .' In the background, Karl heard Jerald shout out, 'I'VE GOT IT, MARIA!' at the top of his voice.

'Sorry,' said Jerald, 'Dad has taken on a Spanish woman to look after the house and cooking. She's trying to learn the language, bless her, but I'm not kidding, it's just like living in Fawlty Towers here sometimes. Anyway, what's up?'

'Just thought I'd wish you luck for uni; you must be off soon.'

'Not going, mate.' Karl was stunned. 'Dad's pulled a few strings and I've started work in his corporation. I plan to work my way up from the bottom, hands-on experience and all that, plus the money's good. I do three days a week in the office and two days in-house training. It's a doddle, mate.'

'Sounds good,' said Karl, trying to sound pleased for him.

'So, what are you doing?'

'I'm trying to set up a practice, some way of using my gift, but its so hard to get a premises to work from; everything is so expensive.'

'How much do you need?' asked Jerald.

Karl suddenly felt very uncomfortable; he didn't want his friend to think that he had only contacted him because he was trying to raise some money.

'I'm all right for money,' Karl lied. 'Charlie was made redundant from the foundry.'

'Yeah, but you'll need that money to survive.' Jerry was already thinking with his father's business head.

'I didn't call you for money, Jerry.'

'I know that, mate; I just want to help. Remember, you helped me once and I'll never forget that. I'll have a word with Dad; you never know, you might just get a little bit of corporate help.'

In the background, Karl could again hear the Spanish voice; Maria was ranting in her native tongue.

'Listen, mate,' said Jerald, 'I have to go. Maria's throwing a wobbler; I'll have to see what's wrong. I'll be in touch, Karl; bye for now.'

With that, he hung up. Karl went back into the kitchen and finished making the tea. Excited by the prospect of Jerald's father getting involved as some kind of financial sleeping partner, he completely forgot about calling Billy. He took the two mugs outside and told Charlie about his conversation with Jerald. Charlie was a little concerned, but at the same time did not want to take away any of Karl's excitement or enthusiasm.

'It sounds great, bro, but don't get your hopes up too high just yet,' said Charlie. 'Jerry's father may be an influential figure, but he's also a very busy man.'

Each day during the following week, Karl continued scanning the papers and searching the Internet for premises. He knew it was just a matter of time before something came along. The problem was, how long? It had been five days now, and there had not been a single property to view.

As Karl and Charlie sat eating bowls of cereal, a clattering from the letterbox caught their attention. The sound of the postman a week previously would have set Karl dashing to the front door, but on this occasion he hardly flinched. Charlie picked up on it straight away. 'Are you going to get that?' he asked, looking up from his bowl.

Without speaking, Karl just shrugged his shoulders. Charlie shook his head and pushed his chair back. As he walked towards the front door he said, 'I hope you're not losing interest; remember what you said last week? Leave it to me, you won't have to do a thing.'

Charlie flicked through the letters; it was mostly junk mail and bills, but one was a hand-written letter addressed to Karl. He walked back to the kitchen. 'This looks interesting, bro.'

Karl leaned back on his chair to see what Charlie was talking about. Charlie handed the letter to him and Karl examined the writing closely. 'I wonder who this is from. I don't recognise the handwriting.'

Charlie shook his head. 'For an educated bloke you do say some stupid things; just open the bloody letter, will you.'

Karl eagerly ripped open the envelope and pulled out a letter and a cheque. He sat in silence, staring at the cheque, the colour draining from his face. After a few moments, he passed it to Charlie.

'What's that for?' asked Charlie in amazement. 'Where the hell did it come from?' Karl opened the letter and read it out loud.

Dear Karl,

Jerald has informed me of your plans to set up a practice using that amazing gift of yours. I know you are a proud young man and would not accept charity, but at the same time you did a lot for my son and I would like to take this opportunity to show my gratitude by helping you to get started. Please find enclosed a cheque for

> £10,000. *Think of it as an investment rather than a gift. I feel sure you will use it wisely.*
>
> *Warmest regards,*
> *Geoffrey Sanderson*

'And there's me telling you not to get your hopes up!' Charlie blurted out, overwhelmed with excitement. He passed the cheque back to Karl, 'If I were you I'd get it in the bank ASAP before he changes his mind.'

'I can't believe it,' said Karl. 'I'll have to give him a call and thank him.'

'I've told you, get it in the bank first and then thank him.' While Charlie was apprehensive about such generosity; the truth was that ten thousand pounds was a drop in the ocean to Geoffrey Sanderson.

Within the hour, Karl was on his way into town. First he went to the bank to deposit the cheque; then he made a return visit to a particular estate agent. He'd liked the look of the properties they were handling, but there had been nothing in his price range. This time, the cash put him in a totally different position. After a short discussion, the details of three properties appeared on the desk before him, all with rents that he could now comfortably manage. From no availability, he was suddenly spoilt for choice with potential locations. He took the details with him and arranged to view them first thing on Monday morning.

That weekend Karl read the details over and over. The first two were a little off the beaten track, and although that was nice and quiet for clients, the opportunity for passing trade was virtually non-existent, and the rooms appeared a little small. The third property was on the High Street, above a parade of smartly maintained Victorian shops, each sporting hanging baskets or window boxes and tidy frontages. It was a converted two-bedroom flat, and the room dimensions on this one were huge in comparison. Consequently, the rent was a third more than the other two, but the location was perfect. He had a good feeling about it and decided that he would ask if it could be viewed first.

Paul Calderwood, the estate agent's representative, grabbed the keys and set off with Karl to begin the viewings. Arriving at the first property, Karl realised that the entrance was quite literally a door to a staircase at the side of a newsagents and convenience store. It didn't put him off, as the advertising potential was superb.

As Karl followed Calderwood up the stairs, he was impressed with the level of decoration. At the top, it opened up into a large reception area with high ceilings, which must have been the living room before it was converted.

'As you can see, it wouldn't take much to get up and running,' said Calderwood. 'The level of décor is the same throughout, and the phone lines are all in place; it's just a matter of furnishing.'

Karl could feel his excitement rising; he knew he had been right having a good feeling for the place.

Calderwood opened the door at the far side of the room. 'This is the main office.'

Karl walked through the door and looked around. In his mind's eye, he could see his desk and, at the far side, a treatment couch. Perfect. They continued through the property, and as they moved from room to room, Karl became more certain. It had a small but well-equipped kitchen, a lavatory with hand basin, and a further but smaller office that would have been a second bedroom. They returned to the reception area.

'I'll take it,' said Karl.

'But Mr Hennessey, don't you want to look at the other properties before you make your decision?'

'No, this is exactly what I want.'

Calderwood was a little surprised by Karl's instant decision, but he seemed adamant. 'If you're absolutely sure, Mr Hennessey, we can go back to the office and fill out all the necessary paperwork straight away.'

Karl agreed, his eyes still scrutinising every part of what he hoped would be a successful business venture.

Within days, Karl was ordering office furniture and making all the necessary arrangements. The plan was to be open for business in two weeks. After contacting a local signwriter for that professional little touch, he had the task of deciding what the business would be called. He had a few ideas but one in particular stood out – TROUBLED MINDS; it was certainly to the point. The signwriter and furniture would arrive on Friday, and the phone would be connected by the weekend. The last and probably the most important thing he had to do was to place adverts in the local newspapers.

Wanting to keep to his word to Charlie about not having to do a thing, Karl told him that when everything was in place, he could come over and see the office. That Friday morning, the signwriter arrived as planned. It was not cheap, but the sign looked professional and made a real statement. The office furniture was first class, as was the therapy couch that Karl had found from an online supplier. The phone was connected, and all he needed now were blinds on the windows, bookcases for the extensive collection of books he had acquired over the years, and a few of Susie's feminine touches to soften the place down a little. Adverts had been placed in three local newspapers; one was a daily, the others weekly. He planned to run them for a month and see what the response was like.

By Saturday morning, Charlie and Susie could wait no longer. The suspense was killing them, so Karl agreed that after breakfast he would take them over for the grand unveiling of the practice. They pulled up in Susie's car, and Karl pointed up towards the office. 'That's it there, come on; I have a little surprise for you.'

Standing at the main door, Susie read out the sign-written company name: 'Troubled Minds; I like it!'

'Catchy, bro, catchy,' added Charlie. Karl told him to carry on reading. 'Psychological Evaluations & Management. Company Directors: Charles Hennessey and Karl Hennessey, BSc Honours Psychology. You can't put my name on there, bro.'

'Why not? You're a company director.'

Charlie shook his head, doing his best to contain a pleased grin.

'Well, I think it's great Karl,' said Susie. 'Now, let's go up; come on, come on.'

Karl got out his keys and Susie anxiously tapped his back with both hands. 'OK, I'm going as fast as I can.'

They went up to the reception area, where Charlie and Susie looked around, both gobsmacked.

'Very nice, bro, it looks almost professional.'

'What you mean *almost*?'

'I'm only joking; I never expected it to be this good.'

'Me neither,' said Susie.

'Come on,' said Karl, pleased with the effect his hard work was having on them. 'I'll show you around.'

The more he showed them, the more impressed they were. Susie had a few ideas that would make Karl's office and the treatment area a little more relaxing, which he took on board. Finally, he asked them to wait in his office. He went into the kitchen and came back with three glasses and a bottle of champagne. 'I know it's a bit early in the morning, but I thought, for good luck.'

'Couldn't agree more, bro.'

Karl popped the bottle and poured the sparkling, pale gold liquid, hoping that this was a sign of things to come. After handing them each a glass, Karl raised his in the air and said, 'To a successful business, Troubled Minds.' The three glasses chinked together.

'Troubled Minds,' said Charlie and Susie in unison.

23

Deception

Emily Stone sat at the breakfast bar sipping a cup of strong, black coffee. Dressed in a bathrobe, her long, flame-red hair was wrapped tightly in a towel. Attentively, she read through the local newspaper. Since finishing university eighteen months previously, she had tried to make it in the world of freelance journalism. It was a hard way to make a living, constantly chasing the next story. She kept her fingers crossed that in the not too distant future, she would get the story that would put her on the map and give her that much-needed break.

Coming towards the end of the paper, she noticed one advert in particular that stood out. In bold letters, it said 'TROUBLED MINDS, Specialists in Psychological Trauma'. It gave a long list of problems that could be managed, from sleeping difficulties to post-traumatic stress. The bottom line read 'Guaranteed results'.

'Damned rip-off merchants,' she said out loud. If there was one thing that really riled her, it was people who exploited others when they were at their most vulnerable. She knew only too well about stress, having lost both of her parents to cancer in less than five years. Being an only child, she had been left to cope virtually alone, and could have easily fallen into that kind of con artist's trap. The area of expertise they claimed to be specialists in was poorly governed; almost anyone could set up in this line of business, and if challenged, they could simply say that they counselled their clients.

Always on the look out for a good story, her mind rushed into action; the public needed to be aware of this kind of exploitation. A little undercover work could generate a good story. She reached over to her handbag, took out her mobile and dialled the number on the advert.

Karl and Charlie were both in the office. It had been almost a week since they opened for business, and they still hadn't got a single client through the door. As the phone rang out, they both stopped what they were doing and stared at it, then looked at each other. Breaking the silence Charlie said, 'Go on then, before they change their mind.' Karl dashed around the desk and picked up the phone. 'Good morning, Troubled Minds, how can I help you?'

'Hi, my name's Miss Stone, Emily Stone. I was recently bereaved and have been having some problems. I saw your advert and wondered if you could help.'

Karl put a thumb up to Charlie, who squeezed both fists. 'Yes,' he said, under his breath.

'I'm sure Mr Hennessey can help you, Emily.' He tried to sound as professional as possible. 'Would you like to make an appointment?' The caller asked him to explain the costs. 'Certainly,' replied Karl, 'your initial consultation is fifty pounds, but that does include your first treatment session. Any further sessions are thirty pounds each.'

Holding the phone away from her face, she put her hand over the receiver and shook her head. 'Robbing bastards.' Putting the phone back to her mouth, 'That will be fine; could I make an appointment?'

'Certainly;' said Karl 'let me just check the diary.' Karl put the phone down and flicked through an empty diary. Again, he picked up the receiver and asked how quickly she would like the appointment.

'As soon as possible, really,' replied Emily.

'Umm, I have a cancellation at 2 pm today.'

'That would be perfect,' said Emily enthusiastically. 'I have your address, so I'll see you then. Goodbye.'

Karl put the receiver down and looked up at Charlie with a smile on his face. 'We're in business.'

Karl spent the rest of the morning moving things around the office for no apparent reason. Charlie turned over the covers on a few magazines and tried to give the waiting area the feel that it was frequently used. Karl knew how much was riding on this client; he had to be professional and confident. Once the client saw what he could do, his gift would sell itself.

Twenty minutes before the client was due to arrive, Karl was in his office waiting for the intercom to bleep. Understandably, he was nervous. Charlie sat behind the reception desk, a fictitious list of client appointments in front of him. He had arranged that Susie would ring the practice every five minutes or so from a quarter to two, the plan being to make the client think that they were busy.

Emily Stone parked her much-loved, beaten-up, old Volkswagen Beetle across the road from Karl's practice and glanced up at the windows. 'Here we go then,' she said to herself. Locking the car, she dodged across the road, narrowly being missed by the oncoming traffic. She read the sign on the main entrance door. It all looked very professional, but these con men's attention to detail usually was.

Taking hold of the handrail, she uneasily climbed the staircase to the reception area. Before reaching the top, she heard the phone ringing; Susie's timing had been perfect. Charlie turned the pages of the diary, pretending to make an appointment. 'Certainly, madam, 2.30 pm on Monday afternoon; I look forward to seeing you. Goodbye.'

Charlie looked up from his diary and smiled. 'Good afternoon . . .' briefly glancing back at his diary he said, 'Miss Stone?' Emily nodded in acknowledgement. 'If you would like to take a seat, I'll let Mr Hennessey know you have arrived.' Emily thanked him and sat down while Charlie went over to Karl's office and knocked the door.

'Come in,' called Karl, Charlie went inside, closing the door behind him. 'She's here, bro.'

'OK,' said Karl, nervously moving a few things around on his desk. Then he took a deep breath. 'Right then, here we go, show her in.'

Charlie opened the door and stepped back into the reception. 'Mr Hennessey will see you now, Miss Stone.'

Looking up from a magazine, Emily smiled and placed it back on the pile. She stood up, straightened her skirt and walked over towards the office, where Charlie, holding the door open, ushered her inside. She glanced at Karl, then around the office; it all seemed very thoughtfully set out and surprisingly tranquil. The combination of office and treatment room had been well designed. Looking back at Karl, she had a problem trying to work out his age. Although very young in the face, his now greying temples made it difficult to determine his years.

Karl stood, walked round to the front of the desk and offered her his hand. 'Miss Stone, very pleased to meet you.' His eyes conveyed a welcoming smile. 'Please take a seat.'

Emily sat down, placing her bag on the floor beside her. Karl opened his note pad and wrote her name at the top of the page. 'Well, Miss Stone, how I can help you?' Considering that it was Karl's first client, he remained remarkably relaxed and professional.

Emily had concocted a story of difficulty in getting off to sleep and vivid dreams concerning her parents' funerals, with friends accusing her of not doing enough for them during the last few months of their lives. In reality, the story was not that far from the truth. Her parents had both died alone. First it was her father, tragically passing away in a hospital bed before she or her mother could get there. Then, all too soon, it was her mother. Not being able to say goodbye had truly haunted her, and the pain she felt was revealed in an expression that passed fleetingly over her face.

Karl noticed it instantly. He had seen the same reaction with Charlie in the weeks following their father's death, interspersed with mood swings, self-accusation and increased anger. If only he could have said goodbye: it just might have eased his mind.

As Emily spoke of her parents, Karl thought that if he could interact with her, he might just be able to reconstruct those last moments when she arrived at the hospital, too late to see her father alive, and guide events within her dream so that she might get some comfort. Karl had positioned a clock on the wall behind where his clients would sit, so that he could glance at it to assess how far through the consultation time they were, without making the clients feel uncomfortable. He could see that it was helping Emily to talk about her parents and let her continue.

Eventually, she stopped and sat quietly. She couldn't believe how good it had felt to talk about her parents' deaths; it was something she had bottled up for such a long time, and she was now feeling calmer. Then, she mentally shook herself, telling herself to be on guard and remember that she was doing undercover research.

'Miss Stone,' said Karl, leaning forwards,

'Oh, Emily, please,' she interrupted him.

'I think I can help you. I use a method that is quite unique, it involves dream interaction.'

Emily thought for a moment. 'You mean that when I sleep you use suggestive statements, aiming to get them into my subconscious?'

'It's a little bit more involved than that,' said Karl. 'All I ask is that you allow me to touch your hand when you're sleeping.'

She almost laughed out loud and asked him if he thought she was stupid, but contained herself.

'The question is,' Karl continued, 'where would you like to undergo the treatment? I appreciate you are having problems sleeping, so here may not be a good environment. It's really up to the client; I can do house visits if that would help.'

She could hardly believe her ears; if only she had recorded this! 'Do you mind if I think about it for a day or so?'

'Not at all,' said Karl, 'but I promise you, you'll be amazed with the treatment.'

Yes, she thought, I'm sure I will. Sceptically, she looked at Karl. He was good. If he was a con man, he certainly sounded very sincere, and she could imagine people being easily taken in. Karl took a business card from the corner of his desk and handed it to her. 'Remember, your first treatment is included in the price of this consultation. Whenever you decide the time is right, call me.'

Karl stood up and extended his hand, which she reciprocated.

'Thank you, Mr Hennessey.'

'You're welcome;' said Karl, 'I hope to see you again soon.'

Closing the door behind her, she took out her chequebook and asked Charlie, who was trying to look busy at the reception desk, who she should make the cheque out to. That put him on the spot; it was so simple, but he hadn't thought of it.

'Err, Mr K Hennessey, please. Will you be making a further appointment?'

'I'll give you a call,' said Emily, tearing the cheque from its stub.

'Goodbye, Miss Stone,' he replied, as she went down the stairs, but she was so deep in thought she didn't hear him.

As soon as he heard the door close, Charlie jumped up and dashed into Karl's office. 'Well?' he asked, excitedly.

Karl looked up from his notes. 'Well what?'

Charlie shook his head. 'How did it go?'

'Pretty good,' said Karl.

'But she didn't book another appointment.' Charlie was becoming irritated. 'In fact, she didn't even say goodbye, but she paid the full fifty pounds.'

Karl looked back at his notes, 'Don't worry, I have a feeling we are going to hear from Miss Stone again.'

That evening, Emily Stone was lying on her living room sofa; between her fingers she held Karl's business card. After meeting Karl, her determination to expose him as a fraudster had diminished. She didn't think for one moment that what he said he could do was genuine, but at the same time, she couldn't see him as an outright con man, purely trying to exploit sick and needy people. But on the other hand, with her journalist's hat on, a story was a story. First thing in the morning, she would make an appointment and see where this treatment would lead.

After breakfast, she phoned Karl's office. Charlie took the call, and they arranged an appointment for the following Friday at Karl's office; the idea of inviting a complete stranger into her home and then going to sleep didn't appeal to her. Karl had requested that she bring a picture of her parents. Emily thought it strange but agreed.

For Karl and Charlie, the rest of the week was quiet, with not so much as a phone call. Karl had some leaflets printed in an attempt to pull in some business, and Charlie had reluctantly trudged from door to door for two days posting them through letterboxes. Karl filled his time investigating relaxation CDs, realising that it would be difficult to get clients to sleep and dream in his treatment room. He found several aimed at people who felt stressed, proposing something similar to a form of self-hypnosis, with calming music and underlying suggestions that the listener should feel relaxed, trouble-free and able to slip into a beneficial period of sleep at any convenient time of day. He would try out one that seemed promising on Emily.

On Friday morning Emily arrived at 10:50 am, ten minutes before her appointment. Uneasily, she sat in the reception area, flicking through a magazine but reading nothing. Karl came out of his office, followed by Susie, who, very craftily, had been asked to come over half an hour before Emily's appointment to give the appearance of being the previous client. As they walked over to the desk, Emily looked up from her magazine.
'I'll see you at the same time next week, Miss Slater,' said Karl, smiling at Susie.
'Thank you again, Mr Hennessey; I'll look forward to it,' she replied.
Karl looked over at Emily. 'Ah, Miss Stone, would you like to come through?' Emily smiled, put down her magazine and went into Karl's office.
As Karl closed the door behind him, Susie gave Charlie a thumbs up and whispered, 'See you tonight,' before quickly making her exit.
Karl dimmed the lights slightly to relax his client, 'Did you remember to bring the photograph of your parents, Emily?'
Opening her handbag, she pulled out a small, framed picture. 'This was taken before my father was taken ill. He lost a lot of weight towards the end of his illness.' Her mood seemed very solemn. 'I like to remember him this way.' She forced a smile and passed it to him.
The image was of two people, taken from around the waist upwards: a tall, strong-looking man with thick, grey hair, his right arm around the shoulders of a smaller woman, presumably Emily's mother, with sunglasses perched on top of her head. The man was smiling, his dark eyes looking directly towards the camera. The woman was smiling too, with her chin tilted up towards the man's face. From what Karl could see of the background buildings, it was probably a holiday photograph. He looked at the faces for a few moments.
'I think you feel that your father resented you not being there at the end.'

Emily stared straight at Karl. He had obviously hit a very sore point, and their eye contact held a little too long for comfort.

'Shall we start?' asked Karl. He directed her to the treatment couch, where she slipped off her shoes and lay down. 'OK, Emily, I want you to try to clear your mind of everything other than your parents, just close your eyes and relax.'

Karl went over to the CD player and switched it on. The sound of soft music and a gently flowing stream enveloped her. Fortunately for Karl, she had slept badly the previous night, thinking about the appointment so, hopefully, all would go to plan.

'Just relax and let your shoulders melt into the couch. I'm going to leave you alone for five minutes. You are completely safe. Think of your parents, then listen to the voice on the CD.'

Emily was amazed just how relaxed she felt lying on the couch; it was so comfortable. As Karl left the room, she stretched out her legs. The restless night, the music and the gentle yet compelling voice on the CD somehow overcame her, and she drifted off to sleep.

Karl waited in reception for five minutes. The CD should have done its work; if she hadn't fallen asleep by then, it wasn't going to happen. Very quietly, Karl went back into the room; Emily was sound asleep. In absolute silence, Karl sat down on a chair he had positioned at the side of the couch. As gently as he could, he placed his hand on the back of Emily's and closed his eyes.

Karl found himself in what looked like a large, old barn. Above him in the hayloft, he could hear the sound of a child's voice. Again he closed his eyes and instantly reappeared in the loft. Choosing whether or not to be seen was a trick he had developed some years ago tormenting Billy and Jerald at school.

A young girl of nine, maybe ten years of age, was crouched on the floor. In her hand, was a small kitten, and at least three others huddled together in a cardboard box behind her. The kittens' mother, a large black cat, lay on her side in the hay barely moving, her breathing desperately shallow. By the size of the kittens, they couldn't have been any more than a few days old. 'Em,' came a voice from below, 'you up there?' Karl looked over the edge, straight away recognising Emily's father, albeit considerably younger than in the photograph he had seen.

'I'm up here, Dad,' Emily called out.

Her father climbed up the ladder, smiling as he put his head over the top. 'I've told you not to come up here on your own; it's too dangerous, you could fall.'

'But, Dad, it's Sooty; she's had her kittens.'

He climbed up and stroked the big cat. 'She don't look good, Em; we have to get her into the house or she won't survive, and if she doesn't, they won't.' Emily looked shocked. 'Come on, help me get Sooty in the box with the kittens. I'll go down first with the box, you follow me and hold tight.'

Emily's father backed onto the ladder, the box laden with cats firmly held under his free arm. It was a good fifteen feet down the ladder. Precariously, he struggled to hold on tight to the box. Emily climbed onto the ladder above him, more concerned for the cat's safety than her own. Suddenly, both her feet slipped off the rung and crashed down onto the one hand her father was using to hold onto the ladder with. He cried out, and his immediate reaction was to pull his hand away. It was almost like watching in slow motion; he cascaded backwards, the box containing the cats still secured under his arm, his other hand searching for anything to grab hold of.

Emily woke with a start, and almost simultaneously Karl opened his eyes. She glanced around the room and back to Karl whose hand was still on hers; a little surprised, she pulled it away.

'Are you all right?' he asked. 'You were dreaming. Would you like some water?'

Now completely awake, Emily sat up. 'No, I'm fine thanks.'

'Was he badly hurt?' asked Karl inquisitively.

She gave him a puzzled look. 'Was who badly hurt?'

'Why, your father of course.'

There was a confused, almost panic-stricken look in her eyes. 'How could you know that?' Her breathing became rapid.

'Please don't be frightened; just try to relax. I told you my methods were somewhat, shall we say, unique.'

She was dumbstruck. 'Are you telling me you saw my dream?'

'More than that, Emily, I was there. I just chose for you not to see me.'

Standing up, she walked around the room, her hands rubbing the sides of her head, wondering if she was still dreaming, unable to comprehend what was happening.

'Just wait a minute,' she said, 'what was my cat's name?'

'Sooty,' Karl replied. 'She had four kittens. Tell me, did they all survive the fall?'

Emily's jaw dropped open. 'You couldn't have possibly known that.'

'Of course not,' said Karl. 'I told you, I was there.'

Emily stared back still in disbelief. Maybe he had used some form of hypnosis to make her talk in her sleep? For now, it was the only explanation she had. Breaking what looked like a very thoughtful stare,

Karl said, 'I think if we are to delve deeper into your subconscious, we need to have you in a deeper sleep.'

Uncomfortable with the idea of having a complete stranger watching over her as she slept, and not understanding what had been going on, she shook her head. 'No, no, I'm not sure about all this.'

Karl interrupted her, 'Why don't you ask a friend to sit in on the session? Then you could have the treatment in the privacy of your own home and a friend to ensure everything was OK.'

Emily thought about it for a moment. Her friend Siobhan would jump at the chance to get involved, especially as she was a freelance journalist herself. 'OK,' she said, 'but I want my friend to sit in on the entire session.'

'That's completely fine with me.' said Karl. 'Give me a call, and when it's mutually suitable, we'll continue your treatment at your home.'

Karl was pleased with the outcome of the session. The first treatment was never intended to put everything right. It was more like a form of reconnaissance; once he was familiar with the client, he would gain their trust, and then he could help them.

Emily wasted no time contacting her friend, and when she explained what Karl claimed to be able to do, Siobhan, equally intrigued, couldn't wait to meet him. The appointment was made for the following Friday evening. Karl jotted down Emily's address and told her he would arrive just after 10 pm. Susie said she knew the area and would drop him off.

Friday evening arrived, bringing with it the most horrendous thunderstorm. Karl was sitting in the back of Susie's car behind Charlie, who had come along for the ride. The rain was so heavy that, combined with the darkness, it was difficult to see out of the windows, let alone see the numbers on the doors.

'Did you say 63A, bro?' asked Charlie, squinting his eyes to see the numbers.

Karl opened out a piece of paper. 'Yes, 63A Sutton Approach.'

'Well, this is Sutton Approach,' said Susie, a little too close to the window screen.

'Ah, here we go, 47, 49 . . .' Susie slowed down. 'Keep going, keep going,' said Charlie, 'and stop.' Susie pulled up. 'That's it, bro,' Charlie pointed into the darkness; 'Good luck.' Charlie got out of the car and tipped the seat forwards for Karl to get out.

'I'll get a cab back later,' said Karl. 'Thanks for the lift.'

Charlie jumped back into the car. Karl pulled his jacket over his head and dashed towards the door. Noticing there were two flats, he pressed the intercom buzzer for 63A. Emily and her friend Siobhan were relaxing with a glass of wine and, of course, contemplating what the rest of the evening would bring. Hearing the buzzer, the two looked at each other for a moment; then Emily went to the intercom.

'Hello?'

Karl put his mouth closer to the speaker. 'Emily? It's Karl Hennessey.'

'Come on up.'

The buzzer sounded, releasing the door catch. Holding the door open, Karl waved back to Charlie and Susie. As they drove off, he closed the door and went up the stairs. At the top of the stairs were two doors, one slightly open. Assuming it to be Emily's flat, Karl gently knocked and pushed the door. Suddenly, the door was pulled open.

'Karl, you found us then?'

'Yes, the weather didn't help though; it's throwing it down out there.' They shook hands.

'Come on in and get that coat off; can I get you a drink?'

'Tea would be nice.'

'You go on in; I'll put the kettle on.'

As Karl went into the lounge, his eyes were drawn to the young woman sitting on the sofa. In her mid twenties, she had a very slender physique and shoulder-length blond hair. Karl stared a little longer than he should have, thinking how attractive she was.

'You must be Karl,' she said. 'Siobhan Tighe.'

'Pleased to meet you, Siobhan.' She stood up and they shook hands.

Emily came in with tea for Karl.

'Oh, you've introduced yourselves. Siobhan and I were at uni together. Sure you don't want something a little stronger to drink, Karl?' Karl refused, adding that he didn't drink.

'I've told Siobhan about your treatment method,' said Emily.

Siobhan sat back down and picked up her glass of wine. 'Yes, when Em told me I was intrigued. How did you learn to do it?' She looked at him steadily, asking more questions about his work, and, without giving away any details, he was able to say that he had a successful track record of helping people with his unique method. He felt as if he was being interviewed, but he didn't mind. Later that evening, any doubts Emily had would be put to rest.

Just before midnight, Karl suggested that Emily should go to bed and try to sleep. It would not be easy to sleep in such an unusual situation, so Karl had brought along a copy of the relaxation CD that had worked well for her at his office. Leaving Karl and Siobhan still chatting, Emily went to bed. She put the CD into the combined radio/alarm/CD player at the side of the bed, turned off the lamp and lay back, trying to relax and think of her parents, as Karl had asked her to.

Karl explained to Siobhan what he would do once Emily was in a deep sleep. Nothing was guaranteed with this type of treatment, and, to a certain degree, Karl relied on his clients to guide him to the right area of their subconscious. It was still not completely clear to Siobhan, but one thing was for certain, she would not leave him alone with her friend.

A good hour or so later, Karl and Siobhan tip-toed into Emily's room; she was fast asleep. Karl pointed to a stool by the dressing table, and, anxiously, Siobhan sat on it, clasping her hands together on her knees. Emily was lying on her back with one arm on top of the quilt, the other raised onto the pillow above her head, almost as if waving. Karl knelt down at the side of the bed and gently placed a hand on top of hers. He closed his eyes.

Karl found himself in what looked like a hospital corridor. Coming towards him with tears rolling down her face was Emily. Recognising him she stopped, a look of shock on her face: 'It can't be you.'

'Never mind about that; listen to me, your father's not here.' She suddenly turned to run back down the corridor. 'Wait, Emily,' he said firmly. 'There's no time; hold my hands and close your eyes.'

Previously, this dream had always ended the same way. She would run through corridor after corridor trying to find her father, only to be told by the medical staff that she was too late. She had to trust Karl.

Karl held out his hands and she took hold of them. He focused on the image held in his head of Emily's father, smiling in the photograph. Just as if she had blinked, she was in another room. Her father was sitting up in bed, and although he looked very weak, his eyes were open. As soon as he saw her, he smiled. Emily couldn't contain herself. Overcome with emotion, she ran to his bedside. They held each other, and he summoned all his strength to raise his frail arms so that he could touch her face and hair.

'Don't cry, darling,' he whispered. 'It's my time. Look after your mother for me, and tell her I love her.'

'I love you, Dad,' said Emily through her tears.

'I know, darling, I know.' He kissed her forehead and again hugged her.

Karl stood by the door; although it was very sad, he was pleased to see her achieving some form of closure. The old man took his last breath and died in his daughter's arms. Feeling his grip weaken, she buried her head into his shoulder and cried.

Some time later, Karl placed a hand on her shoulder. 'He loved you very much.'

Releasing her father, she turned to Karl and thanked him. Karl turned and left the room. Once in the corridor, he closed his eyes and was instantly back in Emily's room, kneeling next to her bed. Siobhan was staring at him. He tried to stand, but his entire body felt weak. Taking a deep breath, he pushed himself up off the side of the bed.

'Are you all right, Karl?'

'I will be; it takes a lot out of me.'

Siobhan looked confused. 'What does?'

Karl smiled; as far as Siobhan was concerned, all he had done was kneel at the side of Emily's bed.

'Come on,' said Karl, 'she needs to sleep.'

As they left the room, Siobhan shook her head. 'Well, are you going to do anything?'

'If you don't mind, Siobhan, I'm going to get some fresh air. Tell Emily I'll give her a call.' He picked up his coat and went towards the door.

'That's it, then; that's the treatment?'

Karl knew she wouldn't understand, nobody could unless they experienced it. 'I'll see myself out.'

'What a joker,' said Siobhan, shaking her head.

Karl stood outside with a pounding head. The rain had eased. He took a deep breath of the cool, damp air; this one had really taken it out of him. He walked down towards the High Street, where he knew there was an all-night taxi office. The fresh air started to clear his head a little, and, although completely exhausted, he was pleased it had all gone to plan.

Emily woke suddenly. The room was in darkness, and all around was in silence. Her dream flooded back to her. Did that really happen? With a surge of emotion, she got out of bed, slipped on her dressing gown and went to find Siobhan. Siobhan was asleep in an armchair, an empty glass of wine on her lap. Emily knelt down by her side and gently shook her arm.

'Siobhan, wake up.'

Slowly, her eyes opened. 'I must have nodded off.'

'Where's Karl?'

'He said he needed some fresh air.' Siobhan stretched her arms. 'What a joker. He knelt at the side of your bed holding your hand for a few minutes, never did a thing, never even spoke, then he gets up and says he's tired and needs some fresh air and leaves. Freaky or what?'

Emily lowered her head and, placing a hand over her eyes, she began to cry.

'My God, what's wrong?' asked Siobhan, sitting up to comfort her friend.

Struggling to control her emotions, Emily looked straight into Siobhan's eyes. 'He was there; he was in my dream, he controlled it. Siobhan, he made it possible for me to say goodbye to my dad. My God, Siobhan, he was actually in my head.'

Emily couldn't control herself any longer. Over the years, she had hidden her emotions over her father's death, and now the guilt and remorse of not arriving at the hospital on time was suddenly lifting from her conscience. With both hands on her face, Emily sobbed. Siobhan could only look on; the thought of what her friend had just experienced sent a chill down her spine.

24

Recognition

The previous evening, Karl had walked and walked. How far he didn't know, but his head had felt as if it was going to explode. After about an hour, maybe two, he wasn't sure, he flagged down a taxi. As he lay in bed the next morning, he tried to figure out what had caused the headache. All he could think of was that he had virtually produced an entire dream and placed it into Emily's subconscious. Normally, he would just interact with other people's thoughts, but on this occasion, they were all his; he just allowed her to be part of it.

He went downstairs and put the kettle on. It was only eight o'clock, but he liked to be in the office by nine just in case there were any calls. When Karl heard the sound of Charlie coming down the stairs, he shouted out to him, 'Tea or coffee?'

'Tea, please,' came the reply. 'Oh, and toast.'

Cheeky sod, thought Karl.

Charlie came into the kitchen and suddenly stopped, staring at Karl. 'Jesus Christ, bro,' he said, 'what's happened to you?'

'What do you mean?' asked Karl, intrigued by his brother's expression.

'Have you looked in the mirror today?' Charlie grinned.

A little disturbed by the statement, Karl quickly went into the living room and looked in the mirror. He couldn't believe what he was seeing. Since leaving school, he had let his hair grow a little longer. But what had previously been a light touch of grey hair on his temples had dramatically spread overnight, so that now it completely covered the sides of his head. As he scrutinised his image in the mirror he thought, what the hell is happening to me?

Karl arrived at the office promptly at 9 am, as usual. Charlie had arranged to go into town with Susie and would be in later. Karl sat at his desk with Emily Stone's case folder in front of him. He needed to write down as many details about the dream as possible, while it was still fresh in his mind, right down to his own headache. Hearing the door open in the main reception room, he closed the folder and got up from his desk. He was half way across the room when he heard a gentle tap and the door opened. Standing in front of him looking very relaxed, but at he same time a little sheepish, was Emily Stone.

'Hello, Karl,' she smiled. 'I have an apology to make.'

Closing the door behind her, they both sat down. Emily confessed to being a journalist and explained that her ulterior motive had been to expose Karl as a fraud. The events of the previous evening had changed all of that. Feeling very embarrassed by her behaviour and attempting to regain a little self-respect, she asked if she could write an article on him. Working on the principle that all publicity is good publicity, Karl agreed, thinking that he had nothing to lose; it might just bring in some business.

Not wanting to give Karl time to change his mind, Emily pulled out a note pad and began asking questions: where he had grown up, how he had acquired his gift and, more importantly, how he had kept it quiet for so long. Finally, she took a few photographs of Karl at his desk. Just before leaving, she plucked up the courage to ask what had happened to his hair. Unfortunately, that was one question he couldn't answer.

Charlie and Susie arrived at the office to find Karl sitting alone in the reception, almost willing the phone to ring. He told them about Emily's pending article, and they both agreed it might be helpful. For now, all they could do was continue placing the ads and wait for the phone to ring.

But it was another quiet week in the office, and the only calls were from Emily verifying one or two points in her article. She told Karl that the article would be in three local papers, and she was working on the editor of a local monthly magazine to get a centre spread on him. Karl had paid out another five hundred pounds in advertising for the coming week. He didn't say anything to Charlie, but he was beginning to feel a little despondent.

The weekend again came and went, and at 9 am on Monday morning, Karl once again unlocked the door to the office. He was about to take off his jacket when the phone rang.

'Troubled Minds, can I help you?'

'Hi, Karl, it's Emily. Did you see the papers at the weekend?' She sounded very excited.

'Sorry, Emily, I haven't'

'Do you have clients this morning?'

'Let me just check.' He paused, not even bothering opening the diary. 'No, I'm clear till lunchtime.'

'I'll be round in an hour.' With that she hung up.

'Who was that?' asked Charlie, appearing at the top of the stairs.

'Emily,' Karl replied. 'She wanted to know if we'd seen the papers over the weekend. I think the article was in, and she said she'd drop in later.'

The phone rang again. 'Hi Emily,' he said, trying to be clever. It was a woman's voice but not Emily's.

'Hello, is that Troubled Minds?'

Karl raised his eyes towards Charlie and took a deep breath. 'Oh, I am sorry; I was expecting it to be someone else. Yes, this is Troubled Minds; can I help you?'

'I hope so. I'd like to speak to Mr Hennessey, if possible.'

At last, they had a breakthrough. The woman had seen the article in the paper and contacted them straight away. Eileen Lynam began to explain that, for the last twenty years of their thirty-five-year marriage, her husband had suffered from night terrors, a condition that Karl had read about some years ago. Nightmares usually happen during the dream phase of sleep known as REM, but night terrors occur before deep sleep, usually within an hour of the subject going to sleep.

Their lives had been blighted by the impact of lack of sleep and fear. They had spent year after year being referred from one specialist to another with no progress, and their doctor could do nothing more. Now, completely at her wits' end, she thought that just maybe Karl might be able to help. Karl said that he couldn't promise to be successful, but was willing to try and help. A consultation was arranged for her husband the following day.

By the time Emily arrived just after eleven o'clock, they had already received five calls, all resulting in appointments; things were really looking up. Leaving Charlie manning the phone, they went into Karl's office. 'I don't know what you wrote, Emily, but it has had one hell of an impact on my client base.'

'I just told the truth, Karl. It was an amazing experience; here, look.' She opened the papers to the pages with her articles, each one a good half page long. Karl smiled at seeing his photograph in print. As he read the columns, he realised just how amazing his gift would sound to a member of the public, especially a desperate one looking for a lifeline.

When Emily left, Charlie waited until he heard the outer door close and then rushed into Karl's office. 'We've got eight appointments now this week!' said Charlie. 'Any more and we'll have to book them in for next week.'

'Excellent!' said Karl rubbing his hands together. 'Here, look at these articles.'

Charlie looked concerned. 'Have you thought about this, bro?'

'Yes, it's great,' said Karl, still preoccupied with his picture in the paper.

'No;' replied Charlie, 'look what happened to you after Emily's appointment.'

Karl looked up from the paper. 'I've thought about that, and I'm almost sure I know what I did wrong. I won't take on so much with the next client.'

Charlie didn't say anything more, but he knew that Karl would do everything in his power to help his clients, and it worried him.

All evening Karl searched the Internet, trying to absorb as much information as possible about night terrors. It seemed that nobody really knew what caused them. Some doctors claimed they were brought on by eating large meals before going to bed, others reported that being overly tired increased their frequency, and some attributed them to stress. This case was particularly interesting for Karl as he was about to discover what happens in the subconscious before people dream.

Eileen and Howard Lynam waited to be called in for their appointment. Lynam, a rotund man of fifty-five, was constantly being warned by his doctor that he must lose weight. He strained his eyes to read the labels on his latest prescribed medication. Since taking early retirement four years previously, the only exercise he took was during his night terrors, when he would move around his bedroom, sometimes at great speed, shouting and swinging his arms as if trying to avoid capture from someone or something. He would wake up with no memory of the event, but sometimes would have injured himself, and was only too aware that he could easily injure his wife without knowing it. He was afraid to sleep and was distressed at how it affected her.

Eileen was a very petite lady and, considering the stress she had been under for the last twenty years, time had been kind to her. But things had reached the stage where sleeping in the same room as her husband was not an option.

As Karl opened his office door they both looked up, 'Mr and Mrs Lynam?' They stood up, shook hands with Karl and he ushered them into his office. Karl noticed they both had a very weary look about them, clearly both in need of a good holiday.

Rounding his desk Karl sat with the couple, putting them at ease as best he could. Eventually, he opened his note pad. 'Mr Lynam, when you experience night terrors, are you able to recall what happens?'

'Nothing,' said Lynam, shaking his head. Karl scribbled a few brief notes.

'He doesn't even remember getting out of bed, Mr Hennessey,' interrupted Eileen.

'I see,' nodded Karl as he continued writing. Karl dotted his pad and looked up. 'I take it your doctor has prescribed medication?'

Lynam opened a carrier bag he had been keeping very close to his chest. In it were four empty plastic bottles. 'I've tried a few over the years.' He handed the bottles to Karl, who examined the labels and again made notes on his pad.

'How long have you been taking these, Mr Lynam?' said Karl

'Over ten years;' Lynam wearily replied, 'probably closer to fifteen.' Again Karl noted it.

'As I've said, my methods are a lot more hands on, and I don't mind saying your condition is a first for me, so it could take a little longer than usual to find out what we're up against.'

The couple nodded in unison. 'Whatever you say, Doctor.'

'I'm not a doctor, Mrs Lynam, more of a specialist.'

'Oh, sorry,' said Eileen, looking a little embarrassed.

'Please, don't apologise,' said Karl trying to reassure her. 'If possible Howard, I'd like to treat you in the comfort of your own home. I find people respond to treatment better that way.' Lynam smiled at his wife, a kind of 'that suits me' expression on his face. 'My receptionist will arrange a mutual time and day; then we can get started as soon as possible. Just one more thing; during the treatment, I'd like you to stop taking your medication; is that all right with you?' Lynam nodded in agreement. Pleased with the consultation, the Lynams arranged for the treatment to begin later that week.

Karl continued seeing clients all week, and each time he asked how they had heard about him, it was from Emily's article. She had turned out to be a real godsend; in fact, it was getting to the point where he had more work than he could cope with, but he wasn't complaining.

On Thursday evening just before 9 pm, Karl arranged for a taxi to take him to the Lynam's house. The cab driver had no problem finding the quaint little housing estate on the outskirts of town, approximately half an hour away. As Karl walked up the drive towards the front door, he noticed the curtains twitch; the couple were anxiously waiting for him. The porch light lit up as he approached the door, and Eileen greeted him, grinning like a Cheshire cat.

'Good evening Mr Hennessey; did you have any trouble finding us?'

'Evening, Mrs Lynam; not at all. I left that to the cab driver.'

Karl followed Eileen inside. Lynam was in the living room, already wearing his dressing gown. As soon as he saw Karl, he jumped to his feet, hand outstretched.

'Would you like a drink, Mr Hennessey?'

Karl accepted and Eileen went off to prepare the coffee, hanging up Karl's overcoat on her way to the kitchen.

'Well, Howard, this will be a little strange at first, but all you have to do is try to go to sleep. Normally, I wouldn't come in till you were fast asleep, but due to your particular condition, I need to be there from the moment you fall asleep.' Lynam gave an understanding nod. 'I've brought along a CD of music that many of my clients find relaxing; it might help you.' Karl indicated to a small CD player he had brought with him. 'Did you refrain from your medication?'

'Yes, the wife said I had a particularly active night last night. All I've got to remember it by are the bruises.' He pulled up the sleeve of his dressing gown to reveal a huge welt of a bruise on his forearm.

Eileen returned with the coffee.

'Howard tells me he had a bit of a lively time last night.'

'Oh, Mr Hennessey, lively is not the word for it.' Eileen shook her head. 'He tried to get out of the window at one stage – that's how he hurt his arm; did he show you?'

'Yes, it looks sore.'

'Then he tried to lock himself in the wardrobe. Nearly an hour this went on for; it doesn't usually last that long.'

'Probably due to not taking his medication,' said Karl. 'Not to worry, we'll see what we can do.'

They chatted for almost an hour, and then Karl suggested that Lynam should try to sleep. It was always going to be difficult due to Karl's presence, but they had to try. Entering Lynam's bedroom, Karl was amazed at how sparsely it was furnished; just a bed, a wardrobe and chest of drawers. There were no lamps or photographs; everything ornamental and unnecessary had been removed, clearly for the couple's safety. As Karl set up the CD player at the side of the bed, Eileen brought in a dining room chair. Lynam, feeling a little embarrassed, slipped of his dressing gown and climbed into bed.

'Now Howard, I just want you to relax, close your eyes and try to go to sleep. I will take care of everything else.'

Lynam awkwardly tried to settle comfortably, and Eileen lowered the lights.

'I'll leave you to it for a little while, Mr Hennessey,' she whispered, then went downstairs.

Around twenty minutes later, tiredness was catching up with Karl, and he felt his head nodding. Suddenly he jumped, wide awake with a start. Looking down, he could see that Lynam was fast asleep. Very gently, he held onto his hand and closed his eyes. Nothing but darkness. Karl opened his eyes and looked again at Lynam; he was definitely asleep. It was strange, just as if his gift had deserted him. He waited a few minutes longer and tried again. This time, as he closed his eyes it was as if they remained open.

In the dream, he was sitting next to Lynam in the bedroom, but Lynam was sitting bolt upright with a look of panic in his eyes as he stared towards the bedroom door.

'Howard, it's me, Karl. I want you to concentrate on what I say.'

Lynam said nothing but continued staring past Karl towards the bedroom door. Karl turned to see what it was that gripped his attention so. Coming from around the edges of the door were shadows, shapes of creatures with grotesque heads, their deformed arms with claw-like hands reaching out and becoming longer and longer. More of them appeared from the back of the wardrobe and around the window, and Karl felt the hairs on the back of his neck stand up.

Lynam started to panic, his breathing becoming heavier and a look in his eyes of total fear. Karl could almost hear Lynam's heart beating in his chest; was this what had haunted his dreams for so many years? The shadows began to engulf the bed like some kind of demonic claw trying to grab at Lynam and drag him into the bowels of hell.

Suddenly, Karl felt a searing pain above his left eye. Clutching his forehead, he opened his eyes he found himself on the floor. The chair he had been sitting on was lying on its side next to him. Lynam was in the corner, his hands covering his face as if trying to blot out what he could see in his mind. Then, without any warning, he dashed across the room to the wardrobe, frantically trying to open an imaginary door on the side of the unit. Glancing over his shoulder, his panic-stricken eyes scanned the room as if he was being chased by the devil himself. With his back against the wall, Lynam edged around the room. Karl got to his feet and backed up to the wall, observing Lynam's every movement. What Karl had seen in Lynam's night terror had frightened him. The poor man was experiencing this almost every night but thankfully, after waking, he had no memory of it.

The bedroom door opened and Eileen peered round. She looked at Karl standing by the wall on the far side of the room, and then, seeing that the bed was empty, she came inside the room to look for Lynam. He was behind the door, frozen in fear.

'Howard, come on dear; it's Eileen. It's all right, get back into bed.'

Like a frightened child, still not focusing on his wife but apparently hearing hear and feeling her reassuring hand on his shoulder, he walked back to his bed. Still scanning the room, he climbed into bed and lay down. She looked at Karl, 'It's not always that easy to get him back to bed.' Turning towards Lynam, they could see that he now looked less troubled. 'He'll sleep now.'

Eileen gently put a hand up to the bruising on Karl's face. 'Come on, Mr Hennessey, let me put something on that eye.'

25

Sweeter dreams

Karl sat at the kitchen table, pressing a bag of frozen peas wrapped in a tea towel against an already swollen eye and cheekbone. Eileen put the kettle on and sat down facing him. 'I'm so sorry, Mr Hennessey; I should have warned you.'

'Don't worry, Mrs Lynam; we'll just put it down as an occupational hazard, and please call me Karl.'

Eileen smiled at Karl's response and friendly attitude. The kettle boiled, and she poured the water into two mugs. Karl put the ice pack down onto the table and blinked his eye a few times. Eileen sat back down placing a mug in front of him.

'Thanks, I need that.' He sipped the piping hot coffee. 'Just before Howard broke my connection with him, I saw into his dream.'

Eileen put her mug down, her attention now firmly fixed on Karl. 'He sees shadows all around him. They come from everywhere: the door, the wardrobe, under the bed.'

Eileen was intrigued. 'What kind of shadows?'

Karl thought for a moment; he didn't want to frighten, her but at the same time, he could tell she was the type of person that would see straight through him if he tried to pacify her with a half-truth.

'If I'm honest,' said Karl hesitating slightly as he watched for a reaction – she remained still – 'demons. That's the best way I can explain it. Not in a solid form, just like shadows trying to catch hold of him. That's why he moves around the room, he's trying to get away from them.'

Although looking a little shocked, Eileen took it very well. 'What can be done?'

'Tell me, Eileen, does Howard have any hobbies?'

'Birds,' she immediately replied.

'Birds?'

Eileen laughed. 'The feathered kind. He's a twitcher. When he took early retirement, he started going for walks round the bird sanctuary, just for a little exercise. Next thing he goes out and gets himself a pair of binoculars. He loves it; it's the only time he really relaxes.'

Karl had an idea. 'Can we make another appointment for next week? There's something I'd like to try.'

The following morning, the Lynams phoned and booked the appointment through Charlie. When Charlie heard how Karl had got his black eye, he jokingly told him he should wear a crash helmet. After thinking about it, with potentially violent clients, it wasn't a bad idea. Karl decided he was going to try something he had never done before. Somehow he had to put a thought into Lynam's mind, so that every time he had the night terrors he would see what Karl had implanted into his mind and not the demons. He couldn't discuss it fully with Lynam, as he was unaware of the content of the dreams when he woke up. Karl had asked Eileen not to tell her husband about the demons, just in case it fuelled his subconscious and increased the intensity and severity of the dream.

On the night of the second appointment, Charlie went along for support and to help out if things became lively. They had come up with the idea of using a Velcro wrist strap to join Karl and Lynam together. This would enable them to hold onto Lynam if he began flailing his arms around and tried to get away, but could be easily released if he became too violent. They arrived at the Lynam's house as arranged, just after 11 pm. Eileen had identified tiredness as being one of the main contributors to her husband's condition, so he had spent the day at the bird sanctuary. The idea was he would get so tired that it would trigger a night terror.

After chatting for a while, Lynam turned in for the night, taking Karl's portable CD player and the relaxation CD with him. They waited for half an hour or so, and then Eileen, as quietly as she could, tip-toed into the bedroom to see if he was asleep. She returned, giving Karl a thumbs up gesture. Karl attached one end of the Velcro strap around his wrist; then he and Charlie quietly went up to the bedroom. Looking through the open door into the dimmed light, they could see Lynam sleeping. Eileen had placed two dining room chairs by the bed.

Karl looked at his brother and whispered, 'If he goes into a night terror, you'll notice him getting restless; that's when I go in.' Charlie acknowledged that he understand with a nod.

Very carefully, Karl passed the other end of the strap under Lynam's wrist and fastened it, joining them both together. If things got out of hand, it was Charlie's job to release the strap. Lynam had been asleep just over an hour, and Karl was beginning to wonder if it had been a wasted journey. Suddenly, Lynam began mumbling, and his legs and arms twitched.

'Here we go,' whispered Karl.

'Good luck, bro.'

Karl firmed his grip on Lynam's wrist and closed his eyes. He found himself standing at the side of the bed. Lynam was sitting up, pushing his back into the headboard, frozen in fear. At the bottom of the bed, the shadows of demonic arms appeared, pulling their way up the quilt. Lynam drew his legs up tightly towards his body in a futile attempt to evade capture, his face contorted with terror.

'Howard, take hold of my hand.' Lynam glanced at Karl and then back to the ghoulish apparitions. 'Howard, listen to me, take my hand, trust me.' Karl thrust his hand forward, and Lynam reached out to clasp it.

'Now close your eyes. Trust me, Howard, close your eyes!'

Terrified, Lynam did as he was instructed. At last, Karl was in control. He had reproduced in his mind an image of how he thought Lynam's bird-watching hide might look. It was a large, wooden hut, with a door at the side and a long, thin, viewing opening at the front. Lynam stood by the opening with a pair of binoculars observing some Canada geese at the edge of a small lake, just in front of the hut. 'Hello, Howard.'

Lynam jumped back, a little startled. 'Mr Hennessey, what are you doing here?'

Karl had experienced this before; Lynam was completely oblivious to the fact that he was in a dream.

'Howard, I want you to listen to me. At the moment, you are in my dream.' Lynam looked confused. 'The next time I ask you to open and close your eyes, it will be your dream.' It was a lot for him to take in, but somehow Lynam seemed to accept it. 'If you see the demons, you are going to close your eyes and think of this place. When you open them, you will be here. Do you understand?'

Lynam took a deep breath. 'Can I do that?'

'You can do anything in your dreams.' Karl gave him a reassuring smile. 'Hold onto my hand.' Lynam did as he was asked. 'Now close your eyes.'

Karl released his mental grip. They were back in the bedroom. The whole room was full of shadows, and Karl sensed Lynam's rapid increase in heartbeat; he was beginning to panic. 'Think of that place, Howard.' The demons were almost upon him, threatening to consume him. Karl grabbed Lynam's hands. 'Close your eyes, Howard!' In a flash, Karl was back in control. Standing back in the hide, Karl could feel the stress flowing through Lynam's body. 'Are you all right, Howard?'

'I will be; just need a moment to get my breath.'

'This is very important, Howard; you have to take control. All you have to do is think of this place when you close your eyes; keep it fixed in your mind. When you open them, if you see anything other than this place, close them and think of this place again, got it?'

'This place,' said Lynam gritting his teeth, 'this place.'

'Ready?' asked Karl. Lynam gave an uncertain nod, and then they both closed their eyes and opened them. They were still in the hide, even though Karl had released his grip. 'Look out there, Howard.' Karl pointed out across the lake where the banks were covered with an abundance of wild fowl. Lynam looked out, instantly absorbed in what he saw.

Karl opened his eyes and released his grip on Lynam's wrist. As he slipped his hand out of the strap, a hot and flustered Charlie said, 'Thank God that's over. I was lying on him at one stage. I can't believe he didn't wake up; what the hell was going on?'

Karl laughed, 'Twitching.'

'Twitching?' replied Charlie.

'Yes. Come on, I'll tell you about it on the way home.'

Karl had one more appointment with Lynam, but it was obvious once Karl interacted with him that Lynam was now in control of his night terrors. At Karl's request, Charlie did one or two follow-up calls, just to make sure there were no relapses, but everything looked good.

Over the next few weeks, the practice really took off. Although thoroughly enjoying his newfound success, Karl was beginning to look very tired. Despite Charlie persistently telling him to take a few days off, the answer was always the same: 'We need to take the work while it's there.' And it was there; the diary was full for the next month, and still the phone was ringing. It seemed the word was out; Karl was suddenly in very great demand.

26

Post-traumatic stress

It was another busy day at the practice; Karl had one client in the office and another waiting. Charlie had managed to talk Karl into seeing only three clients a day. After a heated discussion, Karl had realised that Charlie was only acting in his best interests and agreed. If the clients really needed him, they would wait their turn.

Charlie was sitting at the reception desk updating patient files when the door opened and a woman in her mid twenties came up the stairs. She was very slightly built with long, mousy brown hair, quite attractive in a plain kind of way. Charlie's attention was drawn to a large bruise on her right cheek bone, which she tried to hide with her hair.

Awkwardly, she approached the desk. 'Hello, I wonder, is it possible to make an appointment?'

'Let me see,' said Charlie, picking up the diary; there was no longer any need to make a pretence about being fully booked. 'Mr Hennessey is very busy at the moment; you're looking at three weeks.'

Her face said it all; she looked distraught and tears welled up in her eyes. 'I can't wait that long, but thank you anyway.'

She turned to leave, but before reaching the top of the stairs, Charlie called out to her. 'Excuse me, er, Miss . . .'

She turned around. 'It's Mrs, Mrs Curtis.'

Charlie smiled. Whatever it was, call it sixth sense, Charlie just knew this woman needed Karl's help. 'I've just noticed that we have a cancellation on Thursday morning. Would that be good for you?'

A glint of hope appeared in her eyes. 'It's not for me you understand; it's for my husband, Damian.'

Charlie picked up an appointment card, filled in the time and date, and passed it over. 'I'm not sure if he'll come with me, but I'd like to see the doctor anyway.'

Lots of clients assumed Karl to have some form of doctorate. Unlike Karl, who always corrected them right at the beginning, Charlie left them to assume what they liked.

'It would really help if he was here,' said Charlie.

'I'll do my best, and thank you.'

'You're welcome. Hopefully, we'll see you both on Thursday.'

As the door closed behind her, Charlie was intrigued and wondered what her story was. Over lunch, he mentioned her to Karl, telling him how something inside him had told him she needed their help. Karl was pleased that Charlie had acted on an emotional gut feeling; it showed a gentler side of his brother that was even now still closely guarded.

On Thursday morning, half an hour before the appointment time, Mrs Curtis arrived alone. Looking a little more composed than the last time Charlie had seen her, she introduced herself, apologising for her husband's absence. Charlie told her to take a seat and that Mr Hennessey would be with her shortly. He used the intercom system to inform Karl that she had arrived. She sat in the reception area in silence, her mind apparently at one with her thoughts.

After tidying the papers on his desk, Karl went into reception. Hearing his door open, she looked up and Karl greeted her with a smile. 'Mrs Curtis, would you like to come through?' Returning a thin attempt at a smile, she got to her feet and went into Karl's office.

Closing the door behind her, he gestured towards a chair and offered her a cup of tea or coffee. It was not his usual approach with a new client, but she really looked as if she needed to relax. She declined anyway.

'Right then,' Karl sat back in his chair, 'how can I help you, Mrs Curtis?'

Taking a deep breath, she sat up straight and looked directly at Karl.

'My husband was in the military for just over ten years and was discharged on medical grounds just under twelve months ago.' She looked into her lap, consciously taking control of her emotions. After a moment she looked up.

'As a soldier's wife, you accept that your husband will be away for sometimes months on end. When they come back, it always takes time for them to adapt back to normal family life. He did two tours of Iraq and one in Afghanistan. It was after Afghanistan that it all started.'

Karl listened intently.

'He lost a lot of friends out there, Dr Hennessey, including his best friend. Twelve months ago, my Damian would never have raised a hand to the kids or me, but now . . .' she paused, rubbing a hand on her cheek.

'At times, I'm frightened of him. They released him from the military on psychiatric grounds, post-traumatic stress they called it.' She breathed heavily and shook her head. 'It's as if they've just discarded him, thrown him out. He thinks he's been discharged dishonourably. Why, I don't know.

'He has nightmares and wakes up screaming. Just the other night, I found him sitting behind the door in the kids' room. He was crying like a baby, and when I tried to comfort him . . .' Again she raised a hand to her cheek. 'Whatever happened to him in Afghanistan is destroying my family.' Her eyes were now full of tears. 'I've heard you can do some amazing things, Dr Hennessey, and I don't know who else to turn to.'

Karl could see it was taking every last bit of effort to keep herself together. He pushed a box of tissues from the edge of the desk towards her.

'Thank you,' she said as she blew her nose.

'I really want to help you, Mrs Curtis, but if he won't see me . . .'

'If I could get him to see you at home, would you do a house visit?' she interrupted.

Karl smiled. 'Of course I would; in fact, after listening to you, I would prefer to. I usually get better responses from clients in a familiar environment.'

Finally, her face was showing signs of hope. 'Have a word with your husband first, as I don't think it's a good idea to turn up unexpectedly. You see, to treat him I need to gain his trust. Explain to him that my treatment is completely confidential in the privacy of your own home.' Karl pushed a business card across the desk. 'As soon as he agrees to see me, give me a call and we'll make the appointment as quickly as possible.'

Mrs Curtis picked up the card, squeezing it tightly in her hand. As they both stood up, Karl walked round the desk and shook her hand. 'Please try not to worry, it will only compound the problem. Give him as much space as he needs.' Recalling the times she had set him off by asking what was wrong, she knew he was right.

'Oh, by the way,' added Karl, 'it's Mr Hennessey, not Dr, but I much prefer Karl.' His friendly manner never failed to relax clients.

'Thank you, Karl,' she replied, 'and it's Paula.' They both smiled and went through to the reception area, where another client was already waiting.

'I'll see you very soon, Paula.' She still looked a little worried but at least now had hope.

Karl turned to Charlie. 'I'll discuss Mrs Curtis with you later,' he said, keeping his voice low.

Charlie nodded. 'Right you are,' he replied, turning a file round on the desk so that Karl could read the next client's name.

'Mrs Thompson, pleased to meet you. Would you like to come through?' Karl ushered his next client into his office and closed the door behind them.

It was almost three weeks before Mrs Curtis rang the practice. Although still inundated with work, Karl had the same feeling as Charlie about this woman; she had come across as being very kind but extremely vulnerable, and he felt a need to help her. Karl had arranged his clients so that he could keep the Friday afternoon free. Charlie would stay in the office and man the phones while Karl did a home visit to the Curtises.

They lived at Amberton, a small town around forty-five minutes' journey in a car from the practice. Karl thought about asking Susie to take him, but it meant she would have had to take time off work. He checked and found that Amberton was on the local train line, so he decided to go alone. It was probably for the best as it made the visit feel more professional.

Buying his ticket at the station, he realised that he had not travelled on a train since his school days. It brought back memories of going home for the weekend when his parents had split up and his father rapidly went down hill. Quickly, he pushed the thoughts to the back of his mind and focused on the job in hand. He was a little apprehensive about the kind of reception he would get from Mr Curtis, and hoped that the ex-soldier would not feel that the appointment had been made under duress.

As the train pulled into Amberton Station, Karl got to his feet and felt in his pocket for the paper on which Charlie had written the Curtises' address: 28 Fairview Crescent. A signpost at the far end of the platform indicated towards the town centre. Following the sign, Charlie found himself at the front of the station, where one or two private cabs were dropping people off. One driver was taking his passenger's bag out of the boot. Quickly, Karl ran over before he could drive off. 'Excuse me,' he called out. The cab driver, an Asian man with a turban, nodded towards him. 'Could you take me to 28 Fairview Crescent?'

The driver drew his hand over his beard. 'It is possible, but I'm only allowed to take telephone bookings; you know what its like with insurance and all that.'

Karl was clearly disappointed. The driver looked him up and down and took a deep breath; 'Come on then, just this once.'

'Thanks very much,' said Karl and climbed into the back of the vehicle. Within ten minutes, they pulled up outside the house. Karl paid the driver and took a card from him: 'Give the office a ring next time, mate.'

'Will do,' replied Karl, 'and thanks again.'

The Curtises lived in a typical three-bedroomed semi, with white UPVC windows and doors and what looked as if it had once been a well-manicured lawn. They weren't particularly well off, but with Curtis's military pension and sickness benefit coming in, they were doing OK.

Before Karl reached the front door, it opened, and Mrs Curtis greeted him, 'Hello, Karl; not too much trouble finding us, I hope?'

Standing behind her a little way down the hall was her husband. For some reason Karl had expected a bigger man. He was around five feet eight inches tall, of medium build, with very tightly cropped hair and a small, military-type moustache.

'Please, come in.'

She stood aside, and as Karl stepped over the threshold, he instantly made eye contact with her husband. 'Mr Curtis, very pleased to meet you.'

'Damian, please,' he replied, shaking Karl's hand. The two men sat in the front room while Paula went to make coffee. Already Damian was warming to Karl's open, relaxed approach.

'Your wife tells me you recently came out the forces.'

Damian lowered his head; it was obviously difficult for him to talk about it. He swallowed hard. 'Yeah, it's been twelve months now' – he looked down at his hands as he rubbed them together – 'I had some good friends.' He then fell silent, as if guarding his words.

'It must have been hard. Paula told me you were overseas for a time.'

'Yes.'

'Middle East, wasn't it?'

'For a while.'

Damian persisted with monosyllabic responses, clearly unwilling to discuss what had happened in any detail, but Karl was having none of it and pressed him further.

'Of course, I only see it on TV, but I don't envy those guys.'

This really hit the mark. Damian's head shot up. 'Until you've been there, you can't even start to imagine what it's like.' He almost spat the words out, and the look on his face was deadly. Silently, the two men stared at each other until the door opened and Paula came in with a tray of drinks and a biscuit barrel. She could instantly tell that something was wrong.

'Everything all right, Damian?' He was silent. 'Damian.'

Karl quickly intervened. 'It's fine. Damian was just telling me about his military background.'

Damian was not used to this kind of persistence. 'I always wanted to be a soldier, as far back as I can remember.'

Paula smiled and passed her husband a mug of coffee; finally, he was starting to talk. For nearly an hour, Damian talked about the places he'd been posted to and things he had got up to; it had obviously been a great passion in his life. Karl listened intently. Damian became quite animated, giving an interesting and vivid account of his military career, but not once did he mention Afghanistan.

'What was it like in Afghanistan?' asked Karl. Suddenly all the brightness left Damian's face and his head dropped. Once more, silence fell upon the room. Paula was the first to talk.

'He was there for five months.'

On hearing this, Damian raised his head. 'I can speak for myself.' He took a deep breath. 'One hundred and fifty-six days of hell. Forty-five of us arrived on 1st May, and on 3rd October thirty-two of us came home. It was the biggest loss any regiment had taken out there. We came under attack virtually every day. Helmand Province; you can see where it gets its name from.'

Damian stood up and put his hands in his pockets. He walked towards the window and looked out. 'There's not a day goes by that I'm not haunted by it.'

Karl could see he didn't want to continue on the subject, but he kept pushing. 'When you say haunted, what do you mean?'

Damian turned from the window. 'Dreams, constant dreams,' he said.

'Like nightmares?' asked Karl.

Damian thought for a moment. 'Kind of, but more vivid. Sometimes I'm not even asleep, and its just like I'm there, I can feel it and smell it.' He fell silent once again and bowed his head.

'I don't know if Paula has explained how I work,' said Karl, 'but if it's OK with you I'd like to try something.'

'Go on,' said Damian.

'All I need to do is watch you sleep.'

Damian sat back down looking very confused. 'What will that prove exactly?'

'Let's just say it will all become clear afterwards.'

Damian turned to his wife who, with eyes widened, nodded her head.

'Ok, I'll give it a go.'

'Excellent,' said Karl, 'I'm free this Saturday evening, but if that's too short a notice . . .?'

'No, no, Karl,' replied Paula, 'that will be fine. I'll arrange for the kids to stay with my sister.'

'Right then,' said Karl getting to his feet. 'Oh, one last thing' – the Curtises anxiously looked up as Karl pulled a small card from his pocket – 'could I ask you to call me a cab? I'll never find my way back to station otherwise.'

'Not a problem,' said Paula laughing. 'I'll take you myself.'

The train had been full to capacity with Friday night revellers and the last of the straggling commuters, squeezed uncomfortably together, finishing off the day's work on laptops or sending the ubiquitous 'I'm on the train' message via their mobile phones. Karl didn't envy them; the thought of doing this week in, week out didn't appeal to him one bit.

It was after eight o'clock when Karl arrived home, and Charlie and Susie were curled up on the settee. Karl flopped down into the armchair, kicking off his shoes. 'What a day.'

Charlie was eager to let Karl know what had been going on that afternoon at the office. The phone had not stopped ringing, and word was really getting around about Karl's ability. People were making appointments just for the experience. That was fine financially, but was not really what Karl had planned. It was becoming a circus, and the only way Karl could think of stopping it was to increase his prices. Hopefully, that would lead to only genuine clients pursuing treatment.

Finally, Karl recounted his visit to the Curtises and how sad it was that such a nice couple were falling apart. Susie was touched by the story and offered to drive Karl for his visit on Saturday evening, which pleased him, as he hadn't a clue how he was going to get home afterwards.

Saturday morning arrived, and Charlie and Susie went into town shopping. Wanting to be as fresh as possible for his evening appointment Karl stayed in bed resting. Over the last few months, he had slept well, but from time to time still had nightmares, usually about previous cases, some worse than others. They still deeply upset him, but he just chose not to discuss the matter and tried to push all thoughts of them out of his mind during the day.

Karl had arranged his visit for 10 pm and had let the Curtises know that, due to how late it would be when they had finished, he would bring his assistant and driver with him. There would be no pressure on Damian, and he could go to bed any time he was ready.

Karl, Charlie and Susie left in good time as they were not familiar with the area, but, armed with her trusty satellite navigation system, Susie had no problems finding her way there. As they pulled up outside the house,

Karl saw the curtains twitch; understandably, they had probably been on tenterhooks all evening. Just as before, the front door opened before Karl got there.

After introducing Charlie and Susie, they sat for the next hour or so drinking tea and talking about life in general. Karl tried to avoid asking questions about Damian's military background, but somehow they always got back there. It was obvious it was at the forefront of his mind. By eleven o'clock, everyone was looking a little weary. Damian nervously said goodnight and went up to bed, taking a copy of Karl's relaxation CD to help him sleep.

Karl had explained that if a client was going to relax enough to fall a sleep, it would usually be within the first hour. Patiently, they waited. Over half an hour went by and Paula went up to see if her husband was sleeping, tip-toeing up the stairs, doing her best to avoid any known creaky floorboards. As asked, Damian had left the bedroom door ajar. Looking through the crack of the door, she could see him sleeping soundly, and went down to let Karl know.

Charlie and Susie sat back with the TV remote while Paula showed Karl the way up to the bedroom. Pulling up the stool from the dressing table, Karl quietly sat down beside the bed. Damian was sleeping on his side with the quilt tucked up under his chin, making it very difficult for Karl to find any exposed skin without pulling back the bedding. The danger was that if he moved the quilt back, he might wake him up. Paula nervously stood by the door not knowing whether to stay or leave the room. As slowly and gently as possible, Karl felt under the quilt, close to the pillow, for Damian's hand or arm. Cautiously he watched his face; he seemed to be sleeping soundly. Finding his hand, Karl closed his eyes.

It was barely light. Karl wasn't sure whether it was first thing in the morning or early evening. There was an uncomfortable stillness about the place. What he could see of the terrain was rugged, and a hazy, mist-like smoke swirled around him. Somewhere nearby he could hear voices, some English, but also another dialect he couldn't pinpoint but thought might be Arabic.

Choosing not to fully interact in the dream, Karl scanned the terrain. Suddenly, a loud bang overwhelmed him, then another and another. A series of explosions punished the land no more than twenty metres in front of him. He could see muzzle flashes in the smoke as automatic machine gun fire tore across the open land ahead of him. He was obviously right at the heart of a battle, with the two sides so close that he could hear each giving orders.

To his right, a line of four soldiers dashed forwards. On the ground beside them, others put down rapid fire in an attempt to cover their advance. As the four soldiers hit the ground, they opened fire, and instantly the others were on their feet, advancing at a phenomenal rate. Their enemy scattered, running in all directions. Suddenly, without any warning, a series of explosions of enormous intensity hit the ground exactly where the soldiers were advancing, leaving nothing but four or five huge craters. An eerie silence fell on the battlefield, and the air was thick with smoke, dust and sand.

Still unwilling to materialise in the dream, Karl moved forwards. The smoke was so dense he could barely see more than a few metres in front of him. As his mind's eye advanced across the now virtually silent battlefield, what he saw shocked him. The soldiers had taken a series of direct hits, and those advancing on foot had been quite literally, blown to pieces. Body parts were strewn around the area, and a handful of others had sustained such horrendous injuries they would surely never leave the battlefield alive.

That's when he saw him lying on the edge of a crater. Somehow Damian had avoided the main blasts. His face was covered in blood and dirt, and his right arm was bent at an awkward angle, but apart from that the rest of his limbs looked intact. That was more than he could say for the poor soul lying beside him, who had taken the brunt of the explosion. Somehow still conscious, both of his legs had been blown off above the knees, and where his right hand and forearm should have been was a glistening stump of bone and ragged, crimson flesh. His only useful limb agonisingly scratched at the dirt trying to find a leverage point, his eyes perplexed in shock. Karl felt nauseous; how could people ever lead a normal life after being exposed to such horror?

As Karl looked on, Damian slid up alongside the mortally wounded soldier. The silence of the battlefield was broken by the sound of foreign voices coming out of cover, probably advancing on their position. Damian knew only too well what they would do with them if they found them still alive. Realising there was nothing he could do to his friend's injuries, Damian leaned over to him. 'Come on Paddy, I'm going to have to carry you out.'

Struggling to get himself into a seated position, Damian took hold of his friend's tattered combat jacket and tried to heave him up onto his back. Pain seared through Damian's arm and shoulder, and his friend fell back to the floor. There was no way, with the injuries Damian had sustained, that he was going to carry a man out of the field, even with lower limbs missing. The soldier, shaking uncontrollably, stared straight into Damian's eyes: 'Finish me.' There was an unwritten code they all carried with them – that they would never leave anyone to the enemy.

'No,' said Damian, 'you're coming with me.'

Again he tried to roll the soldier's smashed body onto his back. The pain once more was excruciating, and in frustration Damian slammed his good fist into the dirt. He looked around for a weapon; if he couldn't carry him out he would stand and fight, but there was nothing but an SA80 rifle with a ridiculously bent barrel. Again he grabbed the mortally wounded soldier's jacket, but Paddy's remaining limb grabbed at Damian's arm. Somehow, the soldier stilled his shaking body and in a low, almost composed voice, he said, 'I can't live like this, finish me.' Tears rolled down Damian's face.

The soldier squeezed his arm tightly, staring into his face and willing him to do this one final thing. The voices were getting louder; soon their position would be overrun. Looking once more at his friend's injuries, he made a decision that would haunt him. He took one more look into his friend's eyes, pulled the soldier's jacket up over his face, sealed it around his nose and mouth and lay across his face. There was no struggle. Within a few moments, Damian felt the grip on his arm loosen.

'God, forgive me,' he said as he rolled off his friend and looked into his eyes; they were open but there was no life in them. Damian drew his hand over his friend's face, closing his eyes. The voices in the smoke were almost upon him. Keeping as low as he could, he backed off through the bomb craters, using the smoke as a screen for his escape.

Karl opened his eyes. The bedroom was as he remembered it, and Paula was still standing by the door. How long he had been in the dreamscape? He glanced at his watch and saw that it was just after 12:30. It had been over an hour, but it seemed like minutes. Damian was still fast asleep. To say Karl was stunned by what he had seen was an understatement; this was something Damian had clearly never shared with anyone.

Karl got up from the stool and pushed it back under the dressing table. Paula looked over at him with an expression of hope. He smiled and pointed towards the door. Quietly, they crept out of the room, and Paula closed the door behind them. They went downstairs to the lounge, where Charlie and Susie had fallen asleep.

'What do you think?' asked Paula, a little lost for words.

'Your husband has some issues that we need to address.'

'And you can tell that from just watching him?'

'There are a few things I'd like to talk to him about.' Paula looked concerned. 'Please don't worry.' Karl put his hand on her shoulder. 'I need to discus my findings with the patient before anybody else, so that I can properly understand what's happening and to respect their privacy.'

'I understand,' said Paula.

'Right then,' said Karl, rubbing his hands together, 'let's see if we can wake this pair up; then you might get some sleep yourself.'

Ten minutes later, the three were on their way home, Karl sitting in the back of the car deep in thought. This was by far the most challenging case he had to date. Theoretically, Damian had murdered his friend, albeit compassionately. It was not Karl's job to judge him, only help him. Karl had to tread very lightly; he couldn't even confide in his brother with this one. Overwhelmed by feelings of solitude and anguish, he fell asleep.

27

Dealing with stress

The following morning, Karl was woken at 7 am by his alarm clock. Normally, his body clock would wake him four or five minutes before the alarm went off, but on this occasion, exhaustion had taken over. He reached across, swotted the snooze button on top of the clock and lay back. Memories of the previous evening flooded back to him, and he suddenly realised that it was Sunday and he didn't have to get up.

The Curtises' case had intrigued him so much that it had been 2 am when he finally climbed into bed, and out of habit he had automatically set the alarm. Damian's dream had been so intense and stressful that Karl had felt mentally exhausted. In his mind's eye, he could still see the mortally wounded soldier, the image so clear that it made him shudder. He wanted to see Damian again as soon as possible. His diary was completely full for the week, but he knew this couldn't wait.

Again the alarm went off. Karl jumped up and threw back the quilt. Quickly, he spun his legs over the side of the bed and clicked the off switch on top of the clock.

With the house once again in silence, Karl dressed and went downstairs. It would be hours before Charlie surfaced; if there was one thing Charlie was good at, it was having a lie-in on a Sunday morning, especially when Susie stayed over.

After breakfast, Karl sat at the kitchen table contemplating what he was going to do with himself. With Damian's case fresh in his mind, the urge to go into the office was overwhelming. He wanted to get the details down in writing as soon as possible. At the same time, he could contact the family and arrange another appointment. Leaving a note on the kitchen table, Karl quietly pulled the front door closed behind him and set off.

It was the first time he had been to the office on a Sunday, and it felt strange, almost like a different place. He made a coffee, sat down at his desk and began making notes on the experience he had had the previous evening. He had been absorbed in his work for some time when the sound of a car door slamming outside distracted him. He glanced at his watch; it was almost 10:30 am. Not too early to give the Curtises a ring even if it was Sunday. After gathering up the file, he dialled the number, it only rang once or twice.

'Hello?' It sounded like a young child on the other end.

'Hello there,' said Karl, 'is your Mom or Dad there?'

'Yeah,' came the reply, simply answering the question, then silence.

'Could I speak to either of them? Tell them it's Mr Hennessey.'

Without a reply, the receiver was placed down. All was quiet, and Karl was wondering if the child had hung up when there was the sound of the receiver being fumbled with.

'Hello?' It was a woman's voice.

'Is that Paula?'

'Yes.'

'It's Karl Hennessey.'

'Mr Hennessey, thanks for getting back so quickly.'

'I was wondering if it would be possible for Damian to come into the office?'

Before Karl could say that any day in the week would be fine, Paula said, 'When? Today?'

Karl stopped and thought about it: it would make sense, and he would not have to reorganise his other clients' appointments.

'Well, if that's possible.' replied Karl, hopefully.

'Yes, I'm sure he hasn't anything on today.'

'I don't usually see patients at weekends, but my diary is full all week and I really would like to have a chat with him.'

They agreed to meet at 1 pm. Karl put the phone down and sat back in his chair. If Charlie knew he was seeing a client on a Sunday, he would not be very happy. Charlie had already given him a lecture about burning the candle at both ends. Karl knew he was right, but he had so much to get done and little time to do it.

Karl was sitting in the reception looking through the coming week's client list when he heard the main door open. Glancing at the clock on the wall, he saw that it was almost one o'clock. Getting up from the reception desk, he greeted the Curtises at the top of the stairs. 'Good afternoon, both; I'm pleased you could make it.' Karl shook hands with both of them.

'Thank you for seeing us so quickly,' replied Paula.

'Paula, I'd like to have a chat with Damian on his own.'

'Mr Hennessey, I don't mind Paula hearing what you have to say.' Damian had no idea what Karl knew and was still a little sceptical of his ability.

Choosing his words carefully, Karl continued. 'I'd like to talk to you about Paddy.'

The colour drained from Damian's face. 'How did you know him?'

'I didn't,' said Karl, 'please come into my office.'

Karl turned to Paula. 'We won't be long.'

Looking confused, Paula shrugged and sat down in the reception area. Karl directed Damian into his office and closed the door. As Karl walked around his desk Damian watched him apprehensively.

'Please, don't look worried.' Karl gestured towards a chair, and Damian sat down. Karl leaned his elbows on the desk and gently clasped his hands together. There was only one way to tell his client what he had seen in the dream, and that was straight out.

'I know what happened in Afghanistan with your friend Paddy.'

Damian said nothing but stared directly at Karl. Every second felt like an age. Breaking the silence, Karl said, 'Don't get me wrong, Damian, I'm not judging you. I can only imagine what you and your comrades went through out there.'

Damian looked into his lap, and Karl could almost feel his client's mental pain and anguish. Suddenly, Damian looked up. 'How? Paddy and I are the only people who could possibly have known what happened that day.'

'I have what I call a gift; it allows me to look into people's subconscious as they sleep. All the problems you have had since you got home stem from that one moment. As I said, I'm not judging you, just trying to help you. The decision you had to take would have torn most people apart. I think you are amazingly strong to have coped for this long.'

Damian stood up and paced the room. Hearing Karl talking about it had brought back the memory freshly into his mind as if it were yesterday.

'What could I do?' Tears rolled down Damian's cheeks. He wiped his eyes with the back of his hand and turned to Karl. 'I should have died that day with Paddy; it was my time,' he cupped his hands and rubbed them down his face. 'But no, I disgraced myself and left him there.'

Karl shook his head. 'No, no, you're wrong.'

'What do you know? You weren't there.' Damian's tone became aggressive.

'That's true,' said Karl, 'but your friend Paddy wouldn't have thanked you for carrying him off the battlefield. His body was completely smashed; it was only a matter of time.' Damian sat down and again wiped his eyes.

'I can't change the past,' said Karl, 'but I can help you deal with it.' Damian looked up in disbelief. 'When I look into your dream, my gift allows me to interact if I desire and, of course, if you allow me to.'

'What the hell are you talking about?' retorted Damian.

'I can help you to change things within the dream. It won't change the memory of your friend, just the way you last saw him, and, hopefully, you won't have any more nightmares.'

It sounded unbelievable, but Damian thought that Karl sounded sincere, and how else could he explain how he knew about Paddy? Damian had nothing to lose. They arranged that Karl would visit again the following Friday evening. Damian was unwilling to tell his wife what had happened in Afghanistan, not yet anyway. If Karl really could help him come to terms with it, he just might be able to talk to her about it and move on with his life.

When Karl arrived home, not wanting to annoy Charlie by telling him he had been seeing a client, he simply said that he had been catching up on paperwork. The week ahead turned out to be hectic; even an increase in fees did not deter clients and the phone just kept on ringing. Charlie was becoming concerned about Karl; by Wednesday, he looked exhausted and something had to give. There was no way he could maintain this kind of work rate.

Over lunch, Karl asked Charlie if Susie might run him over to the Curtises' house again on Friday evening. Charlie agreed, provided that Karl promised to take the weekend off and rest. Karl agreed, offering to take both of them for a meal before the appointment – his treat.

By Friday evening, Karl needed no persuasion to take a couple of days off. Choosing to eat at their favourite Italian restaurant, the three sat at a table by the window, watching the world go by, each pleased that the weekend had arrived; just one more appointment and Karl could take a well-earned rest.

'You never did fill me in on the Curtis case, bro,' said Charlie.

'Didn't I?' asked Karl, reluctant to share the details of the case. 'It's boring really. Now, that elderly lady, Mrs Burke, the one with the cat phobia, I know you should face your fears, but she had six of the damned things in the house.' Charlie and Susie both laughed.

'She was strange,' said Charlie. The waiter arrived carrying three large plates in a well-practised manner.

'I'm ready for this,' said Susie placing a napkin on her lap.

After a hearty meal and coffee, they set off for the Curtises. They arrived just before ten o'clock, each hoping that they would get away a little earlier this week. Paula greeted them and took them through to the lounge.

'I don't think there will be any problem with him getting off to sleep tonight; he was up at four o'clock this morning. The kids have been in bed for a while and probably won't even know you've been here.'

Entering the lounge, Karl put out his hand to Damian. 'Evening, Damian. Paula tells me you were up bright and early this morning.' They shook hands.

'Yes, went out for a spot of fishing.'

'Good day was it?'

'So so,' replied Damian, screwing up his face.

'Right, well, any time you feel like turning in, just head on up.'

Karl knew how hard it was for clients to relax, but did not want to pressurise him. He had the relaxation CD, but it was also helpful that this was not his first time. Paula made drinks and, after chatting for a while, Damian, heavy-eyed, said goodnight and went to bed. Just as the previous week, they gave him a good forty minutes or so to get off to sleep and then quietly went up to his room. Paula glanced around the edge of the door – he was fast asleep. Knowing now exactly what Karl was going to do, she went back downstairs.

Karl pulled the stool from under the dressing table and sat down beside the bed. Before taking hold of Damian's hand, he sat for a few moments looking at him. What an amazing thing the human mind was; the stress this man was under and yet he looked so relaxed. Karl reached out and placed his hand on the back of Damian's. This was always the moment he dreaded; if the client was going to wake up, this was usually the time.

Even before closing his eyes, Karl felt a sense of unease; it was another first for his gift, instantly knowing that he was entering a truly troubled mind. As he closed his eyes, he found himself within the confines of what must have been Damian's military base when he served in Afghanistan. There were soldiers running to and fro, some carrying ammunition boxes, others with large packs. A very large man with a bushy moustache shouted out, 'Corporal Curtis.'

Karl spotted Damian sitting on a large pile of sandbags with two other soldiers, pushing bullets into empty magazines. Jumping to his feet, Damian shouted his reply: 'Yes, Sarge.'

'Get your section together; briefing ten minutes.'

Passing the half-filled magazine to one of his colleagues, he dashed off towards a collection of well-camouflaged tents. Karl had a sense of stifling heat; he wasn't actually sweating, but all his senses told him he was. Two minutes later, Damian emerged from a tent followed by five other men in battle dress. They went back to the other two soldiers and began filling their ammunition pouches with magazines. Still not visible to Damian, Karl watched as the soldiers exchanged banter.

'Not long now, Scotty,' shouted one soldier to another.

The man looked up from his task. 'Not long before what?'

'Not long before I go home to see your missus!' A magazine whistled past the soldier's head and they all laughed at Scotty's expense, but it was clear that there was no malice; they were as close as brothers.

'OK, you lads; let's get switched on.' The sergeant with the large moustache approached the group.

'You heard him, lads,' said Damian, fastening the last of his ammunition pouches. The men gathered round in a circle and crouched down on one knee.

'We have one more week in this shit hole, then we hand over to Forty Commando.' The Sergeant looked at each man in turn. 'In two weeks, you'll be filling your boots with your missus.' He looked over at Scotty. 'Except you Scotty; that's Tosh's job.' They all laughed including Scotty. 'Seriously, lads, let's keep it tight out there; don't take any chances. Got that?'

'Yes, Sarge,' they replied in unison.

'OK, we move out in ten minutes.'

They all got to their feet and continued preparing for their mission.

Almost like drifting in and out of sleep, it went dark and back to light. Karl found himself in an area of barren land. In the distance there were mountains, and, about two hundred metres up front, he could see Damian's section spread out in an arrowhead formation. Karl followed, still observing as if a fly on the wall. Every now and then, the soldiers would drop onto one knee. After a short time, the Sergeant would raise his hand, and they would continue to advance as one.

Suddenly, they all burst into running pace. Two soldiers on the right went wide; there was a ridge about a hundred metres in front of them, and, obviously concerned with what lay beyond it, they took evasive action. Weapons at the ready, they advanced in threes, covering ten to fifteen metres at a time, before dropping down allowing the other part of the section to leapfrog them. At all times, fifty per cent of the section's firepower was directed at the ridge. The two soldiers on the right were already in position. Should anyone appear from behind the ridge, they would run straight into their arc of fire.

Finally, they all arrived safely on the ridge. The terrain in front of them was craggy with no vegetation but scattered with small piles of rocks. The men had all been in Afghanistan long enough to know it was ideal ambush terrain. Forward visibility was no more than forty to fifty metres before another ridge or mound.

'I don't like this,' said Damian to his friend Paddy, a few metres to his right.

'Snap,' replied Paddy.

The big Sergeant looked to his left. 'Tosh.' The soldier nodded. 'I want you on that ridge' – he pointed left and forward of their position about forty metres. Every remaining weapon in the section was fixed on the pending ridge, each soldier's attention fully focused on the area, ready to detect the slightest movement or glint of light reflecting off a weapon.

'Ready Tosh?' asked the Sergeant. Tosh nodded and, scrambling to his feet, dashed over the top. His comrades scanned the area. Ten, twenty, thirty metres he ran, dodging rocks and seeking cover anywhere he could find it. Damian saw it first, the sun glinting off the side of an automatic rifle. Without hesitation, he opened fire, laying down a volley of rounds on the position. Suddenly, all hell was let loose. A dozen or more rifle muzzles came over the ridge, and automatic weapon fire rained down on Tosh's position. Bullets ripped through his lower body. Instantly, he fell, rolling behind a pile of small rocks just large enough to temporarily shield his body.

By now, the whole section were firing on the Taliban position, trying to draw the fire away from their fallen comrade. The professional training of the British soldiers went onto autopilot; half the section lay down fire as the other half advanced, leapfrogging each other every five metres or so as they advanced onto the ridge.

Once the ground was secured, one of the soldiers began dealing with Tosh's wounds. Two of the insurgents lay dead. The others had retreated behind yet another ridge some fifty metres away. Realising they were being drawn into a tit-for-tat fire-fight, the Sergeant decided to call in some firepower on the Taliban positions and get Tosh evacuated as soon as possible. Karl watched as the Sergeant relayed the Taliban position to his radio operator. Now it was just a matter of stabilising Tosh's condition and waiting for back-up.

It was not long before the sound of incoming jets screamed towards them. Suddenly, an almighty flash and explosion devastated the immediate area around the British soldiers. Stunned, but fortunately not a participant in the dream, Karl looked around. The carnage was devastating. The section had virtually taken a direct hit. It looked as if the coordinates the aircraft had been given were wrong or had been misinterpreted.

There was complete silence. Tosh and the two soldiers dealing with his wounds were almost completely vaporized. The Sergeant and remaining two soldiers on the edge of the ridge had been blown to pieces. Damian and his friend Paddy were at the furthest end of the ridge. A small mound had protected Damian from the brunt of the explosion, but Paddy was not so fortunate. Karl saw Paddy, just as in the first dream, with terrible injuries, having lost both legs and part of one arm. Karl knew this was his time to intervene.

As the dust and smoke began to clear, Karl materialised on the battlefield. Dressed in full combats, Karl found himself crouching down on the floor. The fear he felt was overwhelming. It was one thing observing, but actually taking part was something else. Although partially in shock, he made his way towards Damian and Paddy. In the distance, he could hear the voices of the Taliban soldiers. By the sound of the disarray, they had also taken a hit, and it would not be long before they rallied and moved on the British position.

As Karl approached through the smoke, he could see Damian trying to haul his friend onto his back. 'Damian,' Karl called out. Exhausted and in pain, Damian gently laid his friend back on the floor. Kneeling beside Paddy, he searched through the dust and smoke for the source of the voice. Then he saw Karl.

'It can't be.' He looked totally confused.

'Never mind that; just help me get him up.' Karl knelt down. As he pulled on the soldier's webbing, he cried out in pain. Karl looked at Damian. 'Help me get him onto my back.'

Responding immediately with his good arm, Damian pulled his friend onto the middle of Karl's back.

'Try and take a little of the weight,' said Karl, struggling to get to his feet.

Half standing, Damian pulled up on Paddy's webbing belt. Karl shrugged the soldier onto his upper back, and again he cried out in agony. Undeterred, Karl retreated from the ridge, staggering more than running, staying as low as possible. Damian followed, glancing behind as they went, aware of the potential counter-attack.

They had not been going more than a couple of minutes when the sound of helicopter rotors assured them that help was on the way. As they cleared the smoke, they saw a large twin-rotor Chinook helicopter hovering about fifty metres off the ground. In the open doorway, they could see eager comrades ready to reinforce them. The helicopter lowered towards the ground, sending a vortex of thick dust swirling into the air. As it touched down, soldiers streamed out, taking up all-round defensive positions.

The commander came running over. 'Get that man on board!' Strong hands lifted Paddy onto a stretcher. He looked at Damian, his arm hanging unnaturally by his side. 'You look as if you need some attention as well, soldier; we've got this covered.'

'Yes, sir,' replied Damian.

Paddy was lifted onto the helicopter, and two medics immediately began working on his injuries. As soon as they were all aboard, the Chinook lifted off, banking hard right away from any potential anti-aircraft missile threat. In the distance, the sound of explosions confirmed that the jets had finally hit their targets.

The medics worked hard to get lines into Paddy anywhere they could, but it was hopeless; their faces said it all. Damian took hold of Paddy's hand, and the mortally wounded soldier slowly opened his eyes. Damian felt him slightly squeeze his hand and saw his lips move. Damian leaned closer.

'Thank you for taking me home.'

With that, Paddy's grip fell loose. The medics instantly went into CPR, but they all knew it was futile. As Damian sat holding his friend's hand, Karl got to his feet and slowly backed away.

Closing his eyes tightly and then opening them, he was once more sitting next to Damian's bed. His client appeared to be sleeping comfortably. Karl's head was thumping; it was by far the most stressful dream he had ever interacted in. As he tried to stand up, his legs buckled under him. Just as if turning down a dimmer switch, darkness swept over his eyes and with a thump, he hit the floor.

Downstairs, Charlie and Susie had been chatting with Paula. The sound of Karl's fall killed the conversation dead. Charlie leapt to his feet and dashed towards the stairs, closely followed by both the women. Taking the stairs two at a time, he quickly got to the bedroom and pushed the door open. Karl was lying face down on the floor. Kneeling at his side, Charlie turned his brother over quickly to check his breathing. The women stood at the bedroom door in a state of panic.

'Ambulance!' shouted Charlie. 'Quickly, phone an ambulance!'

28

The sleeping angel

Karl opened his eyes, and then immediately squinted, trying to adapt to the fluorescent lighting. Feeling disorientated, he sat up and looked around the room. On his right, curled up on a chair, Charlie was fast asleep. Karl lay back and placed his hand on his forehead; he felt very hot and weak. How did he get here? More to the point, where was he?

The door opened, and Susie came in carrying a coffee in a plastic cup. A look of relief spread over her face. 'Thank God,' she said. 'You had us worried.'

'Where are we?' asked Karl, weakly.

The sound of their voices woke Charlie. Startled, he quickly sat up and took a deep breath. 'Blimey, I must have nodded off.'

'About four hours ago,' said Susie.

Paying no attention to Susie's sarcastic wit, Charlie continued, 'Ashbourne General Hospital. We had to phone an ambulance from the Curtises last night. We're not sure what happened to you – we just heard a loud bang. When we got upstairs, you were flat out on the floor; how do you feel now?'

'Not too bad, a little tired and weak, but apart from that OK.'

'The doctor that examined you last night couldn't find anything wrong. Said he was going to do some tests, so it looks like you'll be here for the rest of today at least.'

Karl pulled the sheets back and started to get out of bed. Charlie looked at him quizzically.

'What are you doing?'

'I'm getting up,' Karl replied.

'I don't think so,' said Charlie, pulling the sheets back up. 'You'll stay there till the doctor tells you different.'

'But . . .'

'Never mind *but*; I told you about overdoing it, and look what happened. Now stay there.'

As if on cue, the door opened and Dr Alistair Cummins, Ali to his friends, entered. A painfully thin man who paid more attention to his career than his health, he had worked in the Ashbourne A&E and associated clinics for well over fifteen years. He was never seen without his stethoscope round his neck, and, behind his back, his colleagues constantly joked that he even wore it to bed.

'Good morning.'

'Morning, Doctor,' replied Karl.

Cummins picked up the board hanging on the bottom of Karl's bed. Quickly, his hand searched inside his pocket, pulling out a handkerchief just in time to catch a sneeze. He wiped his nose.

'Excuse me, I have a shocking cold. Well, Karl, I'd like to do a couple of blood tests, nothing to worry about, just a precursory measure. Has this ever happened to you before?'

'No, Doctor. I don't know what came over me.'

'Not to worry; we'll soon have you fighting fit again. Please, no breakfast till the nurse has taken your blood. She'll be along shortly. I'd like to keep you in for twenty-four hours or so to monitor you as you were unconscious for quite some time.' Dr Cummins hooked the board back on the bottom of the bed. 'Get some rest. I'll be back to see you later this morning.'

Almost an hour passed, and there was no sign of the nurse who was to take Karl's blood samples. Karl could see that Charlie and Susie were shattered, so he told them to go home and get some rest. There was nothing else they could do, and they both had to be at work on Monday morning. Karl told them he would phone when the doctor said he could go home.

The nurse finally arrived, took some blood samples and ordered some breakfast for Karl. She said that Dr Cummins would be back that afternoon to go over any findings from the blood tests. As the day progressed, Karl became increasingly bored. It was bad enough being in hospital, but being alone in a room was soul-destroying. Knowing that he would be there for another good few hours, he decided enough was enough.

He pulled on his clothes that had been neatly placed in the locker at the side of the bed. Sticking his head out the door, he could see into the main ward. There were not many staff around, but those he could see appeared to be preoccupied: one busy with paperwork at the nurse's station, another engrossed in the contents of the drugs trolley. Underneath the curtains drawn around one of the beds, he could see the uniformed legs of another nurse, apparently attending to a patient. A yellow plastic sign signalled that the floor was wet, and a glum-looking cleaner unenthusiastically mopped around the beds. One or two patients had visitors busying themselves arranging flowers and tidying lockers. Karl thought he would be able to walk around freely without attracting the slightest attention.

Making a mental note of the ward number, he went out into the main corridor. With a quick glance left and right, he set off with no particular destination, just killing time and taking a look around. A sign caught his attention, 'NEUROLOGICAL DEPARTMENT'. It reminded him of doing tests and puzzles for doctors as a child. It had been fun at first, but he remembered that his mother's mood always seemed to change when they were at the hospital. She had probably not realised, but even at such a young age Karl was finely tuned into other people's reactions and state of mind.

The sign indicated that the department was on the first floor. Inquisitively, Karl pressed the button to call the lift and waited. When the doors opened, he stood back, allowing a couple of nurses to exit. Once inside, he pressed the button for the first floor and the doors began to close.

'Wait!' A woman came running towards the lift and Karl put his hand out. The door automatically opened as it touched Karl's arm. The woman stepped inside and thanked him.

'You're welcome,' replied Karl. 'What floor would you like?'

'First, please.'

Karl once again pressed the button. The doors opened onto a corridor exactly like that on the floor below. The woman gave him a pleasant smile and walked off down the corridor. Karl followed around ten or fifteen metres behind. She stopped below a sign jutting out from the wall marked 'Neurological Ward' and pressed a button on a door entry system. A voice said, 'Can I help you?'

'Mrs Dowling;' the woman replied. 'I've come to visit my husband.'

'Hello, Mrs Dowling; come on through.'

As a buzzer sounded, she pulled on the door and went inside. Impulsively, Karl rushed forwards and grabbed the door handle before it had fully closed, stopping it from locking. Once inside, he expected to be challenged immediately, but it appeared that the reception was at the far end of the corridor. Slowly, he made his way down the corridor, not really knowing what he was looking for. On either side of him were windows looking into individual cubicles. In each one, a patient lay sleeping, surrounded by various monitors and machinery. To his right, a nurse tentatively adjusted one of the machines that beeped incessantly. He walked past half a dozen or more cubicles, each with a patient apparently fast asleep; it was so weird.

Then he saw her. She was the most beautiful thing he had ever seen. Her long blond hair looked like silk laid out on her pillow, flowing down onto her shoulders. Her features were angelic: a petite nose with perfectly shaped lips. Her eyes were closed but he just knew they would be of the deepest blue imaginable. What could possibly be wrong with her? She looked perfect. Come to think of it, why were they all asleep?

As he thought about, it the penny dropped: each patient was in a coma, hence 'Neurological Ward'. What an idiot he was. He placed his hands on the glass and stared through at the beautiful young girl. Guessing her age, he thought she could be no more than eighteen or nineteen. The urge to go into the cubicle and read the notes was overwhelming. The nurse was still busy with the defective monitor. Looking left and right he slowly opened the door, half expecting her to sit up and ask who he was, but that was not going to happen.

Standing at the bottom of the bed, he picked up the note chart and read out her name – 'Nicola Mills'. He looked up from the chart. 'Hello Nicola.' He had read that the last sense to leave a person was hearing, and that sometimes people wake up from a coma when talked to by friends and loved ones. 'I wonder,' he said to himself. He walked round the side of the bed and stood next to her, again glancing around. He reached down and picked up her hand; it felt cold and lifeless. As the warmth of his hand radiated into hers, he closed his eyes.

Karl was in darkness, but it was not his darkness. It was like standing in the middle of an unfamiliar room with the lights off, not knowing where the door was or even if it was filled with furniture. He could hear something; it sounded like weeping. He held his breath in an attempt to heighten his senses. He heard it again only louder. 'Nicola,' he called out, and the weeping stopped immediately. Extending his arms, he felt around in front of him in the darkness. I need a light, he thought; if only I had a torch. With that thought firmly in his mind, he reached into his pocket and pulled out a small torch. 'You're a genius, Hennessey,' he said to himself. Slowly, he shone the beam of light around the room, almost instantly picking out what looked like a crouching figure. He quickly directed the light towards the silhouette. 'Nicola?'

'Who is it?' came the reply. As the light illuminated her face, she turned away, away, raising a hand to protect her eyes from the glare.

'I'm sorry,' said Karl, lowering the torch. He walked over and crouched down beside her. 'Don't be afraid. My name's Karl, Karl Hennessey.'

A glint of light caught her eye and he saw that he was right; they were the deepest blue he had ever seen. Realising he was staring, he smiled.

'Where are we?' she asked.

It had not occurred to Karl that someone in a coma might not actually know they were unconscious, but it made sense. 'You're asleep,' said Karl.

She looked puzzled. 'Why can't I wake up?'

'I can't answer that. All I know is that you're lying in a bed in Ashbourne General Hospital.'

Raising a hand to her cheek, she pinched herself and shook her head. 'But it feels so real.' She thought for a moment. 'If I'm asleep, then that means you aren't real.'

'You're going to have to trust me on that one, but I promise you I'm very real. I have a gift, an ability to enter people's dreams. I saw you lying there and . . .'

Karl was suddenly torn from the dream. He opened his eyes.

'What do you think you are doing?' A man in his early fifties stood over him. 'How dare you touch my daughter! Nurse, nurse!'

The nurse from two cubicles down came dashing round. Karl raised his hands in a submissive gesture. 'I mean no harm; I'm just trying to help.'

'Who are you?' demanded the nurse.

'Please, I'm a friend. Believe me, I only mean to help.'

Seeing the aggression building in the man's face, Karl backed away. The rumpus had attracted the attention of two other nurses, who both rushed to the cubicle.

'Kaz, call Security,' said one nurse to her colleague.

Karl could tell he was running out of time and had to think quickly.

'I take it you're Nicola's father?' asked Karl. 'You have to trust me; I might be the only person who can help your daughter.' Karl reached into his pocket and pulled out a business card. At arm's length, he offered it to the man. 'Please take it.'

The nurse stepped forward. 'I think you'd better leave, Security will be here any minute.'

'OK, OK, I'm going.' Karl placed the card on a trolley and pointed at it. 'I'll leave it there. Call me, for your daughter's sake.'

Karl backed away, maintaining eye contact with the man, and then turned and left. The nurses immediately rallied around their patient, checking that everything was in order. The senior nurse could see the distress on the father's face.

'I'm very sorry, Mr Mills; I haven't a clue how he got in here. I'll get Security to check the CCTV.'

Mills just stood there staring at his daughter. It had been three months now since the accident, but he still blamed himself. She had been the passenger in his car. They had literally just pulled off the drive. As he turned the car into the road, she was reaching for her seatbelt when suddenly another vehicle slammed into the back of them. His daughter was hurled forwards, slamming her head sideways into the dashboard. Being an older vehicle, there were no air bags to absorb the impact, and her head had taken the full force. The external signs of the accident on her body had now healed, but there was still no sign of her regaining consciousness. The doctors could do nothing but monitor her condition and hope that something internal or external would trigger her back to consciousness.

Mills looked up from his daughter and picked up the card. 'Mr K Hennessey, BSc Honours Psychology,' he read 'Psychological Evaluations.' It felt like clutching at straws, but what else had he got? He looked back at his daughter. He sat down beside her bed, squeezing the card tightly in one hand, the other covering his eyes as he quietly wept, engulfed in sorrow.

Karl went straight back to his ward, expecting to be challenged by Security at any moment. He pressed the buzzer at the entrance to the ward. 'Can I help you?' came the reply.

'Hello, it's Karl Hennessey.'

'Ah, Mr Hennessey, we've been looking for you.'

'Shit,' said Karl under his breath; 'now I'm for it.'

The door buzzed. Pulling it open, he went inside. A nurse was walking towards him, shaking her head. He wondered if they had already called the police, and approached her sheepishly.

'Your results came back an hour ago,' she said. 'The doctor wanted to see you, but he's been called away, so unfortunately you're going to have to see him at the outpatient clinic to discuss any problems you may have. He did say your results were perfectly fine and you shouldn't worry, just take it easy for a while.'

'That's a relief,' said Karl. 'So I can go home?'

'Yes, the appointment will be in the post.'

Karl didn't need telling twice. Not wanting to hang around, he picked up the rest of his things and made his way out of the hospital. It was a long way home, but rather than calling out Charlie and Susie, he jumped in a cab. What the hell? He could afford it.

29

Clutching at straws

It was just after 11 pm; Harry and Gloria Mills were watching television. Since the accident, their entire lives had revolved around trips to the hospital, hoping for the slightest sign of improvement. But after three months, there had been no change. For the first two months, they both visited every day. Come rain or shine, they were at the hospital by 9:30 am and did not leave until late into the evening. As time went by, the stress of travelling and long days of waiting in vain was beginning to affect their health. If they were to stay strong for their daughter, something had to give. They decided to each visit on alternate days, so that when one was at the hospital, the other would stay at home and rest. It had been four days now since the incident with Karl, and, not wanting to upset his wife, Mills had said nothing to her. He specifically asked the nurses not to mention it.

'Fancy a cup of tea, Glo?' he asked, pushing himself up out of the chair.

'No thanks, love. I'm going up to bed; I'm shattered. The traffic was terrible on the way back from the hospital this evening.'

'OK, I'll be up in a minute; just going to have a cuppa.'

He went into the kitchen. As he put the kettle on, he heard his wife slowly trudging up the stairs. It seemed to take her a long time to get to the top, a testament to just how much this was taking out of her. Sitting down at the kitchen table, he pulled Karl's business card from his pocket. It had been on his mind constantly since the incident. He had read it over and over again, wondering what he should do. As he drank the last of his tea, he put the card firmly back into his pocket and went to bed. As had been the case for the last few nights, it would be quite some time before sleep finally took him.

The following morning, he was on the road by 9 am, heading for the hospital. The usual rush hour traffic did not faze him; his mind was still firmly fixed on Karl's business card. Arriving at the ward, he buzzed himself in. Having spent so much time there, he was now on first-name terms with all the nurses and carers.

He entered his daughter's room. 'Morning, Nicky.' He always spoke to her as if she were wide awake, in the hope that one day she might answer back. Sitting next to her bed, he read out all the headlines from the newspaper, especially the celebrity scandal. Before the accident, they had often sat together doing the crossword, and he knew she enjoyed it. So now he had a ritual of reading out every clue, giving her the opportunity to answer, hoping that it might just be the key to waking her up.

After about an hour, he folded up his newspaper and placed it on the bedside cabinet. Sitting on the edge of his chair, he took hold of her cool hand. 'I don't know if you can hear me, darling, but I think I have to try this man; I don't know what else to do.' Tears welled up in his eyes. 'The doctors can't help you, so I have to try anything I can.'

He stood up and leaned down, kissing her forehead. Reaching into his pocket, he took out the business card. Without saying another word, he turned and walked out of the ward, squeezing the card tightly in his hand.

After the weekend's exploits, Charlie was in no mood to take no for an answer; he cancelled all Karl's appointments until Thursday. That would give him three days of complete rest. He wanted Karl to take the whole week off but knew that he would be more successful suggesting a compromise. If he had known that Karl had interacted with the girl in the hospital, there would have been hell to pay.

Charlie had stayed at home with Karl; it was the only way he could ensure his brother was resting. When they arrived at the office on Thursday morning, the answering machine was full of enquires from potential clients. They already had a waiting list of between four and six weeks; losing three days work that week, although necessary, only served to put Karl under more pressure.

One of his appointments on the first day back was with the Curtises, who had called three or four times over the week trying to ascertain how Karl was after being taken from the house unconscious. Charlie had reassured them that all was well and arranged an appointment for them.

Karl had just finished assessing his first client. Morning appointments were mostly kept for interviewing new clients. He preferred to do his interactions after lunch, as most people were too fresh in the morning to completely relax. Damian Curtis was his next appointment, and Karl hoped it would be his last as the interaction, although very stressful, went as well as it possibly could have done in the circumstances.

As Karl sat back in his chair sipping a well-earned cup of coffee, Charlie came in. 'Karl, there's a Mr Mills on the phone asking to speak to you in person. He says you met his daughter Nicola at the hospital.'

Charlie raised his eyebrows, a cheeky smirk across his face. Karl put his coffee down on the desk. 'I'll take it in here.'

Smiling to himself, Charlie went back into reception and picked up the phone. 'Putting you through now, Mr Mills.'

Karl pressed the button to put the caller on speakerphone. 'Hello, Mr Mills; I'm so pleased you called.'

'Mr Hennessey, it's taken a lot of thought, and I hope I'm doing the right thing.'

'You are, Mr Mills, believe me, you are. My methods are unique. Is it possible we could meet up and talk?'

The line went quiet, but Karl sensed he was still there. 'Mr Mills?'

It took a few more seconds before he answered. 'I'd prefer to meet at the hospital.'

'Of course,' replied Karl. 'My diary's full tomorrow, but I'm free on Saturday.'

'That will be fine,' Mills answered. 'I'll meet you by the main entrance at twelve o'clock.'

Karl had barely ended the call when Charlie came through the door, grinning from ear to ear. 'You're a dark horse, you are; is she a nurse? No, no, don't tell me, she's a doctor isn't she?'

Karl sat back in his chair and interlocked his fingers. 'I might as well tell you; you'll find out, you always do.'

Charlie nodded his head. 'You're right there, bro.'

'She's in a coma,' said Karl, flatly.

Charlie stared at him, taken aback. 'Hang on, I can feel a song coming on here; I think it was by the Smiths.' He started singing, 'Girlfriend in a coma, aha, aha.'

Karl cut him short. 'Stop taking the piss; she's not my girlfriend, she's a client.'

Charlie turned away and with his jovial manner suddenly changed, turned back. 'Are you telling me that, after being taken into hospital unconscious, the next morning you were prowling round the hospital checking out comatose patients?'

'It wasn't like that, Charlie.'

Charlie got up and walked round the room shaking his head. 'We sat by your bed all night. Do you know how worried we were?'

'I know and I appreciate it, but like I said it wasn't like that. Please let me explain.'

Charlie looked at his watch then sat down again in front of Karl's desk. 'You've got ten minutes before the Curtises arrive. Redeem yourself.'

Karl told Charlie everything that had happened, including the interaction and the confrontation he had with her father. The way Karl explained it to Charlie, it seemed as if it was potentially a whole new area of work for them. What Karl didn't tell him was that he couldn't get the girl out of his mind.

Still annoyed by Karl's exploits but nevertheless having to accept them, Charlie went back into the reception area to await the arrival of the next client. Right on time, the Curtises arrived. They were still understandably concerned about Karl's health but at the same time looked remarkably happy. As Karl greeted them, he extended his hand, which Damian shook. Then completely out of character, Damian pulled him close as if he was a long-lost friend. As soon as he released him, Paula rushed forward and did the same, following it with a kiss on his cheek.

'Gosh,' said Karl, 'I wish all my clients were as friendly; please, take a seat.'

'You really had us worried on Saturday night,' said Paula as they moved towards the desk.

'Don't worry. It turned out to be nothing; I've just been overdoing it a little. Anyway, this is not about me.' He glanced at Damian. 'How have you been?'

Damian smiled. 'It's been remarkable; I feel like a different person. In fact, I feel so good that I've been down to the job centre and registered for some part-time work.'

'That's brilliant,' said Karl. 'So the nightmares have gone?'

'I still have the dreams, but they've changed, if you know what I mean.'

Karl smiled and nodded his head.

'I wanted to show you something,' Damian continued. He reached into his inside jacket pocket and pulled out a small piece of newspaper, which he passed to Karl. Opening out the cutting, Karl began to read.

> *US BOMB KILLS BRITISH SOLDIERS IN AFGHANISTAN.*
> *A bomb apparently dropped by an American fighter jet that had been called in for air support killed 9 and injured 1 British soldier in southern Afghanistan, officials said on Friday. The British unit had been on patrol on Thursday evening in Helmand Province when it came under Taliban attack. The Ministry of Defence statement said that, during the intense engagement that ensued, close air support was called in from two US F-15 aircraft to repel the enemy. One bomb is believed to have hit the British position. Next of kin have been informed. 'There are several possible reasons why this tragic*

incident has occurred, but at present we are not in a position, and I don't think we will be for some time, to establish exactly what has happened,' said the spokesman for British troops in Helmand, Lt Colonel Colin Maidstone. The US Embassy in London commented, 'The United States expresses its deep condolences to the families and loved ones of the soldiers who died, and also wish the injured soldier a speedy recovery.'

Karl finished reading the article and for a few seconds sat in silence; it was very rare he was stuck for words.

Finally, Damian spoke. 'I think I can move on now, put the past behind me.' He looked at his wife and took her hand, and then turned back to Karl. 'Thank you; you've saved my marriage and probably my sanity.'

Realising that his job was done, Karl stood up. 'I mean this in a nice way, but I hope I don't have to see you again.' The couple laughed as they got to their feet. Karl held the newspaper cutting out to Damian.

'Would you put it in the bin for me? I don't need it any more.'

'Certainly,' said Karl. He crumpled the paper in his palm and dropped it into the bin.

As the couple left, Karl's mind wandered back to something his father had said to him many years ago. He said that one day Karl would discover why he had been given this gift. Smiling to himself, he thought it felt good.

On Saturday morning just before 10:30 am, Karl stepped onto a train to Ashbourne. It was only a thirty-minute journey so he would arrive a little early, but it didn't matter as he had the whole day to himself. Charlie and Susie had gone shopping and would not be back until early evening.

As the train pulled into the station, Karl reached out the window to open the door. Being a Saturday morning, it was fairly quiet and he was able to get a taxi straight away. Within ten minutes, they pulled up outside the hospital's main entrance. After paying the driver, Karl glanced at his watch: 11:25, half an hour to kill.

Just inside the entrance, there was a small cafeteria. He bought a coffee and sat down in full view of the entrance, just in case Mr Mills was early. Karl's life had become so hectic that he had forgotten what it was like to just sit down and watch the world go by. He had been sitting there for about ten minutes, beginning to enjoy the enforced inactivity, when a voice from behind him spoke his name. Startled, he spun around. It was Mr Mills. When they had first met, Karl had not really appreciated just how big he was. Mills was at least six feet three inches tall and powerfully built for a man his age. Karl stood up and as they shook hands, the larger man's hand dwarfing Karl's.

'I didn't see you arrive,' said Karl.

'I'm always here early. I have a routine with Nicola.'

'Oh, I see,' replied Karl. 'Can I get you a coffee?' Mills accepted, and once the drinks were ordered they both sat down.

'Mr Hennessey . . .' Mills began.

'Please, it's Karl.' Karl's openness seemed genuine, and Mills nodded.

'Karl, I'm Harry. I'll be honest with you, Karl, and I hope you will be the same. I don't know anything about you except what I read on your business card. I know I'm clutching at straws, but I have nowhere else to turn. I'm not a rich man, but I'm not poor either.'

'Don't worry about that,' interrupted Karl.

'No, please; I won't accept charity, but I won't be made a fool of either.'

Already Karl liked him. He was a no-nonsense, very proud, family man, unfortunately at his wits end.

'Harry, I've never tried to help a coma patient before. Last Sunday was a first for me. You'll find this very hard to believe, but last week I made contact with Nicola.'

Harry looked down at the table, and Karl could see that he was struggling to keep control of his emotions. Composing himself, he looked up at Karl.

'How?'

'By touching people. When they are asleep, I can interact with their thoughts. You have to believe me on this, Harry. Nicola doesn't even know she is in a coma, but I believe I may be able to help her to regain consciousness.'

'Naturally, I want to believe you but . . .'

Karl stopped him. 'Harry, I'll prove it. Think of something only she would know – a pet's name or maybe a shared memory from her childhood. If I can't give you the answer, I'll walk away and that will be the end of it.'

Mills' instinct was to protect his daughter. This man could be a complete fake, yet he seemed sincere. Deciding to take a chance, Mills looked straight at Karl.

'Ask her about her Nan's dog.' Karl nodded his head.

'When do you plan to do this?' asked Mills apprehensively.

Karl lifted his coffee cup, slugged down the last dregs, and stood up.

'Right now.'

30

A sense of hope

Walking down the corridor towards the lift, Karl gave Harry a brief outline of his gift. Still finding it hard to believe, Harry hoped to God he was not being drawn into some elaborate scam. Either way, he would know soon enough.

As they reached the ward, Harry pressed the intercom on the door and identified himself to the nurse inside, not mentioning that Karl was with him. Since the previous week, when Karl had walked into the ward unnoticed, they had re-evaluated their security. Now when anybody was buzzed on to the ward, a member of staff had to watch to ensure that only the person identified entered and that the door closed behind them. Harry walked in closely followed by Karl. Instantly, the nurse recognised Karl from the previous week. 'Excuse me!' she called out, quickening her pace towards the door. Harry raised his hands and looked at her apologetically.

'He's with me, Carol. Sorry, I should have said.'

'Is this wise, Harry?' asked the nurse, looking very concerned.

'It's OK, honestly. Last week was all a misunderstanding.'

She gave Karl a warning look, and then turned to Harry. 'If you need one of us, just ring the bell.' Harry nodded, and she went about her duties.

Harry stood at his daughter's bedside. 'I've brought someone to see you, Nicola.'

'Hello, Nicola,' said Karl keeping to her father's routine, even though he knew from last week's experience that she couldn't hear him. Harry leaned down and kissed her forehead, and then turned to Karl. 'She's everything to me.' It was clear to Karl that Harry was warning him not to harm her.

'I can see that,' Karl replied.

'Right then,' said Harry, 'she's in your hands.'

Harry stepped past Karl and moved to the bottom of the bed. Pulling up a chair, Karl sat down and, with his elbows on the edge of the bed, gently picked up Nicola's hand. Closing his fingers around it, he gave Harry a reassuring smile and then closed his eyes.

The interaction was almost instant. Sensing her presence nearby, he called out her name and heard something move off to his left. He reached into his pocket and pulled out a small torch. As soon as he switched it on, he saw her crouching in the corner, squinting her eyes as she tried to focus on Karl's silhouette. He directed the beam towards the floor and went over to her and knelt down. 'It's me, Nicola – Karl.'

As the torchlight illuminated her beautiful face, Karl could see tears on her cheeks. He had to change her depressing environment.

'Nicola, I want you to trust me.' As she looked into his eyes, he had an overwhelming urge to hold her close. 'I want you to hold my hands, close your eyes and try to blank your mind.' She didn't hesitate, and without saying a word, she firmly took hold of his hands. 'Now close your eyes, and don't open them until I ask you to.' She did as he asked.

Karl thought of a warm, sunny afternoon in the countryside, fields full of waist-length grass and a beautiful flowing river edged with weeping willows. To Karl, it was an absolutely idyllic place.

'Open your eyes.'

As Nicola opened her eyes, the shock of where she was took her aback and she spun round, the tips of her fingers cutting through the long grass. Outside the dream, her father and a nurse stood looking at Karl. Suddenly, Nicola's heart rate on the monitor began to increase by ten, twenty, then thirty beats. Startled, the nurse jumped into action.

'Leave it!' shouted Harry, almost expecting his daughter's eyes to open at any moment.

The nurse stopped in her tracks, shocked by his outburst. 'But, Mr Mills . . .'

'Please,' said Harry, his mood now quieter. As they watched, the monitor slowly returned to normal.

Nicola stopped and faced Karl. 'Where are we?'

'You're in my dream,' he replied. After another quick glance around, she turned back to Karl and, with a radiant smile, thanked him and then turned and ran, her arms parting the grass. Karl moved to the edge of the field and sat down watching her run around the field without a care in the world. After being in darkness for so long, this must have felt like heaven. Finally, she breathlessly made her way back towards him and lay on the ground next to him. He glanced down at her; she was wearing a short, yellow, summer dress that complemented her curvy body. As she turned her head to look at him, he diverted his eyes towards her face.

'Karl, why can't I wake up?'

'I don't know, but I want to try and find out.'

'Why did you leave me so suddenly last time?'

'It was your father, he pulled my hand off yours. If I'm not touching you, I can't interact.'

'So, you're touching me now?' He nodded, feeling himself blush. Reaching over, she smiled and took his hand.

'I have to ask you something, Nicola,'

'Nicky;' she interrupted, 'only Dad calls me Nicola.'

'Nicky, your father doesn't think I'm for real. He's naturally cautious about this, and he wants me to ask you something only you and he would know.'

She was now lying on her side facing Karl and was very close; his lack of contact with the opposite sex made him very nervous. As he looked down, she sensed his shyness and put her hand under his chin, raising his head. Smiling, she asked him what the question was.

'Oh, sorry,' he stuttered, feeling silly about the way he had reacted, 'your Nan's dog, something happened to the dog.'

Nicky lay back on the grass and putting her hands behind her head; she had a little chuckle to herself.

'My Nan came to stay one Christmas. She had a Springer Spaniel called Prince, a really bad-tempered dog. My Nan was an invalid so she couldn't take him for walks. Back home, her neighbour's son used to take him out. Anyway, Dad took him out every morning, but one day when he was getting his coat on, the dog got out of the front door. By the time Dad got out, there he was, gone. We looked for him, but it was no good, and it was three days before we told her. We kept up a pretence, calling his name as if he was in the house, and she was none the wiser. We finally told her he had been stolen. Dad pretended to phone the police. I remember it vividly. He was trying to keep a straight face with my Nan looking on, and it was so funny I had to leave the room.' As Karl watched her telling the tale, she looked so happy.

'He's a nice man, your father.'

'I know,' she replied, smiling.

They walked along the riverbank for what seemed like hours, talking about everything and nothing. Karl felt as if he had known her all his life and hoped she felt the same. Eventually, he knew he had to leave.

'I have to go now, Nicky.'

There was a look of dread on her face. 'Will I have to go back to the dark place?'

The sad look on Karl's face gave her the answer.

'I want you to keep your mind focused on waking up.' He took hold of her hands. 'Don't give up; I won't.'

Through a pained smile, the last thing Karl saw as he closed his eyes was a tear running down her cheek.

Releasing her hand, Karl opened his eyes. Nicky's father had been patiently sitting on a chair at the bottom of the bed, waiting for the slightest glimmer of hope. The nurse had left to attend to other patients, assuring Harry that if he felt any need to call, a member of staff would be there in an instant. As soon as he saw Karl's eyes open, he jumped to his feet.

'Karl, what happened?' Karl glanced at his watch, seeing that almost two hours had passed. In the dream, it had felt like a whole day; no wonder it took so much out of him.

'She's OK, Harry. I reassured her the doctors are doing everything they can.'

He looked at Nicola lying so still. He didn't want to tell her father about what she referred to as the dark place; he was already under enough stress without burdening him with his daughter's psychological torment. Instead, he turned to him and said, 'You really should have told Nicky's Nan that Prince simply got out and ran away.'

Harry stared at Karl, and, with the colour draining from his face, he slumped back down on his chair. Any doubt of Karl's ability was now well and truly expelled from his mind. Karl gave no promises, but agreed that until what had caused the coma had time to heal, he would continue to interact with Nicola and try to find the trigger that would bring her out of her unwilling sleep.

It was just after six o'clock when Karl arrived home. Slipping his jacket, off he yawned; an early night was on the cards. In the kitchen, he found a note propped up against a mug on the table, 'GONE TO PICS DON'T WAIT UP'. I won't, he thought.

He was so tired that even cooking something to eat seemed like too much effort. He made a quick phone call to the local pizzeria; the food arrived within half an hour, and Karl was soon stretched out on the settee with a pizza box on his chest. The day's activities had given him quite an appetite, and he ate heartily while flicking through the TV channels. As the evening wore on, he felt his eyes becoming heavy. Glancing at the clock it was almost ten; it would be another couple of hours before Charlie and Susie came home. He turned off the TV, and, before going upstairs gave the room a fleeting look before flicking off the light switch.

Leaving his clothes in a pile on the floor, he wearily climbed into bed, and within seconds of his head hitting the pillow, he drifted off into a well-earned sleep. He had no idea how long he had been asleep, but was suddenly aware that he was dreaming. He found himself looking across the field that he had mentally produced in Nicola's dream. In the distance, he could see a figure standing in the long grass waving. The person was a long way off, but by the build and colour of her hair, he was sure it was Nicola. He began walking towards her.

Once he reached a hundred metres or so, he could recognise her quite clearly, waving her hands and smiling. Returning a wave, he continued on towards her, but found himself beginning to slow down as the long grass impeded his progress. Suddenly, a figure rose up from the grass behind her. She seemed completely unaware of the person's presence, but Karl's senses told him there was something very wrong. Standing directly behind her, the man's powerful frame overshadowed her. As Karl struggled through increasingly dense grass, the figure reached around Nicola, covering her mouth with his hand and pulling her head back. Nicky reached up with both hands, grabbing at his forearm in an attempt to release herself. Horrified, Karl fought to advance towards her, and then saw the man's face appear over Nicola's shoulder. Instantly, an icy chill ran down his spine freezing him on the spot. It was Mortiboys, the child-molesting master from his old school.

Mortiboys drew Nicola closer to him, a grotesque smile spreading across his face. As panic set in, Karl fought desperately to move faster. It was as if the grass were weaving its way around his lower body, holding onto his legs. He was just twenty metres away. Again he summoned all his strength to battle on. Mortiboys' free hand came up in front of Nicola's face, holding what looked like a razor. Hers eyes bulged as she saw the blade, her screams muffled by the master's other hand. Karl tried to shout, 'NO!', but no sound came from his mouth. As the razor slashed across her throat, blood gushed and spurted from her neck, instantly turning her dress crimson. Her eyes closed, and Karl saw her and Mortiboys collapse into the long grass.

Karl dragged himself on towards them, a confusion of senses racing through him. The terrible feelings from his past experiences with the master were suddenly torn from where they had been hidden away in the back of his mind and were now acutely with him again, swirling around with the fear he felt for Nicola and the rage that was erupting towards Mortiboys.

Finally reaching the spot where he had seen them fall, Karl searched the grass, but there was no blood and no body. Where was she? In a state of panic, he clawed wildly through the grass. From behind him, he heard the sound of sick, sardonic laughter. He spun round; Mortiboys was standing with Nicola no more than ten metres away, both of them covered in blood. Mortiboys held his grip across her mouth, and she was reaching out to Karl with both hands. 'She's mine now, Hennessey,' sneered Mortiboys.

Karl rushed towards them, but again they disappeared into the long grass. They reappeared to his right, and again he tried to reach them. Each time he got close, the same thing happened; it seemed endless. Eventually, nearing mental exhaustion, he screamed out at the top of his voice, 'LEAVE HER ALONE, YOU BASTARD!'

'Karl! Karl, wake up, wake up!'

Karl opened his eyes to find Charlie standing over him, shaking his shoulders with both hands. 'Jesus Christ, bro! What the hell was going on then?'

Standing in the bedroom doorway, Susie had both hands to her face and was clearly concerned.

'I couldn't wake you up, bro; I've been trying for ages.'

'I'm OK, Charlie; it was just a nightmare.'

Charlie shook his head, 'Just a nightmare? It didn't look like that to us.'

'What time is it?' asked Karl.

Charlie glanced at his watch. 'Three.'

'Sorry I woke you both up,' said Karl, still somewhat dazed.

'We weren't asleep,' Susie replied, smiling, 'but are you sure you're all right?'

Karl nodded in reply and Susie went back to bed. Charlie sat on the edge of Karl's bed. He knew his brother only too well, and whatever he had been dreaming about had shaken him up. 'Are you really OK?'

'I'm fine;' replied Karl, 'see you in the morning.'

But Charlie was not convinced. 'Come on, bro, I could do with a cup of tea.'

Karl sat at the kitchen table while Charlie put the kettle on. 'It was Mortiboys,' said Karl. 'Remember him?'

'I remember him, all right,' Charlie replied, pleased to have got Karl talking.

'I don't understand it, Charlie. It's as if other people's nightmares are getting mixed up in my dreams and I don't have any control over the outcome, or the people in them.'

'Or maybe you just haven't learned to do it yet.'

Karl thought about it. 'Good point,' he replied. 'I just wish I could put some people out of my mind forever.'

Charlie finished making the tea and put a mug in front of Karl. 'Here you go, bro.'

Karl thanked him. As they sat drinking their tea, all Karl could think about was Nicola. He wanted to tell Charlie how he felt about her, but in the circumstances how could he? It was just a dream.

31

Bright lights

Two months passed, and to Charlie's increasing but silent displeasure, Karl continued to interact with Nicola, using his gift to free her from the solitude of her own subconscious. Unable to find any clues as to why she could not regain consciousness, he constantly gave hope to her parents by giving them snippets of information from her past, which without prior knowledge he could not have possibly known. The medical staff were still extremely sceptical of Karl but accepted him for the sake of Nicola's parents.

Karl was now only spending three days a week at the office; on alternate Saturdays he might visit a client at home, but this was becoming less and less. Charlie kept his feelings to himself. They were still inundated with work, but Karl appeared a lot more relaxed with his new work schedule. Although he frequently still had nightmares, which turned up all sorts of horrors from past interactions, he accepted them as just another aspect of his gift.

The amount of time he spent at Nicola's side was not just attracting attention from the medical staff. A little further down the ward lay a gentleman called Godfrey Phelps. At eighty years of age, he had had a full and active life. Married for almost fifty years, he had lost his wife Doris just six months previously. The distress and trauma he felt at her death had not left him, and he suffered a stroke, which was in turn the reason he now lay in a deep coma. His four loving children took turns keeping a constant vigil at his bedside, but, three weeks on, there had been no sign of improvement. Word was getting around about Karl's supposed ability and what he was doing at Nicola's bedside. Like the medical staff, most people just dismissed Karl as a fraud and did not give it another thought. That was not the case with Colin Phelps. The eldest son had watched Karl intently on two or three occasions and was determined that any form of hope for his father had to be pursued.

It was just before 7 pm on a Saturday evening. Karl had been interacting with Nicola for more than two hours, and, just as he had done with Blakeway all those years ago, he used his gift to take her to places he had only imagined, trying to make it more exciting for her each time. Every time he left her, he found it harder and harder to let go. As the psychological relationship was growing, Karl realised that he was falling in love with her.

Karl opened his eyes. As he brought them into focus, he noticed Colin Phelps sitting next to his father's bed, staring in his direction. As soon as Phelps realised Karl was looking at him, he diverted his eyes back to his father. Karl knew that he must have appeared a little odd, sitting still for so long with his eyes closed, and just took the staring with a pinch of salt. For the last few weeks Nicola's parents had allowed Karl to visit their daughter alone. It was clear by now that he meant her no harm, and he constantly refused to except any form of payment for his services.

Karl stood up and said goodbye to Nicola; the hospital staff encouraged it, and although they had already said goodbye in the dream, he didn't want to get in their bad books again. Checking his watch, he hurried down the corridor towards the main entrance. It was just after 6:45 pm; if there was a waiting taxi, he would just about make the next train. But unknown to Karl, Colin Phelps was hurrying along behind trying to catch him up.

Just as Karl reached the door, a voice behind him gasped, 'Excuse me.' Karl glanced over his shoulder. 'Could I have a word?' Phelps was out of breath from rushing along the corridor. Karl looked out of the glass door and could see a cab right by the main entrance. 'It won't take more than a couple minutes,' said Phelps, his face almost pleading with Karl. His expression won Karl over and, as courteous as ever, Karl asked how he could help.

'I couldn't help but notice that you've been visiting a young lady in the Neurological Ward.' Karl nodded, suddenly feeling a little defensive. 'Oh, I'm sorry;' added Phelps, 'it's my father – he's on the same ward. A few weeks ago, he had a stroke and has been in a coma ever since. The doctors are telling us he may never regain consciousness, but then again he could wake up at any moment. You see, without his medication, he wouldn't survive for more than a few hours, but how long does it go on?' His head dropped.

Karl could see the hurt in the man's eyes. Glancing at his watch, he could see that he would now miss his train. 'Let's sit down over there, and you can tell me about your father.'

Phelps thanked him, looking as if just having the chance to talk had lifted a weight off his shoulders. They went to the coffee bar, where

Phelps told Karl all about his father. Karl felt almost jealous of how proud Phelps was of his father. The old man had been a massive influence on his son's life, and it was such a shame it was ending this way.

'Well,' said Karl, 'it sounds as if your father has been a good man.'

'He certainly has,' said Phelps, nodding his head in agreement.

'If there is no improvement in your father's condition by next Thursday, I'll see what I can do, but you must be aware, as I tell all my clients, I cannot promise anything.'

'I understand;' said Phelps, 'thank you.'

On Sunday morning, although tired, Karl was up early. Again, he planned to spend the best part of the day at the hospital with Nicola. Charlie enjoyed his Sunday morning lie-ins, but hearing Karl moving around downstairs so early, he decided to get up and have a word with him; his obsession with this coma victim was becoming a little worrying. When Karl had arrived home the previous evening, Charlie and Susie had been relaxing on the settee. Karl was so tired, he had hardly said a word to them but gone straight to bed. Now, barely nine hours later, he was preparing for another visit.

Karl was finishing a piece of toast as Charlie came into the kitchen. 'Mornin', bro.'

'Morning,' replied Karl. Charlie ruffled his hair as he flicked the switch on the kettle.

'You're up early,' said Karl.

'I could say the same about you; it is Sunday, you know, bro.'

'Thought I'd spend a few hours at the hospital.'

Charlie tried to think of the best way to speak his mind without offending his brother. 'Don't you think you're spending a little too much time on this client, bro?'

Karl stopped chewing his toast. 'She's not a client.'

'What is she then?'

Karl thought for a moment, a little stumped by the question. 'Well, she's a friend.'

'But you've never seen her awake; how can she be a friend?'

Karl was becoming agitated.

'Let's face it, bro,' Charlie continued, 'it's been weeks now; if she was going to wake up, it would have happened by now, especially with you spending so much time in her head.'

The thought of her never waking up was too much for Karl to accept. Completely out of character, he snapped aggressively, at his brother. 'She will wake up, I just have to keep trying.'

'OK, OK, calm down.' Charlie was more than a little surprised by his brother's reaction.

Jumping to his feet, Karl grabbed his keys and jacket from the back of the chair. Before he could rush out of the kitchen, Charlie grabbed his arm. 'Karl.' Karl stopped and turned to look at his brother. 'Look at it from my perspective, Karl; I'm only thinking of you.'

Karl pulled his arm away from his brother's grip. 'It doesn't sound like it.' He turned and walked through the living room towards the front door, 'I'll be back this evening.' The door slammed behind him.

Charlie shook his head and sat down at the kitchen table. Running his fingers back through his hair, he gave out a deep sigh. He had never seen Karl like this before, and it worried him.

Hearing raised voices and the door banging, Susie jumped out of bed and went downstairs. 'Where's Karl gone?'

'I'll give you one guess,' Charlie replied.

Susie picked up a cup from the sink drainer and reached across Charlie for the tea bags. 'Don't worry, darlin';' she said, 'it's just a phase he's going through.'

'I hope so,' replied Charlie. 'I do hope so.'

It was after ten o'clock when Karl arrived at the hospital, and the reception area was quiet; there was a very different atmosphere from the bustle of the weekdays. At weekends, Nicola's parents rarely arrived before eleven o'clock; it was the only time they had any kind of lie-in. Karl buzzed into the ward and made his way over to Nicola's bed. Nothing had changed; she lay in exactly the same position as he had left her the previous evening.

'Morning, Nicky,' he said, slipping his coat off and hanging it on the chair at the side of the bed. As he stood looking at her motionless form, Charlie's words were at the forefront of his mind. What if she didn't wake up? They couldn't go on like this forever. It was as if he had entered a world of virtual reality and couldn't find a way out.

As he looked down the ward, the number of people lying there, trapped within their own minds, made the hair stand up on the back of his neck. He thought of his conversation with Colin Phelps and looked towards his father a few beds down the ward. Almost completely surrounded by monitors and feeding tubes, he looked a sorry sight. Edging his way around Nicola's bed, Karl walked down to Mr Phelps's bed. His skin was ashen in colour, and the little hair he had was pure white, a testament to his years.

Being more accepted on the ward now, little attention was paid to Karl as he moved around. He pulled up a chair and sat down next to the old man. Just as happened so many times before, he had the overwhelming urge to touch his hand. Resting his elbow on the bed, he placed his palm on the back of the man's hand and closed his eyes. It was unusually hazy to start with, and Karl felt as if he was trying to find his way through a dense fog. He wondered if it had something to do with the medication or if it was just his state of mind.

Slowly, the mist cleared, and Karl found himself standing on an underground railway station platform, very similar to those in London. It was very quiet, and towards the other end of the platform he could see a man sitting on a bench. As he got closer, he guessed that by the colour of his hair and the frailness of his body that it was Phelps. Slowly, Phelps turned towards Karl; he looked tired and very vulnerable. Not wanting to frighten him, Karl smiled and said hello.

Phelps looked a little startled. 'Who are you?'

'My name's Karl. Your son, Colin, sent me.'

At this, the old man's eyes lit up. 'Where is he? I knew he wouldn't leave me. I've been waiting so long; will he be on the train? It will be here again soon.'

'Do you mind if I sit down?' asked Karl.

'Not at all,' replied Phelps, inching his way along the bench. Karl sat next to him.

'Do you know where you are, Mr Phelps?'

Phelps looked confused, a little like someone suffering from dementia. 'To be honest, no.' There were a few seconds of silence, and then Phelps asked, 'I'm dead, aren't I?'

'No,' Karl smiled, 'you're not dead, but you're not very well. You're in a coma and you have been since you had a stroke a few weeks ago.'

'I had a stroke?'

'Unfortunately, yes.'

Sitting back against the bench, Phelps sighed. 'Now I am confused.' He was deep in thought. 'Doris was on the train.'

'Doris?' said Karl.

'Doris, my wife. When the train arrives, I can see her and she calls to me, but I can't get on.' He sat looking down at the floor. 'It would have been fifty years this year we've been married. Could you help me next time it arrives?'

'I don't know,' said Karl thoughtfully. 'Your wife's dead, Mr Phelps.'

The old man acknowledged with just a nod of his head. 'I'm lost without her. We had a great life together.' His eyes glazed over with tears.

From the tunnel came the sound of static on the tracks. Karl stood up.

'Here it comes,' said Phelps.

Suddenly, the entire platform was engulfed in a piercing, bright light. Karl covered his eyes and turned away, but Phelps stood firmly without flinching. The train pulled into the station and stopped. Once the doors had opened, there was absolute silence. Karl turned to look, still partially covering his eyes. Phelps was slowly walking towards the train. One of his hands was raised as if he was waving to a passenger. Through squinted eyes, Karl scanned the train; what could Phelps see that he couldn't?

Phelps tottered towards the train, but as he got close to the open door, he stopped. It was as if there was a force field preventing him from getting onto the train. With all his might he tried to break through, but to no avail. Slowly, the doors closed, and Phelps was left reaching out with both hands for some invisible goal. The train pulled away, and as quickly as it had arrived, it was gone.

Phelps turned to Karl. 'Did you see her? Did you see Doris? She was standing just inside the train telling me to get on, but there was some kind of barrier across the door; I could feel it.'

'I couldn't see anyone, Mr Phelps.'

The old man lowered his head, slowly walked back to the bench and sat down.

'You say my son sent you?' Karl nodded his head. 'I think I know why I can't get on that train.' There was sadness in the old man's eyes. 'I'm tired, Karl; I believe it's my time. Will you do something for me?'

'Of course, Mr Phelps.'

'Will you pass a message to my son? Ask him to think of what I talked about last Christmas, and tell him this is it. He'll know what I mean.'

Getting to his feet, Phelps put out his hand. 'Goodbye, Karl, and thank you.'

Karl knew it was his way of saying, you've done your job. As they shook hands, Karl closed his eyes. Almost instantly, he was back in the ward. Standing at the bottom of the bed staring at him was Colin Phelps. Startled, Karl jumped up from his chair.

'Colin, I thought . . .'

Colin raised his hands. 'It's OK, Karl, it's OK. I'm just pleased you found the time to sit with him.'

'I was visiting my friend, and while the ward was quiet, I thought I'd come and see your father.'

'Did anything happen?'

'Let's have a chat over a coffee.'

The coffee bar was almost empty. As they sat opposite each other, Karl could see the tension in Colin's face. 'I'm not going to beat about the bush, Colin. If your father wasn't on his medication, he wouldn't survive.

I think it's his time.' Colin looked agitated; he had known for some time what Karl was telling him but it was just too hard to accept. 'Your father asked me to remind you about a conversation you had with him at Christmas; he said you would understand.' Colin covered his face with both hands and lowered his head.

'Are you all right, Colin?'

Colin nodded. Then after a moment he looked up.

'We talked about him growing old, and he told me the one thing he dreaded was becoming incapable and losing his dignity. He said if anything like that happened, I would know what to do. It's a decision I hoped I would never have to make.'

'I'm very sorry,' said Karl.

'Don't be; I appreciate your honesty.' Colin stood up and pushed his chair back. 'At least now I know what has to be done.'

They shook hands and slowly walked back to the ward, each with their own thoughts and agendas.

32

Letting go

Over the next few days, Colin Phelps met with members of his family. After quite a few emotional and tearful discussions, they all agreed that if there was no change in their father's condition by the following weekend, they would allow the doctors to stop his medication and let nature takes its course. After what Karl had told Colin, as hard as the decision was, he knew it was the right thing to do.

As the week progressed, Karl tried to reduce what was quickly becoming a huge waiting list at his practice. People were beginning to cancel rather than wait any longer and Karl suddenly realised that some had been on the waiting list for over five weeks. Charlie had a quiet word with him, but it fell on deaf ears, and once Thursday came around, all Karl focused on was Nicky. Charlie was particularly worried as Karl talked about her as if she was living a normal life. The fact that she was in a coma seemed to have slipped his mind, and he appeared content to accept the, frankly, weird relationship they were having.

Arriving at the hospital with a spring in his step, Karl hurried down the corridor towards the lifts, anxious to see his sleeping angel. One of the nurses buzzed him in, but turning in towards Nicola's bed, he pulled up sharply, the colour draining from his face. She was gone. Fearing the worst, but hoping he was wrong, he moved quickly from bed to bed, desperate to find her, his face frozen in shear panic.

'Mr Hennessey,' called the nurse who had just buzzed him in.

Quickly, he made his way down the ward towards her. 'What's happened?'

'Don't worry,' the nurse smiled, 'she's been moved to a room at the end of the ward.'

Karl took a deep breath. 'Thank God for that; I feared the worst.'

The nurse squeezed his forearm in reassurance. 'When rooms become available, whoever has been on the ward the longest moves in. It's the door on the right' – she pointed down the ward – 'she's on her own at the moment.'

Karl thanked her and she went about her business. He tapped on the door and put his head round, smiling. 'Hi, Nicky.' She lay still, just as he had left her after his previous visit. But now there were more monitors around her: why and what they were for he didn't know. Wasting no time he slipped off his jacket, pulled up a chair and sat down at her bedside. Taking hold of her hand, he closed his eyes.

As usual, he was plunged into darkness. He called out her name. Hearing him, she stood up and moved towards the sound of his voice, searching for him in the darkness. She flung her arms around him holding him tight. 'What's wrong?' he asked.

'I don't know, I keep seeing these intense lights. I thought it was you at first. Something is telling me to go towards them, but as I get closer, I get frightened. What's happening?'

'I'm not sure,' said Karl, holding her tight. 'Close your eyes.'

Instantly, she was transported into a more pleasant environment within Karl's subconscious. Just like a dream induced by sleep, they could spend what felt like hours together in a matter of minutes. Karl had taken her to many locations over the months they had been interacting, but they always came back to the same place, the riverbank where they had first interacted. With the sun shining down on them, they would lie next to each other, talking about everything and nothing.

Later that evening as Karl was leaving the ward, one of the nurses called him over. Colin Phelps had left him a note informing him his father's medication had been stopped, and he was now completely dependent on a breathing ventilator. The family would visit together at the weekend and had agreed to give the doctor permission to turn off the machine. What Colin wanted from Karl was one more interaction. If what Karl had told him was true, he didn't want his father to be alone at the last moment. How could he refuse? But at the same time he was secretly intrigued to know what happened within a person's mind at the point of death. It was something he had thought about on more than one occasion, and this might be his opportunity to get an answer.

Karl arrived home to find Charlie and Susie relaxing on the settee. He showed them the note and told them he intended to do it. Straight away, Susie said she would run him to the hospital that morning for support; it sounded as if it was going be a traumatic day for everyone involved. Karl rang Colin Phelps and told him he would be at the hospital by 10 am on

Letting go

Sunday morning; he would be happy to help ease his family's grief in anyway he could.

Later that evening, Karl lay on his bed in the darkness, thinking. The idea of interacting with someone who was about to die was playing on his mind. Yes, he'd thought of it, but now it was a reality he felt anxious. How would the man react? Would he be able to interact with him at all at such a critical time? A dozen or so stressful, unanswerable questions went through his mind.

The following day Karl was very quiet, still trying to think the situation through, but knowing that he did not have the answers. Trying to make conversation and break the silence, Susie said it would be an opportunity for her and Charlie to see Nicky as they had heard so much about her. Karl instantly cheered up and said that hearing different voices around her might be helpful.

On Sunday morning, as they sat eating breakfast, the only sound to be heard was that of spoons chinking against cereal bowls. Susie had stayed over so that they could get an early start; the last thing Karl wanted was to arrive late. The drive to the hospital took longer than expected, with an excess of Sunday morning motorists and heavy rain compounding the problem. They finally arrived with a few minutes to spare. Charlie bought three coffees and they sat in the coffee bar.

'Do you want us to come down to the ward with you straight away?' asked Susie.

Karl sipped his drink and put the mug back down on the table. 'It's up to you, but I don't think they'll want an audience.'

A group of people came through the main entrance doors; Karl had his back to them but Susie, through pursed lips, said, 'This could be them.'

Karl turned and looked over his shoulder, instantly making eye contact with Colin Phelps. The family seemed dressed for a funeral, the men wearing dark suits and ties, and the women in formal, long coats. Karl stood up to greet them, and Colin shook his hand firmly.

'Thank you for coming,' he said. 'We really do appreciate it.' He turned to the woman stood by his side. 'This is my wife Sheila.' She put out her hand and Karl gently shook it.

The two parties were introduced to each other and then made their way to the ward, exchanging nervous small talk as they went. The uncomfortable silence in the lift was almost unbearable. At last, to Karl's relief, the doors opened. Once on the ward, Colin and his family made their way to their father's bedside. The curtains were already closed around him to provide as much privacy as possible, and a doctor was waiting to go through the necessary paperwork.

Karl took Charlie and Susie down the ward to Nicky's room, greeting her as usual. Charlie closed the door behind them and, as he turned, Susie's expression caught his attention. Her mouth was slightly ajar, and there was a look of disbelief on her face. When he saw Nicky he realised why. Karl had told them about this beautiful young girl he had been visiting. All those months ago, she probably had been so, but now all that was left was an emaciated figure, reminding him of the photographs he had seen of concentration camp prisoners. There was nothing but skin and bone.

Charlie swallowed hard trying not to appear quite so shocked, and stepped forwards. 'Hello, Nicky; Karl's told us all about you.'

Susie was still staring, stuck for words. Realising this, Charlie nudged her with his elbow. Karl was oblivious to their reactions.

'I'll leave you two here with Nicky while I go back to the Phelps family.'

'Good luck,' said Charlie.

'Thanks, I think I'm going to need it. I'll be back soon.'

Once he had gone, Susie broke the silence. 'Jesus, this is a shock.'

'I know what you mean,' replied Charlie.

Susie walked round the bed and gingerly touched Nicky's forearm with the tip of her finger. 'Gosh, she's cold.'

'I'm not surprised,' said Charlie. 'She looks dead.'

'Charlie, don't say that; she might be able to hear you.'

'Karl said she can't hear anything.' He paused and rubbed his forehead. 'I'm going to have to say something, Susie; he's been coming here for months, and for what?' Shaking his head he sat down.

Karl made his way down the ward towards the old man's bed. The curtains were still drawn, and he could make out the silhouettes of the family around the bed. He felt a little uncomfortable interrupting them at their time of grief.

Staying outside the curtains, he gently called out to Colin. A gap appeared in the curtains, and Colin Phelps beckoned him inside. Along with Colin's family, there was a doctor, Andy Childs. Karl had seen him around on quite a few occasions and thought him to be quite an arrogant individual. Childs was completely dismissive of Karl's ability and believed him to be a charlatan. He had no time for Karl, refusing to give him the time of day. On this occasion, he had to accept him at the request of the patient's family and reluctantly greeted him, looking up from the medical charts, over the top of his half-rimmed glasses.

'Morning,' replied Karl, refusing to be intimidated.

Sensing a little friction between them, Colin intervened. 'We're just about ready, Karl. Dr Childs said that when he turns off the machine, it will only be a matter of minutes.'

'Some people pass away a little more quickly than others,' the doctor interrupted, 'but it doesn't take long.'

Karl turned his attention back to Colin Phelps. 'What would you like me to tell him, Colin?' Biting his bottom lip, Childs excused himself and said that he would be back shortly. Karl could see the others looking to Colin for some kind of leadership, and after glancing at each of them, he replied, 'Just that we love him, and tell him thank you for being everything a father should have been to us all.'

It was an emotionally charged situation. Colin's sister, already in tears, stood and held her brother's hand. Karl edged his way through and sat down next to their father. After a quick, respectful glance to each member of the family, he placed his hand on the back of the old man's and closed his eyes.

On entering the old man's subconscious, it was once again very foggy. Then, just as before, the fog slowly cleared, leaving him standing on the railway station platform. Phelps was sitting on the bench with his head in his hands. As Karl approached, he turned his head to one side and half smiled, more like a grin. 'I didn't think I'd see you again.'

'I have a message from your family,' said Karl, sitting down on the bench beside him. He gave him the message.

Meanwhile on the ward, Childs proceeded to disconnect his patient from the ventilator. Once unaided, his breathing became so shallow that his family thought he had already passed away. 'It will only be a short time now,' said Childs stepping back from the bed.

Karl had finished relaying the message, and Phelps looked content, almost happy. Suddenly, and in a quite sprightly manner for his years, Phelps jumped to his feet.

'What's wrong?' asked Karl.

'It's coming, the train, it's coming.'

Karl heard nothing, but Phelps was at the edge of the platform, looking eagerly along the track. Then Karl heard it, and as the sound of the train became louder, the platform was engulfed in light. The louder the sound of the train, the brighter the light became. It was so bright that Karl looked away and had to shield his eyes, squinting before he could turn back.

The train was now standing at the platform. It looked as if the doors were open, but the light was so intense that Karl couldn't be sure. Phelps had both arms extended, as if reaching out for something or someone. Then, through the light, Karl was sure he could see the silhouette of a person reaching out towards Phelps. Glancing over his shoulder, Phelps looked at Karl, smiled a glorious smile, and said, 'Finally, we're together again.' And with that, he stepped onto the train.

It was as if a light switch had been thrown, and Karl was instantly surrounded by darkness. As he opened his eyes, the doctor was removing his stethoscope from the old man's chest.

'He's gone,' said Childs, aware that Karl had opened his eyes at the exact moment that Phelps's heart had stopped.

Karl stood up and turned to Colin. 'Everything you asked me to tell him, he already knew. He's at peace now. I'm sure it was your mother waiting for him.'

It was too much for Colin to handle, and, unable to control his emotions any longer, tears streamed down his face. He took hold of Karl's hand and thanked him. Karl nodded and stepped out from the curtains, leaving the family together. He was making his way back to Nicola's room, when a voice called his name. He stopped and turned, and Childs came towards him, leaning very close.

'I don't know how you did that, but I'm still not convinced.'

'Dr Childs, I'm not in the slightest bit concerned with your scepticism.' They stared at each other with a mutual dislike. Karl broke the silence, 'Now, if you'll excuse me,' he turned and walked away.

'I'm watching you, Hennessey,' called Childs.

'Mr Hennessey,' said Karl, as he continued down the ward.

33

Realisation

Reaching Nicky's room, Karl glanced over his shoulder; he half expected to see Childs staring at him, but he had gone about his business. It felt as if he had been gone for hours, when in fact it had been less than thirty minutes. Gently, he knocked the door, pushed it open and peered inside, where Charlie and Susie sat silently, looking uncomfortable.

'Only me,' said Karl as he came into the room. Relieved to see him, Charlie stood up and asked him how he had got on. 'All doom and gloom, unfortunately.'

Susie shook her head. 'I don't know how you do it, Karl; it must be so stressful.'

'It's not all like that,' Karl replied, with a faint smile.

Feeling uneasy around Nicky, Charlie and Susie had tried to think of a way to leave without appearing cruel or unconcerned.

'What are your plans for the rest of the day, bro?'

Karl looked away from Nicky towards his brother.

'I think I'll spend sometime with Nicky. If you have things to do, get yourselves off. These car parks cost a fortune anyway.'

'Are you sure?' asked Charlie, inwardly relieved.

'Yeah, sure; I'll see you both at home later.' They didn't need telling twice.

'Come on then, darlin';' said Charlie, 'you know what your mom's like if you don't show your face at least once in twenty-four hours.'

'Okey, dokey,' replied Susie. She pulled her coat on then turned and hugged Karl. 'See you at home later.' She was increasingly concerned for him.

Feeling a little silly, Charlie said goodbye to Nicky and then turned back to his brother.

'Don't overdo it, bro.'

'Stop worrying; I won't.'

As Charlie and Susie passed the curtains that still remained closed around Phelps's bed, they could hear the sound of people weeping and others trying to console them. They quickened their pace, both finding the ward an extremely disturbing place. They reached the main entrance without saying a word to each other, but at the same time both feeling that what they had just experienced needed talking about; it was just a matter of finding the right words. Charlie paid for the car park ticket, and then they sat once more in silence, trying to put their thoughts into words. Suddenly, they both spoke at the same time.

'Go on,' said Charlie.

'No,' said Susie, 'you first.'

Charlie composed himself. 'Is it me, or do you think what he's doing here is wrong?'

'I don't think it's wrong, but at the same time I don't think it's doing him any good. I was shocked when we first went into her room; she was nothing but skin and bone.'

'I think Karl only sees what he wants to see,' said Charlie. 'When he gets in tonight, I'll have a chat with him.'

'Don't be too hard on him,' said Susie, reaching over and holding his hand.

'I won't, but it has to be said.'

Susie knew he was right, but knowing how sensitive Karl was about anything concerning Nicky, she didn't envy him. Susie fired up the car, and they headed to Susie's parents.

Meanwhile, back in Nicky's room, Karl sat watching Nicky have her daily physiotherapy. Every day, a physiotherapist came to the ward to help maintain some sort of mobility in patients' joints and stretch their muscles. So as not to set off any alarms, the physiotherapist removed the wires connecting Nicky to the monitors, and switched the alarms onto silent. Karl had seen them do it many times. Depending upon who was on duty, he would often help; they were usually happy for the assistance. Double-checking anything they asked him to do, they would move her joints, massaging muscles as they went, and alter her position to prevent bedsores and improve her circulation. It was a tedious job but very important; if she did regain consciousness it would be absolutely imperative for her rehabilitation.

Once finished, the physiotherapist thanked Karl for his help and left the room, heading for her next patient. Karl sat at Nicky's bedside and took hold of her hand; she always felt warmer after treatment. Closing his eyes, he was once again transported into Nicky's subconscious. But this time, instead of being in total darkness, he was standing in a large hanger. At the far end, there were two large swing doors, with light flooding in from spaces above and below them. About ten metres in front of him, Nicky stood facing the doors, staring hypnotically towards the light like a rabbit in a car's headlights. Was this it? Was she finally going to wake up?

Karl's pulse began to race, but then, putting two and two together, he felt a sickness in his stomach. In the last moments before death, the old man waiting for the train had been bathed in light. Nicky wasn't going to get better; she was going to die. 'Nicky!' he called out. There was no reply. Her eyes were firmly fixed on the intense light. Slowly he walked up behind her, and placed his hand on her shoulder. Startled, she turned round. He smiled. 'I was calling you.'

She turned back to look at the light. 'It's beautiful isn't it? Something's telling me to go over there, but at the same time I'm frightened.' Again she turned to him. 'Now you're here, I feel a little braver.' She put her hand out to him; 'Shall we take a look?'

What should he do? His mind was in turmoil. Not letting her go was selfish, but he loved her. Once she went through that door, that would be it, all over and he would never see her again. He knew it was wrong, but reaching for her hand he pulled her towards him.

'I've got a bad feeling about that light, Nicky.'

'What do you mean?' she looked concerned.

It was the first time he had lied to her and it hurt. 'Stay away from it.'

'But . . .'

'You have to trust me on this,' he said firmly. She put her arms round his waist and held him tightly; there was no reason not to believe him.

'Let's go to our place,' he said, eager to be in the sun-drenched fields by the river. When they were there, she felt safe, and they would laze around on the riverbank, happy in each other's company. She closed her eyes and in an instant they had arrived.

He stayed with her much longer than usual. The guilt of lying to her about the light was consuming him; he knew he should tell her the truth, but it was just so hard to let go. She could sense that something was bothering him, but he assured her that all was well, hating himself for being so selfish.

He was so deep in thought that, on the way home, he did not realise that they had pulled into his station, and he got off the train with just seconds to spare. Rather than go straight home, he decided to take a walk, needing the extra time alone to think through how he was going to deal with the situation. It was dark when he finally arrived home, and he it felt as if he had walked for hours.

There were no lights on in the house. Throwing his jacket over the back of a chair, he went into the kitchen and flicked the switch on the kettle. While he waited for it to boil, he leaned against the sink unit, looking out of the window into the darkness. The reflection that stared back at him far outweighed his nineteen years. The kettle whistled and he set about making a drink, his stomach reminding him he hadn't eaten.

Peering into the sparsely stocked fridge, he heard the front door open. Charlie stepped into the kitchen doorway, and nodded towards his brother, whose head was partly inside the fridge.

'Aha, great minds think alike.'

He was holding an extra large pizza box. 'I guessed you'd be hungry, so we got a take-away.' Placing the box on the table, Charlie took off his jacket. 'Spicy beef with all the trimmings.'

'Great,' said Karl, 'I could eat a horse.'

'Careful, bro, you might be.'

'I heard that, Charlie,' Susie joined them. 'You'll put him off it.'

'That's the plan,' said Charlie with a snigger, 'more for me.' Susie gave a friendly swipe towards Charlie that he just managed to avoid.

They sat down and tucked into a much-needed meal. After eating, Charlie and Susie sprawled out on the settee watching television, and Karl went up to his room to look through some client notes, which he often did during the evening, to brief himself on forth coming appointments. Susie nudged Charlie, who was already half asleep.

'What?' he grunted.

'Have you had that chat with Karl yet?'

'Not yet, no.'

'While he's upstairs, why don't go and have a word with him?'

Charlie made no reply. A while later, Susie nudged him in the ribs. 'Go on, you'll feel a lot better once you've done it.'

'All right, all right,' said Charlie, a little annoyed but knowing he had to do it. He rolled off the settee on to his feet. 'I haven't got a clue what I'm going to say to him.'

'Just be a bit thoughtful,' said Susie. 'You know him better than anyone else.'

Charlie took the stairs quite slowly; he could hear music coming from Karl's room. As he put his head round the edge of Karl's open bedroom door, he could see his brother sitting at his desk going through some files. Karl was so engrossed in the client notes that he didn't notice his brother watching him.

'All right, bro,' said Charlie eventually. The sound of his voice startled Karl.

'God, you made me jump. How long you been stood there?'

'Only a while,' Charlie stepped into the room, feeling a little awkward. 'I wanted to have a word with you.'

Karl spun round on his chair. 'Oh yeah, what about?'

Charlie thought about it for a few seconds, trying to select his words carefully.

'Nicky.'

It was as if Karl knew what was coming and he instantly went on the offensive. 'What about her?'

The aggression in his brother's voice was clear, but it had to be said. 'Mate, you're spending too much time with her, and from what I saw today she don't look too good.'

Karl combed his fingers through his hair. For a few seconds, he looked in deep thought; then he said, 'How can you say that? She's in a coma.'

'Bro, she's nothing but skin and bones. I'm surprised she's lasted this long.'

Karl stood up and began pacing around the room in agitation, rubbing his head. Suddenly stopping, he turned to Charlie. 'She needs me.'

Charlie shook his head. 'No, Karl, it's you that need her; you have to break away. Can't you see she's messing up everything you've worked for?'

Karl looked flustered. His breathing was getting deeper and raising his voice he turned on Charlie. 'She's going to wake up. I can save her, I know I can.'

Frustrated by Karl's stubbornness, Charlie shouted back, 'For God's sake, man, can't you see she's as good as dead already?'

Enraged, Karl lunged forward, grabbing his brother's collar with both hands, pushing him back towards the wall. At the top of his voice he yelled, 'She's not dead; don't you dare say that again.'

Startled by the outbreak, Charlie grabbed his brother's wrists; in years gone by, he would have easily overpowered him, but not any more. Using all his might, Charlie struggled to free himself from the grip on his collar; off-balancing Karl, he forced him to his knees. The thud on the floor echoed down through the living room ceiling to Susie, who immediately jumped off the settee, taking the stairs two at a time she bounded up. Throwing back the door to Karl's room, she couldn't believe her eyes. Karl was kneeing down on the floor with his head turned away; Charlie was standing over him gripping his wrists.

'I asked you to talk to him, not beat the crap out of him,' said Susie.

'It's not how it looks,' said Charlie, shaking his head as he let go of Karl's wrists. Karl got to his feet, both eyes firmly fixed on his brother.

Quickly, he straightened his clothes and grabbed his jacket from the back of the chair. With one final lasting stare at his brother, he stormed towards the bedroom door. Susie was in his way; as he shrugged past her, she lost her balance and held on to the door frame for support. It was like a red rag to a bull. Susie could see the anger in Charlie's face as he leaped across the room towards Karl.

'No, Charlie!' she screamed, putting herself between them. 'Let it go, please let it go!'

Karl glanced at Susie; he wanted to apologise but was so enraged with his brother, he just stamped his way down the stairs. Charlie took a deep breath and sat down at Karl's desk.

'Selfish little bastard,' he said, his fists now clenched with frustration rather than rage.

Susie stood behind him and gently put her arms round his neck. 'It's hard for him, Charlie; we just have to try and help him through it.'

Charlie reached up and held her hands. 'I don't know what I'd do without you,' he said.

'Don't worry,' she replied, 'as he stormed off I could see in his eyes he was sorry; he'll be back later, you see.'

'I hope so, darlin',' said Charlie with a deep sigh, 'I hope so.'

Karl walked, for how long he wasn't sure, but it had taken a long time for the rage inside him to subside. When it did, he hated the way he had reacted towards his brother; Charlie was probably the one person in the world who truly cared for him. Without any real purposeful destination, Karl found himself outside the local park. Looking through the railings, he could see the children's play area, although it had been a long time since any youngsters had played there. He edged his way through the half-closed gate and made his way towards the climbing frames. The authorities had stopped locking the park at night as the local juvenile delinquents only pulled down the fences for access, so it seemed the cheaper option.

Back at home, Charlie was on edge. It had been over two hours since Karl had stormed out, and it was almost midnight. Charlie knew only too well that throwing-out time in their neighbourhood wasn't the best time to be out for a walk.

'I'm going to look for him,' said Charlie, pacing up and down the living room.

Susie looked up from her magazine. 'Stop worrying, he'll be back soon, you'll see.'

Charlie continued pacing, but a few minutes later, he had had enough. 'That's it,' he said, 'I'm going.'

'If you must,' replied Susie, shaking her head, 'but think about what you're going to say to him. I'll wait here in case he comes back.'

Grabbing his jacket, Charlie leaned over the settee and kissed her on top of the head. 'I won't be long.'

Karl was sitting on a climbing frame in the play area. The ground was covered in glass, and the apparatus had been vandalised with aerosol paint. It didn't bother Karl; in fact he hadn't even noticed. His mind was preoccupied with what Charlie had said about Nicky; it really hit him hard. The more he thought about it, the more the realisation of the situation sunk in. In his mind, he focused on the first time he saw her, which was now more than seven months ago. She was the most beautiful thing he had ever laid eyes on. In his mind, her physical appearance had not changed, but on the outside she had transformed dramatically. The months of inactivity had taken its toll on her; the chronic muscle and fat wastage had given her the appearance of someone in the latter stages of anorexia. He now realised that he had known this all along; he had just chosen to ignore it.

'How you doing?' came a voice from close behind him.

Karl spun round, almost falling backwards off the climbing frame. Charlie was standing there with his hands in his pockets. 'I guessed you might be here.' Charlie walked over to the frame. 'Mind if I sit down?'

'No, carry on,' said Karl, his chin dropping towards his chest. For a few seconds, there was an uncomfortable silence, and then Karl looked up and said, 'I'm sorry, Charlie.'

'No, I am, bro; I shouldn't have said what I did. I was out of order.' Again there was a slightly too long silence. 'You're a strong little bugger, aren't you?'

'I'm not a snotty little kid any more, either,' Karl smiled. Charlie got the point and gave a nod of his head.

'I know what I have to do now, Charlie.'

Charlie felt a sense of relief coming over his body.

'Remember I told you about the old fellow waiting on the train platform?' Charlie nodded. 'I think Nicky is in a similar situation.' Karl went on to tell him about the intense light from behind the door and how he had persuaded Nicky to keep away. Maybe it was time that she took a look.

They walked home together. Karl apologised to Susie for his behaviour and received one of her extended hugs, which he made no effort to escape from. She was just happy to have them both home safe. As Karl lay awake, staring at the ceiling, he contemplated what he was going to do; losing her was not an option. What the consequences of his planned actions were, he didn't know. All he knew was, he was willing to give up everything for her, even if it meant his life.

34

Life or love

Karl woke early, his mind still focused on what he planned to do. In the forthcoming week, he had to get his own house in order, just in case things didn't go quite the way he expected. As they sat eating breakfast, the mood in the house felt good; the previous evening's outburst seemed to have finally cleared the air between them.

'Charlie,' said Karl, 'rather than starting any new clients this week, I'd prefer to clear up some of the outstanding ones.'

'Sure, no problem; any reason?'

Thinking on his feet Karl replied, 'I think long-term results will bring in more business, rather than having clients hanging on with two weeks or more between treatments.'

Charlie thought about it and it seemed logical. 'Sure, bro, you're the boss. Soon as I get in, I'll make some calls and adjust the work diary.'

Karl went in his pocket and pulled out a piece of paper. He had already prioritised what he thought he could clear up in one or two treatments. Charlie read the list.

'You're on the ball, bro. Mrs Cahill; I was beginning to think she only comes along for the experience.'

'That's exactly why she's top of the list. Half of them need to be discharged so we can clear up the waiting list.'

Charlie continued browsing the list. Financially, it probably wasn't the best decision to clear out the client list this way, but Charlie always knew Karl didn't start this practice purely to make money, and he had to respect that.

'One other thing, Charlie.'

'Yes, master?' joked Charlie, to which Karl shook his head.

'Wednesday afternoon, keep the diary free will you?'

'What's happening Wednesday?'

'I'm going to take a trip up to Marshdown to see Mr Blakeway. It's just been such a long time since I saw him, thought I'd go and catch up.'

As Karl got up from the table and placed his cereal bowl in the sink, Charlie was deep in thought, trying to work out Karl's motive.

'Right, then;' he said, still none the wiser, 'the sooner we get into the office the sooner we can sort this list out.'

The next few days were busy but very successful. By Tuesday lunchtime, Karl's list was up to date, and Charlie had arranged the diary for the rest of the week, managing to keep Wednesday afternoon clear, as Karl had asked. The plan was to take the train up to Marshdown and hopefully spend an hour or two with his mentor. In his last eighteen months at school, Blakeway had been like a father to him, and without his guidance and financial assistance, Karl would never have finished his education. He felt he could talk to Blakeway about anything, and at the present moment he had a lot on his mind.

That Wednesday, straight after lunch, Karl began his journey. He had not phoned ahead, preferring to surprise Blakeway and trusting that his usual Wednesday afternoon schedule had not changed – finishing classes at 3 pm with the final period reserved for marking work. During the hour or so on the train, Karl reflected on the old days. It would be nice to see the school again, see if anything had changed. For many years, it had been more like home than school and his mind wandered back to his first day there. He remembered waiting in the Great Hall to be sent to his dormitory. For weeks, some boys cried themselves to sleep at night, but it was never a problem for Karl, especially during the last eighteen months when his parents' relationship fell apart; the last place he wanted to be then was at home.

The train pulled into the station, and Karl leaned out the window, recognising the familiar sign of Little Chadbury, a small town about four miles from Marshdown. The platform guard clipped Karl's ticket, and leaving the station, he found a cab waiting right outside. Within minutes, they were approaching Marshdown's main gates. Immediately, Karl noticed the increased security. In his days, a simple wave of the hand would have been sufficient to gain entry, but not any more. As Karl had not made an appointment, the guard contacted the Headmaster's office. A good ten minutes passed before the gates finally opened.

The cab followed the road round the winding path, and as they came through the tree line, Karl had his first sight of the old school. He took a deep breath; unexpectedly, he was feeling quite emotional. As the taxi approached the front of the school, the main door opened, and the familiar figure of Mr Pendlebury, the Headmaster, stood in the doorway.

Karl paid the driver and made his way towards the Headmaster, who came down the steps to greet him.

'Karl, how nice to see you,' said Pendlebury enthusiastically.

Karl was taken aback; in all his years at the school, he had never heard the Headmaster use anybody's first name. They shook hands.

'Mr Pendlebury, how are you?'

'I'm very well, young man. What brings you back to Marshdown today?'

'I was hoping to catch up with Mr Blakeway.'

'I think you might just be lucky, as he should be finishing classes about now.' The Headmaster turned and extended his arm, 'Please, come through to my office; I'll send a messenger for him. Meanwhile, you can tell me what you've been up to.'

Karl followed him through the school towards the Great Hall, gazing at the familiar old portraits, the highly polished side tables and the studded leather chairs with barley twist legs, still in the same positions. Two boys came dashing through the double doors from the Hall. As soon as they saw the Headmaster, they slowed down, eyes firmly focused on the floor in front of them. Pendlebury said nothing; his presence was sufficient to stop them running. Nothing's changed, thought Karl.

Arriving at Pendlebury's office, Karl sat down in one of the luxurious leather Chesterfield armchairs. Pendlebury clicked a button on his phone and asked for a pot of tea for two, and a messenger to be sent for Blakeway. While they waited, Karl told the Headmaster about his practice – just the selected highlights. Pendlebury was impressed. A knock at the door interrupted their conversation, and the door opened to reveal a middle-aged woman with horn-rimmed glasses and meticulously arranged permed hair. She pushed a small trolley into the room.

'Ah, Edith. Tea and biscuits; thank you.'

She poured two cups and looked over the top of her glasses at Karl. 'Sugar, sir?'

'Two please,' said Karl.

She passed Karl a cup and placed another on Pendlebury's desk. 'Mr Blakeway will be with you shortly, Headmaster.'

Pendlebury thanked her, and she nodded, positioned the trolley at the side of his desk and then left the room.

'First-class cup of tea,' said Pendlebury, sipping with obvious pleasure, 'I don't know where I would be without her.' A second knock at the door caught their attention. 'Come in,' called Pendlebury. Blakeway's head came round the door.

'You wanted to see me, Headmaster.' With that, Blakeway realised who was sitting in the office, and a broad smile spread over his face. Karl got up from his chair to greet him, and they shook hands warmly. 'Karl, it's wonderful to see you young man, and what a surprise. How's that practice of yours? Thriving I should think.'

'Very well thank you, sir; it's really taken off.'

They chatted for a while, and then Pendlebury stood up. 'I can see that you two have a lot to of catching up to do. Could I leave our guest in your capable hands, Blakeway?'

'Certainly, Headmaster; I couldn't think of a better way to finish my day.' This brought a smile to Karl's face. 'Come along Karl, I've a couple of book titles for you to check out. Meanwhile, tell me all about this business of yours.'

'It's been very nice to see you again, Headmaster.' said Karl.

'Likewise, young man, likewise. Do visit again any time; it's been a pleasure.'

They left the Headmaster in his office. 'Have you eaten, Karl?' asked Blakeway. Karl made a pretence of not being hungry. 'Nonsense, my boy, I know what you're like. Come on; they'll be serving the evening meal now.'

The dining room was buzzing with pupils of all ages, inquisitive as to who Blakeway's guest was. One or two of the older boys recognised him, fuelling a Chinese whisper that he was coming back to the school as a lecturer. They sat down with a hearty portion of spaghetti bolognaise.

'So,' said Blakeway, 'how's that brother of yours?'

'Fine, thank you, sir,' replied Karl. 'He carries out the administrative work at the practice. We have that much work at the moment that I could do seven days a week and still not get through all the appointments.'

Blakeway knew Karl well and sensed that something was not right; if he had more work than he could cope with, he would not be making unexpected visits. After they had eaten, Blakeway suggested a walk in the grounds, something they had done many times in the past. They reached a bench some way off that had been a favourite lunchtime perch of Karl's and sat quietly for a few moments, taking in the fine architectural view at the rear of the school. Without looking at Karl, Blakeway was first to break the silence.

'Why did you really come back to Marshdown, Karl?'

Karl looked towards Blakeway, who searched his former pupil's face for clues. Karl turned back towards the school. 'I'm not really sure, sir. I've been exploring some other areas of my gift, and I'm not sure where it's taking me.'

'That sounds very interesting,' said Blakeway. 'Can you elaborate a little more?'

Karl explained about the patients he had come into contact with on the neurological ward, but not revealing his feelings towards Nicky; he wanted to, but he couldn't find the right words. Blakeway sensed that Karl might be getting a little too close too his patients. 'You know Karl, it's one thing being close to your work; it's another when you're too close.'

Karl put his hand to an already furrowed brow.

'You should take a holiday, put some distance between yourself and your clients and get away for a couple of weeks; it would do you the world of good.' He knew that his mentor was right; he always was. But the situation with Nicky couldn't wait; it had to be dealt with.

'Gosh is that the time?' said Karl, glancing at his watch. It was almost six o'clock. 'I'm sorry, sir, I've made you late.'

'Don't worry, Karl,' laughed Blakeway. 'There's nobody waiting for me.' He paused for a moment. 'Is there somebody waiting for you?' Karl's head quickly turned; it was as if Blakeway could read him like the open pages of a book.

'No, I was just thinking about getting a train home.'

'Come on,' said Blakeway, getting up from the bench, 'let's walk back.' Slowly they ambled back across the lawns. Blakeway didn't pursue his question; if Karl wanted to tell him more on the subject, he would do so in his own time.

As they reached the school building, Blakeway asked what time Karl's train was due. There was a train on the hour for most of the evening, so Blakeway persuaded Karl to stay for a coffee, after which he would drive him to the station. 'I'd take you all the way home, but I'm on duty this evening.' Karl said that he would take a cab, but Blakeway was insistent, and they spent a further half hour or so engaged in conversation.

They left for the station in plenty of time to get the train. Karl had always felt comfortable in Blakeway's presence; they had so much in common. They barely stopped talking, especially about the books that interested them both. Arriving at the station, Blakeway pulled into the drop-off zone and they both got out. Concerned for his young friend, Blakeway felt that he had to say something. 'I don't want to pry into your business Karl, but if you need advice or just someone to talk to, I'm only a phone call away.'

Karl smiled and offered his hand, which Blakeway firmly shook. 'I know, sir; thank you.' It was one of those awkward moments in which neither of them knew how to move on.

'Right,' said Blakeway, 'don't leave it so long next time, young man.'
'I won't, sir.'
Blakeway jumped into the car, clicked on his seatbelt, tooted the horn and, with a quick raise of his hand, drove off. Karl watched the car drive out of the car park. Blakeway glanced in his rear view mirror at the lone figure standing by the entrance to the station and felt unsettled. What was it that had brought Karl to Marshdown that afternoon? As Blakeway drove back, he went over and over their conversations that afternoon, but to no avail. Whatever it was, Karl had kept it very close to his chest. Karl also had a thoughtful journey. He would be able to finalise his business arrangements over the next two days, and then on Saturday afternoon, when Nicky's parents went home from the hospital, he would sort out his main problem, one way or another.

The following morning Karl was sitting at his desk, chewing his pen and waiting for his ten o'clock client, who was late. The time was not wasted; he had a lot going through his mind. Pulling open the desk drawer, he took out a note pad and began to write. Once finished, he carefully folded the sheet of paper, placed it inside an envelope and sealed it. He wrote his brother's name on the front and slipped it into his jacket pocket. The rest of the day went without a hitch; all the clients were on time, and two-thirds of them he discharged, all content with their treatment.

Friday came around and Karl had arranged to take Charlie and Susie to their favourite Italian restaurant that evening. He told them that he still felt bad about the way he had treated them the previous week and wanted to make amends by buying them a nice meal. Never one to look a gift horse in the mouth, Charlie jumped at the opportunity.
Half an hour after the last client had left, and content that he had done as much as he possibly could, Karl stood at the top of the office stairs.
'Come on, bro,' came Charlie's voice from the bottom of the stairs. 'Susie's double-parked.'
'Coming,' Karl called back. He glanced briefly around the reception area. Was he saying goodbye? But then he just smiled and shook his head. Taking the stairs two at a time, he rushed a little too fast, stumbling down the last couple. Careful, he said to himself. After double-locking the front door, he glanced up at the sky; it looked as if there was going to be a storm. Susie tooted her horn, and Karl raised his hand in response, dashing over the road towards the car.
They arrived at the restaurant just before eight o'clock. It wasn't very often they dressed up to go out, but on this occasion, for some reason, it

felt right. The night went really well. Karl usually abstained from any form of alcohol but was coaxed by his brother into a bottle of wine with their food, most of which was enjoyed by Charlie. After ending their meal with a sumptuous portion of tiramisu each, they sat back in their chairs, feeling their waistlines a little larger for the experience.

'I really do want to thank you both,' said Karl.

'We should be thanking you, shouldn't we, bro? You're paying.'

Susie smiled and tapped Charlie's arm, a little embarrassed by his cheekiness.

'No, I don't mean for coming out tonight. I mean for helping to get the practice up and running, and for believing in me.'

'The pleasure's all mine, bro. If it wasn't for that gift of yours, I'd still be slaving twelve hours a day in a hot foundry, wondering if it was my turn next to have a half a million pound retirement accident.'

'As much as it's my uncle that runs the place, there are definitely too many accidents there,' said Susie. 'I was so pleased when you said you were leaving to help Karl.'

'I'd like to make a toast,' said Charlie, raising his glass. Karl and Susie picked up their glasses too. 'To Karl's gift, may it, like this wine, improve with age.'

Karl smiled as their glasses clinked together. How ironic, he thought, considering that unknown to Charlie and Susie, it might well be their last meal together.

As usual for a Saturday morning, Charlie was sleeping in, while Karl was up bright and early. He had an uncontrollable urge to tidy his room and put everything away just so. Once he had finished, he placed the letter that he had written to Charlie in the middle of his desk. Carefully, as if suffering from an obsessive-compulsive disorder, he squared it up. He looked around the room, took a deep breath and went out, closing the door behind him. It would be another hour at least before Charlie surfaced; as Charlie always said, weekends are for rest and recuperation. Bless him, the lazy sod, thought Karl in an affectionate sort of way.

Grabbing his jacket, he left the house, making his way to the hospital. Nicky's parents usually left her just before lunch. He had plenty of time to get there and spend half an hour with her parents before they left.

Blakeway was looking forward to a quiet weekend. He was still at Marshdown but not on duty. He usually spent his weekends scouring second-hand bookshops or taking long walks, which helped him to think. But since Karl's visit, his mind had been preoccupied. Karl had said he was inundated with work. His exact words were that he could have easily worked seven days a week. Having known Karl for so long, he knew that the unannounced visit was out of character. When Karl had been at Marshdown, if there was something he had to do, it was done yesterday. Blakeway remembered having to take his books away from him on one occasion, as it was the only way he could make him take a break. What the hell, he thought; it was only an hour's drive. He would pay Karl a return visit. If he was not at home, he would leave a note asking him to call.

Karl followed his usual routine when arriving at the hospital and was soon knocking on the door to Nicky's room. Her parents were sitting at her bedside, but at the other side of the bed was a man in a white coat, presumably a doctor, looking closely at a chart. Nicky's mother, Gloria, had tears streaming down her face. Her father looked as if he was trying to keep a stiff upper lip but was slowly losing it. The doctor acknowledged Karl, with a good morning and a nod of his head, which Karl returned.

'I'll leave you to think it over,' he said to Nicky's parents. 'There's no hurry; take as long as you like.' With that, the doctor hooked the chart onto the bottom of the bed and left the room.

Karl looked across at the monitors beside Nicky's bed; he had been coming to the hospital long enough to know that nothing had changed with them.

'Harry, Gloria, what's happened?'

Gloria buried her head in her hands and sobbed. Harry put his arm around her shoulders and looked up at Karl.

'That was Nicky's new specialist, Professor Hammond. He said that even if she comes out of the coma, it's unlikely she would have any quality of life, mentally or physically. Her body is so wasted he doesn't think she could regain much movement, let alone walk. And he's looked again at the CT scans she had after the accident. He doesn't think her brain can recover.' As Harry looked at his daughter, Karl could see that the man was totally devastated. 'He wants us to make a decision to stop the medication and just let nature takes its course.'

Karl felt physically sick, and the colour drained from his face. He had almost expected it, but it was still a shock, and the despair on Nicky's parents' faces was heart-breaking. No parents should outlive their children, let alone be the ones to make the decision to end their life. If what Karl believed would happen next time he interacted with her actually took place, they wouldn't have to make that decision. Which would be a benefit he had not foreseen.

He looked at Nicky, and it was as if he had removed a pair of rose-tinted spectacles. The first time he had seen her, apart from a little bruising around her face, she merely looked as if she was asleep. He had held that vision in his mind for so long, but the conversation he had just had made him see the painful truth. She was emaciated, with sunken eyes and protruding cheekbones. Her arms were so thin they looked as if you could be snapped between two fingers.

Harry stood up. 'Come on, Glo, we need to go home and think.' Gloria half stood up, leaned over her daughter and kissed her forehead. As she did so, a tear dripped from her chin into the corner of Nicky's eye, giving the impression she was crying. Gloria pulled a tissue from her sleeve and very gently wiped it away. With a solemn expression, Harry walked over to Karl and took his hand. 'Thank you, Karl. You gave us both great hope, but next time you see us we will have made our decision.'

Karl understood. 'It sounds as if you already have.'

Karl was right, but Harry still had to convince his wife. Picking up his coat, Harry went over and kissed his daughter's cheek; then, putting his arm round Gloria's shoulder, he pulled her close. 'We'll be in touch,' he said. Karl acknowledged him with a nod. As they left the room, Gloria kept glancing over her shoulder, finding it difficult to accept what now looked inevitable.

Pulling a chair up close to the side of Nicky's bed, Karl sat down. 'I guess the time has come,' he said out loud. Looking at his watch, it was just before noon, a good two hours before her physiotherapy treatment. Suddenly, he remembered the monitor alarms. Having seen it done many times, he got up and went round the bed, quickly switching the alarms over to silent. Whatever happened, nobody outside the room would be any the wiser. Sitting back down, he took a firm but gentle hold of Nicky's frail hand, and closed his eyes.

Blakeway pulled up outside Karl's house. There was no sign of activity. Pressing the bell, he stood back and looked up at the bedroom windows. Charlie had not been up long, and Susie rarely stayed on Friday nights now; it kept the peace at home if she went shopping with her mother on Saturday mornings.

'Who's that, then?' said Charlie out loud to himself. He put his mug of tea down on the kitchen table and, dressed only in his dressing gown, slothfully got to his feet and trudged his way to the front door. He peered round the half open door.

'Hello, Charlie.' Blakeway tried to sound casual, as if his visit was nothing out of the ordinary. 'I was passing, thought I'd drop in on you both.' Surprised but still pleased to see him. Charlie opened the door.

'Great to see you, Martin; come on in.' Blakeway stepped into the hall past Charlie. 'I'm afraid you've missed him, Saturday lunchtime he'll be at the hospital; well, that's the norm anyway.'

Charlie closed the door, and they went into the living room. He offered Blakeway a drink, which he accepted, following Charlie into the kitchen and leaning against the door frame.

'Did you know that Karl came up to Marshdown the other day?'

'Yeah, he said he was going to pay you a visit; got me to work his appointment diary around it. Two sugars, wasn't it?' Blakeway nodded.

'Didn't you think it was a little strange?'

'Martin, it's Karl you're talking about here; everything about him is a little strange.'

Blakeway laughed. 'I wouldn't go that far, but yes, he does have one or two very individual attributes, shall we say.'

Charlie's eyes widened. 'That's one way of looking at it.'

'No, all joking apart, I think he was trying to tell me something. I couldn't figure out what it was, so I thought I'd drop in and see if more light could be shed on it. Has he done anything else out of character lately?'

Charlie handed him a mug of coffee.

'Come to think of it, he has had one or two moments just lately. Only last week, he squared up to me after I made a comment about Nicky.'

'Nicky?'

'She's a girl in a coma at the hospital. He sits with her for hours, every weekend without fail. And this week, he cleared out his client list, said he was trying to get the waiting list down. He must have discharged half the clients in a single week.'

Blakeway's expression showed his increasing anxiety. 'I think I know your brother, Charlie. Gut instinct; call it what you will, but something's wrong. What time do you expect him back?'

'Not till teatime at least.' Blakeway's worried face was now concerning Charlie.

'I don't want to pry, Charlie, but has he got any paperwork here that might provide a clue to what's going on?'

'He brings client notes home and goes through them at the weekend. He keeps them in the desk in his room.' Blakeway asked if he could see them, and they went up to Karl's room.

'Christ,' said Charlie, 'it looks like he's had a spring clean.'

'What's it usually like? asked Blakeway.

Charlie raised his eyebrows. 'I know he's Mr Perfect to you, but come on, this is like a bloody hospital. Hang on, what's this?' Charlie picked up the envelope with his name on and ripped it open. Taking out the letter out he began reading aloud.

> *Dear Charlie,*
>
> *Life and death; how can we compare the two when we have never experienced both? Some people believe that when we die, there is nothing but darkness, the end of a long or sometimes short journey. What if life is just a learning curve for our souls, and death is the beginning of a far greater journey? I believe the comatose people I have been working with are as close to death as we can be in life. My gift has allowed me to tap into the subconscious of people in this state of limbo.*
>
> *I don't find it in the least bit frightening; if anything, I find it calming. As I never knew Nicky in a state of consciousness, I suppose she truly is my soul mate. If it is her time to move into a different level of consciousness, then I plan to attempt to accompany her. I don't know what to expect; I don't even know if it is possible. What I do know is that you'll be OK; you're a survivor. You have your soul mate in Susie, and you're good together. Please don't think badly of me as I truly am at peace with myself.*
>
> *Yours, Karl*

In a state of shock Charlie stared at the letter.
'How far is it to the hospital?' asked Blakeway, urgently.
'It's a good forty-five minutes; that's if the traffic is with you.'
'Quick as you can, get some clothes on; we'll go in my car.'

Karl opened his eyes and found himself once more in darkness. Again, he could see light breaking through from behind a door in the distance. It seemed a little more intense this time. 'Nicky!' he called out. He peered into the darkness but she was nowhere to be seen. She must be here, he thought, this is her subconscious.

Cautiously, he moved in the direction of the light. After fifteen or twenty steps, his eyes became more accustomed to the darkness and he could make out a faint silhouette kneeling down, looking towards the light. He called her again. It was Nicky. She got up and ran towards him, flinging her arms around his neck. 'I thought you'd gone.'

'Don't worry,' he said. 'I'm here now, and I won't leave you ever again.' The light from behind the door illuminated her face. She was as beautiful as the first day he had seen her, nothing like the emaciated figure that lay in the hospital bed waiting for death. 'You know we have to go through that door don't you?'

She nodded, like a frightened child. 'Before we do, I want to go once more to our place, the fields by the river.' She squeezed both his hands. 'I'd like that; I feel safe there.'

'Close your eyes and we'll be there.'

As she closed her eyes, Karl took control of her subconscious. Almost instantly, they were standing on the edge of the field. The smell of freshly harvested hay and meadow grass blew towards them on a soft breeze, and the sound of gently flowing water completed the serenity of the moment, which engulfed them. It felt as if time had stood still, their problems were forgotten, and they were totally absorbed in the wonderful place and each other.

The traffic was horrendous. Blakeway cut through every available gap, annoying other motorists, in an attempt to cut even a few seconds off the journey time. Charlie had only been to Ashbourne General Hospital twice before and was not certain of the route. At last, they saw the A&E signs and knew they were close. Turning the next corner, the traffic came to a complete stop. The hospital entrance was no more than two hundred metres down the round, and completely out of character, Blakeway banged his hands on the steering wheel as frustration finally got the better of him. Charlie glanced over at the schoolmaster, alarmed by the level of anxiety this usually serene man was displaying; Karl was clearly in severe danger.

After a cool, relaxing swim in the river, Karl and Nicky lay on the riverbank in silence, the warm sun quickly drying them. Karl looked up at the clear blue sky.

'Are you ready?' he asked.

Nicky turned her head to look at him. 'I think so,' she replied.

'Don't be afraid,' said Karl, rolling onto his side. 'I told you, I won't leave you again.' Nicky smiled and, leaning towards him, gently kissed his lips. At that moment, Karl knew he was doing the right thing. They got to their feet, and Karl held out both hands towards her, smiling reassuringly. 'Shall we?' Nicky placed her hands in his and closed her eyes.

Blakeway's car inched along in the queue for the hospital car park and then came to a halt. As the seconds ticked by, Blakeway's frustration grew. Charlie leaned out of the window to see what the problem was. A woman at the head of the queue was having problems with the ticket dispenser. Barely able to control himself, Blakeway slammed onto the horn. The driver of the car ahead looked in his rear view mirror and raised his hands as if to say, what do you want me to do about it? Charlie leapt out of the car and ran to the machine; as soon as he pressed the button, a ticket came out and the barrier lifted. With an embarrassed look on her face, the elderly woman tried to thank him, explaining that she hadn't used it before. Charlie urged her on, and after two or three attempts to select first gear, she finally drove into the car park.

Trying to speed up the process, Charlie stayed at the machine and dispensed a ticket to the next driver. Finally, they were in, but every space appeared to be taken. Spotting a space marked for disabled drivers, right by the main entrance, Blakeway drove straight in and pulled on his handbrake. 'You haven't a disabled badge have you, Martin?'

'No,' replied Blakeway, already half out of the car.

'But they'll clamp you.' Blakeway ignored him.

'Come on;' he said, 'we might already be too late.'

Slamming the car doors, they dashed into the hospital.

Karl and Nicky were once more surrounded by darkness. With their hands tightly clasped together, they slowly moved in the direction of the light. 'It will be OK,' said Karl reassuringly. As they arrived at door, the light that pierced the spaces around it was so bright that they had to raise their hands against the glare.

In the hospital room, Nicky's heartbeat was slowing alarmingly. If Karl had not set the monitors to silent, the room by now would have been overrun with nursing staff.

The light was now so intense that they could see each other clearly. Apprehensively, but certain of what he was about to do, Karl reached out and pushed the door. Effortlessly, it swung open. Instantly, they both turned away to protect their eyes, but although they were a little fearful, the light had a calming effect on them, and they looked towards it. There was no pain. They felt compelled to walk through the door and bathe in the rays.

Nicky's heart was barely beating, the monitor display showing no more than ten beats per minute and dropping rapidly.

They stood directly at the doorway. As they took the last step, the light washed completely over them.

At the same moment, totally synchronised as if they were one, both of their hearts stopped beating. Nicky's ECG monitor flat-lined. Karl, still holding onto Nicky's hand, slumped against the bed. It was only for a split second, but for the first time since the accident, Nicky's nervous system reacted, and she firmly grasped Karl's hand.

Blakeway followed Charlie, racing down the corridor. As they approached the lift, with perfect timing the doors opened. Someone manoeuvring a wheelchair to get out held them up momentarily, and then Charlie rapidly tapped the first floor button. The doors closed at a snail's speed. Coming to a halt on the first floor, they were both out before the doors had fully opened. Charlie ran to the ward and held his finger on the buzzer. 'Come on, come on.' he said, beating the door frame with the palm of his hand.
  A voice came over the intercom. 'Can I help?'
  'Yes, my name's Charlie Hennessey. My brother Karl is visiting a patient called Nicky. We want to see her.'
  'Are you related to the patient?'
  'For God's sake,' said Charlie.
  'Her parents gave us permission to visit,' Blakeway interrupted. 'Charlie has visited before.' Charlie looked at Blakeway, who just raised his eyebrows.
  'One moment,' came the reply.
  Charlie looked through the glass in the door. 'She's coming.'
  'As soon as she opens that door, you get to Karl,' instructed Blakeway. 'I'll deal with her.'
  'Got it,' said Charlie, anxiously nodding his head.
  The nurse clicked the latch. Once the door was half open, Charlie burst through and dashed down the ward. As the nurse fell backwards, she slammed her hand on the security alarm.
  'Please,' said Blakeway, 'we think someone may be in danger.'
  The alarm rang out. Medical and nursing staff quickly rallied. Blakeway ran down the ward after Charlie, and once the nurse had regained her balance she gave pursuit. Another nurse stood between Charlie and Nicky's room. Raising his hands in front of him, Charlie called out, 'Check that room quickly.' He gestured with his head towards Nicky's room.
  The nurse quickly pushed the door open and immediately recognised the seriousness of the situation. She turned back and shouted something, but Charlie couldn't make out the words; her lips were moving, but no words appeared to be coming out. From that moment, everything seemed to go into slow motion. All Charlie could see was Karl slumped on the side of the bed, and the monitor with its distinct flat line. Blakeway pushed past, pulling Karl to the ground. The nurse knelt down beside him, and together they frantically attempted to resuscitate him.

More medical staff came into the room, accompanied by security personnel. A nurse dragged in a resuscitation trolley, and one of the doctors, grabbing the defibrillator from the top shelf, took control. Charlie saw his mouth shape the word 'Clear!', but still he was deaf to everything around him. Karl's body jerked as the charge surged through his body. Another team worked on Nicky but it was futile, and he saw them step away and pull her bed to one side, allowing more space for those attending to Karl. Charlie fell to his knees, unable to comprehend the scene unfolding before him. Karl's lifeless body was lifted onto a trolley. Again and again they tried. Helpless, Charlie looked on as they battled to save Karl's life.

Twenty minutes passed, and one of the doctors stood back. 'Are we all agreed we should stop?' Each member of the nursing and medical team gave their agreement. 'Time of death, 13:20. Thank you for your efforts, everyone.'

As the equipment was cleared away, Charlie and Blakeway stood together, distraught in complete and utter shock. Their eyes filled with tears; it was over. He was gone.

The piercing light was no longer hurting their eyes, and it softened to a wonderful glow. Once more, they could smell freshly cut wheat and meadow grass, and for an instant, they thought their eyes deceived them. But no. They were back in the fields they loved so much, once more bathed in radiant sunshine. Looking at each other, they smiled, realising they truly were in heaven.

www.ingramcontent.com/pod-product-compliance
Ingram Content Group UK Ltd.
Pitfield, Milton Keynes, MK11 3LW, UK
UKHW022230230426
12048UKWH00016BA/1175